I0831587

ISBN 979-8-9921806-3-3

Cover Design by Christley Creatives

Editing by Larissa Melo Pienkowski

Hardcover Edition 1

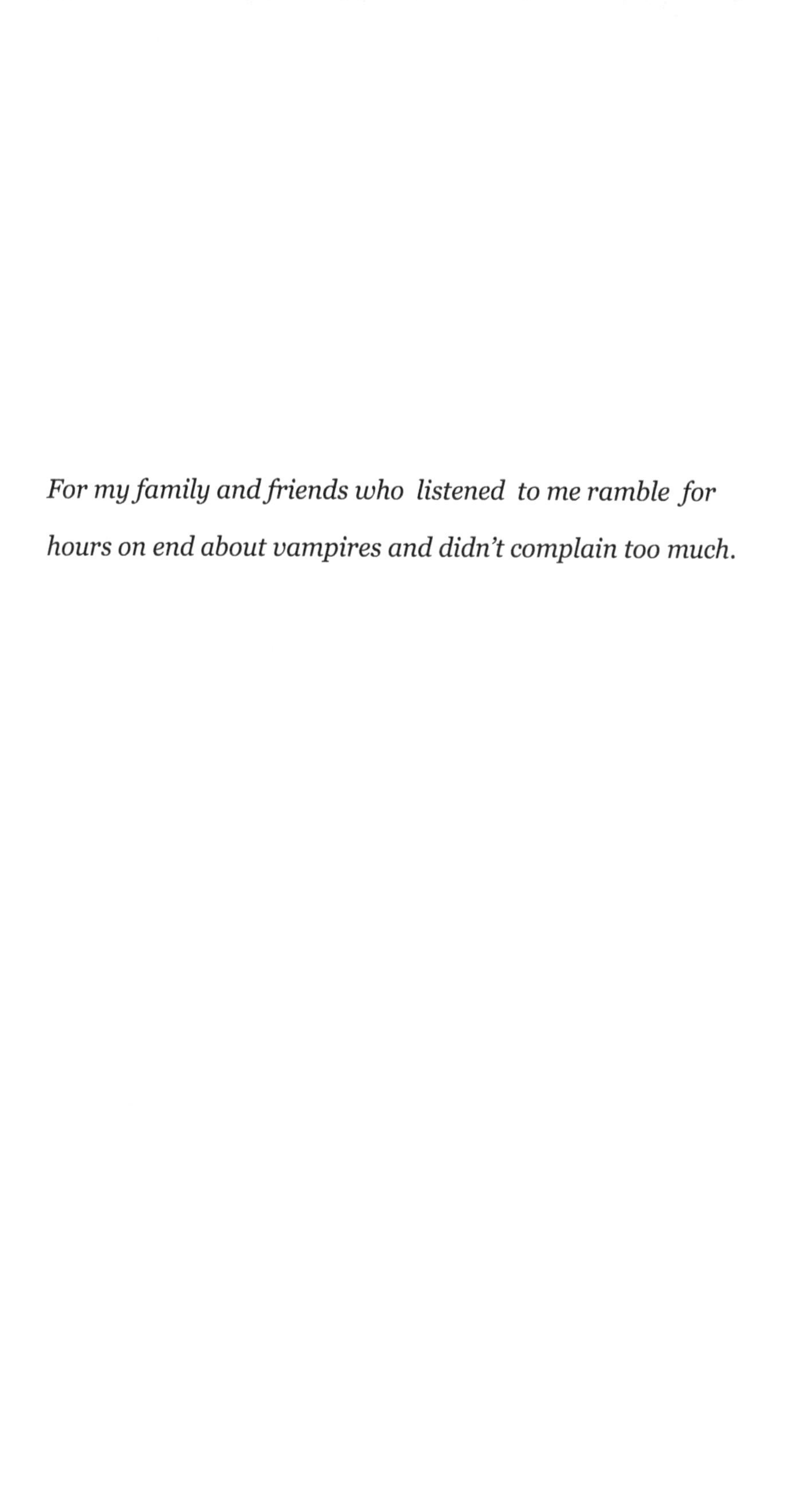

For my family and friends who listened to me ramble for hours on end about vampires and didn't complain too much.

Dear readers,

It would be impossible to thank you enough for your interest in *Just for a Taste*. Out of respect for various mental health conditions as well as individual preferences, I would like to note that this book contains various dark themes.

I have written these topics with as much tact and sensitivity as possible, but this is ultimately a Gothic novel and these elements cannot be removed.

This aside, please enjoy the novel and strap in! If you are so inclined, I would greatly appreciate a review or even recommendation to a friend. As an indie author, your vocal support means the world to me and is my lifeblood in the treacherous (and expensive!) world of self-publishing.

Thank you once again for your time, and I hope *Just for a Taste* was just as enjoyable for you to read as it was for me to write!

Sincerely,

Vera Wolfe

JUST for a TASTE

Just for a Taste

Vera Wolfe

Table of Contents

You ask that I forget you?
[. . .]And this while yet I live?
Ah no! My life would be far worse than death!
Let death come, I await it fearlessly.
[. . .]Fear nothing, my beloved,
my heart will always be yours.

—Wolfgang Amadeus Mozart, "Ch'io mi scordi di te? . . . Non temer, amato bene"

Prologue

Sinfonia

The boy was used to his house being transformed into chaos on a regular basis. The party inside was bustling as usual, bright and loud and teeming with people. Voices overlapping with a roar of laughter, mostly forced. Superficial conversations he found sinful on top of the live string instruments, and lights so bright they made his skin and eyes burn, even from the tree in which he sat.

Zeno resembled the people inside, to some extent. His lanky body, now in the awkward period between boyhood and early adolescence, was fashioned in formalwear. It had taken one of the most talented tailors in Italy to make the suit conform to his figure, and still he had chosen to cover most of it in his favorite antique overcoat—an overcoat now strewn across the branches at his side.

Zeno's white hair had been tamed into a smooth pompadour at the beginning of the night, but now it had deep ridges where he had run his fingers countless times. His pink eyes, long trained to watch the ground, had been powdered in a mostly successful attempt to conceal the deep bags and dark circles endemic to his face. It had taken a special formula to make a foundation that looked natural on Zeno's nearly translucent skin.

There weren't many trees in this area of Florence—at least, not many that were allowed to grow as gnarled as the one outside his bedroom. Zeno wasn't sure why exactly this one had been allowed to twist and turn freely for centuries without intervention, especially when it had always been surrounded by immaculately groomed hedges. Every weed was torn from the ground. This grooming, of course, wasn't exclusive to the manor's exterior. The boy's room itself had the same baroque decor for centuries, the sheets permanently folded. Zeno never slept under the covers.

As usual, he tried to ignore the urge to wash the dirt and bark from his fingers, the crimson from his arms. There was no way for him to climb into the tree without getting scratched up a bit, he had discovered. He looked to the ground and mentally plotted potential paths down but was unable to find any route more efficient than his usual.

The sounds from inside the manor briefly swelled. Another boy, slightly older, crossed the forbidden barrier between them, but at least he had the decency to shut the door behind him quickly.

"Ah, Zeno," he said. "I should have known you would be here."

Zeno, having already found his way to the ground, stared up at the teenager. "Oh. It's just you," he said in a monotone. "Did my father send you to bring me back in?"

The teenager rested his arms along the barrister of the balcony and rolled his eyes. "Why do you think he had to send me? Why couldn't I just want to see you?"

Basilio was barely older than Zeno and had the same condition, yet their appearances could not have been more different. Basilio's shoulders were broad, his body lean yet proportionate, his skin creamy with a healthy flush. Despite all his dancing that night, his medium-length ponytail still didn't have a strand out of place.

Zeno blinked, unimpressed, then brought his attention back to pressing a handkerchief against his bleeding elbows. "I see," the younger boy stated. "So he did send you."

"Well, yeah, but . . . look, you can't hide out here every time there are guests."

Zeno pulled away the cloth, saw that the blood had not yet clotted, and returned to pressing down the handkerchief. Without looking up, he replied, "I'm not hiding."

"Then what *are* you doing?"

"Rotting."

"Rotting?" Basilio chuckled. "How could you be rotting when you're alive?"

"I am dead," was his grave reply. "My body hasn't caught up to it yet, but I died a long time ago."

At this point, Zeno tied the handkerchief around his arm, ignoring the red spots seeping through the white. Instead, he knelt to dig through a pile of leaves with a stick.

After realizing his cousin had little interest in speaking to him face-to-face on the balcony, Basilio easily scaled the tree to the ground. "What are you talking about? You've been acting so peculiar lately. Did you hit your head or something? Have a bad transfusion?"

"No," Zeno's grumbled. "And I didn't have a transfusion this month."

Basilio tied Zeno's handkerchief tighter and scoffed, "You refused *again*? No wonder you're bleeding so much."

Finally, Zeno met his older cousin's eyes. "How can you stand it? Every single month, another transfusion . . . looking forward to a life of pain and needles . . ."

Basilio shrugged. "You're going to be fourteen in, what, a year? I hear it isn't so bad once you get a *beniamina*. I'll let you know once I get mine."

"I don't want one," Zeno responded immediately.

"Why not?"

After several seconds, it became apparent Zeno wasn't going to bother with responding.

With a grimace, the boy finally used his hands to brush aside the leaves. "Where did you bury her? You told me you were going to get her a gravestone. Where is it?"

Basilio laughed. "Is all this about the *bird*? Of all the—you can get another bird!"

Zeno looked up and met his cousin's gaze. For the first time, Basilio could see that although his eyes were empty, tears had gathered in the corners.

"Carmen wasn't just a bird. She was mine."

Basilio kicked a nearby pile of leaves, causing them to blanket the spots Zeno had uncovered. Zeno forgot all about cleanliness and plunged his hands into the dirty leaves to clear them away again. Basilio groaned loudly and threw his arms out to his sides.

"Come on! I told your father it would only take a few minutes to get you back inside. We need to get you cleaned up. There are people who want to meet you. How are you supposed to get a *beniamina* if you hide out here every time?"

No response at all but the skittering leaves. Basilio nudged his cousin, who gave him a glare but continued what he was doing.

"I was so foolish to think that you would be normal once those damn birds were gone," Basilio grumbled to himself.

Zeno's head snapped up. "What did you just say?"

Basilio quickly took a few steps back to widen the space between them. He held up his hands. "Look, i-it wasn't my idea."

"What the *fuck* did you just say?" Inch by inch, vertebrae by vertebrae, Zeno lengthened his spine.

"It was painless! I had them use natural gas, so it only took a few—"

Basilio didn't get the chance to finish the sentence before his collar tightened around his neck. He gasped and clawed at his throat, trying in vain to dig his feet into the ground rather than be dragged back onto the tile beneath the balcony, but the very leaves he had kicked prevented him from getting a grip. Dead silent, Zeno grabbed his cousin by the hair and bashed his head into the base of a column once, twice, three times. He only stopped once he saw teeth through Basilio's split lips, his chin a crooked mess of blood and bone, Zeno's own knuckles broken.

He picked Basilio up with his intact hand and dug his fingers into his cousin's scalp until blood gathered beneath his fingernails. Then, he threw Basilio to the side and kicked him as hard as he could in the stomach until vomit and gurgled sobs spewed from Basilio's lips.

Just as Zeno lurched forward to start another onslaught of punches, a large hand pulled him back. Another hand grabbed his other arm, seamlessly pulling them back into an uncomfortable cross

behind his back. Zeno kicked and fought despite the risk of dislocating his arms, then went limp when he realized who was holding him.

"All this where guests could have seen you?" came the unmistakably low voice of his father. Every time his father spoke, the boy thought, it sounded like a dirge.

Zeno wilted to the ground. His father let go of him and knelt close, so close his lips were almost touching Zeno's ear.

"You're so fucking lucky that nobody else heard this," he hissed. "You're so lucky that I even call you my son."

Several people crowded around them then, numerous guards lifting Basilio and rushing him off. Zeno's father shoved his son so he was belly-up and spat in his face. "You're disgusting."

Zeno didn't wipe it off, even once his father's back was turned to him. Those familiar footsteps, slow and even, faded into the distance, leaving the boy alone.

Curled up in a ball, face covered in tears and vomit and blood and spit, Zeno whispered back, "I know."

BOOK ONE:
SERENATA

Chapter One

In bocca al lupo

I wondered how my mother would feel if she knew what I planned to do with these vampires. Would she throw back her head and laugh that all the time and money I spent on school had gone nowhere? Would she spit at my feet and tell me that selling my body, my blood, month after month, was no better than what she had spent her life doing after Pa died? Or would she muse that it only made sense for the girl she had surrounded with Gothic novels and Bibles to wind up in an abbey?

When I left that morning, I didn't think my interviewer was correct in assuming I would arrive so late. After all, Sicily was a small island, and the abbey of Santa Dymphna was well-known, so why would I need to rely on all the maps she had laid out for me to guide my path to such a massive building? But as I had discovered, my formidable grasp of Italian was useless when conversing with the inhabitants of rural Sicily.

I couldn't speak a word with the man who was driving me the whole way. After saying something I couldn't fully understand about the wind, he cracked my window. Cool mountain air rushed into the car, carrying with it the earthy scent of tilth. Intermittent clouds floated overhead, casting sunlight erratically over the already patchwork land. I could see the tree-lined border of a distant town, but little else of interest. For all its beauty, the only sights Sicily had given me were predominantly farmland, and that wasn't enough to stop my racing mind.

I turned away from the gust and dug out my phone. Considering the remoteness of my destination, this would probably be my last chance to use it. A stock photo of heirloom roses shined

through the spidery cracks on my screen. I had finally changed my lock screen a few weeks ago, but it still jarred me every time I checked the time or looked at a notification. Holding it close to my face, I wondered if the picture of me and Emily in our favorite cafe was burned into the screen or if I had simply imagined its shadow image overcasting everything. Just like I wondered if the smell of her strawberry shampoo still lingered on my clothes or if I had just willed the familiar scent into existence. At least I knew the sensation of a ring on my finger was just a phantom–she had taken that with her when she left me last month.

I unlocked it, then grimaced as it opened to the mail app. There were a handful of emails written by my thesis advisor, trailed by the various drafted responses spawned by each. In all of them, she maintained her usual professional tone, but over time, they had gotten increasingly terse. Between cordialities and academic prose, the underlying message was clear—

"You've run out of funding, Cora. We can't keep giving a stipend to a no-name, so get results sooner rather than later."

Many of my abandoned drafted responses were lengthy explanations about how I was only missing a few key documents, ones that surely existed to prove my theory. Others were outright excuses about crashed computers or sick grandmothers. Some were just embarrassing pleas and empty promises. I had almost sent a lengthy response explaining how this thesis was all I had in this world, what I had left everything behind for. The eventual response was two sentences sandwiched between the auto-generated salutations:

"I have a lead. We'll talk when I find something."

Less was more, I supposed, with a "lead" as sketchy as mine.

The letter I received in the mail a few weeks ago, written in gold ink on black parchment, had initially seemed like a prank:

"Hello Miss Cora Bowling,

I am mailing you to inform you of a job offer. I have looked through your credentials and find them satisfactory. Here is the description:

Healthy adult wanted for paid blood donations in rural Sicily. Room and board provided. Long-term gig with a generous salary. Discretion required.

Please respond as soon as possible via mail if you are interested. I am of the understanding that you will be.

–Doctor N."

There was no start day, pay, or even the first name of the sender. The only shred of information was the return address on the envelope. I should have thrown it away at first sight, but genuinely, what did I have to lose? I had recognized the insignia on the wax seal—the Medici coat of arms. The exact family I was at a dead-end on. Sure, it could have been a dupe, but at the same time, what if it *wasn't?*

We exchanged a few letters, with every reply increasingly bizarre. First, there was a basic questionnaire regarding my knowledge on a variety of topics, an official application form for me to fill out, a request for my blood work, a written entrance essay about a subject of my choice and, finally, an NDA. Each one with only a vague acknowledgment that I had sent the previous requirements and no sign as to when the correspondence would end. The last letter, in an envelope even flowerier than the rest, contained a series of airline tickets, car vouchers, and a small note:

"See you soon for the interview

—Doctor Ntumba."

I stuffed the letters back into my bag and sighed. Coming here was stupid and dangerous—I was fully aware of that. But for someone in my situation, this was too valuable of a chance to pass up. This provided too many opportunities for an authentic look into the world I'd spent my entire life studying, and an income to boot.

As soon as I tried to switch to another app, my phone died—not that I had internet service anymore, anyway. I returned it to my bag and watched the clouds pass, trying to steady my breathing. By the time I reached my destination, the sky was a mottled mixture of pinks and blues and the abbey itself was rendered a bare silhouette against the orange sun. It was only thanks to the old-fashioned lantern Doctor Ntumba held that I could spot her among the shadows.

After I gathered up what little luggage I possessed and hopped out of the taxi, it puttered away, leaving me alone to approach the abbey and my interviewer. With a gulp, I sized up the woman before me.

Doctor Ntumba was a curvy woman wearing a white button-up shirt, knee-length tweed skirt, and matching fitted jacket. The conservative color scheme of her clothes brought out the brightness of her hot pink heels and the deep red ombre of her braids. Behind a pair of rectangle glasses were heavy-lidded discerning eyes that were equally rich in color as her umber skin.

"It's a pleasure to meet you, Signorina Bowling," she said in Italian, her deep tone lilted with an accent I couldn't decipher. Even so, I was relieved to hear a more familiar dialect.

"Please," I replied, shifting my suitcase into my left hand and holding out the other. "Call me Cora."

"In that case, call me Noor." She accepted my hand with a robust shake.

To call such an esteemed woman by her first name seemed like an impossible task, but I didn't protest outright. The doctor opened a heavy iron gate, leading me into the front perron. I stared in awe at the land around me as streetlights flickered on. I had seen images of fantastic duomos and basilicas from Rome and other major Italian cities, but I had not expected such majesty from a rural abbey. In the middle of the garden was a massive fountain with a plume of water bursting from its center. It was surrounded by a ring of gravel, followed by a flawlessly trimmed wall of flowering shrubbery. On the periphery were flowerbeds as intricately woven and colorful as a tapestry, and on either side of me were two symmetrical lanes, a bosquet of evenly spaced alternating rows of trimmed hedges and olive trees.

And the chapel—it was completely and utterly magnificent, the sort of Sicilian Baroque architecture you could write a thesis on. A beautifully detailed lava stone stairway led up to a gardened terrace with large wooden doors set between an even larger façade. Elaborate statuary featuring grinning masks stared down at me from above, and numerous sets of eyes and swirling vines were embedded in pillars. Through large curve-topped windows, I could discern paneled murals all along the ceilings, clearly inspired by the central dome of the

Sistine Chapel. All this, stretching impossibly long and tall in every direction.

In my moment of awe, Doctor Ntumba's words had slipped past me entirely.

"English or Italian?" She repeated, though not harshly.

"English please," I replied a bit too quickly, picking the first word that came to mind. "Or whichever you prefer, I suppose."

"English it is then."

She led me into the chapel, and despite my desire to stop and marvel at every historical inch, Doctor Ntumba's swift pace and numerous turns allowed little more than glimpses at the art crowding every inch of the walls and the flowery engravings on the twisted columns. After what seemed like a dozen lefts and rights, I was swept quickly into what I later learned was a minor scriptorium.

Doctor Ntumba stepped out briefly, giving me a chance to look around the small room. I sat in a floral armchair facing a broad oak bureau and a large outswing window. Two bookcases spanned the walls beside me, crammed with books that appeared as if they would fall apart if even touched. Dust-covered cobwebs swayed against a scarcely open window panel, the only source of freshness in an otherwise murky room. A stained-glass lamp provided the only artificial light in the room, for all the candles had been snuffed out long ago. I could tell the furniture had only received a single, cursory sweep of dusting.

My eyes immediately sought the contents of the shelf closest to me, but before I got the chance to examine the titles, the door behind me gently closed. Doctor Ntumba took her seat in a simple wooden chair in front of me rather than in the plush chair behind the desk. Perhaps this was meant to make me feel more comfortable, but it had the opposite effect. For a second, it seemed like she would berate me and point out the obvious truth: a mere peasant didn't belong in such a castle.

Despite my fears, her focus immediately shifted to the clipboard in her hands. Doctor Ntumba glanced over my labs and resume so quickly that I knew the act was purely for show.

"These look quite excellent," she said, looking up at me. "You have some excellent hematology labs and no discernible nutritional deficiencies."

"Yes, I try to keep a healthy diet despite my . . ." I paused, trying to find the right word. "Limited budget."

At the mere mention of money, the student loan debts and immigration fees I had accumulated over the last few years burned at the forefront of my consciousness. Seeing the extent of the riches around me, I couldn't help but fear that Doctor Ntumba would look down upon such a high number if she knew it. I took in a shaky breath and tightened my fists, painfully scared that she could tell my dress was thrifted.

Doctor Ntumba set aside the lab results and tapped my resumé with the back of a ballpoint pen. "I see you attended the London School of Economics, but you don't have any major listed."

Heat rushed to my face. I had deliberately *not* written down my major because I feared my intent would become clear. Maybe leading honestly was the best idea, but I didn't know if Doctor Ntumba was as tight-lipped as the rest of the Medici family. *Shouldn't you know, anyway?* I wanted to ask. *You're the one who reached out to me!*

"I majored in Renaissance vampiric history," I finally admitted. "With a minor in biology."

She gazed at me for a pronounced period, expression inscrutable, then finally replied. "That sounds interesting. And what brings you to Italy?"

"I'm doing my thesis on Italian history, but I'm on an . . . extended break. I came here to save up for a bit and organize my current research."

I conveniently neglected to mention the specifics, and she did not pursue them, instead returning her attention to another document. After several moments, she spoke once more. "You realize that given the remote nature of Abbazia di Santa Dymphna, you are effectively cut out from the outside world, correct? No Wi-Fi, no phones, no mail? And you are okay with the fact that you will not be receiving any guests?"

I nodded, a bit more eagerly than intended. “That isn’t an issue at all! I have more than enough paperwork to keep me occupied. And I’m not exactly the most social person either, so that won’t matter.”

Again, a pronounced silence. Unlike the former, this one was interrupted by a series of rapid-fire questions.

“Do you have any allergies?”

“No.”

“Do you follow any particular diet?”

“I try to eat healthy and avoid alcohol. Otherwise, no.”

“Do you smoke?”

“No.”

“Blood type?”

“B negative.”

“Any scheduled medications that could transfer?”

I bit the inside of my cheek. “Yes.”

She raised a brow, and I continued.

“100 milligrams of sertraline, daily at night.”

“For?”

“Panic disorder.”

Doctor Ntumba made a brief note of this, then said, surprisingly jovially, “Duca de' Medici could probably benefit from a dose or two of that, as you’ll soon find out.”

My heart leapt to my throat. Did this count as a success? Perhaps I should have felt some inner sense of fulfillment, but all I felt was unease. I reminded myself for the dozenth time that I *needed* this job and rose to my feet.

"I'll take you to the piano room to meet Duca de' Medici for the second part of the interview. Follow me."

Chapter Two

Crepi

When I entered the piano room, I found myself engulfed in darkness. The sound of orchestral music played on an old gramophone. A woody, spiced scent hung in the air, some long-faded cologne now lingering among the musty abandonment. It was neither warm nor cold but rather a strange lukewarm temperature that made me feel like I was swimming in myself. I had the sensation that this was what it was like to be dead.

But, I supposed if I *were* dead, I wouldn't hear the blood surging through my ears. I couldn't help but shiver. Was this really the room I was meant to be meeting a member of the illustrious Medici family in?

Just as I was about to retreat, a low, serious voice reverberated throughout the room. "Would you like some light?"

Before I got the chance to answer, a match was lit, and the warm glow of a beeswax candlestick sprang forth. Although the lighting was dim, I could discern a figure amongst the shadows.

Duca de' Medici was sitting in a wingback chair, his head resting against the top rail, his arms spread wide along the wings. Despite the awkwardness of the pose, he looked utterly at peace, practically as though he were sleeping. Or maybe, given the formality and the archaic nature of his outfit—canvas trousers held high at his waist by suspenders atop a white button-down shirt—I was staring into a massive open coffin.

"Sit, please." The man gestured with a wave of his hand to the chair opposite him.

As I sat, his white lashes fluttered open. The quick movement of his pale, ruby eyes struck me as strangely lupine. He stared at me

with his head at a peculiar angle. Even from the corners of his eyes, I saw him watching my every movement.

In a sudden yet fluid motion, he uncrossed his legs and shifted toward me.

Seeing Duca de' Medici's slender body, it was hard to believe the stories in my textbooks of vampires overtaking entire villages in their search for blood. And yet, with those elegant, calculated mannerisms, it was easy to understand how they had maintained power in the church and kingdoms for hundreds of years. Per my thorough research on this Medici before me, I would argue the link was rather direct—if you included bastards, that was.

Duca de' Medici bore no small resemblance to the art commissioned by his illustrious forefathers. He had the same thin Roman nose of Michaelangelo's *David*, the same prominent Cupid's bow as Donatello's counterpart, and the same heavy brow as the statues on the chapels of his relatives. Like those statues, he was depigmented compared to his Italian brethren. If memory served, oculocutaneous albinism type 1A was the exact mutation commonly associated with vampirism.

He ran a porcelain hand through pale blond hair.

"So," I said, wringing my hands. "You must be Duca de' Medici."

"Please," he said, resting his head back onto the wing chair with a tone of disdain. "Zeno. Or, if you must use a title, just Duca."

Where I was from, plenty of people shed their given names. I had done so myself. But here, in the realm of titles and nobility, it felt odd to do so. I scoured my brain to come up with an explanation, but was unsuccessful.

Another huff from the vampire prompted me to reply, "Which do you prefer?"

He closed his eyes again with a sigh and replied, in a thoroughly exasperated tone, "I don't."

This time, I allowed the silence to linger. Strangely, it was the act of doing nothing that changed everything in the vampire. He leaned forward with an acutely interested gaze and gingerly lifted the needle from the gramophone.

"Pardon my manners," Duca de' Medici said once the record stopped spinning. "Your name is?"

It took me a moment to reply, for the candlelight had glinted off of a pearly fang. I hadn't ever seen one in person before now. "Um . . . Cora. Cora Bowling."

"Signorina Cora Bowling." He spoke my name slowly, enunciating every syllable. When his eyes flickered to me and he said nothing more, I realized he was commanding me to speak.

I nodded and gestured to the now-motionless record player. "Was that Tchaikovsky?"

"Not a terrible guess, actually," he replied, popping a chocolate truffle into his mouth from a tray on the coffee table. "Rachmaninoff, *Rhapsody on a Theme of Paganini*, Opus 43, Variation 18. You can tell it's him because of the wide chords and use of 'Dies Irae.'"

Not a terrible guess, actually. I held back a sneer. What a pompous ass.

Duca de' Medici nudged the tray of chocolates closer to me after carefully selecting another one for himself. "They're raspberry flavored," he noted.

"I should make more 'not terrible' guesses in the future, if this is what I get," I said without thinking.

He didn't laugh, or scowl, or make much of a response at all. I stuffed a truffle in my mouth, then another, trying to bury the lump in my throat. *Positive thinking, Cora.* Another truffle down the gullet. *I guess if I fail this interview now, at least I've tried these damn good chocolates.*

"Which composers do you listen to?"

I jumped when he spoke—not that having been mentally present would have made answering much easier. I chewed my cheek for a bit. His gaze remained steady on me.

"Not very many," I finally replied. "Pretty much just Vivaldi."

He frowned and said, "I like more recent composers than that—like Chopin—because you can hear recordings of them performing the works."

"I think it's nice to hear subjective interpretations."

Duca de' Medici scoffed again and folded his arms. "Why wouldn't you want to hear the songs being played as they were truly meant to be heard? Does that not defeat the purpose?"

"But isn't it fascinating that someone heard something in their head, transcribed it, and then someone lifetimes away tried to hear it again?"

"I want to listen to the work of a genius individual, not an unintended collaboration."

"But that's the entire point of music! It's part of humanity that we can touch and change that transcends time!"

There was a pronounced silence. My shoulders were drawn up like a cat with raised hackles. I had been *yelling*. Heat spread over my cheeks.

To my surprise, Duca de' Medici tossed his head back and let out a soft, short laugh. With an impish grin, he lifted the candle to his face. "Aren't you a peculiar one? Interesting enough to keep around."

The appraisal struck me as similar to the way Pa would talk about a strange cat that had wandered onto our farm. *What a weird-lookin' critter! That one's interesting enough to keep around.*

I had absolutely zero idea what a reasonable response to this would be, so I said, "Thank you?"

Another chuckle. "It's a pleasure to have you as my guest tonight, Signorina Bowling."

"Um, it's a pleasure to be here, Duca d—" I paused. "Signore."

There was a soft *whoosh*, and the candlelight vanished, immediately followed by the sweet ringing of a bell.

"I've summoned my butler. He'll show you to your room. Doctor Ntumba will talk to you tomorrow about future steps."

"Future steps? What—" I squinted my eyes into the darkness, but the vampire was already gone. "—future steps?"

Did this mean I had passed the interview? The reality of my situation struck me: I hadn't expected to get this far. I hadn't even thought they would let me in. And I'd been so desperate to find some sort of solution to my problems that I hadn't considered what it would entail.

I had barely left the room when a portly man with a neatly groomed beard and combed hair greeted me. He gave a small bow and introduced himself, but my mind was swimming with too many thoughts to absorb any information. I'd have to get his name from Doctor Ntumba tomorrow, I reminded myself.

"How was the trip? Was the driver agreeable?" he asked, leading me down the hall.

With my head so full, even answering this was a challenge. "Um, good, I guess," I managed. Then, with a bit of effort, I added, "I've researched this area a lot, but . . ."

The butler wasn't listening and didn't seem to notice when I trailed off. It was only when the silence became painful that he probed again. "Where are you from?"

"I lived in London before this, but originally, I moved around several small towns in Appalachia. Er, that's a mountain range in the United States. What about you?"

"Florence." Such a simple response, yet it sounded as though he had to wrench it out. Clearly, the man was not interested in disclosing much about himself.

That made two of us.

Neither of us made any further attempts at small talk. He led me through the abbey in silence and brought me to my room: an old monk's cell with appropriately minimalistic furnishing. There was a single cot across from a window and a small altar beneath it. The stone walls were almost entirely undecorated, save for a cross on the wall and a simple shelf. A rosary dangled over its edge above a Bible. The sight gave me chills.

I imagined a monk clutching those beads a lifetime ago, whispering to himself in Latin. The vision was so unnervingly clear, his breath heavy in my ear. I wondered if his body was resting in the catacombs below, along with his brothers and dozens of locals.

"Sorry we don't have something better to give you," the butler said behind me, jolting me from my thoughts. "You see, we've seen many people come through these halls over the past few weeks. A few have gone past Doctor Ntumba, but none any further. Who was I to guess Duca de' Medici would permit a guest to stay the night?"

My brow quirked. I hadn't registered that other interviewees had walked through these very doors. Were there others like me who wanted to comb through family trees and catch fleeting sights of the heir of a famous vampiric family? I had a hard time imagining any other reason someone would so willingly sign up for such an unusual job square in the middle of nowhere.

Unfortunately, he perceived my expression in the worst way possible. "And I have already spoken out of turn as well. My apologies, Signorina." He sighed softly, manually forcing his manner to return to the stuffy tone of servitude as from before. "We will have the Abbess' suite prepared for you to move into by tomorrow evening."

I couldn't help but grimace. Every ounce of this interaction had been awkward if not downright painful, and there was little point in trying to salvage it. Maybe tomorrow we could start again, and I could pretend like I was comfortable talking with strangers.

"Thank you, sir," I replied, lips tightening. "Good night."

With a small bow, he was gone, leaving me alone.

I took off my shoes and placed them by the door, which consisted of a cloth curtain. I shuffled through my bag in search of a change of clothes, toppling over a rabbit's foot and my trusty binder. Most of its contents were old work–snippets of information I had scrounged together from old textbooks and university archives. The final section, however, was stuffed with all of my research on the building I was in.

There wasn't much information on the abbey to be found online, only that it was built shortly after the 1693 Sicily earthquake by a Spanish noble whose name I couldn't place. Only a small walk away from his equally magnificent palazzi, it stood proudly atop a cliff, distantly overlooking the then bustling city of Poggioreale. La Abbazia di Santa Dymphna was for a time, adored by the town and lovingly maintained by the locals. When the earthquake of 1968 struck, the town itself and even the noble's palazzi fell into ruins, yet La Abbazia di Santa Dymphna stood, entirely untouched. With no priest, no monks, and no congregation to attend, locals and the church alike abandoned it.

How Duca de' Medici had funded such a venture was undeniable–the Medici were a rich family of bankers who practically patronized the entire Renaissance, funding the likes of Leonardo da Vinci, Galileo, and even the invention of the piano. If the family were

to have even a fraction of their historical wealth–they would have been a dynasty full of billionaires in contemporary times–then the cost of this abbey was mere pennies to them.

My true curiosity was about why Duca de' Medici was here. Plenty of Medici lived outside of Florence, but to go somewhere with no company, no internet, and no interaction with the outside world was entirely contrary to the Medici goal of subtle influence over the church and state that had persisted since the Renaissance. The implication that one of the most important heirs of such a family had cast aside the political life that he and all of his forefathers had been groomed for since infancy was one of many puzzles that had drawn me to La Abbazia di Santa Dymphna. Perhaps, I theorized, insidious documents lingered among the imported inventory from wherever the heirs had been living before. It seemed silly now, but I had pinned my entire future on the vague suspicion this haunted place held the secrets I had been searching for. After all, how could you research the underbelly of a family by keeping your head above board?

But after such a long day, with my head a mess of unfinished thoughts, replayed scenes and imagined futures, I just wanted to enjoy what remained of the night. The window creaked open in a greeting I found welcoming rather than suspicious. I knelt onto the bench, folded my arms on top of the windowpane and placed my head on the backs of my hands, breathing in the fresh Sicilian air. Time passed at a bizarre rate as my thoughts gradually morphed into the sorts of daydreams that had kept me company since childhood. I imagined what it would be like to be in this place back in its prime, that I was some abbess who had overcome her gender limitations to reign over the hills stretching endlessly beyond my window. I imagined, conversely, that I was a lost damsel in distress, tucked away in the corner of a strange, haunted land. Just as I had shifted to another dream, a nearly imperceptible icy drizzle struck my fingertips like pins and needles and jarred me from my reverie. By now the moon had now reached its epoch in the sky, my forearms were covered in goosebumps, and my knees were aching. I didn't need to glance at my watch to know I needed to get to sleep now or face the consequences.

It was surprisingly easy for me to go to sleep that night. Despite the cold, despite the stiff bed, and above all, despite all the millions of questions swirling around my head.

Chapter Three

Da Capo Aria

No matter how long I stared at them, those changeling shoes weren't mine.

Last night, I'd left my cheap Mary Janes by the door, two little brown mice standing watch by the closed curtain. But when the alarm on my nightstand rang in the morning, the curtain was slightly ajar, and my tiny guards were missing entirely. In their place was a pair of designer Mary Janes, exactly my size: six wide.

Something about all of this—the strange, cold nature of the butler, the way the abbey had enveloped me overnight, the bizarre nightmares that wracked me last night—struck me as oddly predatory. On the other hand, I had never been to such a beautiful place. Both the Sicilian mountains and the abbey were jaw-droppingly gorgeous, and I had the feeling the Abbazia di Santa Dymphna held something for me. It was probably a good idea to ignore my anxiety for once and throw myself into the opportunity.

But what really got me was those damn shoes.

"Good afternoon, Signorina Bowling," a deep voice said from behind the curtain. "I'm here to escort you to breakfast."

I grimaced at the butler's voice and momentarily considered retreating under the covers.

"Signorina Bowling?" he repeated.

I closed my eyes and let out a small exhale. My bag and its contents were seemingly untouched. *I* was untouched. If anyone wanted to kill or hurt me, I reminded myself, they would have done so by now.

I quickly changed, slid the shoes on, and stepped out to meet the butler in the hall. The moment I was in sight, he began to depart.

"Please follow me to the refectory," he said over his shoulder. "We'll be cutting through the garden to the west wing."

The afternoon sun made the already dramatic sight of the western courtyard garden seem even more fantastical. Elongated shadows stretched askew from the statues amongst the flowers. As much as I wanted to stop and explore the scenery, I had to focus on the broken stone path weaving through the garden. The butler, whose name I still did not know, walked at a swift, long-legged pace. Maybe he was not used to short-legged guests like me, or maybe he was not used to guests at all.

In a contrastingly considerate gesture, he held the door open for me once we reached the refectory.

As I entered, the ancient, musty smell that permeated throughout the abbey intermingled with the scent of something rich, hearty, and utterly delicious. I was in the largest room I had seen so far, with two long tables spaced generously apart and many chairs stationed around.

Light poured through the stained-glass windows that practically took up the entire wall, casting intricate patterns onto the richly colored rug. To my surprise, dozens of candles were lit on an altar, surrounded by scripts and other religious paraphernalia. On one table was an absurd amount of food: bowls overflowing with fresh grapes and other fruit, steaming bread next to herbed olive oil, a bottle of cider, and a full charcuterie board. Given all of this magnificent food, seeing a solitary set of china and polished silverware seemed bizarre. I turned around for guidance, but my chaperone had already departed.

It was hard to fathom such an exquisite setting was just for *me*. I was on a stage with no lines to read, and I had never been great at improvising.

Then, as soon as I raised my fork to eat—*creek. Creeeeek.*

My eyes darted to the door. Still closed. The sound had come from the stained glass beside it.

Bony fingers rattled against the window and dragged their claws across the other.

Panic erupted in me. I wanted to scream and run away, but nothing came out. My legs didn't move. I stared at the beast before me, frozen in fear as it clawed harder and rattled faster.

But then, just as soon as it came, the illusion dissipated: it was not a pair of skeleton hands clawing at the windows, but branches.

And yet the horror lingered within me.

For most of my life, I hadn't been particularly superstitious. Sure, I avoided walking under ladders and ate my share of black beans on New Year, but it wasn't until I entered my mid-twenties that my mother's folkish nature began to emerge in me. For years, I had tried to view religion through an academic lens, as the man-made catalyst of all the papal revolts and social revolutions I was so drawn to learning about. I had battled to see the church as my colleague, and superstition as a relic of the past. *That God claimed Eve was sinning for eating the apple is the reason I cannot believe in Him*, I told my heartbroken mother one night.

But now, in such a haunted yet holy place, my intuition won.

I put my fork down and keyed in on my surroundings properly. The enormous feast in front of me, combined with the long table, conjured up the image of *The Last Supper* in my mind. I felt compelled to say something to the silence. But should I say grace in Latin, as the monks who sat here would have? Or should I speak the English Protestant prayer taught to me by my pa?

As the rattling became louder and more aggressive, I settled somewhere in the middle. "Bless us, O Lord, and these, Thy gifts, which we are about to receive from Thy bounty. Through Christ, our Lord, amen."

As the words left my lips and I crossed myself, the room once more fell into silence.

After a moment of pause, I resumed eating. My mind wouldn't stop racing. What if the abbey was haunted? My hands were shaking, and when I drank, cold apple cider met cold sweat on my hand and chin. What if this place knew I didn't belong here? I picked up my fork and tried to spear a cube of cheese, but I missed and ground the prongs into the plate. What if something bad was going to happen, and I deserved it? The door creaked open steadily, and my thoughts galloped.

Would anyone care if I went missing?

At the sight of someone in my periphery, I screamed and sprang to my feet. The fork flew from my hand and hit the ground with a clatter, along with the rest of my meal. Fat grapes radiated like marbles, bread sat soggy in a pool of olive oil, and colonies of risotto clung to tile and walls. On the other side of the room, an island amongst a sea of food and with a trident at his foot, stood the butler.

"Oh my God," I cried, clapping my hands to my mouth. "I'm so sorry!"

He had somehow dodged it all—the fork, the food. His suit was spotless, his demeanor no more uneasy than it had been all day.

"No need to apologize. You did not do that on purpose," he replied, surveying the wreckage. "I can clean it up. In the meantime, please follow me. I will be bringing you to your room."

"*My* room?" I repeated, getting up to join him.

"Assuming you will take the position, you will be residing in the abbess's suite and abiding by its schedule."

That only raised more questions. I considered pressing further, but it seemed easier to just follow along with the machinations of this place. I pushed myself into silence and shoved my anxiety into the back of my mind.

When we reached the abbess' suite, which was in the wing opposite the one I had stayed in, the sight of my potential lodging drew me into the present.

The suite was comfortably large with decorations much more ornate than I had expected. Partitions compartmentalized the space into three areas: the bedroom, a reading area, and another room to which the door was currently closed. A queen-sized four-poster bed stood on top of an Arabian rug, complete with a matching armoire and a wingback chair. Everything was silk and satin and mahogany—certainly not the modest accommodations I had anticipated.

More fittingly, the paintings were all reverent—portraits of someone I assumed was Saint Dymphna herself. The reading alcove was more bare-bones, clearly unaltered from its original state. Rather than rugs, the floor was plain tile, the furniture unvarnished. My heart raced at the thought of what ancient treasures the bookshelves beside the fireplace held. Perhaps I could fascinate myself with a diary from the abbess herself, or a first-edition copy of some Latin epic. I might stumble upon some hand-scrawled poetry, or even an old almanac. If I

was extraordinarily lucky, I could even find something to help my thesis.

"The maids are waiting for you in the bathroom, signorina."

I was so lost in the fantasy that when the butler spoke, I jolted. "Huh?"

"Your maids are waiting for you in the bathroom," he repeated with a scowl. "I will leave you to bathe."

I couldn't help but laugh. *My* maids? Getting a big fancy breakfast and a beautiful suite already seemed excessive, considering I hadn't yet accepted the gig, but adding maids to the equation was downright comical.

The butler didn't return my laugh. He ended the conversation with a small bow.

Was that supposed to be a joke? Joke or not, I heard water running in the other room. I couldn't just let it overflow.

When I entered the bathroom, white noise filled my ears. My round lenses fogged up within less than a second, blinding me. But this didn't matter, as they were snatched off my face immediately. Now the world looked as blurred and moist as the surrounding air, which was heavy with fragrance. In other circumstances, I would have found the scent of rose and sandalwood delightful, but now it felt like that sense had been overwhelmed to compensate for being robbed of my hearing and vision.

Then I was invaded by touch. Suddenly, two pairs of hands were on me, unzipping, unbuttoning, unclasping, and undressing me. They were swift and efficient, yet so gentle that I only felt my clothes themselves move. I didn't even have the time to squirm or cry out before my clothes were in a heap on the ground in front of me.

Then those hands were lifting me in the air as if I were weightless. I took in a deep breath to scream, but the hot air was stifling in my lungs, and all that came out was a strange croak. I thrashed my head from side to side, squinting to view my captors. The small hands clasping my arms were attached to a bright, round-faced girl in her early twenties. Holding onto my legs was a stern, eagle-nosed woman who appeared wiry yet strong. Their hair was tightly plaited and pinned to their heads in flat, uniform updos, and they wore identical, taupe cotton dresses featuring dark twill aprons and a practical yet elegant design.

I relaxed just a hair. Maids. They were maids.

But this relaxation didn't last for long, as I was quickly lowered into a massive claw-foot tub. Steaming water enveloped me, rushing up past my chin. Rose petals danced in the swirling water, and before it settled, the older maid poured in a jar of honey, followed by buttermilk. As I curled up to shield myself from both sets of curious eyes, I almost expected to see a massive spoon stir the delicious concoction I was getting mixed into.

"Please relax, Signorina Bowling!" said the youngest maid. "It is our duty to ensure you have a relaxing day."

I wanted to point out what a ridiculous task it was to make me *relax*. As if I could relax when no one had told me why I was being treated like a goddess for no apparent reason, when I was quite literally ass-naked and defenseless. Yet she spoke so earnestly that I allowed myself to settle into the tub a bit more.

"You can call me Cora," I told her.

"Of course, Signorina Cora! I'm Lucia Circelli, your lady's maid. I will be responsible for feeding, bathing, and dressing you."

I stifled a nervous laugh into an awkward smile. "It's a pleasure to meet you, Lucia. But I don't know that I'm going to be staying here, and I don't think I'd have a maid even if I did. I'm not—" I wasn't the abbess, or a duchess, or anyone noble, and that fact was at the forefront of my mind.

"You are Duca de' Medici's guest," she said, smiling warmly. "Please, let yourself relax a bit."

I was so confused and exhausted it didn't take any further convincing. My younger self, the little girl huddled in the corner of the school library reading sloppily taped-together regency novels, took over. As I sank into the tub and let the water lap at my chin, I allowed myself to indulge in the daydream.

Unfortunately, the reverie didn't last when I realized the older maid would not even look my way. She stood by the far end of the tub, tidying my rumpled clothes with a peculiar air. Was it disgust? They were freshly washed. What had offended her so much? Had my Italian been too touristy? Was my desperation palpable? Or was the problem just . . . *me*?

A small hand pressed down on my shoulder, and Lucia's dulcet tone whispered, "Signora Carbone is distant, but I promise she is happy to have someone in the abbess's suite. She has kindness in her, even if it doesn't always show."

It was probably a lie, but it was a lie on my behalf, so I allowed it. I smiled as best I could and let her pull my arm from the tub to gently scrub it. All the while, Signora Carbone stood back from the tub, scratching away at some unknown document on a clipboard.

When my bath was done, she left to prepare pastries for afternoon tea, and Lucia enthusiastically gathered the outfit I would be wearing. It probably should have struck me as unnerving that the clothes she'd returned with were not my own, but it didn't. Unlike the shoes which had materialized on their own, I felt that this pleasant young woman was my sister playing make-believe with me. Lucia dressed me in a fine dress I did not dare ask the price of.

Staring in the mirror, I frowned. The dress was wasted on someone of my short, boyish stature. But then, when I saw Lucia's utter pride and satisfaction behind me, I could see the good qualities in it too. The lace choker around my neck accentuated what was now a surprisingly elegant jawline and high cheekbones. The emeralds brought out the green in my hazel eyes. And to my surprise, the coquette gloves and stockings actually looked flattering.

"Um, thank you," I told Lucia over my shoulder, who grinned in return.

"Of course, signorina! By the way, Doctor Ntumba thought you might want to visit the libraries before meeting with her. Would you be interested in that?"

Libraries? As in plural? Despite not having accepted the job yet, my heart soared at the thought. Aside from my dire need for thesis material, I had already read all the books in my satchel several times over, and the idea of having access to more was exhilarating. No matter the genre, books were my solace, and they always had been. Books didn't bully, books didn't leave, books didn't need, and books didn't die. Instead, they transported me to fantastical realms and allowed me to live hundreds of lives within my own, ones with problems that solved themselves and people who spoke freely without expecting anything in return.

"Yes!"

The smaller library lived up to its name. It barely exceeded the size of my room, and its cleaning had been mostly neglected. Even so, its shelves teemed with countless volumes of various ages. Lucia left me there to explore, and I did so eagerly.

To my surprise, most of the books were not the things I could find in normal libraries. They were exactly what I had spent hours in fruitless pursuit of: old banking transactions, family trees, copies of letters . . . anything and everything related to the Medici family since the Renaissance.

I filled several pages of my notebooks with titles of documents to examine more closely, and many more with notes from what I had already scavenged. I had to remind myself I hadn't signed any sort of contract, but the prospect of saying "no" to the job was growing more and more outlandish.

This inkling only grew stronger when it came time to see the large library. The room was a bibliophile's sanctuary. Books covered every part of every wall, save the few sections with paintings, sculptures, or sitting areas. The room was scattered with wheeled ladders, and their pale bodies and yellow posts reminded me of a flock of storks. I followed the imaginary line to where they were staring. Overhead, in the middle of an oil-painted mural clearly inspired by the Sistine Chapel, was a massive golden chandelier. Even the floors themselves were decorated; the areas not covered by rugs or tapestries had been carved into with tiling, and Latin script surrounded each tile. In contrast to the study area by my room, this library appeared immaculately maintained. I would have bet money each individual book was dusted.

I didn't notice Signora Carbone until she walked in front of me, handed Lucia a small stack of papers—busy-work, from the look on Lucia's face—and marched to a desk in the corner.

"I manage this library," she said, "and I manage it well."

I felt a pang of betrayal at such a cozy sanctum being managed by such a standoffish woman, but I smiled and nodded anyway.

She beckoned me over. I stood awkwardly by her desk.

"As you may have noticed," she continued, picking up a binder from a shelf behind the desk, "the books here are all organized. Each row is marked, and each book is assigned a number. I intend to keep it that way. Accordingly—" she dropped the binder onto the desk with an

emphatic *thud*, and it swung open to reveal a gridded chart. "—any book or record you check out or even *touch* must be recorded within our logbook."

Signora Carbone trailed her finger along each box as she spoke. "Here, you must put the name of what you have taken. Here, the EAN or whatever number it is assigned. Here, the location you have removed it from, the expected return date, the actual return date . . ."

She outlined, in excruciating detail, the hoops and ladders I would gladly leap through to read these books. Then she showed me a small receptacle to return it all. "Do you have any questions?"

I shook my head. As confusing as she had made it sound, the library's system was straightforward enough.

"I see. So long as you follow these rules, you should not see me here."

I gave her a tight-lipped smile, counting the seconds until she left. I went to work immediately, identifying each section and mentally notating a map of every shelf. To Signora Carbone's credit, she had organized it beautifully, not just by author and whether a book was fiction or nonfiction, but by artistic classification. All the Arthurian legends were in one row, New Wave records in another. The placement made logical sense; I understood why she didn't want it disrupted.

But before I got the chance to fully dig into it, Lucia returned. "Please come with me, signorina," she said. "It's time for you to speak with Doctor Ntumba."

Chapter Four

Obbligato

Doctor Ntumba was waiting for me in the tearoom. She was as elegant as yesterday in a flashy, geometric-print pantsuit. Even her pose—sitting on the edge of a recliner with her legs folded tightly at the ankles—looked out of a magazine. Of the half dozen rings on her fingers, only one lacked a gem corresponding to a color on her pantsuit. Instead, it was identical in shade to her electric-green earrings and shoes. Her braids were meticulously styled and pinned in a tight up-do. It was no less intimidating meeting her for the second time, but at least I felt prepared. As invasive as my run-in with Duca de' Medici's maids had been, I was grateful for it now. Doctor Ntumba looked the picture of professionalism, and I actually matched her.

She trained her eyes on some figure in the behemoth of a textbook in her lap and only broke contact with it once she'd dog-eared the page, shut the book, and placed it on the ground beside her.

In a fluid gesture, she beckoned me closer and poured some tea into two cups from a china pot. I sat in a recliner perpendicular to hers and gave a small nod in greeting, hoping to look as nonchalant as she appeared.

"How was your afternoon?" she asked after taking a long sip of what smelled to be freshly brewed hibiscus tea.

I mirrored her action, relishing in the chance to have a bit more time to think of my response. How had the afternoon been? Lonely, lovely, jarring, eerie? Many possible answers swirled in my mouth, alongside the floral taste.

"Strange," I answered, truthfully. "It doesn't feel like I'm supposed to be here. It's like I'm playing pretend. Like I'm in some childhood daydream."

Doctor Ntumba cast a meaningful gaze to my hands and

revealed her own. Thick lines creased them, the calluses permanently embossed. Their general coarseness mirrored mine. I saw this reflection of her upbringing for only an instant as she turned them to reveal the smooth, perfectly lotioned and pampered backs of her hands.

"Your palms may remain like mine, but you'll get soft skin within a few weeks of milk-and-honey baths."

Within a few weeks. It was presumptuous of her to assume I would agree before actually discussing the deal—but not entirely untrue. My wallet was empty, and my mind was full of intrigue. I had nothing to lose and she knew it.

"Now, for the details of your offer," she said. "As previously mentioned, your position would entail you living here full time. The specific duration of your employment is to be continually negotiated by both parties on a quarterly basis but has the potential to be indefinite if both parties are amenable. During this period, you are considered a member of the abbey, and you will be following its schedule, along with a designated maid."

I forced my lip not to curl. Based on all of my past experience, a job usually involved some sort of sacrifice: Burns from frying grease at the local fast-food joint. Being uncomfortably hit on by an old man at a cash register, only to be scolded by my manager for being "rude" when I wasn't receptive. Headaches and heart palpitations from excessive caffeine while grading essays at three a.m. Clearly—unless I was missing a detail in the job description—someone was being taken advantage of here, and it was probably me. I was becoming more and more frustrated at being invited all this way, only to have the reasons why hidden behind smoke and mirrors.

"Okay, but what is my actual job?" I countered once I could no longer bite my tongue. "You haven't touched upon my duties, and I have a hard time imagining you're giving me room and board to try on fancy clothes."

Doctor Ntumba stared at me intently, and for a moment, I considered apologizing for the interruption. While I certainly had a temper, it was typically smothered by a strong distaste for confrontation, and wielding such bluntness felt incredibly awkward.

I feared I'd enraged my interviewer irreparably, but her reply was as cool as ever.

"Your secondary responsibility as an employee will be to maintain your health by having as little stress as possible. You will maintain a strict regimen of supplements and exercise planned by

myself, as well as eat at least 70 percent of all meals prepared. You are required to abstain from all aspirin, alcohol, and other blood thinners. All of this will ensure your blood is of high quality for donation." Doctor Ntumba followed my gaze to my inner arm, where faded, amber-greenish smudges still remained a week after an apologetic nursing student had butchered my veins.

"My primary duty is to donate blood?" I asked, quirking a brow. "That's it?"

"It is an important duty. Zeno requires one quarter of a liter of whole blood every month to replenish the blood cells he cannot adequately produce as a vampire."

"Even so, having me live here full time and giving me all these luxuries doesn't make sense," I retorted. "It would be less expensive—not to mention easier—to get monthly transfusions."

Doctor Ntumba gave me a peculiar expression, which I could only assume was a combination of annoyance at my interruption and some sort of amusement. She laced her fingers, leaning forward in her chair. "You assume correctly. However, it is not truly the blood itself that is your purpose."

"What's my purpose, then?" My tone sharpened.

To my surprise, Doctor Ntumba furrowed her brow. "I have been searching for someone to be Zeno's *beniamina*."

Images of famous *beniamini* flashed through my mind: muses, courtesans, concubines, assistants, confidants, advisers. All the main blood sources for powerful vampires. More than that, *beniamini* were the right hand of their vampires. They had waged wars, and wars had been waged over them. Hell, some medieval Christian cults argued Peter had been a *beniamino* of a vampiric Jesus, connecting Him with humans.

There was really only one interpretation of her words, one I refused to accept. It was simply impossible that one of the wealthiest families on earth would have any interest in appointing *me* as the partner to its presumed heir. There must have been some grave misunderstanding, and the only way I would look more naïve than

sitting here, wordlessly, would be by acting like I knew what the hell was going on.

Silence proliferated. Doctor Ntumba tapped the inside of her teacup with a spoon, and Lucia immediately refilled it.

"It's a coming-of-age ritual for vampires to gain a *beniamino* during confirmation, typically, or otherwise around fourteen or fifteen years old," she said. "And it is a responsibility that Zeno has opted to push back for the past fourteen years."

"Why would he do that? I've never heard of such a thing."

"For the same reason that he is living in an abandoned abbey in rural Sicily rather than at a gathering in Venice. Zeno is not fond of the expectations of vampire society. He would much rather continue to go to a blood transfusion center than bother with the human component of the partnership, and he doesn't hide that from prospective *beniamini*. Of course, he still requires a source of blood, and the Abbazia di Santa Dymphna is not a family heirloom. Zeno wasn't able to purchase it and leave Venice without behaving. That includes fulfilling the step of getting a *beniamina*."

A dull ache emerged behind my eyes. I pinched the bridge of my nose. Doctor Ntumba was knocking down questions quickly, and all that remained were the ones that had spawned the moment I opened that first letter.

I finally let out those two simple words: "Why me?"

Doctor Ntumba let out a strange, exasperated combination of a laugh and a scoff.

"The mere presence of someone with the title of *beniamina* is enough to placate upper society and his family, regardless of who they are or if they even interact with Zeno. The only truly relevant requirement to this position is that the individual's presence is

tolerated in the abbey. Several candidates have interviewed for this position, but you are the only one he has permitted to stay."

I had a hard time seeing how immediately arguing with my host made me worth tolerating, but that wasn't something to complain about. More importantly, I hadn't received an answer to my question.

"But how did you find me? Where did you get my address?"

"I saw you last fall at a conference in London," Doctor Ntumba replied so quickly, I wondered if I was only imagining her trying to be evasive.

Last fall—and London—both seemed decades away, but even in the haze of distant memory, that conference was clear. Along with manning the lab's table, I had given my first and only presentation that day, earned through the luck of having my thesis adviser get sick at the last minute. The booth had been sequestered away in the corner of the dingiest hall, and it was clear I was just taking up space. The paper I was presenting on, *Perspectives on Vampiric Syndromes in the Papal Conclave of 1492*, was a crowd-pleaser I wasn't proud of. But none of that had mattered. Drenched in sweat beneath the nicest suit jacket I could rent, I had the time of my life, thrilled at sharing and being heard.

But only a few people had stopped by my booth, and I didn't remember Doctor Ntumba amongst them. I studied her features carefully in the hopes that some previously unnoted freckle or dimple would unleash a memory, but nothing did.

"We did not exchange words," she clarified, "but I saw you throughout the night. There was a manner in which you spoke that made me believe Zeno might be fond of you. You were astonishingly vibrant when speaking about your work, only to fade into the background entirely whenever you stopped speaking. You never joined in on conversations uninvited, but I also never saw you with a lack of opinion when prompted."

She continued on, explaining how she had found my name on the lab website, but I wasn't paying attention. My mind was already racing, and it couldn't handle much more information.

Seeing the look on my face, Doctor Ntumba shot me a pointed gaze and stated, "Cora, this position is incredibly straightforward. I was telling you the truth when I talked about your sole duties—you'll be a *beniamina* in name and blood bond alone. There are no parties to

attend, no formal meetings, and no decisions to make. Zeno may not even speak to you on a regular basis."

"I see."

A complex array of emotions washed over me, crossing and knotting like sloppy weaving. The warp was disappointment and the weft was relief, with countless other embedded feelings. But what had I expected out of such a bizarre situation?

"Think about it," Doctor Ntumba said, organizing her papers but pointedly leaving one behind. "I'll meet you tomorrow morning with either a contract or passes for a ride home." With the rest gathered neatly into her arms, Doctor Ntumba rose from her chair to leave.

"W-wait!" I stammered, taking a step toward her.

She swiveled to look back at me, brow raised. "Have you made up your mind so soon?"

I shook my head and wrung my hands, nervous under the intensity of her gaze. "No, I just wanted to know the name of the butler."

Her confused expression remained, now slightly mottled with annoyance. "There is plenty of help. It doesn't matter whom you bring it to."

"I meant the name of the one who showed me to my room the other night. He had dark brown hair and seemed nervous, but he was nice to me. I should at least know his name."

A strange smile crossed her lips. "That would be Signore Urbino. He will probably be ordered to keep a distance if you choose to stay."

"What?"

She shrugged and turned back to the door. "I won't say much further, as it isn't my business. Good night."

I muttered my goodbyes as she left and, as before, found myself alone. I lingered for a moment on the strange detail regarding

Signore Urbino, but it passed through my mind quickly, overtaken by the more pressing matter at hand. I had a decision to make.

I ate dinner in the same dining hall I had eaten breakfast in earlier. Like before, there was an excessive amount of food to eat, and like before, I was eating it alone.

Beniamina. I traced the word on the table in front of me until my fingertip felt numb. I mentally combed through the job description that had brought me here: *Healthy adult wanted for paid blood donations in rural Sicily. Room and board provided. Long-term gig with a generous salary. Discretion required.*

It was an accurate description, wasn't it? One day out of the month, I'd get a needle or fangs in my arm, and for the remainder, I'd be spoiled rotten by maids and have access to a whole host of treasures. Nothing would truly change for me to decline what seemed to be godly intervention, other than that one word: *beniamina.*

I dissected the job description again, sentence by sentence.

Healthy adult wanted for paid blood donations in rural Sicily.

Paid blood donations were what I did in college. This wasn't really so simple, though, was it? Being a *beniamina* was something far beyond such a simple thing; *beniamini* were partners to the powerful and elite. Whether that partnership was platonic, romantic, sexual, or solely economic was private information. Many considered the pact between a *beniamino* and their vampire to be as deep, if not deeper, than that between spouses. I doubted anyone had ever interviewed for it like this, especially someone like me. And even now, one month after our breakup, I couldn't help but feel a twinge of guilt at the notion of a pararomantic relationship when Emily still existed.

Room and board provided.

That was the easy part, wasn't it? But why was Doctor Ntumba rushing me and pushing so hard for something so nice?

Long-term gig with a generous salary.

Doctor Ntumba said my position was to be reviewed quarterly, but how long did it have the potential to be? Oculocutaneous albinism and pancytopenia—an inability to produce blood cells—were the core

mutations involved in vampirism, and neither was inherently life-shortening if managed. But even with modern medicine, many subtypes of vampirism led to significantly shorter lives, often with much of them spent in hospitals. Would I be wasting their time when I inevitably left after getting all the information I needed?

A trio of sharp knocks shattered my trance. Instinctively, I sat up straight and folded my hands in my lap. Signora Carbone greeted me with a vaguely annoyed glance, so I tried to make myself as small as possible as she tidied up my dishes and cleaned around me.

"Signora Ntumba says you have not made up your mind yet," the older woman said in a low tone as she continued to scrub. "Please do so quickly so I can know whether to fully prepare your room."

"It's . . . not a simple decision," I replied, fidgeting with my skirt.

"It would be if your resolve were firmer."

As offended as I was, I couldn't argue with her assessment.

"My family has been associated with the Medici for generations," she continued. "For generations, we have sweat for them. We have bled for them and by them, and not once have we had the honor of being *beniamini*. For you to so lightly look at such an opportunity—"

"I'm *not* looking at it lightly. I would have said yes by now if I was." My tone came out sterner than expected.

Signora Carbone rested a fist on her hip but allowed me to continue.

"I know more about the Medici than you might think. I know about the centuries of death and life and power that have followed the family, and how much influence the *beniamini* within it have held. But you must understand that this was never a possibility I could have imagined."

"Then why hesitate if you understand what a chance you have?" A combination of perplexity and exasperation sharpened her tone. "Why turn down what so many others have only dreamed of? Why deny me my chance to perform my duties as a *conservatrix*?"

I clutched my phone to my chest and said nothing. So she was a *conservatrix*, meaning she'd trained for years on the minute details of rituals associated with housing *beniamini*. But even so, how could she understand? How could I even communicate the feeling of treachery pulsing within me at the mere notion of getting into some farce of a relationship when I had only just gotten out of one? And why even bother explaining it to someone who seemed so predisposed to judge me?

The older woman sighed and loosened her fists. "I am sorry, signorina. You must have a reason. Pardon my impertinence." She returned to scrubbing with greater diligence and avoided my gaze altogether.

I, in turn, rolled my food around my plate with a fork.

You're not wrong, signora, I thought as I stabbed a trio of peas. *This should be a simple decision.*

After gently placing my fork on the table, I closed my eyes and inhaled slowly through my nose. There was the musty scent of the ancient abbey, the spices from my food, even my own perfume, but beneath that all, the Sicilian air was distinct. I was, I reminded myself, in Sicily. Not in London, not in Emily's apartment. Not in her arms, her bed. I would be cheating on the memory of her, nothing more.

This position, unorthodox as it was, was the answer to everything I had been searching for. If I said no, what would I be left with? I had no apartment, no funding, and no one waiting for me beyond the abbey walls, other than an increasingly stressed thesis adviser. *Beniamina* or not, I would be a fool to turn this down.

The sound of pen scribbling on paper caused Signora Carbone to whip her head in my direction. I folded it tightly once, twice, and thrust it into the stunned woman's hand. She waited for any sort of explanation, but I knew the resolve on my face was enough.

Despite having only cleaned half the room, she set down her supplies and left to deliver the message.

Chapter Five

Tessitura

I was woken three times the next morning, twice by chance and once on purpose. The first time I woke up was at the crack of dawn, when Signora Carbone entered my room. I pretended to be asleep as she placed the full contract for employment at my bedside, and soon enough, I was. The second time I woke up was when Lucia gently called my name and shook my shoulders at the expected time. She quickly gave up when my somnolent protests made it apparent jet lag still clung to me. The third time was a few hours later, when Lucia cheerfully whistled as she folded my laundry in the other room.

I groaned as I sat up in bed. No matter how comfortable this mattress was, it couldn't counteract a night of tossing and turning. I rubbed my eyes in a vain attempt to push out the exhaustion, then decided the better option would be to lighten the room a bit. I threw open the curtains on the eastern wall, wincing as the afternoon sun poured in.

"Ugh." My chin was sticky and wet with drool. I knew instinctively my hair was a mess, and although I would have a bath later in the day, I should at least attempt to tame it somewhat. With another groan, I stumbled to my vanity.

In the mirror, a flash of someone: sallow cheeks, yellowed skin and eyes, matted hair.

I blinked in shock. Between frames, she changed. Light sunspots across a round, dimpled face, bright green eyes, dirty-blonde hair plaited into loose braids.

With another blink, it was just me. Me, with the freckles along the bridge of my nose and prominent features, tight black curls, intense gaze. I staggered back and reached for something solid but found only air. I hit the ground with my tailbone at an awkward angle, and for a second, I feared it had shattered. But by the time the adrenaline wore

off and I could fully assess my pain, it was already fading. I ran a shaking hand across my forehead and wiped away the cold sweat.

"Signorina Cora?" Lucia burst into the room and immediately fell to her knees beside me. "Are you okay? Are you ill? What happened?"

I exhaled and shook my head. "It's fine, Lucia. I just got a little startled, is all."

"Do you want me to get Doctor Ntumba?"

Surely I hadn't woken up entirely, right? Surely my nightmares had just lingered a moment past waking up.

That was what I told myself, anyway.

"No, I'm fine, really." I pinched the bridge of my nose and closed my eyes. "Sorry to worry you." She hovered by me for a moment, clearly restraining the urge to help me up. She only relaxed when I gave her a small smile.

"What's the plan for today, Lucia?"

Instantly, she brightened. "Oh yes, I heard you accepted the position, Signorina Cora! Congratulations!"

"Thank you," I replied as I got to my feet. "I'm excited to be here."

"Anyway," she continued, "Doctor Ntumba thought you might want to settle in, so she didn't want to have you follow the schedule very strictly today. Signora Carbone was going to write it up for you."

I felt my muscles tense at the sound of the conservatrix's name. Our last encounter had been . . . strained, to say the least.

"Speaking of which," Lucia added, "she's on her way to speak with you."

I couldn't help but grimace. Luckily, Lucia wasn't looking. I didn't know what to expect, nor was I emotionally prepared. Would Signora Carbone now regard me with respect, or would the rudeness continue?

I briefly considered finding some sort of escape route, but before I could do so, Lucia looked behind me and said, "Good afternoon, Signora Carbone!"

Signora Carbone had her arms folded tightly behind her back but was seemingly unaltered from our previous exchange. I searched her face for any sign of anger or discomfort and was slightly disturbed to find none. Lucia beamed, evidently clueless.

"Good afternoon, Lucia," Signora Carbone said coolly. "I need you to go to the kitchen and finish preparing breakfast."

Lucia pursed her lips in a childlike pout—she hated cooking, she had told me—but didn't protest further. Once we were alone, Signora Carbone finally addressed me. "Signorina Bowling. How are you today?"

"I'm well," I lied, shifting from foot to foot.

"Good. I was just coming to inform you that breakfast will be ready soon, and that I will be delivering your daily schedule this evening."

Her eyes trailed me up and down, and her lips tightened. I wasn't sure if her thoughts were transparent for once, whether her actions showed she thought I was inadequate to be a beniamina for the most powerful family in Italy, or if I was transposing my own insecurities onto her. But then she showed the first true ounce of incertitude I had ever seen from her.

"Signorina Bowling," she said with a funereal air. "I apologize for yesterday. Going forward, I will remember my station. I hope you remember yours."

She walked away before I could ask what she meant by that last bit.

I wondered if she knew the truth. As lovely as this week had been, my goal here was not to be a beniamina, or even get the salary. I was here to find clues for my thesis, and even if I hadn't dug into them so far, that was my sole reason for staying. Doctor Ntumba had told me both parties would review the job quarterly, and I planned to take full advantage of that leniency. But if Signora Carbone had caught on, I couldn't help but wonder if—or when—anyone else in the house would. I hadn't mentioned the details of my thesis, and I couldn't help but fear that if I did, certain documents would mysteriously go missing from the library—or worse, I would be out of a job entirely.

With this uncomfortable possibility in mind, a sense of urgency burned in my chest. Knowing Lucia and Signora Carbone would be busy in the kitchen for the foreseeable future, I grabbed a notebook and made a beeline to the large library to investigate its innards. The fiction section dwarfed the large library's non-fiction section, and much of the

non-fiction section focused on the sciences, not history.

I crouched in the most promising area and scanned the books, writing down anything that looked unusual or relevant. Within seconds, I spotted a pair of promising titles that hadn't been available at my university.

I scratched them down quickly. Just as I was about to start on the second row, a strange feeling bored through my excitement: the feeling of someone watching me.

Duca de' Medici's eyes were piercing, especially in the light. How I hadn't noticedthem before was a mystery. He sat in the corner of the room in front of a small tea table, sprawled out in a casual position—one arm extended onto the table, chin resting on his fist, and one leg dangling over the other—that seemed mismatched with the formality of his clothing. The vampire wore a gray button-down shirt with plaid charcoal pants and a matching suit jacket draped over his shoulder like a cape. I hadn't noticed his earrings before: ruby-and-gold studs that matched the gem on the end of his bolo tie and brought out the sharpness in his jaw.

In front of him was a tray of biscotti, many with the corners nibbled off in tiny, mouse-like bites. A series of records were fanned out in front of him, but I couldn't see the titles at my angle. Even if I could, it would have been impossible to focus on anything but the terrifyingly angelic man before me.

"O-oh!" I stammered, my notebook nearly slipping from my fingers. "I wasn't expecting—um, good morning. How long have you . . .?"

Duca de' Medici blinked at me a few times, then returned his attention to the biscotti. I almost thought he wouldn't reply, but a few seconds later, his voice rang out, clear yet in a monotone, "However long you've been here, along with an additional ten or so minutes. Not that I tend to linger here, normally. I would have finished my meal and picked out music by now, but your uninvited presence was distracting."

My jaw fell to the floor. All that came out for several seconds was incoherent sputtering. But once I could actually talk, the wrong words came out, a sharp riposte instead of the intended apology or small talk.

"I'm sorry my presence was distracting, but I didn't realize I had to be invited when the door was wide open. And for that matter, I didn't realize a plate of cookies counted as a meal for a grown man."

A faint rosy shade spread across Duca de' Medici's cheeks, and

he jerked away.

I was terrified he was enraged until I noticed the quiver in his lips, the fine knitting of his brow, and the way he was averting his eyes from me entirely.

"Consider the library yours during your stay," he grumbled, his voice surprisingly even for how flustered he appeared. "I'm . . . not fond of sharing, and I doubt my company is desired, regardless."

Duca de' Medici's coat billowed as he strode quickly to the door. I reached out for where he had been.

"W-wait!" I cried, hoping to salvage the conversation. This was my employer, after all. "What about your cookies and music? You haven't chosen—"

"I don't have an appetite anymore," he snapped. "And I have a collection of records that serves me well enough."

Once again, I was at a loss for words. An awkward silence hung between us. I considered apologizing and discounting his former assertion that I wouldn't want his presence but feared it would look forced. Then I thought about inviting him back in and starting the conversation anew, but I knew I was far too rattled to come up with anything to discuss.

Instead, I asked the question at the forefront of my mind. "You know I accepted the position, right? I'm technically your beniamina?"

He gave me a single, quick nod. "If that is acceptable to you. I'm sure Noor informed you that the title won't require much of you out here. You're welcome to change your mind, but I will gladly keep my distance for the time being if you find that preferable."

"I don't want . . ." I trailed off. Maybe I did want him to keep his distance. Doctor Ntumba had insinuated that Duca de' Medici only needed to tolerate my presence, and it was possible he would keep interactions with me to a minimum. Had she been wrong in guessing there was something about me he would be fond of? Perhaps in future discussions, Duca de' Medici would discover he found me neither "peculiar" nor "interesting enough to keep around." Perhaps I would continue to flounder in conversation after conversation and get kicked out before I even finished a single book.

I should at least clarify I didn't hate him.

I didn't get the chance to finish my sentence, or any other for that matter. With little more than a tense nod, Duca de' Medici departed.

In the two conversations I'd had with him, he had shown himself to be many things: pompous, peculiar, and blunt. But over the next few days, I discovered another trait: he was true to his word. I didn't see him in the library or anywhere else, and soon it felt like our conversations were some imagined figments of the past.

Of course, that couldn't last forever.

Chapter Six

Libiamo ne' lieti calici

Despite the rough start, the next several days of my stay were an utter fantasy. The morning progressed as seamless clockwork, where I played the role of a gentlewoman–I'd be awoken and brought down to a gourmet breakfast, then have a bath drawn for me. Then, once being preened and dressed by Lucia, Signora Carbone would provide a light afternoon snack paired with some sort of local drink.

After that, Lucia would bring me down for afternoon tea with Doctor Ntumba and the two of us would chat briefly. Mostly, I would listen as she explained to me Sicilian culture, the latest advancements in medicine, and her surprising interest in anthropology. But now and then, I'd get a peek into her personal life—the antics of her two college-aged sons, the crafts she liked to do with her late husband, and her young life as a Christian in Egypt. She stated to me often that she had an unusual and even controversial specialty in medicine, but did not go in any further depth. She served as a grounding point, someone whose pragmatic presence would remind me the wrapping outside my window at night or the scratching in my walls were likely twigs and small animals respectively–not specters I had conjured.

But for as much as I would enjoy these conversations, I was always more eager for what came after—the rest of the day in the library. At this point, I wasn't brave enough to venture into the Medici family documents themselves, but I was content enough with a seemingly unlimited supply of novels from the past five centuries on all four walls around me. I had a good idea where to start, and confidence my eventual search would be fruitful. There were ample CDs and records along with the books, and in the room's corner were enough art supplies to last me a few years. I had dabbled in painting back during my undergraduate years and was pleasantly surprised to find I had a bit of technique in me still.

Yet despite being surrounded by the richest of architectural

beauties I could ever imagine, I found myself time and time again sketching the illusive Duca de' Medici. I would set out to paint the interior of a lovely greenhouse, but by the end of the painting, he would be a statue standing in the middle with ivy twisting around his legs. I would try to paint a sunset on the beach and his intense eyes would find their way to swirl into the crimsons in the sky. But soon enough, the illusive vampire turned into a fictional character in my mind along with Beowulf and Heathcliff and Tristam.

Occasionally, I saw flashes of him. He would regularly pass me in the hall with his chin raised high, not giving me a single glance. There were a few instances where I walked in on him stretched out like a cat in front of the fireplace with a book in his hand, and he had simply tossed me an annoyed glance for the intrusion and angled the cover away from me. More often, I heard music coming from his room and saw trays of chocolates and tea placed at the foot of his door.

By the time I was brought down one day into a jarringly modern exam room within the abbey, I had almost forgotten my purpose.

"I'm just going to run a standard CBC and CMP on you," she informed me. "Assuming your labs are good, I will be drawing a liter of blood from you tomorrow to transfuse to Zeno."

Transfuse? I had never heard of a beniamina donating blood via any route other than direct drinking. It would be a lie to say I wasn't a little bit relieved at the prospect of this untraditional donation, but I also felt strangely wounded. I couldn't help but wonder if somehow, I wasn't good enough, or if Duca de' Medici found me repulsive in any way. Doctor Ntumba attempted to walk me through the process, but I was too distracted by the elephant in the room.

When she finished tying the tourniquet, I couldn't bear it any longer and had to ask, "Is it normal for vampires to get blood like this? I've never read of beniamini donating blood so..." I paused, looking for the word. "So clinically."

"You're correct. This is inefficient," replied Doctor Ntumba as she scrubbed my inner elbow with an alcohol wipe. "Transferral can damage platelets, for instance, and it's easy for fluid overload to occur."

"Then why are we doing it like this?"

She chuckled more warmly than I had ever heard.

"Because Zeno is foolish and shy."

"Him? Shy?" I exclaimed without thinking.

"That and terrified of intimacy. Drinking someone's blood is very... familiar."

Portraits of the process with romantic or even erotic undertones filled my mind. I had written an entire paper on the artistic significance of Ritus Sanguinous—the first public drinking, simple and sweet, marking the bond between a vampire and their beniamini, which could be a massive, multi-day occasion.

Capping a vial I hadn't realized I had been filling, she looked up at me.

"But you knew that already, and you will do your duty soon."

I flinched. "What exactly do you mean by that?"

"Nothing unusual. Zeno wants to drink from you, and he wishes for you to offer him company."

My entire body grew hot. Company? Did she mean in a romantic or even more intimate sense? I was neither my mother's child nor my father's when it came to emotional or physical openness. From a young age I admired from afar, in the same non-replicable way as I would a circus performer, the way the two had gushed over one another like newlyweds. And while I had never experienced such a relationship, I was doomed to repeat its end—not the literal death that ended their love, but the death of intimacy. Emily and I hadn't slept together for months before we broke up, and it had been years since I was with a man. God knew I hadn't even considered the possibility of sharing a bed with Duca de' Medici. With the face an angel but the temperament of a devil, was I even attracted to him like that?

"I thought I was a beniamina in name alone. I thought you said Zeno may not even interact with me. A-and when you say company, do you mean...?"

She replied after swiftly removing the needle and instructing me to hold a cotton ball to where it had been: "He just wishes to talk with you, Cora. Zeno has been getting to know you, albeit from a distance."

I only felt relief for an instant before I considered the implications of the latter sentence. Had he seen what I had been up to? Did he know how he was in all of my paintings? Doctor Ntumba keyed in on my panicked expression and was quick to elaborate.

"I've seen him looking at the library's logbook. Anything you've listened to here, so has he, often while reading what you've read. Truthfully, he's so busy studying your tastes that he barely speaks to me

at all anymore."

"That's..." I wasn't sure what the end of my sentence would be. Invasive? Weird? Flattering? "...Unexpected. Why didn't you tell me this sooner? How long did you know?"

A twinge of guilt flickered onto her face briefly, but her expression quickly returned to its usual stoniness. "It wasn't my business. You're going to be having tea in the main library this evening with him before dinner. I have other matters to attend to."

I felt lightheaded. "I thought he hated me."

"Far from it," she replied with a chuckle.

"I mean, he always glares at me or outright ignores me and—"

"Keep pressure on that cotton ball," Doctor Ntumba cut in with an uncharacteristically stern tone. I pushed down the cotton as she explicitly ordered and followed the implicit one to shut up.

I watched in silence as Doctor Ntumba carefully stowed away the blood bags and retrieved a set of fresh supplies. Once she had laid everything out, she turned back to me with folded arms. "How do you feel?"

"Okay?" My answer sounded like just as much of a question as hers.

"Well enough to walk?"

"I guess."

"Good." She pulled a string on the wall I hadn't realized was there. Another bell.

From across the hall, I could hear two sets of footsteps nearing. Shit. I'm only half of the transfusion. Duca de' Medici was presumably coming to the exam room, and the two of us would have to cross paths. Per my racing heart, this was not the time or the setting for a small talk. I needed some buffer time between this bizarre conversation and our scheduled teatime, after all. I closed my eyes and charted an escape route. If I left the room right away, I could make it out the side door. Then, I could cut through the garden and hopefully make it into my suite entirely unseen.

I leapt off the exam table.

"Thanks! I'll let you know if I have any issues."

I snatched the bandage from the doctor's hand and, to my relief, she did not stop me as I raced out the door. Once I made it to the courtyard, I looked at my watch. I had two hours before tea. Two hours to figure out how the hell to talk with my strange host.

Chapter Seven

Chiaroscuro

Duca de' Medici was late for our meal. I had the feeling *he* would have said he was fashionably so, but I filed away that he was exactly five minutes late—to the second, according to my watch. Five extra minutes for me to plan my reconnaissance.

I had no clue how this would go. For reasons that stumped me entirely, this conversation was two weeks in the making. Both times we had spoken had ended in me blowing my fuse, but now that I knew the vampire was more awkward than antagonistic, I'd have to force myself to be open-minded. And of course, I'd have to plan.

When Duca de' Medici finally arrived, he carried himself with a nonchalant air and tossed his coat over the back of the chair before sitting. Good. I had prepared a casual yet upfront way of approaching the conversation.

"I heard you've been looking at the library logbook," I said, giving him a sideways glance. Studying his face, waiting for a reaction.

"I heard *you've* been painting me."

I grew as red as the carpet at my feet. Maybe if I stared hard enough at the floor, I could bore a hole into it and curl up into a ball.

"No, no need for that look," Duca de' Medici exclaimed, voice loud and dripping with mirth. "I'm flattered, really. It's very Degas, you know, with the heavy chiaroscuro."

He tilted his head up and to the side, which revealed the elegant curve of his jaw I had tried to capture time and time again.

"Don't worry," he continued, stifling a laugh. "I won't send a cease and desist or anything. All I ask is for a cut of the profits for my likeness!"

Never mind the floor now. It was time to launch a grenade at this man with my eyes. But rather than explode, he simply softened. Laughter subdued into a nervous chuckle, but the red in his cheeks remained.

"Joking aside, I am, though. Flattered, I mean. Degas is one of my favorites."

"Thanks, I think." A small but genuine smile came to my lips. Though mildly mitigated, the embarrassment mostly remained. "I don't know why I did it, honestly."

He shrugged broadly and said, "I don't know why I did what I did either."

The mood in the room had palpably shifted to something alien, but quickly turned awkward upon its recognition. I considered venturing further into this uncharted territory when the vampire quickly backpedaled.

"Have you explored this corner of the library before?" he asked, dipping a scone into his now lukewarm tea. "Or do you still hide out in that little section of yours?"

It was as if the massive, untouched tray of cookies and earl gray had materialized before my eyes. I shook my head and took a sip from my cup.

"No, I haven't read anything in this section." I searched for the subterfuge in this strange mixture of authenticity and pretense. "But you knew all of that already, right? So I don't know why you're asking."

"I did know all of that," he admitted. "I just asked to make conversation."

"Why not ask something you don't already know if you want to make conversation?"

He didn't respond, but the way he bit his lips was enough for me to parse the implicit reply: Anything I don't know can't be in the script.

“I’d like you to ask things you’re actually curious about,” I pressed firmly. “Or else I’d rather you just ignore me again than try to have some pre-planned discussion.”

“I wasn’t ignoring you.” His voice was unexpectedly soft. “I just... didn’t know what to say or do. I still don’t.”

In that moment, with all that uncertainty swimming around him, Duca de' Medici reminded me of myself when I was younger. When I skipped recess and hid in the back of the class every day the year my sister started middle school and left me behind. When I reread the same few books over and over, hoping in vain someone else would talk to me, or better yet, pull up a chair beside me.

Without another word, I stood up. Panic painted the vampire's features until he realized I wasn’t heading for the door. Instead, he watched with interest as I went to the return shelf and trailed my finger along the spines of records. A few of them were those I had checked out, but mostly there were unknown records. I thumbed through them. Plenty of Grieg and Chopin, but also contemporary composers and even singer-songwriters I had never heard of.

“Can I ask you a question?”

“Of course.”

“Did you listen to the music I picked out when you were reading those books?” I glanced over my shoulder at him, and all the confidence melted away. “It might sound silly, but I liked to match the books to the music.”

“It isn’t silly.” He answered quickly. “I tried to match them too, but I’m a slow reader with poems. So I supplemented the songs you picked.”

Remembering everything I had read over the past few weeks, I felt my face grow hot. There were so many books in this library, and yet I had read the Three Crowns almost exclusively.

“If I had known I was leading a book club, I would have chosen a bit more variety. I mean, I can’t imagine you liked all of that old poetry. It was probably pretty tiring reading all that Petrarch, right? And I can’t imagine how pretentious you think–”

“No,” he cut in with an unexpectedly sharp tone. "I liked them. I liked every poem and every word you chose. I learned a lot.”

About me or literature? The question coagulated on my tongue, and anything else I could think to ask or reply was clotted behind it.

“Signorina Bowling,” Duca de’ Medici broke the painful silence. “Can I keep reading with you? And please, only read what you wish to. Nothing to please me.”

Now, my reply came easily: “Only if I can keep painting you.”

We said little after that, but somehow, the rest of the hour passed quickly. He had picked out a record to match what I had been reading. *Mahler’s Symphony no 5,* he told me. *Conducted by Bernstein, of course. Why listen to any other version?* To my relief, the small library had two copies of *A Long Fatal Love Chase*, so we could sit across from one another and read together. Occasionally he would point out something from the symphony, such as “Listen to this part–Bernstein wished to be buried with this Adagietto pressed against his heart,” or I would comment on the unusually modern pacing of the book, but otherwise the music was punctuated only by the flipping of a page or long sip of tea.

I hadn’t realized a distant bell had rung until the vampire stood, bowed, and left the room. I remained in my chair for a moment. teatime was over? I could continue reading at the dinner table, so why was I so disappointed? Why was it I felt alone for the first time in this abbey now that he was gone?

Chapter Eight

Opera Buffa

I didn't see Duca de' Medici for many days, but when I went to evening teatime the following week, I didn't have to ask who my guest would be; the tray Signore Urbino carried out with him was enough of an answer. Doctor Ntumba was a light snacker and tended not to like overly sweet foods. I was, therefore, used to things like sesame cookies and chai every afternoon. But now, the tray in front of me was overflowing with a wide selection of chocolates and freshly baked cookies. A light, fruity fragrance wafted from still-steaming teacups, next to another teacup exclusively full of sugar.

Trying to extinguish the proliferating butterflies in my stomach, I plucked a smaller cookie from the middle of the tray, a thumbprint cookie that looked like the kind my mother used to bake. As nauseous as I felt, the raspberry jam and buttery pastry went down easily.

"Those are good, aren't they? I ordered them from a bakery in Salemi."

Duca de' Medici had entered without me noticing. I was surprised when he didn't immediately take a seat across from me. Instead, he lingered at my side with a small plate and tongs.

"You should try those." He grabbed a few small chocolates from the tray. "I had them custom-made from a chocolatier in Switzerland. They're Couverture chocolate bonbons with a lingonberry liquor filling. Oh—or perhaps those petits fours from my favorite patisserie in Paris? And those macarons there have a lovely ganache. Ah, and those ladyfingers have a deceptively nuanced vanilla undertone. Or maybe—"

The list of sweets, all intricately described, continued on for several minutes, and the plate became more and more crowded. Once it couldn't hold a single other confection, Duca de' Medici placed it in front of me.

I blinked at him silently several times before realizing what that meant.

"I uh... I can't eat all this? I haven't even finished the cookie. This is all a lot."

"Oh, I see," Duca de' Medici responded somberly, taking his seat. "I should have been a more attentive host; I didn't mean to overwhelm you."

At how genuinely crestfallen the man looked, I felt a pang of guilt. I took another empty plate, migrating the sweets with my tongs.

"That's alright, we can split them," I told him. "I'm excited to try this one here–I've never tried lingonberry! And the Petit fours look wonderful... Not to mention the macrons! I wish the climate was this wonderful when I used to make these at work."

"You worked in a bakery?" He brightened once more after plopping a Petit fours into his mouth and spooning two scoops of sugar into his tea.

I continued to separate the chocolate, halving them as needed.

"Just a few months before college, to make ends meet before my scholarship kicked in. I did a few odd jobs, but that one was actually quite fun."

"Did you not live with your family at that point? Were you kicked out at 18?" His voice was casual, far calmer than it had been only minutes before. "Or was it a matter of your family being poor and having to rely on you for an income?"

I froze, causing a truffle to fall from my tongs and roll off the table. I didn't bother to pick it up. Duca de' Medici eyed the truffle, then gave me an inquisitive look, but didn't press the issue. This was not an acceptable topic, which must have shown on my face. For a moment, we sat in an unsteady silence, so I attempted to fill it.

"Um, I've been pretty fruitful with painting lately. With the weather changing, it's been pretty fun to dabble with landscape paintings. I haven't painted since I was a freshman, so it's been nice to return to."

I watched as he looked around the room at each painting, then finally rose to his feet and strode across the room. A small swell of anxiety pulsed through me as I charted his course of action—he was about to uncover my work in progress. I balled up my skirt in my hands as he tossed the cloth over the canvas.

It was a still-life oil painting, clearly in the early stages of shading. I hadn't put the details on it either, other than the focal point of the work, an open pomegranate with a chunk grotesquely removed. Beside it was a China bowl partially filled with red seeds. Barely visible in its reflection were a pair of slender, pale hands, which were in the process of picking out more of them. Duca de Medici regarded it for an agonizing half-minute while I counted the shapes on the carpet.

When the vampire turned back, I saw an unexpected fury in his eyes, saw his hands tightened into balls. Had the painting somehow offended him? Was he so egocentric to dislike any work of mine without him as the focus? But to my surprise, the flash of anger was subdued into mild annoyance.

"You're out of carmine. I'll have Urbino pick you up some more." Then, to the door with an exaggerated huff: "He should have known not to let my guest run out. What does he think I keep him around for, anyway?"

There was a strange vitriol in his voice, and one I did not care to explore. Awkward silence proliferated, and I quickly sought a more pleasant topic.

"So, what did you think of Il Canzoniere?"

I had always been incredibly fond of the poem collection by Petrarch. The sonnets composed to his unrequited love were ones that touched me since I read them when moving to London. They had given me a shred of hope that beauty and romance existed in a world so dark, and I could recite a few sonnets by heart–not that I had ever done such a thing in front of a living soul. I had truthfully been terrified to check it out, knowing someone else would read with me, but I was harboring the vague hope that maybe I had found a truly kindred spirit who would be just as eager as myself to discuss it. Instead of answering as quickly as I had hoped, Duca de' Medici dug through his sweets to find a perfectly shaped lady finger and replied,

"I imagine you chose that to satisfy me, which I expressly told you not to do when we last spoke. But it was an acceptable read, nonetheless."

I folded my arms and didn't even attempt to soften my glower.

"What makes you think I chose it for you? And I don't think 'acceptable' is an accurate description of Il Canzoniere."

Duca de' Medici took a long sip of tea, then added a third spoonful of sugar.

"My assumption is based on the fact that you've not once read poetry here, nor have you read anything from the 14th century. That said, I acquiesce on that second bit."

"How generous of you to acquiesce."

"What more did you expect me to say? Au regarde, I'd rather you not attempt to butter me up with sonnets of all things."

I narrowed my eyes. First, this man forced a large plate onto me, then he pried into my past, then accused me of trying to kiss his ass in the most pretentious way, and above all, he had the gall to scoff at something personal I had been terrified to share?

"For your information, I chose it because I've never been able to get my hands on the original, just translations. What I wanted to read had nothing to do with you. And what exactly was your point in coming here if you didn't want to talk about books? You know, other than just to eat a bunch of sugar and brag about all your fancy desserts?"

Once that last sentence left my lips, immediate regret set in. Shit. Not again. While he was not directly my employer, Duca de' Medici's opinion of me was still imperative to my being here. Aside from that, getting angry over something so stupid was just... embarrassing. I felt a lump in my throat, an abomination of chocolate and cookies and sweets threatening to break through. I stuffed another cookie in my mouth, swallowed it without chewing. It was dry, like swallowing sandpaper, and I coughed. Crumbs flew from my mouth, soaring all the way across the table. And, I wagered, right onto Duca de' Medici's face. My eyes had watered from the coughing so that I couldn't see his reaction, but I couldn't imagine it was anything good.

The door was screaming my name. I leapt up and shoved the table away from me, causing a clatter of shifting plates and cups. I didn't wait to see how many chocolates I had overturned, how much tea was dripping down the table.

"I'm sorry! Thanks for the cookies! I think it's time for dinner now, actually!"

With a pained expression, Duca de' Medici stood and held out a hand.

"Signorina Bowling, I–"

I didn't hear the end of the sentence, as I had already run off.

Chapter Nine

Bisbigliando

Even if I hadn't felt sick with regret, my stomach was so full of chocolate I couldn't eat a bite of dinner. And of all the days to have done this, I chose one where my favorite dishes were being served. A delicate and fragrant risotto was being served alongside eggplant Parmesan and butter chicken.

"Stupid Medici..." I grumbled, to no one in particular. Complaining to the air felt better than scolding myself internally for the umpteenth time.

I tried to force myself to eat, but it soon became apparent doing so would be a graver sin than having my meal cold. By the time I had finished rolling around bites, the sun had set entirely. With an unfortunate amount of food remaining on my plate, I left the dining hall.

The second the door behind me shut, fear kicked in. Combined with the shift in seasons, walking through the abbey at night felt as if I had been transported to another world entirely. Moonlight reflected so coolly against the statues in the courtyard, and the darkness surrounding me made it seem like I was trespassing. A weak breeze whistled through the air, stirring piles of dried leaves and making strange scratching noises reminding me distinctly of mice scurrying. I had to look past plumes of my breath to see the stars. A sudden, powerful gust felt like it was eating through my clothes and burrowing into my bones. Since when did Sicily get so cold?

I relied on memory alone to navigate through the gardens and jog into the main building. It took only a slight push for the main door to rush open, inviting all the chill of the night into the entrance alongside me. Even after making it to the end of the hall, the air had

gotten no warmer. As I took turn after turn down the halls, I rubbed my hands along my forearms in a futile attempt to warm myself.

In the distance I heard a chorus of chirps, as jangling and melodically irregular as wind chimes. It sounded like there was a flock of songbirds just outside the building. I looked for the nearest window, then remembered this hallway was in the middle of the abbey, that there was no passage to the outside for several minutes.

And yet the birds continued singing as if separated only by a single wall. Or perhaps as if they had been flitting around in the recesses of my mind. My stomach turned at the thought. How many novels had I read about widows or governesses or whatever on earth I was going crazy in these types of places? This wasn't just a few avian stowaways hiding out in a nest in the rafters—I could pick out at least a dozen chirps and multiple different species. Surely I had to find the source, right?

For all the curiosity burning within me, there lingered an ounce of hesitation. Some part of me felt like somehow I would step onto forbidden ground if I went any further. Like anything living and jovial inside this dead abbey was too good to be true. But I had to know. I jogged toward the song, but was quickly cut short.

"Birdie."

The word echoed through the hall and snaked down my spine. Goosebumps pricked along my arms and the back of my neck, and I searched the darkness for signs of life. There was nothing. Nobody. By all indications I was completely alone in this hallway, but I knew I wasn't.

"Birdie," whispered the voice again, somehow sounding further and closer at the same time. It was soft and sad and echoed around me, and it was Opaline.

"Peachy?" I called out, taking a step forward.

I swore the air around me was growing even colder by the second, and my hands shook. Silence engulfed me. Even the birds had hushed. I stood still for one beat. Then another. Out of nowhere, a gust of wind rushed from the end of the hall. Rows of sconces shut off in a wave toward me.

"Birdie!"

My mother's voice.

I spun on my heels and ran, but before I made it to the end of the hall, I crashed into someone.

For a moment, everything was dark. Dark and warm. Then, Duca de Medici grasped me by the arms and separated me roughly from his chest. A slew of curses rang through my mind. Of all the people to find me like it, it had to be him. He regarded me momentarily with a sharp, exasperated gaze, but when he searched my face, it softened.

"Signorina Bowling? Are you okay?"

No, was my immediate thought. I'm not okay! I wanted to explain everything that had happened, but I knew there was nothing to explain, anyway. Behind me, the lights were shining like usual and the air was still.

"I-I'm fine. I just thought I heard something."

The vampire's expression darkened, and he looked past me.

"A voice?"

The sincere concern in his tone elicited me to answer, somewhat truthfully, "I don't know. Or birds, maybe."

Duca de' Medici met my gaze again, eyes swimming with unease.

"Would you like me to investigate?"

Before I could reply, he gently placed me away from him and turned to walk off in the direction I had run from. I grabbed his sleeve, stopping him.

"No, please. I-I just want to go to bed."

With a solemn nod, he returned to my side and moved my hand to his forearm. I leaned against his arm. I hadn't realized I was wavering so much.

"Of course. You live in the Abbess' suite, correct?"

"Y-Yes."

"Understood."

Wordlessly, he led me through several doors, tossing his head behind his shoulder every now and again just to confirm I hadn't

spirited away. I was grateful for this, as I didn't think I'd be able to utter a word. After several turns, we stopped at my door. Even with the security of a familiar setting, I hadn't let go of his arm. He waited and didn't move until I finally unglued myself. Then, he held my door open for me but stood decidedly on the outer side of its transparent threshold. Duca de Medici remained for a moment, clearly on the verge of saying something, then simply nodded.

But before he could leave, my arms sprung out from in front of me and I grasped his sleeve again. With the thought of being alone again for a mere instant, the air felt heavier. Darkness encircled my sight. No, not now. A familiar sense of dread filled my chest. No, no, no. It had been months since my last panic attack. I had mastered this. 100 mg per day of Sertraline was bitter on my tongue every morning, no matter how quickly I chased it down with water. I had done everything right, had gotten therapy. The refills for the bottle of lorazepam above my sink had long expired.

You're fine, I told myself. You're safe.

You're going to die, was the response. Your heart is going to explode.

My body grew hot, my breath grew shallow, and a sharp ringing filled my ears. Everything was rushing away. I stumbled back and groped behind me for stability, but even the vanity I found wasn't enough to keep me steady. Its knobs ran painfully along my spine as I slid down, rolling sharply across each vertebrae. Something slipped past my fingers and hit the ground with a trill. A bookmark. A bookmark with beads, just out of reach.

"Please," I croaked, staggering into my bed. "The bookmark. A- and the pills in the bathroom."

I faded in and out, and in an instant the bookmark was at my side along with Duca de' Medici and the lorazepam.

"How many?" He asked, voice just above a whisper.

I knew the bottle wanted me to take only one, but logic was elusive when faced with the end of the world.

"T-two!"

He popped open the cap and poured a pair into my hands, and I popped both of them under my tongue. They dissolved quickly, leaving behind only a faint vanilla taste and the anticipation of relief.

Some of the swimming in my ears had abated, and I faintly heard Duca de' Medici's voice saying,

"You're safe here. It's going to be okay."

The words from my unlikely savior helped, and I felt another step closer to avoiding death. Finally, I grasped the beaded portion of the bookmark between my fingers and counted as I breathed. One-two-three-four, I inhaled. One-two-three-four, I exhaled. One-two-three-four. I held my breath and slid one bead through my finger. I repeated this and by the time I had reached the base of the bookmark, the world had grown softer, cooler, closer. But warmth still lingered on one half of me. Duca de' Medici was holding me against him, grip on my shoulder and hand sturdy yet gentle. As it became clear my breath was stabilizing, he put space between us.

"Are you okay? Is there anything I can do? Do you need Noor?"

As he rambled on with questions, his words faded. Not because I was going into another panic attack, but because I had taken too much medication. Even though its effects might have lessened because of expiring, one dose of Lorazepam—a potent benzodiazepine and sedative—would have been enough to blunt the fear. Two wasn't dangerous, but it was clearly an anesthetic, and even without medication, I always crashed after getting through a panic attack.

"No. It's fine." I murmured, forcing my eyes to stay open until he left. "You can go now."

"Are you sure?"

I nodded so Duca de' Medici wouldn't have to hear my speech slurred. After a moment of hesitation, he rose to his feet. The last thing I heard was the door shutting softly behind him, and when he flicked the light off, it engulfed everything.

Chapter Ten

Arietta

That night, my sleep was shaky and fragmented, with vague nightmares broken up by even vaguer moments of lucidity. I remembered waking up at one point bound in my own sheets, and startling myself awake at another by kicking the wall. By the time something other than myself woke me up, I sensed it was early evening. At first, I mistook the gentle knock for ethereal footsteps, but then the sequence repeated.

"Hello?" The hesitation of whoever was on the other side of the door was palpable.

I sat up and fluffed up a pillow beneath me. "Come in."

Duca de' Medici opened the door and took a tentative step into my room, then another. Then he froze and turned beet red.

I followed his line of sight to a pair of freshly folded panties and a bralette, frilly and lacy and riding the fine line between nice undergarments and lingerie proper. I had worn them to my interview to increase my confidence. I was now also acutely aware of how my shirt was drooping off my shoulder.

In a movement I hoped wasn't too conspicuous, I shrugged the sheets around me a bit tighter.

"Good evening," Duca de' Medici said after gathering himself again.

This was the first time, I thought, that the vampire's flamboyant visage had reduced to something more somber. No—I had seen this expression last night as he led me to my room. Pity, worry, and something else I couldn't name.

Suddenly, the events of last night had turned back from a distant nightmare to a concrete memory. I shoved them down and focused on the present.

"Good evening," I replied. "Can I help you?"

"No. Rather, I'd like to help you."

I tried my best to suppress my doubt, but still felt myself grimace slightly. Duca de' Medici appeared for a moment as if he might call me out or otherwise comment on it–there was a valid point he had helped me last night, I realized–but pressed on with his original point.

"I feel in part to blame for what happened last night."

The doubt had not receded. Unless you can do a spot-on impression of my sister, I'm not too sure of that.

He turned his head to the side and folded an arm across himself.

"The birds you heard, they're mine. I feel at fault for what happened last night, and would like you to see them at least."

A small, startled "Oh," escaped me, followed by an, "Okay?"

"Carbone will bring you to the aviary for afternoon tea." His usual grin reemerged. "I'm sure Noor won't miss you too much."

Despite its jarring beginning, the first part of the day slipped back into its usual machinations. Breakfast, morning bath, being dressed by maids, time in the library and a small lunch. Out of habit, I started toward the usual afternoon tea spot, but when I walked out the door, I crashed into a seemingly impenetrable barrier.

"Eep!" I let out a pathetic, high-pitched squeak and leapt back.

In front of me stood Duca de' Medici, biting his lip to suppress a smirk.

I flushed, folded my arms, and glared at the corner of the room.

"If you're going to laugh," I grumbled, "Just do it."

I released a torrent of laughter from the vampire, and despite myself, the melodic noise made me feel better. Even his laughter is pretty, I thought, taking advantage of his head being thrown back to

examine the man. He wore black dress pants and dress shoes with a simple white button up. Tossed over his shoulder in a distinctly aristocratic manner was a beige overcoat. His sleeves bunched up past his forearms and the shirt was unbuttoned midway to his sternum. What elegant collarbones, I noted. But what was that between them? A gold chain of some sort. But before I got to see what was on its end, he had turned away and walked off. I got a whiff of his cologne, musky but slightly fruity, like a cask of well-aged mulberry wine.

I jogged a few steps to catch up to his long-legged pace and trailed closely behind as he returned to where we had been last night. It was as if the door he was leading me had materialized entirely overnight. How hadn't I noticed it before? In my defense, it was the same old cork as those beside it, and unremarkable. But, sure as day, I could distinctly hear birdsong on the other side. When he opened the door, my expectations were dashed entirely. The room was practically swimming in light, and it seemed so organically warm I feared Duca de' Medici's skin would blister. The room, which was about six meters long and wide, was fashioned into a cageless aviary. In its center was a massive driftwood stand with food and water and fruit hanging from each branch. Birds flew freely around the room, flitting from perch to perch. Some chirped cheerfully from the entrance of nests, others foraged for seeds among hay scattered around the ground, and a few bathed in large stone fountains.

I may not have known what these birds were, but they certainly weren't Sicilian. The surrounding birds honed in, curious but not anxious. I gripped my skirt with my hands, which had now become cold with sweat. I didn't do birds. Not this close, anyway. But of course, I couldn't escape for what I knew sounded like a silly reason.

"This room used to be another scriptorium," explained Duca de' Medici, after gently closing the door behind us. "Noor threw a fit when I turned it into a room for my finches. She said this used to be the most beautiful room in the abbey. She wasn't wrong, truthfully."

"Then why this room? Why not one of the plainer bedrooms with windows?"

He visibly darkened at the suggestion.

"No. Here they are safe from any pests or predators, and I can visit them at all times of the day."

One of the braver birds, a member of the species of vibrant bright green birds with purple breasts, red heads, and yellow

stomachs that dominated the aviary, hopped closer to him. Duca de Medici gingerly grasped a spray of millet, and the bird flew to his finger and began pecking away without an ounce of hesitation or fear. I, meanwhile, had backed up against the wall. I forced myself to speak as casually as possible.

"Well, it is beautiful. Are these really all finches? I've never seen anything like them."

He nodded and said softly, "This one is a Lady Gouldian finch. His mate is waiting for him in that nest back there."

A red bird with white speckles landed on his shoulder and hopped down along his arm toward the millet.

"This one is a strawberry finch—it's probably what you heard last night. And those foraging on the ground over there are double-barred finches and society finches."

It took me a moment to reply, as it all took me aback. By the lovely aviary, the happy little birds, and most of all, the warmth emanating from the man in front of me. I would have to paint this later. An expectant look spurred me to talk.

"They're lovely," I quickly noted.

"Yes. They're my treasures."

By this point, the millet had been stripped clean and the two birds—now quite content with themselves—flew back to their mates. The vampire turned back to me with a child-like grin and held out a spray to me.

"Would you like to try?"

No, was my immediate thought. No way in hell. I took it from him anyway, but immediately clutched the millet to my chest.

Duca de' Medici gave me a strange look and pulled another spray from his pocket.

"Here. I can do it with you."

"No, it's okay." I made my voice stern. "I can do it myself."

I held out my arm, squeezed my eyes shut, and focused on the pounding in my ears instead of the rush of wind around me. When I opened them, a representative of each species had already claimed

their spot at the buffet and was chowing down. They didn't seem to be bothered by my trembling. Less than a minute later, the birds flew off and my arm fell limp to my side. My cheeks felt moist.

"S-sorry," I stammered, roughly wiping my sleeve across my face. "I didn't mean to cry."

He gave me only silence, and I rushed to fill it as tears fell more quickly than I could wipe them away.

"I'm sorry, I'm grateful, I promise!"

Words tumbled out, made worse because I couldn't see the vampire's reaction through the blur of my tears. I had no idea if he was glowering or laughing, or something worse. All I could do was vomit out words in my native tongue and native accent.

"It's just that when I was little, I gardened a lot and I got attacked by one of my ma's roosters 'cause I went too close to the coop one day. I know what you're thinking—'how bad could a chicken attack be?' But it was actually bad. I needed seven stitches on my face, an' my granny made chicken an' dumplin' soup that night but she called it Robert an' dumplin' soup since the rooster was named Robert an—"

"It's fine," he cut in. "Truly. You did well, Signorina Bowling."

The world was still blurry, so I had to rely on touch to realize he had put a silk handkerchief in my hand.

"Use this, please. Your sleeve is too rough, and I don't want you to scratch your face."

With newfound caution, I blotted at my eyes until I could see again and my crying had reduced to sniffles. He was sitting on one end of a bench and I joined him.

"Sorry," I repeated as a few more tears rolled down, burying my face in the handkerchief. "I'm just embarrassed now. Again."

The vampire shook his head with a frown and a furrowed brow. "Don't be. It's a waste."

"Huh?"

"Sadness is like absinthe. It stings and burns and yet somehow brings comfort. Happiness is sweet, and anger has an exhilarating spice, but shame? It's a useless emotion. It sullies every other."

"I… see. I'm not sure what to say anymore then."

He sat further back on the bench–a clear sign there was no plan to leave soon.

"Then tell me about your garden."

"I've had a lot of gardens. The one when I was a kid was a vegetable garden. Originally, it was because my Pa told me I wasn't allowed to read new books until I started going outside more, but I started finding it really relaxing and rewarding. After the chicken attack, I was too scared to go close to the hens that ate around the garden, so I moved areas and changed the type of garden."

For a moment, I became acutely aware I was rambling and was afraid I would bore Duca de' Medici. But surprisingly, his gaze upon me was intense–he seemed genuinely curious, latching onto every word.

"What other types of gardens did you have?" he prompted gently.

"In college, I actually had a rock garden. When I first moved to London for college…" I paused, unsure whether to go on. But then I remembered last night and pressed forward. "When I first moved there and left my family, my panic attacks started getting really bad. My therapist was the one who suggested the rock garden, but it didn't feel alive enough for me. I added some bonsai, but their upkeep actually made the panic attacks worse."

I watched Duca de' Medici carefully, for his reaction at this moment would be pivotal. Mental illness was a taboo subject, and I didn't know if it was one I could trust him with. But to my shock and relief, he casually responded,

"Oh, so that's what happened last night. I'm sorry you've experienced that kind of fear."

I shook my head quickly. "No, it's okay! Ever since I got diagnosed with panic disorder, it's become a lot easier to get through. And um, thank you for helping me through it. I didn't think you would do something like that."

The vampire chuckled and gave me a small, lopsided smile. "I was afraid I'd given you that impression. Despite how I come off, I'm not that wicked."

My face grew warm, and my eyes widened. "N-no, I didn't mean that! Well, I guess I did think you were an ass, but–"

Duca de' Medici threw back his head and laughed. "I knew you were interesting."

Though I was still a bit flustered, I couldn't help but smile. "Anyway, I also had a stint with microgreens, but that didn't last long. Turns out they taste pretty gross."

Tone softening again, he asked, "Do you miss gardening?"

"Yes. It's funny, but even though it's associated with one of the worst parts of my life, I miss my rose garden the most. I felt almost close to those flowers, since I really didn't have anyone else at that point."

Although he had just laughed at me, Duca de' Medici had no clever quip, no sarcastic remark for me. He just tilted his head toward me and flickered his eyes across my face until I felt hot. Then, finally:

"I see. Why not?"

I was grateful then, for the curtain of hair that fell out of place from being tucked behind my ear, for the shield away from his piercing gaze. It was for that protection alone I could speak normally.

"My pa had just passed, and Ma stayed in bed all day. Well, in bed or at the kitchen table with the moonshine our Pa used to make. My older sister Peachy–er, Opaline–kind of became my Ma even though she was only two years older. She was too busy with cooking and cleaning and even mailing out the bills to spend time with me anymore. Outside of books, I was never really one for friends outside of her. Ugh, that sounds so pathetic."

He shrugged broadly and gave me a reassuring smile. "You had roses and a sister for friends. I had birds and a cousin."

I chuckled. "At least yours were animals."

I looked over, expecting him to have mirrored my casual expression, but was met with a slightly furrowed brow and faraway look.

"But thorns aside, roses aren't cruel, Signorina Bowling. Not like Basilio became. He was my dearest and only friend once, and now I am left with birds."

I had absolutely no idea what to say or do. As much as I wanted

to ask about this cryptic statement, I was terrified to overstep and ruin all the progress we had made. As the silence lingered, his gaze on me intensified.

“I would like to make your acquaintance with someone important,” said Duca de' Medici finally. “If you are willing.”

If sadness was absinthe, then confusion was like cooking wine. As much as I wanted to retreat, it wasn’t as though I had grounds to decline other than the fact I was nervous to meet someone with my face still sticky with tears.

“Uh... okay?”

Without another word, Duca de' Medici gestured for me to follow him and crossed the room, toward a planted area I hadn’t noticed before.

Chapter Eleven

Sempre Libera

Despite the lack of plants elsewhere, leaves curtained the corner of the room. He carefully gathered the branches and held them to the side, making a soft clicking sound. Keeping ample space between us, I squinted my eyes into the darkness, where a small bundle of bare twigs came into view.

After allowing the branches to whisk back into place, Duca de' Medici looked over his shoulder and gave me a reassuring nod. I took a hesitant step forward.

"No need to worry," he spoke, softer and sweeter than I had known him capable of. "She won't go any further. I'm astonished she was even willing to come out this far."

Cupped in his hands, tilting her head toward me, was the aforementioned *she*. The bird was smaller than a pigeon, with shiny white feathers, and a pale pink beak. Her cherry-wine eyes gazed up at me intently, and her wings twitched with my every movement. Despite this clear vigilance, her eyes closed as he pet the back of her head, and she cooed in delight.

"As I said, these birds are my treasures, but amongst them, Leonore is my gem."

I couldn't help but smile. "She's beautiful."

"Indeed." He beamed with pride. "She's a Barbary dove."

I peered around the corner and looked into the darkness with a small frown. "Was she hiding from me?"

As I should have expected, Duca de' Medici did not hesitate to answer, nor lighten the blow. "Yes, she was."

Then, huffing in mild amusement at the guilt on my face, “That isn't a personal offense. As I said, I’m astonished that she was willing to climb into my hand with another soul present. Leonore has been timid since her mate died a few years ago. It took me several months to gain the slightest of trust with her, and several more to be able to hold her.”

I leaned in a bit closer, slowly so as not to frighten the small creature. This proved unnecessary, as the small bird was far too enraptured with being stroked to notice me.

“Florestan and her were truly opposites. I’ve never seen anything quite like them. He was a nasty little thing, biting and attacking everything that came near. I presume nobody told him he was a species meant to represent peace. And yet, with her, he was gentle and sweet. She has always been quiet and shy, but with him, she was mischievous and playful. They worshiped each other and made each other exist. Doves mate for life, but widows rarely die unwed. Of course, I presented Leonore with several candidates after this.”

“Did she not like any of them?”

“All of the suitors I showed her were far brighter, larger, and healthier than Florestan, yet she had little interest. Perhaps animals cannot understand death, but I think her love for him is true, and she is waiting for him, nonetheless.”

Duca de’ Medici planted a small kiss along her wings, then lowered his hands slowly. As if on cue, Leonore fluttered away, leaving a single long feather in her stead. Duca de’ Medici plucked it from the air and held it before himself between his thumb and forefinger.

“Or perhaps,” he said, tone strangely bitter, eyes falling sharply onto mine. “Perhaps I am projecting something idealistic onto an animal, and perhaps you think I'm foolish.”

I hadn’t realized I had been making a face.

“I don’t think you’re foolish! But there’s no way of knowing how she feels, Duca de’ Medici. There’s a strange balance between trying not to anthropomorphize animals and denying them feelings. Your guess is as good as any other.”

“Is it now?” he chuckled darkly, playing with the feather. “What would your guess be, then?”

"I don't know. Like I said, there's no way of knowing what she feels."

He scoffed. "That's quite the noncommittal response. Tell me what you actually think."

"I think it's silly to assume animals can't feel or love. But to equate love to waiting... No. That sort of entrapment is unreasonable. Moving on is more realistic, especially if that love wasn't true."

Head still tilted away, he gave me a sideways glance and smiled cooly.

"Are we speaking of birds or people now, Signorina Bowling?"

My eyes widened. "Uh, birds. Both. Neither. I don't know."

The feather shone in the light as it fell from his fingers and slowly pirouetted to the ground. Duca de' Medici faced me finally and gave me a small bow.

"Thank you for meeting her, Signorina. She doesn't see guests very often. Neither of us do."

It took me a moment to register that I was being dismissed, albeit in a painfully courtly manner. It was hard not to laugh, and despite myself, I found it strangely endearing.

"Of course. Thank you for introducing us. I uh, guess I'll see you tonight for tea."

"Yes, I've kept you far too long."

He returned to his former spot on a bench, and in turn, I stepped away. I lingered at the door. I had fully intended on simply saying goodbye, but curiosity brought out other words entirely.

"What do you think, then?" I asked, glancing at him over my shoulder. "About whether love requires the ability to wait?"

Duca de' Medici leaned forward with his elbows on his legs, laced his fingers together, and propped his chin on them.

Then, closing his eyes in thought, he asked, "True love, or something lesser?"

My clarification came quickly: "True love."

Duca de' Medici opened his eyes halfway and stared at me through pale lashes. When he spoke, his words were just as heavy and intense

as the look in his eyes.

"I think, Signorina Bowling, that true love is a rapacious thing. The stronger it is, the further it crawls into your chest and infuses into your every breath. It pulses through your veins and embeds itself into your heart, your lungs, your liver, your organs. When it dies, whether by choice or by mortality, all it leaves behind is a mass of rotting, necrotic flesh. It is a beautiful, inoperable cancer. That is what I think."

I held his gaze for several moments, and he returned it wordlessly. Then I broke it and placed my hand back on the door.

"I see," I murmured before leaving. "So we feel the same after all."

Chapter Twelve

Serenata Notturna

The tea and tarts that evening were fruity, but not as overwhelmingly sweet as that disastrous meal. I glanced at the clock. 7:33. Based on his pattern the previous times we met, Duca de' Medici would be here in exactly two minutes.

I poured another cup, took another sip, and closed my eyes. Despite how strangely amicable our conversation had ended today, the disaster of the day prior still swirled in my stomach.

"My apologies for the other day. With saying you were trying to butter me up, that is."

I jumped, spilling a bit of tea on myself (luckily, it had cooled), at the realization that Duca de' Medici had materialized before me. He was dressed differently than on previous days—more casually. At least, his equivalent of casual. He had already allowed his suspenders to slide down the shoulders of his loose button-down shirt, and his dress shoes were propped up on a footrest. A vintage suede jacket was around the chair behind him, paired with a matching flat cap on the ear of the chair.

After attempting in vain to wipe the pinkish stain from my white skirt, I gave him a small smile. "It's okay."

"It isn't, though. That was presumptive of me." He ran his fingers through his hair. "I'm not ...used to having people around me. I'm not used to talking to people."

I shrugged as casually as I could manage and pushed the plate of cookies toward him. "Me either, in case you couldn't tell. Like I said yesterday, I was never very good at it."

Duca de' Medici gingerly plucked a cookie and took a small bite. He tried not to grimace at its lack of sweetness, but I still caught the small twitch of his lip. "I've lived here now for over a year. Noor talks to me on occasion, but otherwise, there's no one."

"Noor mentioned there isn't any mail or phone line up here. Is that not possible to install?"

"It was an elective decision not to do so. It's difficult to rot with company present."

He spoke with an air of somberness I hadn't seen in him before—not flamboyant or exaggerated, despite the dramatic wording, but genuinely desolate. Duca de' Medici returned the cookie to his plate with an air of finality.

Unsure of how to follow up on such a comment, I opted to return to the previous topic. "I'm sorry for spitting cookie all over you."

He echoed my previous shrug. "No, I entirely deserved it."

I raised a brow at his unusual gravity. Sure, he *was* rude, but this sort of reaction was... excessive, to say the least. And, by all appearances, not put on. "It really isn't that big of a deal."

Duca de' Medici's response was instantaneous, as keen as it was quick. "It is if it upset a guest."

I stammered over my words for a few seconds, then swallowed them down with tea. How could one reply to such a statement? I had been upset, sure, but awkwardness lingered more than any resentment, especially after his kindness earlier. I lifted my cup to my mouth, but there was no tea left. I feigned swallowing it anyway.

After a while, Duca de' Medici spoke once more. "I reread several of the sonnets. They're quite beautiful. His love for Laura, for a dead woman, oozes from every word. I confess I hadn't given them a proper chance." He paused to see if I was going to cut in, running his fingers through his hair yet again. "Um, when I was younger, I wrote a lot of sonnets around when I stopped talking to my cousin. I don't associate that form of poetry with pleasant times. But, uh, I digress. What are your thoughts?"

I studied the man in front of me. He was a nervous wreck, just as I had been.

"We don't have to talk about them if you don't want to," I said slowly, then picked up my pace when an idea struck. "We don't have to stay here at all, actually. It's kind of intimidating, you know? Maybe it would be good to try something else."

Duca de' Medici's eyes flickered back and forth, and he scrunched his brow. Finally, as some unknown thought passed through his head, everything relaxed. "I could show you somewhere outside, near the abbey," he said cautiously, deliberately, every word dripping with hesitation. "If you would be okay with that."

I smiled. "That would be lovely."

The night was temperate, and if it not for the gentle breeze, the air might have felt heavy with humidity. I closed my eyes and took a deep breath, savoring the petrichor. *It's been far too long*, I thought, *since I've been outside, especially after the rain.*

When I opened my eyes again, I could see Duca de' Medici studying me in my periphery. I glanced over to meet his eyes, and he looked away quickly, running his hand through his hair. He finally stepped to my side.

"It's . . . nice out. It rained. From the sky and all."

I bit my tongue to stifle a laugh. Was this his attempt at small talk? If so, it was a rather pathetic one.

"Yes, it did," I replied, tilting my head at him with a smirk. "Didn't plan what you were going to say this far, did you?"

"No," he grumbled, blushing. "I didn't."

Finally, my laugh broke free as a giggle. "That's okay. Why don't you tell me about what kind of music you would play right now? To capture the night, I mean."

Instantly, he brightened. "Hmm . . . let me think. While I do, let's walk down."

He headed down the path, and I followed closely behind. An owl in the distance hooted loudly, which I took as an invitation to continue. It was a gravel path, slightly downhill, which wound back and forth through stone pines as we descended into forested land. The trees were massive and ancient, with moss climbing at their bases.

Thick underbrush—a combination of grasses and flowers—tickled my ankles. Duca de' Medici held the lantern at a distance in front of him, illuminating beyond the path. At the sight of it, small animals skittered away audibly, occasionally letting out an annoyed squeak or chirp.

After a few minutes, Duca de' Medici finally spoke. "I think," he said, "tonight's song would be Liebestraum No. 3, Notturno."

I sped up a bit to walk at his side and make eye contact, despite the narrowness of the path, but he continued to look straight ahead. "I've heard that before. By Liszt, right? It's very pretty if it's the song I'm thinking of."

"It is quite beautiful."

"Why did you pick it?"

He halted, truncating our conversation. "Ah, here we are."

The path beneath us tapered off, overtaken by downy grass. The invisible line it followed curved over a hill, with a small pond at its base. Trees encircled us with such breadth that the hill still felt open, and the sky was in full view. With the moon full and close to the earth, our lantern could have easily been snuffed, and every blade of grass and drop of dew would have still been visible. Light even radiated over the edges of the water, the surface of the pond rendered into an impression of the sky above.

"What is this place?"

Duca de' Medici continued beyond the path without me and found a flat area. "I think it was once a graveyard, based on the inlaid stones, but the names have all faded by now. I have Signore Urbino keep the grounds here maintained, just in case."

"It's beautiful."

Duca de' Medici knelt to the ground, then his face twisted. "Ugh. I neglected to consider the rain."

I folded my skirt under my legs and crouched closer to him. "Well, the ground isn't muddy," I observed. "Just wet."

"And now so is my ass. But at least yours won't be. Here, lie down."

In a swift motion, he undid his jacket and swept it over the ground to form a makeshift blanket. After a moment of hesitation, I did as I was told.

Beneath me, the jacket was soft, dry, and still warm. I tried to hold my breath so I wouldn't get overwhelmed by the intermingling smells of cologne, suede, and the vampire himself, but when Duca de' Medici opted to lay with the tops of our heads touching, that became impossible. Accepting my fate, I extended my legs to get comfortable, then quickly recoiled. The weather may have been warm, but the grass was cold and uncomfortably damp.

Despite his calm demeanor, the vampire was trembling.

I turned my attention from terrestrial to celestial. There was nothing comparable to the sky in places like this. Even in the mountains where I grew up, there was more light pollution than here, where the heavens were not solely blue or black, or any single color. Instead, they were fresco ceilings of infinite depths and shades, stippled with gold-and-silver clusters, distant galaxies marbling beyond comprehension.

The soft sound of Duca de' Medici's breathing brought me back to earth. "Do you know any constellations?" he asked before I could say something.

"Um." I searched my memory but found nothing. "Just the Big Dipper and Little Dipper."

"Ah, brilliant!" Even without seeing Duca de' Medici, I could hear the smile in his voice. "So you won't know the difference if I make it all up, and I can impress you immensely for once."

He wanted to impress *me*?

"Pfft. Of course I'd know the difference! I may not know where the constellations are, but I know the myths they're based on."

"I'm aware," he replied with a sigh. "You've been checking out so much in ancient Greek lately, and I'm terribly rusty."

"I guess I didn't think about that." I felt my face flush. "Aren't you tired of all this old stuff? Like you said, I just stay in that little section."

"Forget I said that, please," he responded, firm but not harsh. "Read exactly what you wish to. Nothing else."

Feeling a strange mixture of comfort and more vulnerability, I tucked myself into his jacket. "Okay."

No doubt hearing the confusion in my tone, he sighed. "I don't care what it is you're reading—I care *why*. This library existed before you came. It will after you leave. So tell me, why do you stay in that section?"

I gulped audibly. As cloistered as my world was, the notion of someone gazing upon it was as exhilarating as it was horrifying. Under normal circumstances, I would have changed the topic. But right now, beneath such a massive sky, it didn't feel like there was reason to.

"I think classic literature is really special because it's lasted so long, you know? So many people have died, but these stories are still read because something about them exemplifies humanity."

I wished desperately now that I was sitting beside Duca de' Medici, so that I could look over and gauge his reaction to see if he thought I was foolish, or pretentious, or talking out of my ass. Maybe it was better this way.

I took a breath and continued, "What's changed about people over the centuries is interesting and all, but I think what's stayed the same is the most beautiful part. No matter how many times I read the *Aeneid*, it feels like the first time. Every time I read it, I cry harder and dread the ending more."

Duca de' Medici said something indistinguishable beneath the dulcet warble of the surrounding crickets.

"What?"

He repeated himself, just a hair louder. "*Sunt lacrimae rerum et mentem mortalia tangunt.*"

Book one, line 462 of the *Aeneid*, a line practically tattooed beneath my skull. A line with no direct translation due to its dual meanings, where a translator had to choose one over the other, and, in my mind, the most beautiful line of poetry to ever exist, written by a dead person in a dead language about a dead city. All to express the abstract entanglement of mortality and reality from the perspective of both man and the world he inhabited.

I had to restrain myself to not shout with excitement. I suppressed my tone to a whisper. "*Sunt lacrimae rerum*. You know, I learned Latin for that line."

Though Duca de' Medici spoke rather than whispered, his voice was softer than my own. "I wish I could say the same."

I sank into the quiet, allowed it to linger for a time, then finally said, "You know, you never answered me about why you chose that song for tonight."

Now the silence felt different. Guarded. "Why do you want to know? Is my answer itself insufficient?"

I closed my eyes, trying to remember the exact phrasing he had used. "I don't care what it is you chose, I care why."

Duca de' Medici laughed loud enough that a nearby nightingale fluttered away. "Ha! Using my words against me? You really are an amusing one, Signorina Bowling."

I puffed out my cheeks. "Well? What's the reason?"

Another chuckle, but gentler now. "I don't know. I don't have a reason. I could pretend to, but it just makes sense."

It didn't seem like he was lying, but a small shred of me still wondered. "Really?"

"I wish I did, signorina, but I do not. Thank you for sharing your thoughts with me nonetheless."

My face went hot. "Um, yeah, of course. I mean, I am your *beniamina*, after all. It's the least I can do."

Suddenly, Duca de' Medici sat up. I noticed how the back of his shirt clung tightly to his skin with moisture, and how the moonlight glistened across the fine dew clinging to the white hairs of his arms. I did not, however, see his face.

"Yes," he stated plainly. "You are. Let's return to the abbey."

As he quickened his pace on the way back, I attempted to initiate idle conversation. "That tea was really good. It uh, wasn't very sweet, though. You have a sweet tooth, don't you?"

"Yes, I suppose." While curt, his response didn't seem as though he was upset. Rather, he seemed in a trance.

Just in case I was wrong, I tried again: "I painted a picture of Leonore, actually. I'm not sure I got her eye color right."

"You'll have to show me some other time."

Once again, a polite termination. I decided not to make a fool of myself and keep trying, so we walked back in near silence. The only words beyond that point were a mutual, *good night,* followed by him quickly departing.

I settled in my room, my stomach flipping. Most nights, I would read before bed, but I hadn't checked out another book yet. That didn't matter, though, as I was too busy replaying our conversation to uncover where I went wrong, a task that continued until the moment I fell asleep.

Chapter Thirteen

Crescendo

I squinted my eyes, trying to ignore the pounding in my head. It seemed like the text before me had grown smaller, closer, and lighter with every page, and now the letters were battling and overlapping.

I need to get a new pair of glasses, I thought, flicking on a lamp. I sighed. Who was I kidding? The glasses weren't the problem here. I had been at my desk in the abbess's suite with my latest thesis lead, and while I didn't know exactly how long it had been, the sun had set, and I had entirely drained a highlighter. I hadn't seen Duca de' Medici since that night on the hill, and instead of continuing to dissect our truncated conversation, I distracted myself with my work.

"Hello."

I raised a brow and turned toward the door, unsure if Lucia was directing her dulcet tone toward me. My heart thudded in my chest; I hoped to God that wasn't the case. I doubted she would understand the significance of the book in front of me, *The Unexpected Heir: The Untold Story of Enzo Armando de' Medici,* but that wasn't something I could risk. I slammed it shut, looking around the room for a hiding place.

"Signorina Bowling." Signora Carbone's voice came through the door this time, crisp and sober as always. Everything she said sounded like a statement, a command.

I quickly stuffed the book in my drawer and replied, "Come in!"

Signora Carbone entered immediately, with Lucia waddling awkwardly behind. A flat, pink box was in her arms, tied loosely shut

with a white ribbon. Balanced atop it were smaller boxes of various sizes, all of which were pink with white ribbons. Presents, quite literally overflowing in Lucia's arms so I only saw her lower half.

"Where should I put these?" asked the stack of boxes.

Heartbeat returning to normal, I flickered my eyes pointedly between the present and the end of my bed. Lucia practically fell into it. Boxes tumbled every which way, and she quickly knocked aside any stragglers when she tried to escape the fluffy mattress. I bit my lip to suppress a laugh, but eventually joined in her fit of giggles.

"I'm sorry!" she exclaimed after finally rolling off.

"Are you okay?"

"Yes, I am! Now I know why you sleep so deeply in that bed!"

Signora Carbone glared at the younger maid, but she had no room to talk, considering her empty arms. Instead, she gathered up the presents that had joined Lucia on the floor, examined each briefly, and placed them gingerly with the largest present. I looked up at her, awaiting orders from the true mistress of the house. Surely not all this could be for me?

"Open them, Signorina!" Lucia crooned beside me. "Signora Carbone wrapped them just for you!"

"And Signorina Lucia flattened them just for you," the other maid added, monotone.

Was that a joke, a jab, or somewhere in between? I searched her face, attempting to discern her intent but found something entirely unexpected; Signora Carbone looked excited. Sure, she was trying to maintain her normal stony visage, but just as surely was the shimmer in her eyes and her fidgeting hands. In fact, I sensed something more profound than the enthusiasm of the younger maid beside her.

What the hell was in all the boxes and why had they materialized? I opened my mouth to ask as much, but a sharp look from Signora Carbone stopped me. In an attempt to transform anxiety into anticipation, I tore into them. Inside the largest box was a violet satin dress. Holding it up to the light, intricate embroidered patterns and inlet gems adorned every inch. The borders of the sleeves and collar were crafted with a web of black lace. I carefully opened the other boxes to reveal my treasures: black high heels, violet ribbons for my hair, golden rings and bracelets, and a gorgeous amethyst pendant with matching earrings.

"What is all this?" I asked once the awe had subsided. "Who is this from?"

Lucia clasped her hands together and murmured something to herself in Sicilian. Signora Carbone stepped forward and gathered up the gifts.

"This," she said with a small smile, "is something I never expected to take part in."

"Huh?"

"It may not be Ritus Sanguinous, but I did not expect that Duca de' Medici would allow me to perform my duties." She was speaking mostly to herself, and to the dress in her arms. "How proud would my Mother have been?..."

I hadn't realized I was making a face until she reacted to it. If the abrupt, forced sobriety said anything, I had been gawking. In my defense, however, even Lucia appeared taken aback by the whimsy that had possessed such a normally stoic individual. Signora Carbone spoke again then, more soberly to me:

"Now, we must prepare for tonight. You must have the traditional meals. There is sizing to be done. We must bathe you and give you sacrament."

Signora Carbone pulled a list from her apron, muttered to herself a bit more, and left after giving a quick bow. I looked down at the silks and satins surrounding me, not entirely unconvinced I was dreaming. Lucia helped me up, and I dazedly followed her through the gardens to the dining hall.

The table was more abundant than usual–I hadn't thought that was possible before–but the food was also simpler. Rather than the herbed omelets, eggs benedicts, or mascarpone tarts I was used to, my breakfast consisted of various cheeses, boiled eggs, fresh breads, and local fruits. Instead of the fine china I was used to eating from, all the plates were metal. All this atop a white tablecloth. I recognized it immediately—Panis largitoris. The traditional meal given before vampires drank from their beniamini, an ascetic meal meant to cleanse the spirit of worldly sin. Now this felt real.

"You will do your duty soon," Doctor Ntumba had told me last month, when drawing my labs. "Zeno wants to drink from you, and he wishes for you to offer him company." But even after that conversation, I had convinced myself she was wrong. There was no way a Medici would want to drink my blood, no way my host would want to engage in something with such romantic undertones after we had just had such

an awkward exchange. But now, with the meal before me, I couldn't deny it any longer.

That meant the dress in my room had been chosen in lieu of more traditional robes, the bath would be filled with traditional cleansing herbs, that I would be given Eucharist, and most of all, that my blood would soon be on the Duca de' Medici's tongue. Too stupefied to do anything else, I forced myself to eat before I was fetched for the next steps.

Rather than the usual mixture of milk and honey, my bath was filled with a fragrant mixture of frankincense and hyssop, and Lucia scrubbed me more aggressively than ever before. For as much as the oils burned against my chapped skin, what came after was far more uncomfortable.

Signora Carbone was ruthless in her efforts to fit my dress. She tied measuring tapes taut, pricked pins through fabric with little consideration to the flesh beneath it, and ripped ribbons every which way. On and off the dress came, with such minute alterations that I could not discern them, no matter how hard I looked. But by the time she finished, Signora Carbone's skills were undeniable. Everything fit perfectly, and once Lucia added all the accessories and a touch of makeup, a doll was staring back at me in the mirror.

For the first time, I saw myself as beautiful as my mother had.

"Thank you," I said to them both.

Both women beheld me with such reverence they didn't need to respond. I wondered who had been the one to choose these clothes and how they had known what colors complimented my eyes, or how the dress would render my boyish frame into something elegant. For some reason, I didn't think I wanted the answer.

After this, Signora Carbone led me to the room I had spent the first night in. How shockingly small it seemed now, how utterly plain. When had I gotten so used to luxuries? The bed was stripped clean and the only inhabitant of the room was in a single plate which held a single piece of bread and glass of grape juice, meant for sacrament. The door shut behind me quietly and now, left alone, I was dumbfounded. I had prayed in this abbey out of fear before, the first time I ate, but this was different. I wanted to honor this tradition, but I certainly wasn't Catholic and had long forgotten how to pray. After teetering from foot to foot for a bit, I made the executive decision to kneel at the altar. This proved to be an immense challenge considering the dress, but I committed to it, nonetheless.

"Hello, God. Or Jesus, I guess?" I whispered, pressing my

forehead against my clasped hands. "I don't know. I'm not really sure what I'm supposed to say when I talk to you all by myself like this. I guess, thank you for the flesh and blood? It looks tasty, and I appreciate it not being alcoholic."

Where were crickets when you needed them? The silence was painful, so I cleared my throat.

"Um, anyway, hopefully this drinking goes well. Wish me luck?"

I inhaled and exhaled sharply, whispered the Lord's Prayer as I could think of no other, and ate the cracker and juice. A stray droplet of juice ran down the side of the glass and onto the back of my hand. I quickly licked it off before it could roll off and stain the unfinished wood.

I wonder, I thought, if my blood will be so red or taste so sweet.

There were three soft raps at the door and a soft, "Are you ready, Signorina?"

"Y-yes!" I jumped to my feet.

Duca de' Medici's room was exactly as I remembered from that first day. Like before, darkness blanketed the room almost entirely, staved off only by the dim light of a few candles. The sweet scent of leather and wood wafted throughout the room, and Duca de' Medici sat in his usual spot.

There were differences, too. Instead of Tchaikovsky, some aria I could not place filled the air. Instead of truffles, there was a plate of shortbread cookies on the table. Most different of all, however, was Duca de' Medici.

When I entered, he had been sitting with both feet on the ground, his elbows on his thighs, and his head in his hands. His hair was visibly parted from having run his fingers through them so much. At the sound of my footsteps, he lifted his face up so that his chin rested on his thumbs and his fingertips pressed against the bridge of his nose.

Our eyes widened in synchronization.

"Wow," he said, sitting up slowly.

Feeling my face flush, I folded my arms tightly and bit my lower lip.

"Yes?"

A smile spread across his face.

"I chose your clothes well."

Duca de' Medici and was looking at me just like he had on that day in the aviary, just like when we walked to the hill. With warmth and something else I couldn't decipher. When the slender man rose to his feet and stalked gracefully toward me, I froze. He knelt on one knee as if to propose and looked up at me with a jarringly sincere expression.

"May I?"

"Yes." The answer leapt from me automatically, despite my not knowing what he was asking permission for. Half of me would have said yes to almost anything, and the other half cowered.

Duca de' Medici's slender fingers slid beneath mine. He turned my arm palm-up, exposing my wrist. Prominent veins pulsed beneath chestnut skin. His cool thumb, contrasting in temperature and tone, rested lightly along my radial artery and the pointer finger of his other hand traced along my artery. Duca de' Medici's breath was hot against my wrist, and for as poised as he was, his body radiated eagerness.

"Relax, I'll be gentle."

He must have felt the uptick in my heart rate when I realized what was happening. I didn't know if I should watch or look away, but I didn't have a choice either way—my body was frozen. Duca de' Medici looked up at me with those silver eyes, filled with an emotion intense yet indiscernible, and plunged his teeth into me. My body went hot, then cold, and I closed my eyes. I felt his tongue gently caressing the flesh of my inner wrist, his long eyelashes fluttering dreamily against me, his soft lips pressing into me. And yet for all this tenderness, his grip upon me was strong and he drank in greedy gulps.

This was nothing like donating blood had been. This was intimate and somehow vulnerable for both parties. A soft whimper escaped my lips, and instinctively he pressed his lips onto me harder and began drinking more feverishly. My legs began to shake, and the shaking traveled up my body. When my arm faltered, his free hand traveled up my dress and between my legs to grip the back of my thigh so tightly the keen pain of his fangs on my arm was mirrored by his nails digging into me. He scooped me close, chest heaving and his body surging with electricity. I moaned, soft and quivering.

We sat like that, with him clutching me tightly against him for only a few more seconds. When he separated from me and pressed a piece of gauze against my wrist, a mixture of relief and disappointment struck me. He retreated into the darkness, expression flat and entirely

unaltered.

For all the world, it appeared nothing had happened at all. Or maybe that it meant nothing.

I touched my shaking fingers to the indents on the back of my thighs and trailed my fingertips across the grooves. The heat of his hands still lingered, and the remaining blood in my body all rushed to my face, burning in the tips of my ears. I fell to my knees, cupped my face in my hands, and squeezed my eyes shut. Humiliation washed over... whatever I had been feeling. The noises I had made! The way my body had reacted! To have acted so lewdly with a man I barely knew, one who likely had no interest in me in that way, was beyond humiliating.

I feverishly planned, in a matter of seconds, my resignation from this position and subsequent move to some remote cabin in the woods where I would never see another living soul.

Just as I was midway through my mental packing list, something I hadn't noticed before jarred me. I held my breath, listened beyond the heartbeat in my ears, and peeked through my fingers. Despite Duca de' Medici's cool appearance when he stalked across the room, I heard his heavy breathing and smell the intermingling of sweat and cologne. He had unbuttoned the collar of his shirt down to his sternum and had flung himself onto his sofa. Even with only the flickers of candlelight across his features, I could see his normally opalescent face was bright as a tomato.

I caught his eye and he quickly shifted into the darkness. "You can go now."

I stood quickly, staggered back a few steps, cried, "Yes, of course, thank you!" and rushed to the door. I slammed it behind me, shielding myself from the peculiar dimension I had clearly wandered into. Light crashed into my vision, and I crashed into someone immediately.

I fell hard onto my ass and hit my head against the door.

"Shit..." I hissed between my teeth, hand leaping to a freshly blossoming knot on the back of my head.

Since when was remaining standing such a challenge? I squinted into the light, saw the blurry figure of a hand reaching out toward me, and grasped it. As I rose to my feet once more and my vision adjusted, Doctor Ntumba came into view.

"You're going to need an ice pack and some ibuprofen for that," she said with a frown.

I rubbed the bump again and winced. It had already grown. But that wasn't my concern right now–I had forgotten Doctor Ntumba had been waiting in the hall for me. I had forgotten anything else but he and I existed.

Chapter Fourteen

Diminuendo

I required a full bag of saline after the vampire drank directly from me for the first time; Duca de' Medici had been far too greedy, Doctor Ntumba later informed me, but I could have discerned as much. The world was a blur of sound and color, and I could only gather snippets of Doctor Ntumba's snappy Italian scolding.

Stai attento! In my current state, I could not translate.

She carried me into my room and gave the IV in my bed. I drifted in and out of sleep until the following afternoon, strange staccatoed dreams being broken apart by a handful of minutes where I would drowsily listen to bird calls outside my window until I fell back into slumber. Even after recovering from this, I struggled to resume my studies for the rest of the week. My focus had waned entirely, all thanks to Duca de' Medici's confusing behavior. We had shared, I thought, a noteworthy few days, and yet I hadn't seen him hardly at all since then.

He did not even allow me brief daily glimpses or stilted conversation around the abbey like he had at the beginning of my stay. I saw him through my window at night once, stalking around the grounds and scrawling furiously in a notebook. But even if I had gotten the chance, I wouldn't have called out to him. No, I had instead relegated myself to replaying every moment together over and over in the desperate hopes of finding where I had gone wrong. Had it been how pathetic I looked by bawling in front of him in the aviary? Perhaps I had been too informal and offended him. Most horrifyingly of all, had it been my reaction to his teeth plunging into me?

I tried to speak with Doctor Ntumba about it once, but she pointedly changed the topic. By the way everyone was dancing around the question, I was alone in trying to answer it. After that point, Signora Carbone and Signore Urbino had also been unusually absent.

Prior to that first feeding, I had seen them daily, and now I only crossed their paths when I went through the gardens for meals. Even then, they always huddled together, muttering inaudibly to one another.

Lucia had noticed the difference in me long before the others. She pointed out the torrents in my moods as astutely as a weatherwoman, and sometimes I swore she could predict where they were going from one morning to the next. I theorized at one point she had been gossiping with Signora Carbone about the differences in the music I checked out. Maybe she had mentally cataloged how much I had been eating. Or perhaps I was simply that easy to read. Regardless, I quickly came to appreciate her jokes and the general pleasantness of her company.

"Would you like to go on a walk or have dinner with me?" I asked her one day during my bath.

She had been scrubbing me gently today, which meant she could tell today had been difficult for me. She paused what she was doing and gave me a strange look.

My face felt warmer than the water.

"What is it?"

Lucia simply smiled, then picked up my other arm and resumed her scrubbing.

"I just never expected you to ask me that, Signorina. How come?"

I shrugged, lowered into the water past my chin and blew bubbles out of my nose.

"Signora Carbone says you've been so needy because you don't have teatime anymore." Lucia's tone was light, and I imagine she had expected any reaction other than the one I gave her.

Needy? I had been called many things in the past by many people–distant, reserved, avoidant. But needy was a first, and I wasn't sure how it made me feel.

I sat up in the tub, and to my dismay, the minute movement had a dramatic effect. Water rushed to fill the space I had left, a cascade of bubbles rolled down my arms, and steam rolled out around me. "I'm done with my bath, Lucia."

"I'm sorry, Signorina Cora!" cried Lucia, holding up her hands.

“I shouldn’t have said that!”

After rising from the tub and wrapping a towel around myself, I looked Lucia dead in the eyes.

“No, it’s okay. You’re right.”

Lucia studied my face for a moment, searching for traces of anger, but finding nothing. She visibly relaxed and continued her tasks. She helped thread my arms through my robe, fresh from its designated towel warmer. Occasionally, I would forget how spoiled I was in this abbey, but the simple joy of a warm, fluffy robe always reminded me of how much of an outsider I was to this place. With a hint of residual caution, she said,

“I don’t think it’s a bad thing. When you first came here, Signorina, you were always nice, but I don’t think you ever spoke with me without a reason. For many days, it was like you weren’t really there. But now I hear you laugh and complain, and sometimes you even talk about silly things with me. It’s nice to be taking care of a house that feels like it has people in it. I can tell Signora Carbone is happier too.”

My reflection tilted her head to the side.

“What makes you think that? I don’t think I’ve seen her very much at all lately. When does she even go to bed?”

“She’s always busy like that,” Lucia responded with a giggle. “It means she’s happy. One time when I was a child, I dreamt she didn’t sleep. That she actually spent all night working in her room, and only pretended when others were around. The next night I hid in her closet, but she was asleep every time I looked out. When she found me, I had to scrub the floors myself for a week!”

I tried not to wince as Lucia plaited my hair. No matter how gentle she was, the feeling of my hair being touched felt painful and vulnerable. She was used to my jumping by now, at least.

“So you grew up with Signora Carbone then?” I asked.

“Yes,” Lucia replied. “For as long as I can remember, I lived with Signora Carbone. We took this position together so that I could return to my birthplace. It was her dream to work as a head conservatrix, and mine to come home.”

“Do you...?” I trailed off. How could I ask her if she enjoyed her job and how hadn’t I considered it this much before? Truthfully, I supposed I spent most of my time trying to forget that it was me getting pampered, and that it was another person doing the pampering.

"I do like being a lady's maid, though," she said, somehow reading my mind. "It's nice to be a part of making someone happy every day, and the pay is quite good. The only bad thing is that I don't get to leave very often, and when I do, it's to a town with only one bar!"

Yet another thing I had never considered came to mind—the possibility of Lucia leaving the abbey before me.

"Are you going to stay here long term, then? Now that you're home?"

"Until I have enough money saved up to open my own salon," she replied. Then, adding with a cheeky smile. "Or Signora Carbone gets tired of dealing with me and tells Duca de' Medici to fire me."

At the sound of that name, I sank into the chair. The robe had gone cold again, just like how my blood felt.

"I don't know," I mumbled. "I think I'm the one more at risk of being kicked out of this place."

Lucia gaped, nearly dropping the hairbrush.

"Why would you get kicked out?"

Uninvited, unannounced, a familiar feeling pricked the corner of my eyes. I winced at the uncomfortable feeling in my throat but suppressed it.

"I..." My voice came out soft, hoarse. Even though I had held back tears, it was a dead giveaway. I cleared my throat, despite knowing full well it wouldn't help.

"I think I did something wrong, Lucia, but I don't know what. Duca de' Medici hasn't talked to me in days. It's like he hates me. Nobody is talking to me anymore, and it feels like I'm going crazy just for asking about it. The thing is, I don't have a plan B if I get kicked out of here. I don't have anyone or anywhere."

I expected Lucia to either come swinging with refutations or comfort me without addressing the issue, but she did neither. Instead, she simply stood there, not saying a word, with her gaze on the floor. I stared at her, brow furrowed, until she finally met my eyes and spoke.

"I wish I could tell you what is going on, Signorina, but I can't. I promised it would be a surprise."

"Huh?"

"I don't see Duca de' Medici around the house very often—Signora Carbone told me long ago to keep my distance from them. I can promise you, though, nobody here hates you. Especially not Duca de' Medici. You'll just have to see."

Chapter Fifteen

Ombra mai fu

I peeled myself out of bed and wandered into the hall without bothering to change out of my nightgown or put on slippers. The air smelled like freshly cut wood and dirt—like my pa used to when he came back from his workshop. I felt the prick of phantom splinters in my heels and quickly grabbed a pair of shoes to vanquish the echoes of childhood scoldings from the corners of my mind.

I followed the scent to an open door next to the aviary. It was the hall leading to the conservatory, currently illuminated by lantern light on account of its glass walls being covered with tarps. I had poked my head in before occasionally to admire the stained-glass ceilings, but the room had been in disarray, and I had the sense I should stay away. Obviously, there was little point in a vampire maintaining a sun parlor. But now things were different. I examined the scene of the crime: A pair of dirty boots, one on its side. A hammer lying beside a fan of nails, many crooked and deformed. A pile of wood chips in the corner, and beside it, a book left open, its pages sinfully touching the ground.

I approached what I expected to be the most illuminating clue but could decipher nothing. The text of the book was in Sicilian, and it lacked pictures. I stepped over it and followed a trail of scattered mulch, which led me into the conservatory itself.

The culprits came into view: a handmade garden bed, filled to the brim with potting soil. The wood was new, with a fresh layer of sawdust coating its surface. There was a large potting bench flush against another wall, complete with brand-new shears, trowels, pots, and just about anything else I could imagine needing for every step of the gardening process—empty pots, bags of soil, heat lamps, and supplementary lighting.

The room had been restored to its former majesty, and many steps beyond.

A familiar voice rang out from behind me. "Will it suffice?"

I hadn't noticed Duca de' Medici approaching. His clothes were as formal as usual; I recognized his white button-down and trousers with suspenders from the day he showed me his aviary. Nothing else about him appeared the same. His skin glistened with sweat; his sleeves were rolled up to reveal surprisingly muscular forearms. His face was crossed with lines of dirt where he had pushed his hair out of his eyes until it finally slicked against his forehead.

In those hands, those powerful hands that had gripped me so tightly, were a folded pair of gloves. He leaned against the doorframe, and I wondered why I had ever thought he was fragile.

It's because of me, I realized, *that he is able to stand so strong.*

As bitter as the feeding had been, this realization made everything feel a bit more worth it.

"Will it suffice?" Duca de' Medici repeated.

"I, uh—" I swallowed, moistened my lips, and caught my breath. I could barely look at him. "What is it?" I finally mustered.

He frowned and turned his head away. "You can't tell?"

"N-no, I—"

"It's a garden," he said, voice sharp. For an instant, I wondered if he was actually mad until I saw the faint glow of a blush across his cheeks. Then, he added, almost inaudibly, "For you."

Numerous variants of *thanks* swam alongside dozens of *why*'s. I grasped into my psyche for anything to say, but all that came out after several seconds of dead air was an empty, "Oh."

But by the time I could muster that single syllable, I was speaking to his back. Duca de' Medici was walking off toward his aviary, and while his strides were even and confident, I saw the bright red tips of his ears.

He stopped for a second and said over his shoulder, "Feel free to take some cuttings from outside. There's a map on the table. I'll have Urbino remove the tarps."

With that, he folded his arms behind his back and stalked off, leaving me to gawk.

I studied every corner of the room, feeling more and more overwhelmed by the second. Just as Duca de' Medici had said, there was a folded piece of paper on the table—or rather, the potting bench—that contained a map of the abbey and its surrounding gardens. I had seen one of them many times when researching the Abbazia di Santa Dymphna. This map differed from the usual image, however, in that the tight, elegant scrawl of the Duca de' Medici covered it. He had circled various areas and written on them:

Rosa x odorata

Soliel d'Or

Zépherine Drouhin

La France

And so the list continued.

It was an annotated map of the location of every rose cultivar in the abbey.

I crammed into my pocket and ran to the library. I flipped to the back of the logbook—the section Duca de' Medici wrote in—and saw nearly a dozen books checked out on rose cultivars, rose horticulture, and gardening in greenhouses. All checked out within the last week.

So that was why I hadn't seen him.

The text in front of me blurred, the pages developing several dark spots. I touched my fingers to my cheek and was alarmed to find them moist. When did I start crying? What could I even call the emotion pouring out of my eyes—relief, shock, gratitude, confusion? Maybe a strange mixture of all of this, and more. Regardless of what I should call it, the feeling burning inside me spurred me to drop the logbook and race back to Duca de' Medici's room. I burst through the door and looked around the dimly lit room, but the vampire was nowhere to be found.

I was hit with a flash of the other night and heard the echo of my own cries, but shook them and every other thought away. For the first time, I ventured further into the room, beyond the satin curtain I had seen him retreat behind so often.

"Duca?"

I couldn't see him—or much of anything in such dim lighting, for that matter—but I still sensed his presence. I was not surprised in the slightest when I heard him reply, "Signorina. You realize our feeding is tomorrow, do you not?"

"Uh, yeah. Can I turn on the light?"

"There's a lantern on the table in front of you."

I touched my face again and found it sticky but dry. Hopefully, my eyes wouldn't betray me. Squinting into the darkness, I discerned the faint outline of the aforementioned lantern and switched it on.

He was sitting on a bench, one leg drawn up with a notebook resting gently on it. And in front of him—"Whoa."

A grand piano, which certainly lived up to the title.

It was antique, so much so that the keys were genuine ivory, but beautifully maintained, without a speck of dust on it. The piano bench he sat on appeared to be made from the same wood and had the same detailed carvings, with the addition of velvet cushioning. A massive four-poster bed was directly perpendicular to it, along with a nightstand, upon which was a record player. The rest of the furnishings formed a crescent around the trio: a large desk overflowing with papers, a sofa, and a coffee table with a vase of dead roses.

Light flickered across Duca de' Medici's face, revealing an annoyed expression. He placed the notebook on the bench with a loud sigh. "What is it?"

What had I walked into? I took a deep breath and returned the lantern to its place on the table.

"Before today," I said, "I thought you were mad at me."

In response, the vampire tossed his head back and harrumphed. "Who says I'm not?" he replied with a glare as sharp as his tone. "You came into my parlor unannounced."

I folded my arms tightly over my chest, feeling the glow of embarrassment and indignation wash over my cheeks. "It's not like I could knock!"

Immediately after, I stepped outside of myself and saw the scene before me. Once again, Duca de' Medici had me stomping around like a child. My face grew hot.

"Look, I just wanted to say thank you for the garden, okay?"

He didn't reply and instead just stared at me. I pivoted and was about to retreat from this failure of a conversation when I saw Duca de' Medici rise in my periphery.

"Wait," he said, taking a step toward me. "I'm sorry—you caught me off guard. I've been meaning to show you this place. I just wasn't expecting to do so today."

He placed the papers in his hand to the side, sat on one end of the sofa, and patted the spot next to him. I joined him but positioned myself as far away as humanly possible, practically hanging off the edge. I hugged a pillow to my chest and mumbled,

"It's okay. I hate being interrupted too. I'm sorry I didn't ask."

"It isn't just that. I must admit. I'm sorry I wasn't able to speak to you recently. And I'm ashamed of my behavior when I saw you last."

"My hand. I got carried away. I won't let that happen again."

"N-no, it's my fault! I'll sit down next time and be quiet."

He chewed on my words and eyed the space between us. Then, with a small sigh. "I see. If that is what you wish."

I scooted a bit closer to him to return the pillow to its original spot in the corner.

"Thank you for the garden. I can't imagine how long it took you for all of that."

"As an excellent host, who would I be to deny my guest her hobby? We need our passions, or we'd go mad. One must fill their life with beauty to forget the ugliness of the world, correct?"

I bit my lip to hold in a grin and gestured to the piano with my chin.

"Is that yours, then? Your passion, I mean."

"Yes. Her name is Eulalie."

"Oh, after the poem?"

He smiled at me so warmly it was a wonder I ever thought he'd hated me. "I thought you'd know."

I fidgeted with my skirt, growing hot. It was hard to converse casually when it had been so long, when I had been so confused. Most

of all, when such beautiful eyes were regarding me. I did my best anyway.

"I didn't realize you liked poems," I said. "I thought you didn't."

"I always have. Poe and Dante are favorites, as you've likely gathered, but I've become quite fond of Petrarch. Of the sonnets he wrote for Laura."

"You don't have to say that."

"I have yet to say a thing for your sake. I don't have it in me to mindlessly flatter you. Anyway, I wanted to read Petrarch again, to see what you saw. And I get it now, I think."

He leaned forward and craned his head to the side to meet my eyes with an inquisitive look of his own.

"Do you think Laura ever existed?"

"No." Yet another question I had always wished someone would ask me, had always wanted to answer. "I don't think she ever really did. At least not entirely. I think she had originally been based on someone he barely knew, but eventually..."

I returned his gaze steadily, studying his reaction to see if he agreed, but as I should have known, he offered no clues. That was, not until he continued my thought for me.

"Eventually, through all those years of obsession and worship, she became something else. A homunculus formed from love and a corpse. That was what I missed before, Signorina Bowling. In my eyes, having such love for someone who never existed is far more tragic than, say, Dante and Beatrice. And of course, tragedy and beauty are lovers in their own right."

I shook my head. "I don't think it's tragic at all. I think Petrarch is lucky—how many people can say they've loved someone or something so deeply? I certainly can't. So I don't pity him. I envy him."

I was expecting a laugh, a riposte, some acute reaction, but

there was none. Duca de' Medici simply darkened and stared at the lantern on his table. After a long, painful silence, he finally said,

"You shouldn't. That sort of love devours everything around it."

A chill snaked up my spine, crawled along my arms and legs and brought with it goosebumps. I didn't like this seriousness, this gravity threatening to suck in everything around it. I wanted to return to that time only moments ago, where we were talking so light-heartedly about his piano.

My eyes fell on the papers on the table beside us. "What's that?" I asked as I pointed to it.

Instantly, jarringly, he brightened.

"That would be my composition. Speaking of Dante, it's based on his life."

I grinned.

"You'll have to show me! I'd like to hear it."

"No. I wouldn't dream of sharing unfinished work. It's only a few songs now, but it will be a symphony, eventually."

He gathered the papers up quickly and crossed the room to place them on his desk.

"Anyway," He resumed, "I don't expect you'll still be here for its completion, regardless. You may be my beniamina, but I'm not forcing you to stay."

"Who knows?" I reached into my pocket and ran my thumb across my pen. The one I had used since I started writing my thesis back in London. "I have quite a bit of reading to get through."

Chapter Sixteen

Dolce

True to his word, Duca de' Medici was practically as clinical as an IV for the next feeding. Even the clothes he chose for me were plain and modest. I felt immense shame after that feeding—shame for using up all the carmine in my portraits, shame for the dreams I had been having that made me wake up with warmth between my legs.

My routine had become transparent to the household. In the morning, there was breakfast, gardening, and my morning bath. Afternoon consisted of lunch, time to research, and tea. Noor and I had grown closer, and I finally felt enough like peers to speak with her on a first-name basis. I became more and more transparent about my work, and soon it was an open secret between us. Then I had my unofficial book club with Duca de' Medici in the aviary, dinner, and several beloved hours alone.

One night, Duca de' Medici left the door to his parlor open, with an untouched charcuterie board and sparkling cider. From then on, I would spend the early hours of the morning in his room with a book and listen to the sweet sounds reverberating through that corner of the abbey. Sometimes he played a familiar tune; other times, I heard him stumbling about for hours to perfect a single section of an original piece. Both sounded just as enchanting to me.

I forced another bite of *pasta alla Norma* and grimaced. Even with its tangy sauce and delicious capers to tempt me, I hadn't had an appetite for a while—not before evening tea, when my stomach seemed to be upside down. I looked at the *pane siciliano*, a sweet, nutty bread I normally devoured by the loaf, only to see it was entirely whole and still steaming. Lucia emerged from the kitchen.

"You need to eat more," she teased playfully as she took away the dishes, "or Signora Carbone will scold you."

"I know, I know," I grumbled.

Signore Carbone had given me more than a few lectures on my duties as a *beniamina*, and Noor finally stepped in at one point to report my bloodwork was still adequate. After shoveling in a few more bites, I grumbled my thanks to Lucia and rushed off to the aviary. *Idylls of the King* was already in my bag, waiting for our meeting.

A delicate coo sounded from the corner of the room when I entered. "Hello, Leonore," I said, as gently as I could, eliciting yet another satisfied coo from the dove.

As the weeks passed, she had become more and more comfortable with my presence. Though she still spooked if I moved too quickly or spoke too loudly, she had clearly become fond of me from afar. On one or two occasions, she even built up the courage to fly close to me. I smiled at the bird, who was peeking her head out from beneath a branch and eyeing me, and I whistled softly as I waited.

"What did you bring today?" I asked the second he walked through the door.

Duca de' Medici chuckled warmly and unpacked his satchel. "Aren't you an impatient one? Let me get situated, at least."

He laid out his belongings slowly, in an organized manner. First was his copy of *Idylls of the King,* then a packet of sour grape drops—my favorite candy, I had disclosed one day, as they tasted like the happier days of my childhood. After that, he brought them every day to our time in the aviary, even if he winced with every bite. "I picked a few selections from *Tristan und Isolde* by Wagner, starting with the 'Liebestod,' of course," he said, holding up a vinyl.

"Bit on the nose, isn't it? Choosing that opera when we're reading about 'The Last Tournament?'"

"Pah," he scoffed, plopping down next to me. "I prefer their story as a full-length romantic tragedy rather than some side plot."

"I think both are pretty, in their own ways," I replied with a shrug. Then, once it became too difficult to hold back my enthusiasm, I added, "But I think the full story is so much prettier—just wait until we finish it!"

Duca de' Medici chuckled. "I'll give it a chance for your sake. I must admit, though, the reason I picked out the 'Liebestod' first is more so because I'm quite the fan of a good Tristan chord, and—"

After having watched us from afar so long, Leonore landed on his shoulder.

Duca de' Medici held out his finger, and the dove quickly hopped onto it with a satisfied coo. "Do you have any millet?" he asked without looking away from his beloved pet.

I was already taking it out of my pocket. I wasn't sure if Duca de' Medici noticed, but I had always been prepared for this possibility.

His eyes softened, and one corner of his lips curled ever so slightly. We listened far past the 'Liebestod,' well into the opera, as more and more finches gathered around Duca de' Medici. Eventually, my stomach gurgled audibly, causing Leonore to flutter away.

Duca de' Medici gave me a sideways glance, and now his lips were curling the other way. "Sorry," he repeated, an echo from tens of minutes ago. "It's already teatime for you, isn't it? I didn't mean to be distracted."

"That's okay," I said with a small chuckle. "There's always tomorrow."

"Yes," he murmured, handing me my book and giving me a strange look. "I suppose there is."

Just as I was about to leave, Duca de' Medici tossed his book aside, shot up, and said, "Wait, Signorina Bowling."

I looked him up and down, searching for the urgency, then finally asked, "Yes?"

"Can we have the feeding in here?"

"I guess?" I shifted from one foot to the next, not relinquishing hold of my bag. "I mean, I haven't had *panis largitoris*."

"Does it really matter? I only have you eat it for Signora Carbone's sake."

"Okay." I couldn't find anything objectionable, but a pressing question came to mind. "Why, though?"

He sat and ran his fingers through his hair. "This is my favorite part of the opera. I would like to listen to it with you in my presence. But I understand if you'd rather not."

I tossed my bag to the side and sat next to him. "No, it's fine!" I said a bit too quickly.

Despite my initial hesitation, I warmed up to the idea quickly. After all, I couldn't trust Duca de' Medici's room not to bring to mind certain undertones, and the exam room we used the second time had felt uncomfortably antiseptic. I looked down at my hands, trying to decide the best option to offer him to drink from. There was the inner wrist, like he did the first time. There was my inner elbow, like the second time.

And there was my femoral artery in my upper inner thigh. I saw it in my head, the scene of him on his knees on the ground, the ghostly feeling of his lips, his soft eyelashes fluttering against me.

I banished the thought with such ferocity, my face scrunched up.

"Are you okay?" Duca de' Medici raised a brow.

"Uh, y-yes," I stammered. "Just got an extra sour piece of candy, that's all." I thrust my hand toward him quickly, giving the choice over to him.

Duca de' Medici carefully took my hands in his and looked me in the eyes. His breath hitched. It brought me relief to see he was also anxious, that there was also something in his mind that brought him unease. I was okay with this, as long as he couldn't read mine.

He raised my hand slowly toward him and placed his lips on the most sensitive part of my inner wrist. Duca de' Medici's eyes closed, and I closed my own, tuning in to the sound of the music and the feeling of him.

He continued to press his mouth against me, then finally parted them, softly sucking on my skin. I tried my best not to squirm and focus on staying still, but I couldn't help but let out a staggered exhale.

Then came the sharp pain of a single fang piercing my skin, one I had forgotten to expect. I grasped his hand, and he rubbed a gentle thumb across my fingers. I expected this subconscious movement to elicit an electric response from the vampire, but it

seemed to have the opposite effect. Duca de' Medici drank from me slowly and steadily, pausing now and then to squeeze my hand and swipe his tongue across my wrist, all the while not moving from where his mouth had originally touched.

"You were right," I murmured.

"Hmm?" His mouth buzzed against me with a strange tickling sensation.

I suppressed a giggle, then explained, "The opera. It's really pretty."

"Yes, it really is." After one last sip, he parted from me and looked up with a smile. "Have a lovely day, Signorina Bowling."

And then he departed, leaving me a mess of dizziness and fluttering butterflies.

Even after dinner, I didn't have it in me to take off the cotton ball or bandage. Not that it would hurt or anything—I just didn't want to. When I sat down for tea with Noor, she gave me a strange look but didn't inquire. I was too distracted to explain myself, anyhow, as my attention was immediately drawn toward the satchel of books at her side. I didn't recognize any of the titles, but they appeared to be archival, the sorts of things Noor had brought from local libraries in the past to help me.

"Are those for me?" I asked, taking a seat.

"I thought they could be," she replied, her mouth set in a line. "But now that I've examined them more closely, I don't think they would be of interest to you."

"Why not?" I reached out and glanced at one. It looked old and said *Medici*, which was typically my only criteria.

"They are more recent than documents you are typically interested in—those from the seventeenth century."

"That's not necessarily true," I replied, carefully reading her expression. We had tiptoed around the precise topic of my thesis, but if Noor was to help me and I was to avoid leaving the abbey anytime soon, she would need to know what to look for. I took a long sip of tea to steel myself. "What do you know about the Medici line?"

Noor shrugged. "Not more than most. They were a wealthy and influential family in Italy during the Renaissance, and they are still wealthy and influential today."

I leaned forward in my chair. "And?"

"And nothing more."

I frowned. "Don't you know any details about what happened between then and now?"

"I do not need to know such details to care for Zeno." Then, seeing my disappointment, she acquiesced. "But I am willing to hear them."

"Really?!" I clasped my hands together.

"Yes, if it will help you."

I ran and grabbed several books, which contained Medici portraits, and sprawled them out along the table.

"You see, I was recently researching the family in the seventeenth century, but my interest actually stretches a century beyond it. I'm mostly fascinated by the Medici succession of the seventeenth and eighteenth centuries."

I gave her a moment to butt in and make some excuse to leave, like so many had before her, but to my joy, she remained silent and still. I was flustered to have an audience for my lectures for the first time in so long. "Um, well, at that time, Cosimo III de' Medici faced an unusual problem, right? More specifically, the likely extinction of the Medici dynasty. Cosimo and his wife had three children—Ferdinando, Gian Gastone, and Anna Maria Lucia. Sorry, that's a lot of names to remember, isn't it? Please stop me if you get confused. Actually, I guess these portraits here can help? Um, anyway, Ferdinando, the eldest son and presumptive heir, died before Cosimo could pass along the throne, and in desperation, Cosimo proposed a bill to allow for female-line succession so that Anna Maria Lucia could inherit the family name. Unfortunately for him, this law was revoked after his death, leaving the Medici name in the hands of Gian Gastone."

By this point, I had fully fallen into my lecture and forgotten to feel self-conscious.

"Like his sister, Anna Maria Luisa, Gian Gastone's marriage was barren—in his case, because he was not interested in women, and

in her case because she was infertile, probably because of syphilis. After Gian Gastone's death, it was known to all of Italy that although Anna Maria Luisa may have inherited the Medici family's treasures, the dynasty was already dead. That was, however, until Anna Maria Luisa revealed Ferdinando had secretly sired a child prior to his death. So it was that in 1740, Enzo Armando de' Medici, a bastard and a vampire, emerged from the shadows to claim his title as Grand Duke and revive the Medici family.

"There was plenty of mumbling at the time that Enzo Armando was an imposter introduced by Anna Maria Luisa on her deathbed, but the nobility was too afraid to say anything. The Grand Duke had several children and grandchildren who became artists, bankers, and even popes. It was at this point that vampirism became associated heavily with the Medici family. Now, centuries later, historians are even more skeptical. After all, the Medici family had been sparse on vampires, and many doubted Ferdinando would have been a carrier for the mutation, much less have encountered a presumed prostitute who was also a carrier. So, many wonder who the mother of the Grand Duke was, and why Enzo Armando kept himself secret. Being a bastard was scandalous but not worth abandoning a fortune, right?"

I could've sworn Noor grew darker by the second, but words were spewing from my mouth uncontrollably. I had already said this much.

"Well, when I was doing a research paper on Enzo Armando as an undergraduate, I read through quite a few letters that one of my professors had found between Anna Maria Lucia and Enzo Armando. Nothing was explicitly said, but there were enough clues left that I have a theory. I believe that Ferdinando himself was the result of an affair between Cosimo's wife and a French vampire noble—you know that French nobility has a lot of vampires, right? Furthermore, I believe that Ferdinando unknowingly had his child with the niece of that noble, his own first cousin! Enzo Armando wanted to go into the clergy, so of course he couldn't admit he was the product of incest."

"That's—"

"—a stretch, I know. But there's more evidence floating around too! Genetic records, family trees . . . I *know* I'm close to making a proper argument. I just need a few more things. I think I have a good lead too! See, there was this vocalist nicknamed La Bambagia that Ferdinando fell in love with—he adored music—but nobody knows who she is. Anyway, I know there's this daughter of a famous French

opera singer he was a patron of who died of syphilis shortly after Ferdinando died, and Ferdinando was a known carrier of syphilis, and—"

"Cora," Noor finally cut in, her voice low and serious, "I will help you find what you need. I will even search around Sicily and Tuscany. Just don't tell Zeno. He may find all of this a bit too . . . familiar."

"What do you mean?"

Noor gave a long, slow sigh, as though blowing out the smoke of a cigar, and moved her chair from the table. On cue, Signora Carbone entered the room, gathered up the porcelain, scooped up the tea caddy in a swift motion, and hastened out with it. I wondered how long Signora Carbone had been lingering outside of the room with a tray, or if she'd heard any of what I had said.

I wondered how much I would regret mentioning any of this.

Noor stood, looked me deep in the eyes, and repeated, "Don't tell Zeno. Your thesis is none of his business, and his past is none of yours."

While her words were not cruel, the whiplash of the day made me feel sick. She pressed the satchel of books into my chest.

"I need to put these away, I think," I grumbled. I ran away before she could say another word.

Chapter Seventeen

Recivativo

Even though they were leather bound, the books Noor brought me were small and thin, not much larger than the cheap thrift-store novels that had crowded my college dorm. Yet this trio felt heavier in my hands than textbooks. The three-month mark of my arrival was coming up soon, when I'd have to tell Noor if I wanted to renew our contract.

Nearly three months, and what did I even have to report to my thesis adviser? I couldn't help but wonder if the problem was me, or if this place really was a dead end. I looked down at the books again only to discover my nails had embedded a series of deep crescents in the leather.

I cursed beneath my breath and awkwardly shuffled them into my arms to avoid any further damage. As I shifted, one end of the bandage on my wrist unfurled, causing the cotton ball to dangle askew off my arm.

"Oh no!" I cried, trying to maneuver the books and free my hands. When a gust of wind threatened to peel off the other half, I let the books crash to the ground. I was too late—the bandage fell in an unceremonious heap on the floor, curled up around the cotton ball like a dead bug.

With a gasp, I snatched it back up, but its sticky interior was now encrusted with dust and cotton fiber. It was only when I tried to force it back on that I realized the absurdity of it all. I had abandoned potentially invaluable artifacts for a bandage. A meaningless bandage.

It isn't meaningless, though, is it? I thought, caressing the spot where his lips had been. Some sort of feeling toward Duca de' Medici grew stronger and stronger within me every time we spoke, and I

didn't know what it was. All I knew was that it wouldn't—and couldn't ever—be reciprocated. At the end of the day, this was a job, one I would have to leave eventually.

I left the books on my desk in the little library and left immediately, knowing full well I wouldn't be able to read a single page with my mind jumbled like this. As opposed to to the gentle yet bright glow of the lights in the little library, the sconces around me had been turned down to their lowest level. Each one alternated with minute differences in brightness, which caused the overall direction of light to ebb and flow irregularly. My shadow, barely visible, wavered back and forth out in front of me, creating a disorienting effect.

I took a slow, deep breath that was meant to be grounding but had the opposite effect. The air was thick with dust; the floors had been freshly swept, which combined with the abbey's usually comforting odor to create a stifling feeling. I sneezed, and despite how soft the sound was, it echoed around me.

When I opened my eyes again, the sconce nearest to me had a sudden burst of brightness, and the shadow at my feet darkened. But it was not my own.

A tall, slender man's shadow stretched to Giacometti proportions. His hair was short and kinky, and he wore loose work clothes. A ferric, tangy, *wrong* scent intermingled with the car oil he smelled like after work. His figure was pitch black, but the blood seeping from him was as crimson as the day Ma found him.

He stood motionless. Everything was quiet. The air had chilled, and my breath came faster and faster by the second. My legs shook, and I didn't know whether to run before or away from him. All I could manage was a wide-eyed, whispered, "Pa? Is that—?"

A door slammed down the hall, and I swore the ground itself shook. The lights beamed blindingly around me, and I winced, my eyes squeezing shut.

When they opened again, the shadow was my own. He had vanished, without leaving even a drop of blood behind.

Stifling sobs, I collapsed into the memory of where he was.

"Signorina Bowling!" Signora Carbone called out as she rushed to my side.

Relief met regret, and it took everything in me not to cry out at her, to pretend I was remotely fine.

"I'm not hurt," I said, cooperating with her firm yet gentle touch to help up. "I just got scared."

Her brow creased. "I apologize. I would have closed the door more softly if I knew you were there."

"N-no, it wasn't you. It was . . ." I trailed off. How could one explain what I had just experienced? Even though my body was still surging with adrenaline, my mind was already beginning to doubt what I had seen.

"I understand," Signora Carbone said. She led me to a bench, and I shakily took a seat beside her. I noticed tea stains on the rag tucked in her pocket, presumably from wiping down the table after my conversation with Noor.

"Did you hear me talking with Noor?" I asked. "About my thesis?"

She nodded.

I took in a breath with pursed lips before saying, "Do you think it's wrong of me to be working on that topic . . . here?"

Signora Carbone set her eyes upon me, and the tiny scowl on her lips would have answered the question sufficiently. "I do not think it is befitting of a *beniamina*. I have no intention of assisting you with it."

There was that word again: *beniamina*. One I couldn't escape. I felt bitterness paint my features. "I'm considering resigning anyway. I don't think the abbey holds any real secrets, so there's nothing here for me."

I knew the last sentence was a lie, even as I said it. This place had all the things I had forgotten I wanted: a beautiful garden, an endless library, and kind coworkers I had actually befriended. Most entrapping of all was the gentle vampire who I wanted to be around more and more, who listened and cared, even when he was sulking or making fun of me. I couldn't fall into this place, couldn't risk having it torn from me.

"And truthfully," I added, "I've seen things here. Things that make me wonder if I'm even welcome."

Signora Carbone's brow knitted, and there was a prolonged pause before she said, "I have been told by locals that the Abbazia di Santa Dymphna shows people their ghosts."

I sat up straighter. While strange, her explanation made sense. I had seen Ma, Pa, and Peachy—living or dead, they all haunted me. But if this were true, why was everyone else acting so normal? Why did it seem to be just me?

"Do you have ghosts, then, Signora Carbone?" I asked with great hesitance. "Do the others?"

She chuckled darkly. "We all have things that keep us up at night, and I am no exception. But they do not show themselves to me here, and if Duca de' Medici, Doctor Ntumba, or Signore Urbino see them, they do not show it. Some people are more sensitive to the effects of this place. I know Lucia has seen—" Signora Carbone faltered, voice hitching when she spoke the name of her adopted child. She looked into the distance, expression hardening. "You stated there are no secrets in the Abbazia di Santa Dymphna, that there is nothing here for you. But the Medici family has a history written in blood. I do not doubt that its ghosts also linger here. I do not know if I would want you to uncover them, but that is not my decision." Then, facing me again, she said, "I implore you, Signora Bowling, please stay for Lucia's sake. We have moved from town to town since she was a child, and she has never truly had a friend. Please, at the very least, do not leave without giving her warning."

The light from the sconces illuminated the moisture gathering in the corner of her eyes. Signora Carbone's voice was shaking, and I finally saw how tired she truly was.

Seeing her sincerity and her desperation, I felt a lump in my throat. "I will," I said without hesitation. "At least until the end of these six months. I can't make any promises beyond then, but I'll do that much."

Her fists tightened, and she averted her gaze from me. There was a prolonged pause between us, and she opened her mouth several times without finishing a single word. Then she blinked several times before tears could fully gather, flattened her brow and lips, and said in a low voice, "Thank you. I will leave now to attend to my duties."

There was nothing more to say, so I nodded and went to bed. I would speak with Noor tomorrow and tell her I wanted to renew my contract for this quarter, and I would focus on finding the secret of the

Medici family. Most importantly, I would banish the silly idea that Duca de' Medici could ever feel for me the way I did for him.

Chapter Eighteen

Bel Canto

"Ouch!"

My shears hit the ground, and crimson bloomed from my fingertip, forming a fat droplet that threatened to run along my palm and onto the floor. The lava-stone flooring here had a way of soaking up pigmentation as readily as the carpet in my childhood home soaked up wine.

A rag in one pocket, mottled with dirt and oil, wouldn't be appropriate to mop up the blood. The folded pair of gloves in my pocket were even worse. In desperation, I stuck my finger in my mouth and grimaced at the taste, salty and sour.

"You should be more careful. You'll get an infection one of these days." Noor approached, already prepared with a bandage and generous globule of antibiotic.

"I know. I was spoiled by thornless roses growing up." I held out my wounded hand to her, cupping the other underneath just in case. This was, of course, unnecessary, considering the speed at which she worked. "What are you doing here?" I asked, returning the shears to the drawer. "I don't think I've seen you in here before."

"I stop by now and then," she replied with a smile, "to see how things are growing."

It was early afternoon, and the air in the greenhouse was hot and thick. I ran my sleeve across my forehead to intercept sweat from a well-used path along my brow, then joined Noor's side to see the gardens from her perspective. Various cultivars were growing at different rates, noisettes wrapping themselves around the trellises and

bourbons reaching proudly toward the stained-glass roof. As indicated by the trimmings that littered the ground, all of them were uncontrollably thriving. Virgin buds interspersed the greenery, ready to burst at any moment, and there were even a few young flowers.

Signora Carbone scolded me regularly when cleaning the dirt out from beneath my nails, but I knew even she could admire how well the cuttings were growing. I discovered she and Signore Urbino shared the duties of tending to the gardens outside, and she would often offer me snippets of advice. On one occasion, Signore Urbino attempted to do the same, but he was quickly dismissed by the sharpest glare I had seen from Duca de' Medici. I hadn't spoken of either of those tense conversations with Signora Carbone or Noor since that night, and they passed from our collective consciousness. The decision to continue working here had been little more than a nod and a signature at the end of the quarter.

"There are still a few spots I need to plant in, mostly in that far corner there," I said, pointing toward it. "I haven't figured out what type of roses I want yet. Maybe tea roses?"

Noor put one hand on her hip, tilted her head to the side, and pursed her lips, like she always did when she was thinking. "There is a plant nursery in Partanna. I've heard it has some rare seeds."

"I see." Roses rarely grew from seeds. It would most likely be a futile effort.

Noor frowned. "I see that look, but the cultivar is old, and you could use a challenge. Regardless, you could stand to leave the abbey for once."

Now it was my turn to frown. How long had I been here? Time blurred in this place. I counted the number of blood donations on bandaged fingers. Four total months in the abbey. Four months since I was connected to any sort of cellular network, since I'd messaged my thesis adviser. *I'll respond to her next month,* I told myself, *once I've examined this current lead.*

Noor was staring at me, clearly expecting a response, so I stammered, "W-would you be willing to get some for me next time you go to Partanna?"

Noor glared. "You won't be getting those seeds unless you go to Partanna yourself. I don't want you to get too anxious here. Stress will compromise your health."

"Okay." *I'll just have Lucia or Signore Urbino grab them for me.*

Per usual, Noor was quick to read my deception. "And don't try to get away with asking any of the maids or butlers to purchase them. I'll know."

I sighed, put my hand on the back of my neck, and forced a smile. "Fine. I'll go at some point."

Noor sighed, shook her head, and left, muttering, "Oh, Cora . . ."

If only disappointment wasn't contagious. The bench screeched in protest as I dragged it toward the center of the room. I sat, drew up my legs, and hugged them to my chest.

"It isn't really that bad, is it?" I asked the roses. I finished the rest of the sentence in my head: *I mean, I've been working on this thesis for eighteen months, so what's another one?*

The flowers were bright, immune to the contagion of disappointment. How enviable. The sun was at my favorite point in the sky, where it hit the stained glass just right and cast an array of color across the greenhouse, rendering it dreamlike. That meant afternoon teatime was soon.

"I think today is supposed to be hibiscus tea. I know Noor doesn't really like it very much, but I think it's delicious. Maybe I can talk to her about—"

"So, you really do talk to your flowers," a voice boomed behind me. "How cute."

I leaped to my feet, turning as red as the roses themselves. Duca de' Medici was leaning in the doorway at such an angle that he was just out of the sun.

"W-what are you doing here?" I bristled.

"Just passing by." His smile was audible in his voice. "I'll see you in a bit. I was wondering—"

The sharp click of Noor's high-heeled footsteps was barely audible through the wall behind me. A quick glance at my watch revealed she was on time, of course.

"Oh no!" I exclaimed, jumping to my feet. "I haven't even changed!"

"Ah." Duca de' Medici's voice softened with poorly veiled disappointment. "You'd best be off, then."

I hesitated. "But wait, what were you going to ask? I interrupted you."

Duca de' Medici stepped out of the light entirely. "Never mind. It was foolish anyway. I'll tell Noor I held you up."

He left before I could gather my thoughts or say anything, and with little else to do, I mentally tucked away the encounter and left to change.

As I had expected, the library greeted me with the pleasant scent of hibiscus layered over the usual mustiness of old books. Shortbread cookies peeked out from underneath a neatly folded napkin.

I was surprised to see that Noor didn't appear annoyed that I was late. On the contrary, she was sipping her tea in an unusually jovial mood. Despite the strangeness of our previous conversation about my thesis, I decided to try once more.

"I've found a promising lead," I ventured, taking a bite of a cookie. "There was an exhumation of Enzo Armando's body a few years ago to gather his genome. I'd like to see which mutations—"

Noor drank the rest of her tea in a painfully large gulp, then slammed the teacup onto its plate. When she spoke, her sharp tone was as jarring as the sound of porcelain against porcelain. "You're dabbling in things you don't understand the gravity of, Cora."

I was speechless. She had rebuked me when we first talked about my thesis, but since then, I thought we'd established a mutual understanding. As long as Zeno was not involved, everything was fair game.

I took a sip of tea, but it did little to wet my dry mouth.

Noor locked onto me, brow furrowed and eyes intense. "Do your thesis, find your information, but do not involve me in anything relating to vampirism itself."

She paused for a moment and softened just enough to jar me from my state of paralysis, then asked me a straightforward question: "How long did Enzo Armando live?"

No matter how taken aback I was, this sort of concrete information was seared into me and came forth as easily as my name. "Enzo Armando lived to the age of forty-two."

She nodded slowly. "And what did he die of?"

"It's widely debated. If you look at one of his portraits later in life, he has an unusual marking on his face, and some scholars assume it's from syphilis. I think it could be melanoma, though, since he was known to spend time outside with his children in his thirties."

"Well, then," she said, donning her usual mask of detachment. "Connect the dots, and don't step over any lines you've made. You should leave now. Zeno will be expecting you."

My arms and legs burned, my chest heaving. Although I may have needed the exercise, jogging had been futile. Duca de' Medici hadn't even arrived by the time I found my spot in the corner.

I gulped in the air and dropped *War and Peace* onto the bench. It hit the stone with a satisfying thud. *At least*, I thought, *how sore my arms are is justified*. Shoving my unusual discussion with Noor from my mind, I plopped down next to my adversary and waited for my friend. Leonore flitted over to me immediately, nesting happily in my lap. The shy little thing had finally warmed up to me and was sure to demand affection the instant I sat down. She had especially come to adore those five minutes before Duca de' Medici arrived and she had me all to herself.

But for the first time since I'd met Duca de' Medici, he arrived exactly on time. He entered the room, eyes to the ground, and took a seat.

He was as horrible at hiding his moods as I had become skilled at reading them. This was, I deduced, neither pouting nor anger, but mild discomfort, presented with Medici's usual flair.

"What's this about?" I joked, trying to lighten the mood. "Not a fan of the latest chapter in the book?"

Duca de' Medici glanced up at me and appeared to be on the verge of speaking, then tightened his mouth in a line. "No, actually, I'm quite fond of how the story is moving along. I've picked out an excellent record for today. Some Debussy, in fact."

That's a pretty good impression of being normal, I thought, *but not good enough*. Then it hit me. "What were you going to ask earlier?"

He froze so jarringly that Leonore was startled away. "I, uh—I heard your conversation."

I rolled my eyes. "You already made fun of me for talking with flowers, remember?"

"No, before that. With Noor."

My heart leaped to my throat. The notion he had heard about my thesis, for reasons I couldn't fully parse, felt acutely sinful. To my combined relief and confusion, the look of Duca de' Medici was not anger, but embarrassment. "Yes, I was reading next door, in the aviary. I was going to ask if you wanted to go get the seeds with me."

Oh. *That* was the conversation he heard.

Somehow, this wasn't any clearer.

"I mean, that would be lovely, but can you really go outside during the day? Is that . . .?"

I knew it wasn't safe for him, but I didn't know exactly how unsafe it could be. On top of albinism, some vampires had lupus-like photosensitivity or solar urticaria. This was bad enough, but there even existed some rarer subtypes of vampirism with anaphylactic responses to certain ultraviolet rays. While I would appreciate having a friendly face accompany me, I didn't think Noor would appreciate me using up all her epinephrine.

Duca de' Medici gave a dry laugh. "I'll be fine. I'll look foolish, certainly, but I'll be fine." Then, shooting me a sideways glance, he added, "So, uh, did you want to? There's still time. The shop closes in a few hours."

"I guess?" It came out as a question, but this didn't seem to bother Duca de' Medici at all. In fact, he was glowing.

"You should get ready. I'll have Signora Carbone wash your pink dress. Lucia knows what to get for accessories."

Chapter Nineteen

Lascia La Spina

By the time Lucia finished my makeup, the dress had already been washed, dried, and ironed. It was a floral baby-doll dress with puffed sleeves, tailored to fit me. Despite my never having worn the dress before, Duca de' Medici's assumption that Lucia would know how to accessorize with it was correct. She had chosen a sun hat with a creamy, white ribbon that matched uncannily well with the heels. Around my neck was a gold necklace with several diamonds I hoped were fake, a matching gold bracelet, and several rings. I twisted in the mirror, searching for exactly where the flaw was that made me feel so much like someone in a costume, but could pin nothing down.

Duca de' Medici's words echoed in my mind. *I'll be fine. I'll look foolish, certainly, but I'll be fine.*

Maybe I shouldn't be so concerned about how I looked at the moment. Perhaps the more pressing concern would be comforting my counterpart.

The moment I saw Duca de' Medici, I understood what he meant. His garb was, in a word, bizarre.

Rather than his usual dress clothes, he was wearing a thick, full-length jacket with a hood over his head, which wouldn't have been too abnormal—a bit out of season, granted—if not for what was underneath the hood: a combination of a balaclava and sunglasses that entirely obscured Duca de' Medici's face. He had also covered the rest of his body. His hands were covered by leather gloves, his pants were tucked into comically large boots, and not even a single strand of hair or an inch of skin was visible.

I found myself unable to say a word.

Duca de' Medici said nothing, either, but carried himself with a nonchalant air, movements loose as usual. "Are you ready?" he asked in a muffled voice.

I nodded wordlessly and followed him outside. It was difficult not to reach out to the man and grab him by the wrist and try to pull him back inside. But of course, I knew the clothing he wore provided ample protection against the sun, far more than the high-quality sunscreen and sunglasses most vampires got by with.

He opened the back door of a fancy black sedan awaiting us. I ducked inside and slid across the leather seats to the far side for him to follow suit. Duca de' Medici took his spot beside me and stretched out.

"Good afternoon, Signora Rafia," he said to the driver, a middle-aged woman with short brown hair I had never seen before. She wore a uniform much like the other drivers I had seen. Noor had a driver, the butlers and maids had a driver, and evidently, so did Duca de' Medici. But how often, I wondered, did she actually drive him anywhere? I'd thought my job was easy, but this salaried woman who I'd now seen for the first time after months of living at the abbey clearly had me beat.

She turned around to look at him, clearly unfazed by his outfit. "Good afternoon, Duca de' Medici and—"

"—Signorina Bowling," he finished her sentence.

"Cora is fine," I replied with a forced smile. "It's a pleasure to meet you."

As we rolled off, I stared out the window out of habit, but it was so darkly tinted it felt as though it were night. I focused instead on the barely audible smooth jazz and the rhythmic bouncing of the car.

"The ride shouldn't be long," Duca de' Medici said. "Fifteen minutes at most."

With a strange nostalgia, I remembered the winding road I had taken to the abbey for my interview so many months ago, and though we must have been going the same route, it felt entirely different. In fact, despite the perfection of Signora Rafia's driving, my body reacted as though our ambling descent was a roller-coaster ride: heart palpitations, a bit of sweating. But so far, nothing akin to a full-blown panic attack.

"Could we grab some water?" I asked, mouth feeling dry.

"There's some in the cooler," Duca de' Medici answered. "It's built into the wall of the trunk. We can pull over and I'll show you."

Oh, my bad, I thought with a sneer. *I shouldn't have forgotten to check if this car has a refrigerator.*

"No, it's fine." I finished the rest in my head: *The sooner we get cellular connection and the sooner I can see my messages, the better.*

I closed my eyes and focused on my breath. My heart rate evened out by the time the car slowed to a final halt. When I opened my eyes, sunshine and cool air alike poured into the car. Outside and holding the door open, Signora Rafia stared down at me expectantly.

Next to me, Duca de' Medici shook his head at her, and the door shut again.

"Are you ready?" Duca de' Medici's tone was far too soft and attentive to be anything but an acknowledgment of my anxiety. "We can wait here for a bit."

I wished desperately that I could make eye contact with my ally through his sunglasses to truly and properly thank him, but I gave him a smile.

"Yes," I replied, realizing my phone hadn't buzzed. "I'm ready."

We stepped out into the unknown, and I was surprised to find that the bricks were almost identical to those surrounding the abbey. Disparate, weed-filled furrows in the ground were visible evidence of the earthquake from decades ago. In contrast, the bustling market square nearby was young and quaint, surrounded by hand-built booths and small traditional buildings, none of which had any sort of professional signage. Clearly, this was an area for mostly locals. Laughter and conversation sounded from all sides, a mixture of joking, hard bargaining, and day-to-day rural gossip.

Although Signora Rafia had intentionally parked in a tucked-away area, a few of the locals directed their attention toward us. Why wouldn't they? The car I had just exited was clearly worth more than anyone in this town had ever seen, and Duca de' Medici's clothing was strange, to say the least.

"Come," Duca de' Medici said. "I'll show you where it is."

I focused my attention on my breath, the cracks in the ground, and Duca de' Medici's shoes as I followed behind him. The chattering of the people around us swelled, hushed, then swelled again. The crowd gave us ample breadth, but I could only assume this was to stare.

"Here we are."

The stone building was clearly one of the few that had survived the earthquake untouched. Above the door was a wooden, hand-painted sign: PIANTI DI CARUSO. Climbing roses crawled along the bricks, and potted plants of every type were above, below, and aside all the outdoor displays. Local pottery crowded one side of the door, fountains and sculptures on the other, and bags of fertilizers and mulch were propped against the side of the building.

"Ah, shit," Duca de' Medici grumbled. "I forgot my wallet in the car. Go on without me. I'll be right back."

He picked up a half jog and left toward the car. Once he was out of sight, I pulled my phone out of my pocket. No bars, no Wi-Fi. For at least another month, I could pretend my thesis adviser was patiently awaiting any updates. All that mattered today was those seeds. I took a deep breath and entered the shop.

Upon the bell ringing, the shopkeeper quickly wiped dirt from his hands with an old rag and beamed at me. "*Assa binidica!*"

He was round and bright like the sun, with one of those trustworthy faces that seemed perennially on the verge of laughter. Hours of squinting during bright Sicilian days had creased his tanned face, and minute scars covered the backs of his large hands, battle wounds from wars with weeds and thickets.

The shop around him was similarly welcoming. It was small, little more than a single room, but filled to the brim with life, both literally and figuratively. Dozens of plants teemed from every corner, with ivy even climbing around the legs of furniture and along the old brick walls. Trinkets and local art were situated around sporadically, invading the few organized sections of the store.

I nodded my head and gave my best smile. As the shopkeeper gestured enthusiastically around the store and continued his rapid-fire Sicilian, panic set in. How helpless could I be to not even know how to tell him I didn't speak his language?

Just as I was on the verge of running out to find Duca de' Medici, the door opened behind me.

The shop owner froze immediately, and his crescent eyes turned full. He let out a small gasp—a cross-cultural expression, at least, as was the pallor that covered the man like a sheet. Various trinkets and pamphlets hit the floor as the shop owner rushed past his counter to shut off several grow lights and close the curtains.

"I'm sorry, Duca de' Medici!" he cried out in mainland Italian.

The aforementioned vampire took off his jacket, draped it over his shoulder, pulled off his balaclava, and shed all of his protective gear. Then he browsed wordlessly.

The shopkeeper rushed to his side, nearly pushing me aside. "Good afternoon, Duca. I am Ugo Caruso, and this shop has been in my family since before the earthquake. I heard you moved into the abbey, but I did not know such rumors were . . ." He trailed off as Duca de' Medici walked the other way mid-sentence.

Instead of regarding the man, Duca de' Medici picked up a packet of commercial seeds from the shelf and inspected it. "Hmm," he said to himself. "Imported, but at least at market value."

He returned it to its original spot and crossed to the other side of the store, Signore Caruso tottering around him in close orbit.

"What is it I can help you with, Duca de' Medici?" Signore Caruso asked as the vampire sifted through various books and continued to mutter to himself. "It would be a pleasure—no, an *honor* to assist you! You are interested in purchasing seeds, it seems?"

Duca de' Medici silently removed his sunglasses, hung them on his collar, then finally addressed Signore Caruso. "You should help the customer who was here before me," he said in a monotone, gazing through the man as though he were nothing.

Signore Caruso whipped his head back and forth to look between us, mouth falling open into a horrified *O*. It was like I had existed again for the first time since the vampire entered the store. "I'm so sorry! Are the two of you together, Duca?"

After an exaggerated sigh, the vampire resumed studying the contents of a weathered book. "Yes, but that is irrelevant. She was here first, so assist her first. It's common sense."

Signore Caruso stammered a few syllables, then rushed to me. I remembered, for the first time in months, that Duca de' Medici had ever spoken so coldly to someone before, that he had once spoken to me like that.

But to contradict this memory immediately, Duca de' Medici looked over at me with the intensity and warmth for which I knew him. He extended the book he was reading far from him before closing it to avoid the small cloud of dust that puffed out, then returned it to its spot.

"What would you like?" he said upon joining my side. "Pots, seeds, any of the books, tools, however many plants . . . I'll have another car come fetch it all for you. Feel free to get some of the decor as well. You can pick out one of the fountains outside. We can figure out plumbing, hire a contractor if need be. I'm sure Noor will throw a fit, but what does that matter if your garden is how you wish it?"

I nodded at him dumbly, then finally returned the attention of Signore Caruso, who was visibly sweating away some of the dirt along his hairline. Nothing here had price tags, and I couldn't even imagine the resulting cost of all the things Duca de' Medici had so casually thrown my way.

"I just want a bag of some seeds," I said to them both. "Rose seeds. That's plenty."

As the world grew wobbly and time intangible, Signore Caruso's rambling voice faded. I focused on the various packets of seeds he was showing me. There were countless flowers, and I finally had to repeat, "Rose seeds, please."

Duca de' Medici echoed what I said in Sicilian, and something finally clicked in the man. He rushed behind the counter, and tucked away in a small, dusty box was an unmarked, pocket-sized linen satchel. He opened it to show me what initially appeared to be several tiny, brown stones. It took me a moment to recognize the irregularly shaped brown objects: seeds.

"*Rose di Santa Dymphna*," Signore Caruso informed me.

He didn't have to tell me these were the heirloom beauties I had heard so much about. The pride on his face said as much. He held them out to me with both hands, as though they were fragile.

Accordingly, I took them carefully. "How much?"

"For you, Duchessa?" Signore Caruso grinned broadly. "Free."

My heart fluttered at his assumption that I was a duchess, wife to the duke beside me. It was an impossibility in so many ways, and I struggled to get out any syllables. "D-Duches–?"

"Thank you, signore," Duca de' Medici cut in quickly. "I'll have the payment mailed to you." He was already putting his protective gear back on, but he wasn't fast enough for his crimson-tipped ears to escape my attention. He turned back to me after fully garbing up and said in a cool tone, "Signorina Bowling, the car should be here momentarily."

I gave a small smile to Signore Caruso, tucked the seeds in my pocket, and rushed out. Today had been intense, to say the least.

Chapter Twenty

Cogli la Rosa

Now that dusk had fallen, it was safe for us to roll the windows down in the car. If Duca de' Medici could tell how strange the events of today had made me feel, he did not show it. The vampire looked utterly at peace as he watched the trees go by.

"Would you like dinner in the gazebo?" he asked suddenly.

I looked back from the window and raised a brow at him. "Dinner in the what?"

"There's a gazebo by the graveyard. I enjoy a candlelit dinner there from time to time. I imagine you would too."

"Sure. That might be an agreeable change of pace."

It was strange how quickly this unlocked something within me, some calling for something lost. Here I was in a designer dress, designer shoes, and jewelry worth more than I had made in years, but I suddenly craved what I had lost: simple foods, simple activities, simple joys.

"This might sound kind of silly, but could we have a picnic? It's been such a long time. Peachy and I used to love them."

He studied me, not showing any immediate sentiment. I no longer found this lack of emotion off-putting; he was waiting for all the information before giving me anything in return.

I gave Duca de' Medici a coy smile and said, "I can make some *mean* deviled eggs."

He chuckled and returned my smile. "I'll have to take you up on it, then. What shall I bring?""Whatever you can make." *Which I imagine isn't a lot.*

"Well, I can make a *fiendish* PB and J."

"Perfect! Let's see . . ." I recited a theoretical packing list to him and wasn't surprised to find most of my choices for fruit and snacks unavailable at such short notice. The feast we were going to pack would be enough regardless.

The path to the hill was similar but different from my memories. The trees, rocks, and plants were all the same, but fall had transformed them. The oranges and reds were stark against the deep blues of the sky above, and only the tips of the stones were visible from fallen leaves. Instead of the small, wiry stems that had poked from green grounds on the farmlands to our sides only months ago, rippling oceans of wheat surrounded us. Although the seasonal change had altered the appearance of the environment, the autumns and winters here were supposed to be ridiculously mild. In fact, it was unlikely I would see any of this land covered in white.

Setting up the picnic was second nature to me, and all the dishes were quickly visible: trays of deviled eggs, various sandwiches, fruits and vegetables, two pitchers of lemonade and iced hibiscus tea, and shortbread cookies. Duca de' Medici ate in the strange way he always did, able to peck at an entire meal without spilling a crumb. Meanwhile, I ate my large bites slowly, trying desperately to keep the jacket he had again loaned me clean. A cloud crept along the sky above, with stars peeking through sheets of gray for brief seconds. Those flickers, however ephemeral, were sweet enough that I kept my attention to the sky.

When Duca de' Medici spoke, low and clear, I found myself caught off guard.

"I have never really cared for others. Perhaps if I could go outside as you can—if I could blend into the crowd—I would. Or perhaps I simply do not have it in me. Either way, the vast majority of people are little more than an annoyance to me. Absurdity plagues the human race, and once you realize that, Signorina Bowling, the game of small talk and smiles gets rather Sisyphean. We often speak of Greek myths, and that one is my favorite for a reason."

The yolk of the deviled egg I was holding jiggled just like my hand, then plopped into my lap. I returned the white to the tray, got

yolk all over my fingers while brushing it off, and attempted to steel myself once it was clear he was going to continue.

"I must sound rather melodramatic to you, and I know that I am. 'One must imagine Sisyphus happy,' Basilio often quoted to me when I said as much to him. 'The pride of attempting to save humanity from death, and the fact we speak his name, must make it all worth it.' But I cannot imagine the king to have felt anything but remorse as he pushed that boulder up the hill, day after day. Remorse for his hubris, and remorse for how foolish he was to attempt to surmount an unchangeable truth."

"Why are you telling me this?" I couldn't hide the offended undertone in my voice. To spring something like that on me without warning was tactless, to say the least.

He met my eyes and spoke evenly. "I saw the look you gave me back at the shop when I spoke to the owner as I did. I felt you were afforded an explanation."

I tightened my mouth into a line and sat up fully. Why bother pretending with Duca de' Medici? But agreeing to that much didn't mean bowing to the rest.

"It wasn't just the coldness that caught me so off guard. I mean, offering to buy all that for me was a lot. I'm not used to *any* of that." I gestured broadly with my arms.

Duca de' Medici sat up, looked toward the abbey, and pointedly placed his high-end silverware on the fancy china. He then removed his many rings one by one and placed them in his napkin, allowing each gem to shimmer. "All these riches around me, the designer clothes, the fancy sweets—they make me happy for a moment, but they mean nothing. On the other hand, watching you wear them, eat them, enjoy them . . . that's something."

I wilted. "The fact that I'm getting paid to be in my paradise, surrounded by books and archives, feels selfish enough."

"Signorina Bowling." His voice was unexpectedly stern. "I need you to understand that I could not possibly spend a portion of the money allotted to me within my lifetime, even if it were full."

The statement alone was shocking, sure, but my mind clung to the end of what he said. *Even if it were full?*

I forced myself not to look at the vampire and lie back down behind him. Then I said the only thing I was thinking: "Okay."

We lay there in silence, and the moon peeked through the clouds for the first time. Despite how hazy the rest of the sky was, the full moon was crystal clear. The quiet became layered and complicated, yet neither of us seemed to want to fill it.

Eventually, Duca de' Medici was the one to break it.

"I've never had a picnic," he admitted, voice muffled, as though this were some massive shocker.

I couldn't help but laugh. "I'm not exactly surprised. I imagine there's a lot of things you haven't done, just like me. I've never ridden in a car with a refrigerator before, and I doubt you've ever taken public transportation."

A strange thought came to me then, one that made my stomach twist in a knot: he had probably never been pushed on a swing, or had a nickname. I imagined him being called by his full name by a butler, even while taking his first steps.

"I'd like to do this again," Duca de' Medici said, so sincerely that my former trepidation melted. "We don't have to, of course, but it was nice. For however long you plan to be here, that is."

I finally looked at him for the first time in a while with a smile. "We can have plenty of picnics, and movie nights, and even bake cookies together, if you'll have me."

Duca de' Medici averted his gaze to a rabbit in the distance and clenched his jaw.

"Can I?" he asked, voice scarcely above a whisper.

I blinked and peered my head around to catch his eye. "Can you what?"

He continued to watch the rabbit, which was grazing serenely on fallen fruit from a wild strawberry tree, and didn't reply. Despite the silence, I realized what he meant: *Can I have you?*

I bit my lip, burrowed into Duca de' Medici's coat, and slowly nodded my head. "Yes. For now."

He lay down again, face turned away from me. "That's enough."

Chapter Twenty-One

Sepolcro

The next few days passed normally for Duca de' Medici and me. Per usual, we had our book club in the aviary; we'd shifted from reading *Idylls of the King* to *Julius Caesar*, then to *North and South.* Respectively, we'd shifted from listening to *Tristan und Isolde*, to Mussorgsky, to Beethoven.

But on the inside, my stomach flipped every time I remembered that day in Partanna and our conversation on the hill. I didn't know if I regretted my answer, if I was making a mistake in promising something I couldn't really give. All I knew was that at the moment, I'd meant it—for at least another month, I was his. And when the next donation came around, his words haunted me: *I need you to understand that I could not possibly spend a portion of the money allotted to me within my lifetime, even if it were full.*

I never ceased to be impressed by how chilly the exam room was. I used to assume my old fear of doctor's offices was responsible for my goose bumps, but the cold was the actual culprit. Even the side table my arm rested on was sickeningly cool. I looked at Doctor Ntumba next to me, envy striking at the sight of her warm outfit. It was per her demand that this feeding was being done by IV—retribution, I assumed, for the horrifically unsanitary feeding we'd had in the presence of countless birds.

"Doctor Ntumba," I said before she began, "I have a question."

She looked up from what she was doing—preparing the IV itself—curious yet slightly irritated. "What is it, Cora?"

"Well, actually, I don't know if we can talk about this. I mean, is there some European equivalent to HIPAA?"

She tied the tourniquet masterfully, as usual, and I tried not to wince at its vice grip, preparing my arm for the prick of the needle. I focused instead on the cold, rough sensation of the alcohol wipe across my arm.

"There's a near equivalent, GDPR. But your job acceptance included mutual ROIs. In fact, the same applies to you and Zeno with this entire household. So, what do you want to know?"

Doctor Ntumba pierced my vein with ease, then tossed the tourniquet aside as though it were a victory flag. I was never squeamish with blood, but my stomach always turned at the sight of red traveling down the tubes into a bag.

"I, uh—how long could my employment last? Like, if I were here for a long time, how long could that be?"

"Ah. You're asking how long Zeno has to live."

I wished, suddenly, that I wasn't sitting there with a massive tube in my arm so I could abort the conversation if it wasn't successful, but maybe both of us being forced to sit here would work to my benefit.

"Yeah," I replied. "I guess I couldn't find a polite way to ask."

"Zeno's health has long been a subject of contention." With the blood flowing easily, she sat across from me and coolly said, "Some specialists believe he'll live into his fifties, others believe he should have already died."

"But I thought most vampires had a normal lifespan?" It came out as more of a question than a statement.

"Most, but Zeno has an unfortunate set of mutations on top of the typical oculocutaneous albinism and pancytopenia—xeroderma pigmentosum and congenital immunodeficiency. To vastly simplify both conditions, the former means his skin struggles to repair damage caused by ultraviolet light, and the latter means his body cannot fight off infection or abnormalities."

My undergraduate biology degree wormed its way out of my subconscious. "In other words, he's incredibly likely to get skin cancer?"

I wasn't sure when Doctor Ntumba had pulled the IV out from me, but she was already patching me up.

"He's been lucky so far. Set up to thrive, as it were. Vampirism is known amongst nobility, and houses tend to prepare for it. This entire house is powered with UV-free lighting, as has every house he's grown up in. Even the candles here are designed to burn at a low enough temperature so as not to emit any hint of radiation. It is likely that if he only had xeroderma pigmentosum, he would have a normal lifespan, but I believe it's only a matter of time."

My patience was already wearing thin, and Doctor Ntumba gathering up the bags made me unable to hold back from cutting her off. "But how long do you think he'll live?"

Doctor Ntumba's countenance finally darkened. "As many doctors have projected, he could probably live until his late fifties, but knowing Zeno, I think he'll only last until his mid-to-late thirties."

The pit in my stomach blossomed, its branches coursing through my body, making my fingers numb. Like I felt when Pa died, before pangs of sorrow radiated through me.

"Why? Isn't he set up for success?" I demanded. "He doesn't even look like he has any sun damage!"

Doctor Ntumba gave me a small smile, more pitiful than any tears could have been. "He *is* set up for success, more than any client I've ever seen, but he's . . . negligent. Even convincing him to have transfusions, much less blood from a *beniamina,* took months."

"I don't understand," I said, shaking my head and crossing my arms tightly.

I did, of course. I just didn't want to.

With a deep sigh, Doctor Ntumba put her hand on my shoulder. "That is why your presence here is so important, Cora, and I must apologize for understating it when you were hired. But truthfully, you are responsible for giving much more than just blood to him."

I wanted to ask what exactly I was responsible for, but I already knew the answer. He had told me that night on the hill: as briefly as we had known one another, our time together was motivation for him to fight for every day.

I felt myself shaking. Sweat gathered on my brow and hands. "That's *way* more than I signed up for. I—I can't handle that kind of responsibility! You said this wasn't a permanent position."

Doctor Ntumba stepped away from me with guilt, exasperation, annoyance, and countless other emotions flickering across her features.

"I didn't think he would take to you so strongly. I didn't think he was capable of it," she admitted with a frown. "Zeno has been my sole patient since he was eight, and I knew him even as an infant. For as long as I've known him, he has only let a few people in, and those were all so long ago."

We both held our breaths, and another sound became audible.

Drip. Drip.

I looked down to see crimson pooling on the tile at my feet, the result of a spidery path of red trailing down my arm. The cotton ball was dangling, half attached to my arm, entirely ineffective in damming the deluge of blood I had forced out by gripping my fists. I cursed under my breath, and Doctor Ntumba quickly gloved up and patched me up again.

"Sit," she ordered. Then, more politely, "Please."

I was grateful for this request, as the weight of my body and the entire situation had already impressed itself upon my limbs. The blood loss made things worse, of course, but everything Zeno had said to me over these past few weeks fully came to a head. I allowed myself to go limp, slouching in the chair with defeat.

She worked quickly as I sat there and eventually closed my eyes. "Do you feel okay?" she asked.

"Yeah," I mumbled. "This is just a lot to take in."

"I understand. I am true to my word, and your contract will continue to be renegotiated on a quarterly basis." She paused and met my eyes. "You should consider whether or not you wish to be a *beniamina* in *all* senses of the word."

How could you understand? was the immediate riposte in my mind. I bit the thought back the second it emerged; Noor was not to blame for any of this, I realized. In fact, *blame* might not even be an accurate term. Even without a contract, I had accepted this role, both to myself and to Zeno. I just hadn't allowed myself to consciously acknowledge it.

"It's okay," I finally asserted once she finished. "I already have, for the time being."

I remained seated but gave her a nod of dismissal. After a moment of hesitation, she wheeled away the blood, leaving me alone with my thoughts in that cold, cold room. So cold it reminded me of the mortality of the man who was getting my blood.

Whether I remained here—whether I left to pursue my PhD after finishing my thesis—his body would join the others in the graveyard. But he would continue to fight for at least another month. What would I do after that?

I stirred the soup in front of me, long gone cold. I had taken a few bites of the *macco di fave*, and the fava bean soup was delicious as everything else I had been served. My portion sizes had lessened to account for my waning appetite, and I felt more obliged than ever to try to finish what I had. But unfortunately, today was one of those days where neurosis had nestled into my stomach and made the thought of eating unbearable. I plopped my spoon into the bowl and ran my thumb across the bite marks on my wrist, strangely comforted by the familiar grooves, the remnants of that feeding in the aviary, as sweet and electrifying as the feeling of when I had signed the contract renewal.

A plate descended from above, carried by a set of tiny hands. I glanced behind me at Lucia, who was grinning broadly, first at me and then at the plate. It had a few truffles on it—my favorite. No matter how full or nauseous I was, I couldn't resist the little treasures.

"Don't worry, signorina," Lucia told me, stealing one for herself. "I know you've been having late-night snacks. I won't hold your appetite against you."

I gave her a small smile but didn't outwardly acknowledge her comment. She was entirely correct, as the charcuterie boards I devoured each night were meals in and of themselves.

While clearing away the bowl of *macco di fave*, Lucia whistled a tune I didn't know the name of—some local folk tune I would hum when she wasn't there. By the time she returned with cleaning supplies, I had already finished the remaining four truffles. Raspberry-vanilla with white chocolate. How she could predict the exact sort of flavor profile I was craving was a mystery.

"It's Friday, isn't it?" I asked, reaching for a washcloth. "I heard you were asked on a date when you were in town the other day. Signora Carbone is a gossip."

I realized what a pretty blue Lucia's eyes were now that her face was so pink. I also realized how booming her voice was now that she spoke so softly. "I had to turn it down. I can't leave the premises until you are asleep, signorina."

I shrugged. "Tell the others I told you to fetch me some more paint."

"So late at night?"

I wiped down the tables, but because of Signora Carbone and Lucia's thoroughness, there were only a few crumbs. "I'm a silly American. I didn't know any better."

She fidgeted with her apron. "Are you sure?"

"Yes, I insist." I shoved the washcloth in my pocket. "And since you were already out and about, you ran a few errands for me. You know, fetching me some cuttings, dropping off some letters, grabbing some spring water."

Lucia sighed softly, and her eyes darted around as the cogs in her head turned. That was one of my favorite things about Lucia. She couldn't hide her thoughts even if she wanted to.

She paced toward the windows. Night had fallen, but the purplish hue in the sky showed it was still young. Still plenty of time to make it to town and either meet this mysterious belle at a bar, or text her once she could get reception. Then she looked down at her clothes, held out her uniform, and stared pointedly at the dirt in its creases.

"You're about my size," I offered. My wardrobe was filled with countless clothes, most of which I hadn't picked out myself. They seemed to appear as if by magic.

She smiled and shook her head. "I have my own dresses, Signorina Cora. And I think Duca de' Medici would be angry if anyone but you wore yours. Anyway, are you sure?"

"Yeah," I replied with a small smile. I finished the rest of the sentence in my head. *And I just want to be alone.*

"O-okay!" Lucia could barely conceal her excitement; she appeared on the verge of literally jumping for joy. She looked at me

once again as though to confirm permission, and I gave her a nod. With only a, "Thanks!" she gathered up my dishes and hurried off toward the maids' chambers, leaving me alone.

For as quickly as she had dashed away, the door behind Lucia shut softly. And as quiet as the noise was, it seemed loud to me. I kept repeating my conversation with Duca de' Medici over and over, scouring every sentence I had spoken and every sentence he hadn't, until eventually, I couldn't handle mulling on the subject any longer.

Reading proved to be a fruitless activity with my limited focus, so I tried to track down every crumb and scrub every inch of that table. Once I completed that task, I watched as Lucia's tiny car disappeared deep into the horizon and its sputtering became inaudible.

I continued to stare out the window after that, hoping to see any movement, but not even the grass was fluttering. I didn't want to be alone with my thoughts. I glanced at my watch and was satisfied to see it was just late enough for Duca de' Medici to begin his playing. Now, if nothing else, I could focus on something other than the way the chocolates felt heavy in my stomach. With more hope than I had felt all day, I rushed off toward his room.

Chapter Twenty-Two

Gia nella notte densa

The door was closed. I stared at it, stunned, then finally opted to knock a few times. *Rap rap rap*. Even after a few seconds of waiting, there was no response. Another pause, another round of knocking. Still nothing.

After taking a deep breath, I peeked my head in to see the room was shrouded in darkness. The usual lantern was nowhere to be seen. There was no scent of pastries to overshadow the room's standard fragrance. And most of all, there was no music to be heard.

I hadn't realized how much I loved this part of the day until it was swept out from under me. I let the door fall shut.

I mentally flipped through various activities, but nothing seemed like the correct replacement. With nothing but the old standby of taking a walk, I crept out into the courtyard between the main abbey and the dining hall. It was a cool night, at least by Sicilian standards, and a gentle wind caressed my face, carrying with it the fragrance of blooming flowers. Despite how sweet the fragrance was, there was some complexity in its undertones, some distinctly musky sourness. Flowers, yes, but they were older blooms, only days away from falling.

The bittersweet realization that the seasons were changing behind my back struck me. How long had it been since I had walked through the gardens at night? Goose bumps pricked along my arms when it came to me—the last time was the night when I had heard my sister's voice.

Birdie.

With that thought, my chest tightened. I knew the burning feeling between my breasts wasn't mere anxiety but rather the start of an episode. I took in a sharp breath in a slightly successful effort to delay that feeling of imminent doom for a few seconds, to stave away that loud ringing. *I need beads. Everything will be fine if I have beads, just like it was last time*. Unfortunately, my room was on the other side of the abbey, and I knew that by the time I reached it, I would be reduced to a hyperventilating wreck. I would need to look closer.

I ran into a building I had never entered before: the church itself.

Darkness was closing in on my vision, and I relied on instinct alone to navigate the new place. I focused on putting one foot in front of the other and pressed my hand against my chest. A wooden table emerged before me, and to my relief, so did a rosary. After shoving past a curtain, I fell to my knees and began my ritual.

One-two-three-four, inhale. One-two-three-four, exhale. One-two-three-four, hold my breath, rotate a bead.

After one full rotation, everything came back into view—more specifically, a lattice appeared before my face. Great. Not only had I been using a rosary in a literally unorthodox manner, but I had also been doing so in a confessional. If I believed in God, I would have apologized to Him, but I relegated myself to trying to find my way back.

The confessional gave way to a small hallway, which gave way to another. It was astonishing that I had wound through this labyrinthine place amid a panic attack, and more astonishing still that I was struggling to return to the entrance. Left, right, right, left. I turned in random directions at the end of each hallway until finally, I entered a novel area.

It took me a moment to realize that the beautiful white figure kneeling at the altar was not a ghost or a statue, but Duca de' Medici. Blue moonlight poured through the stained-glass window above and candlelight from below, giving his face a strange, ethereal glow and highlighting every delicate feature. The sight stole my breath away.

"What are you doing here?"

The rosary fell to the ground. I didn't realize I was still holding it.

"Sorry!" I blurted out. "I didn't realize anyone else was here."

He sighed. "I didn't say it was a problem." Through his veneer of exasperation, I detected warmth. "Please, sit."

As he requested, I chose a nearby bench. Duca de' Medici resumed his previous position, hands folded and head facing the wall. But rather than praying, he spoke to me.

"I came here with my father once as a child, long ago. Some young, ambitious local priest asked him to bequeath a massive donation to the town to reconstruct this abbey. I'm sure my father knew he would never fund such a venture. What good would repairing a place no one could see be? After the priest gave us a tour, my father laughed in his face and told him the favor of the church couldn't be won with money, especially someone else's. At that point, he cited some obscure *latae sententiae* suspension to censure the priest. My father made a teaching moment of this—I think he had planned that all along. In bringing me here, he meant to show me that idealistic fools would reach for my pockets all my life. But that wasn't what I got out of it. I knew, ever since that day, that I wanted this to be my casket. At the end of the day, that priest fulfilled his wish, and the Abbazia di Santa Dymphna was restored."

Maybe it was the remnants of adrenaline clouding my mind, but I couldn't force the puzzle pieces together, not when I had so few.

"Why here?" I finally asked. "Why not somewhere closer to your home?"

He chuckled, and the sound sent a chill down my spine. It lacked any warmth. "Since the moment I understood shame, I knew it was attached to me. I have no home, Signorina Bowling, not even now. That's why I chose this place."

At that moment, I wondered why I had ever mistaken him for an angel. Then again, the look in his eyes right now did not seem earthly. Something in me felt the need to claw at his skin until a drop of humanity bled out.

"Do you ever get lonely?" I pressed.

"Yes. I'm never not."

For as quick as his answer had come, nothing followed it. I was unsure how to respond, and a palpable pause held in the air. The

irregular rattling of branches against the windows and the distant calls of an owl seemed loud.

"You said something when we first met—something about why music was beautiful." His gaze flickered over to me. "Do you remember what it was?"

My heartbeat doubled with a mixture of feelings I couldn't fully identify. He remembered that conversation? Truthfully, I did too. Something about it had stuck with me—something about every word we shared had. I didn't reply.

"About how its beauty lies in its ability to cross time? I don't know if that's what you meant, but there's something like that to these places." He pressed his hand against the lava-stone wall and traced his pointer finger along the intricate embossments, leaving only the sound of my heartbeat in my ears. Then, suddenly: "Do you believe in ghosts?"

Even if I told myself I was used to the tricks of the abbey, the sights and sounds I had experienced here were engraved in my mind. The rosary sat on the ground, taunting me. "I don't know."

"I don't either. I just know I feel them all around me when I'm here. I feel them in the stones and the altar and the rosaries and the Bibles. That doesn't sound stupid, does it?"

Since when did he care what anyone thought of what he said?

"No, not at all," I answered. "I think I get what you mean."

"The ghosts that live here feel more real than the other nobility I talk to. Yes, I get lonely here, but it's less lonely than out there."

I held out a hand to him. "Duca de' Medici, I—"

A nightingale flitted along the stained glass, calling loudly and casting a shadow over our heads. Seeing its outline fly across the tiles, up through the apex of the church's triumphal cross, I remembered where I was, who I was talking to. My hand returned to my side.

"I need to go to bed now."

"Cora," he said, voice scarcely above a whisper. "Please stay."

In another circumstance, I may have faltered or frozen, but there was not a moment of hesitation in me now. Not when his voice

was so vulnerable, so pitiful. Not when he had called me by my first name.

Wordlessly, I sat on the bench in front of him, and he sat beside me. From the corner of my eye, I saw minute, halted movements as he considered and second-guessed a thousand different actions. I smoothed down my skirt, an invitation for him to lay his head on my lap. After briefly meeting my eyes, as if to ask for permission one final time, he accepted it.

Seconds later, Duca de' Medici melted into me, closing his eyes. Looking down at him, at his long, white lashes and the fullness of his lips, it struck me that Zeno was only a few years older than me. I saw blood was pooling into his cheeks, and I remembered that some of that blood was my own. I brushed my thumb across his sleeve, feeling how soft it was and wondering how soft the skin beneath it would be.

"You smell good," he mumbled, voice muffled by embarrassment and fabric. "You always do."

"Strange," I replied with a small smile. "I was thinking the same thing about you."

"Cora?" the vampire murmured dreamily.

"Yes?"

"You can call me Zeno."

I chuckled and ran my fingers through his hair. "Okay, Zeno."

As if I had commanded it, his breathing slowed and grew even. Up close, the contrast between his translucent skin and the dark crescents beneath his eyes was even starker. How long, I wondered, had it been since he had a good night of sleep? From afar, his hair always looked sculpted, so I was pleasantly surprised to find it silky to the touch. As I carefully braided a few stray strands, Zeno snored softly through parted lips. I gently combed through the braid to loosen it, then began another.

By the time dozens of braids were done and undone, the moon had risen to its apex, the purplish hue of the sky had deepened, and the lanterns around us flickered as their power diminished. All the while, Zeno slumbered in near-perfect stillness, save the occasional languid mumble.

"Cora." When he spoke, clear and lucid, after some time, I flinched. "Sorry," he mumbled. "I didn't mean to startle you."

Zeno peeled himself from my lap, yawned wide enough to show every fang, and straightened his hair. "How long was I asleep?"

"Only a few minutes," I lied.

He looked at where the moon was in the sky and shot me a skeptical look but didn't bother arguing. Instead, he stated, "Thank you, Cora. I'll walk you back."

Zeno's pace through the gardens was steady, which I sensed was for my sake rather than his own. That flash of childlike fear he had shown was absent now. Meanwhile, my anxiety had heightened, a Pavlovian response to the twilit gardens. I sighed and focused on the tiles at my feet and the sound of Zeno's shoes on them. No more moonlit walks for me through this courtyard. What a pity.

The checkerboard of tiles ended, and Zeno held the door open for me.

"Aren't you a gentleman?" I teased.

"Only for—" he cleared his throat. "I try."

When we made it to my room, he lingered at my doorway, and I smiled. Déjà vu. When I turned to say good night, I realized Zeno was holding out his hand. The rosary. "I didn't realize you were religious."

"I'm not." I took it quickly and shoved it into my pocket. "Counting the beads helps when I get nervous. Sorry, I'm not trying to be disrespectful. I'll get a normal bead bracelet soon."

"I don't believe He minds. I don't, anyhow." Zeno shook his head and reached into his shirt. All along, he had been wearing a miraculous medal. "It helps me to rub my thumb across this as well."

"I didn't realize *you* were religious," I echoed.

"Ah, so I'm still a mystery to you? How amusing." He smirked. "In another life, I would be standing here in a cassock." I studied him to see to what extent he was joking about becoming a priest. Seeing my prying eyes, he added, "Probably further from your bed at this time of night, of course."

I gasped at the implication and pointed past the door. "Out!"

"Hey!" Zeno said with a guffaw. "I *am* a gentleman, remember? You said so yourself."

"It doesn't matter! If anyone sees you here—"

He put his hands up, stifling further laughter. "Okay, okay. I was just joking, I promise." He closed the door partially but peeked his head in for a moment. "Thank you."

It shut softly behind him.

"You're welcome," I said to his memory.

Chapter Twenty-Three

Brindisi

The virgin paper felt rough against my fingertips, but I pushed further into the weft to find an abnormality in the pattern. As I'd suspected, using my sketchbook as a journal in the heat of the moment had backfired, and my heavy-handed writing had transferred between pages. I sighed. What a waste of good watercolor paper. I traced my finger along to find the extent of the damage and landed upon distinguishable letters.

E.N.Z.O.

I traced over them again in a different order.

Z.E.N.O.

Don't tell Zeno, Noor's voice echoed in my mind. *He may find all of this a bit too . . . familiar.*

"What are you doing?"

As if on cue, Zeno's voice rang out beside me.

I hadn't noticed him take his normal place beside me in the aviary, and for once he was on time rather than five minutes late. On instinct, I jumped and slammed my sketchbook shut, nearly dropping it. Zeno raised a brow at me, curious but not concerned, as was his usual reaction to my jumpiness.

"I was just checking the paper in my sketchbook. The page has some indentations from writing on top of it, so I can't use it for watercolor." I neglected to say what exactly that writing was—that the indentations were notes from his family tree and scrawling his name.

From the way he leaned closer to me and glowered, I knew

Zeno saw the string of thought I was biting behind my teeth, and that he wanted to reach into my mouth and yank it out.

"You've been acting peculiar for over a week," he finally stated. "More than usual, that is."

"Sorry," I mumbled with a shrug.

Zeno scoffed and rolled his eyes. "I'd prefer an explanation over an apology."

I sighed and hung my head. "I can't get anything past you, can I?"

He smirked crookedly, revealing a single fang. "I'd take that as a compliment if you weren't so easy to read."

I wrung my hands, and this time, Zeno was patient enough. I must have been scrunching my face together the way I often did when I was trying to compose a sentence. I soon gave up on trying to find a subtle way to say it. Probably because there was none.

"I want to know about your past," I finally said. "What you said about how you would be in a cassock in another life."

Suddenly, Zeno stood and walked to the door.

"W-wait!" I cried out. "I didn't mean to upset you! Please come back!"

He tossed his head over his shoulder at me and gently shooed away a finch I hadn't noticed before. It fluttered away with an annoyed chirp. "I'm not upset. I'll be right back."

He left me alone for several painful moments with only the finches. It seemed like they were glaring at me for scaring off their beloved keeper. Just as I was about to accept Zeno wasn't coming back, the door opened halfway, and Zeno stuck his head through.

"Come on. Hurry."

At his appearance, several Gouldian finches jumped from perch to perch, aligning themselves on a visible trajectory to his shoulders.

"Where are we—"

"*Hurry*. They're fond of you now, so they may try to follow you out."

I gathered my belongings hastily and rushed out, looking behind me all the while. An arm stretched over my head, and I felt like a rabbit who had seen an eagle flying overhead. I instinctively spun on my heels and stepped back against the door, which was now shut.

Zeno leaned over me, gripping the frame of the door above my head, staring down at me with a casual expression. As if standing over me, only inches from my face, was a daily occurrence.

Too close! every cell of me screamed. "What are you doing?" I snapped.

One of his brows arched. "Closing the door? It's not my fault you stood there for so long."

I tried to avert my eyes from the towering man, but they fell onto his left hand. Zeno's arm was slack, his fingers curled loosely around the neck of a bottle. The light of a sconce glinted across the shiny glass surface.

"Burgundy pinot noir, 1963," Zeno read, holding the bottle up. He spun on his heels and headed down the hall. "Follow me."

I followed him to the little library, where a small dining table and duo of chairs were waiting for us. He placed the bottle between two glasses and took his seat at the far end of the table. I mirrored his actions and looked at the unusual setting. The table was new to the room. Its tablecloth was as crimson as the wine in the bottle, with the crystal glasses probably never used. In contrast, a thin film of dust covered the room, which consisted almost entirely of grays and browns—all except the books on the shelves, which had been opened and wiped clean of dust by yours truly. I hoped Zeno didn't notice.

The cork let off a satisfying *pop* as it dislodged and flew onto the table. Zeno poured the wine in a smooth arc, and it pooled at the bottom of my glass, revealing a deep red color with purplish undertones. The fragrance wafted up toward me, delicately floral yet earthy. Nothing like the cheapo wine Emily used to drink.

"Should you really be drinking?" I asked, trying to ignore my watering mouth.

Alcohol was a known blood thinner, and Zeno was nearly due for his next donation, meaning he was probably borderline on clotting factors as it was.

Zeno scoffed and filled his glass. “Pah. If I had to go without wine, I’d rather not live.”

“Did Noor say it was okay?”

“She would rather have a living patient—” he sat across from me and gave his glass a swirl “—so she acquiesced. I get my cheese and wine once a week.”

I took the chance to study Zeno as he took a slow, even sip with closed eyes. What a lovely painting that would make. He opened them, and I quickly reached for my glass, spilling a few drops of wine on the tablecloth. If the vampire cared, he didn’t show it. Instead, Zeno sat forward with his elbow on the table and his jaw resting on the back of his fist. In his other hand, he continued to swirl his glass.

“Try some,” Zeno implored, gesturing toward my drink.

I took a sip, and a complex array of flavors washed over my tongue.

“Good, isn’t it?”

“It’s delicious.” I returned the glass to its original spot and tried to ignore the fresh stains on the table.

“And?”

I folded my arms tightly. “I don’t know. What else am I supposed to say?”

“You could have pointed out its raspberry notes, or comment on its smoothness.”

“I’m not a wine connoisseur,” I grumbled. “I avoid drinking when I can.”

Zeno took another sip, tilted his head to the side. “Because of what happened to your mother?”

The query was as cool and dry as the wine we were drinking, as though he were simply asking me what I did for a living, or if I had any siblings. I gave him a strange look. “I thought we were talking about you, not me.”

Zeno shrugged so broadly that I thought his wine would tip over, but it didn’t. “Tit for tat,” he crooned. “That’s what you say in English, right?”

I took a gulp of wine, disappointed not to feel it burn as it went down. I grimaced at the dryness filling my throat, the tannins tasting like cotton balls. Bitter, just like my answer was about to be.

"Yes, because of what happened with my mother. She drank herself to death. It started out with wine, but after Papa passed, wine didn't cut it anymore. That's when she turned to his moonshine."

Guilt marred his features ever so slightly. "I'm sorry, Cora."

"It's all right. I wasn't there for it, anyway." I forced a small smile. "I ran away, I guess."

Zeno ran his fingers through his hair, his usual nervous gesture betraying his attempt to look impartial. "What happened, if you don't mind my asking?"

I fidgeted with my skirt, glancing back and forth between my hands and Zeno, who was growing more anxious by the second. The only person I had spoken about this with was Emily, back when I first moved to London. Sweet Emily, who had held my hand and whispered, *It's going to be okay* as I cried into her chest. Who only spoke of it again in the heat of an argument: *I should have known you'd run away from me. You always do.* Time hadn't dulled the sting of those words.

I met Zeno's eyes and noticed how his eyelashes fluttered as he quickly blinked (another nervous habit). It was only last night that I had seen them so close, had run my hands through his hair. He had told me so much about him, and I owed him the same. Tit for tat.

I drank another sip, took a deep breath, and tried to speak without letting my voice shake.

"My family always told me I'd be the one to go to college first. First in the family, first in Red Creek—that's in Appalachia, by the way. Mama wanted me to become a lawyer, or a doctor, or something that would get all of us out of using food stamps, but Pa—Pa told me to do whatever I wanted. He was a great man. He never really hugged me, but he loved all of us so much, I swear it warmed the house in the winter.

"He used to buy me history books for my birthday or Christmas, or even when he got a raise. He taught me how complicated the past was, and how beautiful its secrets are. Pa always wanted to be a history professor, but he had to take a job at the local factory. I used to make him give me lectures, though, and the only

time he shined brighter than when he talked about ancient Rome was when he looked at Ma. He, uh, died when I was ten. He was killed, actually, by Ma's ex-husband."

That part, I hadn't told even Emily. As far as she knew, it was a misfire from a friend. I took another deep sip and pointed at my glass. He refilled it.

"Anyway, that was when Ma slipped into it. She had experienced depressive episodes before, of course, but nothing like this. She just went back and forth between sleeping and drinking. That's when Peachy stepped up to do all the housework and even did our taxes, and all there was in this world was me and her. She never applied for college, since she had to take care of Ma.

"I graduated at the top of my class with a ton of credits, and I got all these applications for all these schools. Prelaw schools, premed schools. But when I was filling them out, I saw a picture of Pa, and I remembered what he told me. I threw away all the applications but one, to a nearby liberal arts college. Ma was *mad,* and once her liver started acting up and medical bills started piling up—"

A new flavor overshadowed the aftertaste of wine. It was strong and salty. I touched a finger to my lower lip and found my fingertips were stained red, but not from wine.

"Shit," I hissed. Even that small amount of blood was jarring against the white of my sleeve. A handkerchief appeared before me. I pressed it against my mouth with one hand and found my glass empty with the other. "More wine," I said through the cloth.

"I don't think—"

"More wine, *please.*"

"Cora, I'm not going to give you more."

I shut my eyes, swallowed back tears, and grabbed the bottle myself. Once my lip clotted, I chased down the ferric taste with a mouthful of wine.

"Cora, I'm sorry, I didn't mean to—"

"It's fine," I cut in. "Tit for tat, right?"

"Right." His uneasy tone betrayed the certainty of the word. Carefully, as though I wouldn't notice if he were slow enough, Zeno

moved my glass away. It was a strange decision, I thought, for him to be swaying. Or was that me?

"As I was saying, Ma was mad. She was downright *furious*, an' I couldn't handle it, so I went to London. I got a call from a doctor a few months later sayin' Ma had died. Peachy called an' called an' called me—she still does sometimes—but I ain't ever answered. Maybe I could'a gone there in person, but—"

All at once, the amount of alcohol in my system overwhelmed me. I felt my brain floating in my head, my head floating on my body, my body floating around the room. I heard my native tongue emerging uninvited. Sitting up straight with my ankles crossed and hands in my lap like Ma had taught me had become a challenge.

I looked across the table at Zeno, sitting with perfect posture, looking horrified.

"Oh," I whispered. "I gotta go."

Chapter Twenty-Four

Che Gelida Manina

When I stood, the world spun, and the ground rushed toward me. I squeezed my eyes shut in anticipation of the hard stone against my face, but the blow never struck. Instead, I was smothered in warmth.

Zeno gently separated me from him but still held me up by my shoulders. I squinted but couldn't read his expression beyond the haze.

"I shouldn't have let you drink so much," he sighed.

"Too cold," I mumbled. I grabbed the back of Zeno's shirt and pulled him back toward me. He stood rigid and awkward, *not* comfy like he had been only a few moments ago.

"Hey!" I looked up to glare at him but laughed instead. "Your face is so red! Are you drunk, too, Zeno?"

His eyes widened. "I'm not—Cora, we're done. You should lie down."

"No!" I hit his chest with the side of my fist in protest. "Tit for tat! Your turn to talk!"

"Don't be ridiculous. You won't even remember what I said. I'll walk you back to your room."

"Tit for tat! I ain't going nowhere 'til you tell me everything. I wanna know if you've been in love, an' your favorite food, an' where you get your clothes."

"Cora, come on."

"Not 'til you tell me!"

I tried to stamp my foot for emphasis, but the second one foot was off the ground, the other tried to follow. In a smooth, sweeping motion, Zeno lifted me off the ground. I squealed for a moment, but drunken drowsiness quickly superseded stubbornness. I became a rag doll in his arms, allowing him to carry me bridal style.

How warm, I thought as I nuzzled against his chest and closed my eyes. As Zeno walked, I inhaled his scent and let out a satisfied sigh. My attention turned to his shirt against my face, his breath on the top of my head, and the steady rocking of his even gait.

"To answer your question," Zeno whispered into the top of my head, "I was in love once, in a sense. Whatever love looks like for someone like me."

The sober person within me wanted to say and ask so much, but all that came out from my drunken self was a muffled, "Mmmph?"

"I told you I wanted to become a priest. I don't believe in God in the same sense as others, but to devote my life to Him would have been so much better than fumbling through Medici politics."

My foot bumped into a wall when we rounded a corner, but I was listening too intently to say anything.

To my joy, he continued, "I stopped trying at that when I was young—why bother being a socialite when everyone knew I was a bastard? A cuckoo, really, trapped in my victim's nest. To get any closer to truth, or perfection, or whatever ascension a higher being could offer—why wouldn't I want such a thing? Why didn't everyone want to become priests? To me, the sacrifice of chastity was irrelevant. Preferable, even." He paused. "Wait here. I'm going to get you some water."

"Wait where?"

It took me a moment to realize I wasn't in his arms anymore. My bed, though soft and more expensive than any bed I had ever slept on, now seemed cold.

A few seconds later, the warmth was back. Zeno slid an arm behind my back and held a glass to my lips. Greedily, I sipped at the icy mineral water.

"There you go," Zeno whispered, stroking my head. "Good girl. You can lie down now."

"You're so sweet." I grabbed his hand and rubbed it against my face, then kicked my heels off and lay down as told, curled up in a ball. The air felt cool on my legs, pleasant against the heat of the alcohol coursing through me. My fingers were sloppy and inefficient at undoing the buttons of my blouse, but I succeeded in the top few.

"Oh, for fuck's—"

I huffed in protest when Zeno's fingers slipped through mine, and the bed squeaked and shifted. He had already made it to the door, redder than I had ever seen him before.

"Come back!" I called after him, sitting up halfway.

Zeno kept his gaze pointed straight at my wall. "N-not until you get dressed."

I shot him my best glare and cocooned my blanket around myself. "I'm nice an' decent, alright? Come back."

Zeno pinched the bridge of his nose and cursed beneath his breath in a combination of Italian and English. He sat on the corner of the bed, his gaze entirely averted from me, hands curled into balls around the edge of my sheets. My eyes felt heavy, and the layer of blanket around me only added to my drowsiness.

"Hold my hand."

The words escaped without me thinking. A cool, shaky hand lingered above mine, barely touching my skin. I felt my breathing deepen and slow ever so slightly, and the hand over mine tightened, finger by finger. That was the final step to lull me into a gentle sleep.

When I came out of it, sobriety was creeping onto me, along with lucidity. I shifted, emerging slightly from the blanket, and raised my head. Zeno had sunk into the mattress beside me on his side, his hand still holding mine. Studying the rise and fall of his chest, I could tell he was awake, even though his eyes were shut. I tried not to make any sudden movements, for the man at my side was a deer and a wolf. Selfishly, I enjoyed the basic sensation of human touch.

"Feeling better?" Zeno's hand retreated from mine, and he migrated to the edge of the bed again.

"A bit," I said to his back. "How long has it been?"

Zeno turned back toward me, his silhouette striking. "I don't know. A few minutes, maybe?"

It had definitely been longer—long enough that the drunken haze was gone from my head—but I appreciated Zeno attempting to spare me from the embarrassing disclosure that I had actually fallen asleep.

"I'm still a bit tipsy. Can you stay with me a little longer?" I asked, knowing full well it was a lie.

Zeno sighed softly and placed one of my throw pillows between us. "If anyone saw me come in here, they would assume something horrid of me. I'll stay just a little longer, okay? Just to make certain you don't get sick."

"I'll be good, I promise," I grumbled at the pillow and its scratchy linen cover. "Just continue what you were saying before."

He shot me a glance and bit his lip. "You remember that?"

"Yes. I remember all of it. You were talking about wanting to join the church . . . well, I guess you were talking about being in love before that?"

"I was hoping you didn't remember that." Zeno flushed. It seemed like since he'd entered my room, his skin was more often red than its usual white. "But yes, I was in love once. I was in my late teens, and a girl from the Salviati family invited me personally to a banquet. I declined, but the invitations continued for six months."

Salviati. A name known to anyone who researched the Medici, myself included. In the fifteenth century, the family had been rivals with the Medici, both in banking and the church, and were even involved in an assassination. They were banished from Florence and, much like their rivals, nearly died out until the nineteenth century. Slowly but surely, however, the family scrounged back their gold and a more noble reputation.

The photo of the current Salviati heiress I had seen during my research emerged in my mind: Serafina Rosa Salviati, a doll-like Frenchwoman with loose, white-blonde ringlets, crystal-blue eyes, and an ever-present glow not even makeup could replicate. She was tall and slender, with the sort of figure a model could only dream of. She *had* been a model at one point, if memory served correctly.

"Was she . . ." I trailed off. I didn't know why, but I didn't want to know the answer.

"Beautiful?" Zeno filled in the gap, and I nodded eagerly despite the strange feeling in my chest. "Yes. Beautiful and wild and wicked. She only saw me for my name and my wealth, and I loved her for that. She was open about it, at least. It was more interesting than the usual politics anyway."

"What happened?"

"I left to join the church, as I had originally planned." He pulled out the medal from his shirt and ran his thumb across it. "I loved her, but I could never have her. Nobody could. She got her wish to gain Medici power anyhow, albeit with my cousin. So I sought out mine. Unfortunately, there was politics there, too, especially when aspiring popes learned I am Medici. I've found more of God in this abbey than in any of the ones I studied in. So, here I am."

"Is this really what you wanted?" I hadn't even fully processed his words before guilt crept in from my periphery.

"A solitary life, away from noise and people who care only for my name, surrounded by music and everything I love? To be away from the world, to fill my life with beauty and forget its inherent ugliness? That is *all* I have ever desired."

Past conversations echoed through my mind, weaving together and connecting into a terrible web. *Just don't tell Zeno. He may find all of this a bit too . . . familiar*. Without thinking, I traced my finger into the pillow once again. *E.N.Z.O*. A vampire who was forced out from the clergy because of his family name, who carried the weight of the Medici family despite being known as a bastard. Who, according to all my research, hated every second he spent amongst nobility. *Z.E.N.O*. He had loved Serafina because she admitted she saw him for his name. Yet here I was, in his sanctuary away from people like *me*, who had been drawn in by the name *Medici*.

"Zeno, I have something to tell you."

At the solemnity in my tone, Zeno tensed. His eyes searched my face. He remained silent but seemed resolved in some conclusion—this was, I imagined, that I was actually entirely sober. I met his gaze and held it.

"You know I have a thesis, right?"

"Yes. I assumed in literature—possibly the *Divine Comedy*?"

"I wish that was it."

He leaned back and tilted his head to the side. “You came here for access to my library, did you not?”

“I came here because I knew you’re a Medici, because your library is about the Medici. My thesis is on the Medici succession in the seventeenth and eighteenth centuries. I’ve been researching the origins of Enzo Armando.”

“Ah, the famous bastard. I see,” Zeno spoke evenly, with no discernible emotion. “How is it going, then? Has my library serviced you well?”

“Yes. It did, for a long time.”

“And you’ve been so curious about me because I’m Medici? That’s why you’ve been insistent on speaking with me and learning about my past? That’s why you chose to stay in this abbey?”

I clenched the blanket tightly. It sounded so much worse coming from him, especially when he wasn’t yelling, or crying, or reacting at all. There were so many things I wanted to reply, but I couldn’t parse what was an excuse, or what sounded like one.

So I just nodded and said, “Sorry.”

I expected yelling or crying, but Zeno stared at the floor. “No need to apologize.”

“Aren’t you upset?” I asked, almost offended by the lack of impact my treachery seemingly had on him.

But then, looking more closely at his knitted brow and the miniscule quirk of his lips, I realized what I had initially perceived as a lack of feeling from Zeno was instead an overabundance of competing emotions. As some conclusion visibly sorted itself out in his mind, Zeno finally met my gaze and responded, “I can’t be upset because this brought you to me.”

It felt like the floor had fallen out from beneath me, like I had been punched in the gut.

“I enjoy having you here, Cora,” Zeno continued. “As much as I despise being around everyone else, I treasure every second with you.”

The blanket fell from my shoulders, but I felt no more naked.

“I like—” Those first few words came out soft, almost inaudible even to myself, but the rest died on my tongue.

If Zeno expected any further response, he didn't show it. In fact, I wasn't entirely certain he had heard me at all until I saw him mouthing the rest of the sentence to himself in my stead: *You too.*

Zeno's brow furrowed once more, this time in the same way it did when he was puzzling out a measure of music. "Your research has dried up, has it not? You said my library serviced you for a long time, so I imagine it no longer does. And that's why you came here in the first place."

I swore I could hear the gears clicking in his mind as I retreated to the other side of the bed to make myself presentable. Without Zeno's hand on them, my fingers felt too cold and numb to button up my shirt with any speed. I took my time to finish working my way up to the collar, savoring the brief pause from impassible seas before I had to address the torrent of emotions that had washed into the room.

"Yes," I finally answered. "I've gone through all the Medici documents here several times over."

It was Zeno's turn to pause, to force me to wait for a response. *How cruel*, I thought. I tried to predict his next sentence but failed horrifically.

"I've been a pathetic excuse of a vampire," Zeno said, rising to his feet. "You've been my *beniamina* for nearly six months now. It's time for your *ritus sanguinous*."

I froze at the last few words. *Ritus sanguinous*—rite of blood. For most *beniamini* and their vampires, who were typically paired at the cusp of adulthood, this was a rite of passage. The ceremony with the first public feeding was the point of the practice, but what was arguably more important was the burgeoning network that could emerge from such a gathering.

My hands fell to my side, and I stared at Zeno, slack-jawed. "What? Isn't that the epitome of everything you hate?"

"Gaudy, expensive, ornate—what's worth hating there? Not to mention the hors d'oeuvres. Why, I could hire a private chef!"

I narrowed my eyes into slits and folded my arms. "Loud, busy, *socializing*. I'm pretty sure your skin would turn inside out."

Zeno shrugged and leaned against the frame of my door, body as loose as his words. "Pah. We'll have to see."

"But *why*?"

"I cannot give you more documents, Cora, but I know several people who can. This is the only chance we have to gather them in one space."

I frowned and shook my head. "That's not what I asked. Why? Noor told me that having a *beniamina* was enough to satiate your father. Why would you go so far out of your way for me? What could your reason be?"

To my shock, my question was returned with a laugh.

"Why do I need a reason to go out of my way for a beautiful girl, one who turns every line of a book into its own poem when she reads it? For a girl who brought a garden full of life into the dead room of an abbey, who charmed a dove who trusts no one, and who managed to lure a wretched bastard out from his hiding place?"

My heart rate doubled, maybe even tripled. Perhaps the fluttering in my chest was caused by the beating wings of the butterflies that had started up in my stomach.

"I—uh—" I stammered, not even certain what words I was trying to get out.

Even if I had managed, Zeno was already starting to leave.

"Why would I bother, hmm?" he chuckled to himself just before shutting my door. "What a preposterous question."

Chapter Twenty-Five

Cabaletta

Signora Rafia took full advantage of our generous timeline to drive at an ambling pace. Flickering streetlights interspersed the path sparsely, so we were cast into complete darkness for a full second before entering the glow of the next. However, the darkness around these parts felt welcoming rather than ominous.

Zeno had begun planning the *ritus sanguinous* on his own, much to my combined relief and disappointment, as it meant I saw him less and less in the final month before the ceremony. This would be the last time we saw one another until the ceremony in a week, I knew.

"It's surprising you were able to find a museum that has such late admission time," I said after a bit. "After dark is odd for a place to be open, isn't it?"

"That was only per my request. The gallery is famous for its glass walls. I wanted us to be able to see them in the moonlight, at least." He paused, chuckling. "If only someone had told the sky that it shouldn't be so cloudy tonight."

The lights outside were growing closer and closer together, the roads more manicured. We were approaching a small city. Signora Rafia turned into a small, overgrown alleyway I hadn't even seen through the tint of the windows. As we approached the wrought-iron gate, an attendant of some sort took a cursory glance at us, not even bothering to check the plate upon seeing Zeno's face, and unlocked the fence. It squealed open with a bit of force from the attendant. Our car wheeled toward the back of the building.

Part of me wished I could see it in the daylight. The museum had been built in neither the elegant baroque styling of the abbey nor

the simplistic, homey style of the rural houses. Instead, it had been built in a delightfully over-the-top art nouveau style that had clearly been inspired by Museo Casa Lis. The entire building was made of stained Tiffany glass. The front door was already propped open for our arrival, and I couldn't help but rush in.

"Wow!" I cried upon entering.

The interior of the building was as garishly extravagant as the exterior, with vivid furniture and countless chandeliers. I spun to Zeno, who was giving me his usual smile—one side of his lip curved up, a single fang visible.

"Are you ready for your tour, Signorina Bowling?" he asked, strolling over with his hands folded behind his back.

It had been so long since he called me by that name, and now it made my face feel hot. I rubbed the back of my head and stared at the ground. "Yes!"

Zeno walked slowly to the first work, a tall oil painting, and tilted his head up. "Here we have the 1862 oil painting, *Sir Galahad* by George Frederic Watts. Beside it is the *Lady of Shallott*, painted only twenty-six years later by John William Waterhouse. As you may have guessed from the chain in her hand, it is based upon the tragic death of Elaine of Astolat, Galahad's mother."

My eyes widened at the seemingly extensive research Zeno had undergone. "Have you been here before or something?" I asked.

Zeno shook his head and replied, "No, I have not."

I shot him a skeptical look. At this, Zeno gave me his usual lopsided smile, one fang visible, and looked around meaningfully.

It took me little time to recognize what he was trying to show me. All the works were anachronistic and stylistically disparate, and there was only one connection between them all: each and every masterpiece was related to something I had talked about. *Dido* from the *Aeneid* on one wall, *The Death of Julius Caesar* on another. Every work, song, and book we had ever discussed had its own representation. Even titles or ideas I had mentioned only once or twice in passing had their places amongst the gallery.

"Holy—how did you—when—? How long—?" No matter how hard I tried, I couldn't finish a single sentence. I sputtered out half questions and whole expletives, and Zeno's gaze softened.

"It took a while," he answered once it became apparent I wouldn't be able to talk. "But it was worth it if you like it."

Zeno sat patiently and wordlessly for the few seconds it took me to gather myself fully, then resumed the tour with a softer, more genuine tone, albeit with the occasional joke scattered throughout. I spoke rarely, but this did not seem to discourage Zeno from asking me about my thoughts or knowledge. When we approached a recreation of *Landscape with Orpheus and Eurydice* by Niçolas Poussin, however, the torrent poured forth.

"Look how beautiful it is!" I cried. "I did a paper about this a long time ago, in my art history class. I got a bad grade on it because I focused too much on the legend itself."

"Well, what were your thoughts, then?" he asked, giving me a sideways glance.

"The story can't be separated from the art. It's the moment just before Orpheus realizes Eurydice has been bitten. Before you see that, it's beautifully idealistic, but once you realize it, all that's left is just pure and utter dread."

Zeno listened intently, then responded, "I must argue with you, signorina."

I rolled my eyes but still smiled. "Of course you must, you contrarian. Let's hear it, then."

"I think everything you need to know is in the painting. The artist does a good job of making you focus on Orpheus and how happy he is outside of the shadows, but when you look into the background—"

"I know, I know," I cut in, making sure my tone was audibly teasing. "The castle is burning, and the clouds are overcast. All the dread is already in the painting. That's what my professor said too."

He reddened slightly but tilted his head up for show. "Sounds like quite the brilliant professor. Have I impressed you with my artistic eye, then?"

I laughed and shook my head. "Maybe you would have impressed me if you used the big words she did."

After several paintings, we approached the last piece, *Dante and Beatrice* by Henry Holiday. I stared up at Dante, gazing lovingly

at the angelic Beatrice. The idea that Zeno had looked at *her* like that made me feel sick.

"I never thanked you for telling me about Serafina the other night," I told him, continuing to stare at the painting and trying not to tear up. It wasn't my place, not when he and I would never be together.

In my periphery, I saw Zeno's expression alter slightly, frowning with worry. He masked it with a smile once I looked over at him and shrugged. "Tit for tat. I did not tell you about my family, and you did not tell me about your love life."

"There's not much to tell," I muttered with a dry chuckle. "A casual ex-boyfriend in my early college days and a serious ex-girlfriend in London who had the gall to break up with me last Valentine's Day."

"There's not much to tell for me either. A father, stepmother, and cousin who despise me, and an extended family who want nothing to do with me. That, and a mother who is either out of the country, in the ground, or both."

"Your father didn't tell you where she is?"

He laughed bitterly. "Sure he did. He said she was an actress who left shortly after I was born, when she learned he was engaged. But even as a child, I never believed him. The death in my veins came from her just as much as him. I'm sure she died long ago."

"Oh," I replied.

What else was there to respond to such a thing? *I guess we can bond over our mutual dead-mommy issues*, maybe? Or perhaps, *Good thing you're the one drinking from me, since death isn't known for having the best flavor?*

No, that one syllable certainly sufficed.

Zeno walked in no particular direction, clasping his hands behind his back once more in what I assumed was a futile effort to brighten the mood. Unfortunately, he wasn't the best at actually steering conversations.

"Last Valentine's Day wasn't long before you came here. I'm rather surprised you were living in London before then."

I joined his side but stared at the ground, rather than any of the art around us. "That's why I left London. Emily and I were together for three years, living together for two. And she wanted us to go out *constantly* when we were together, so it seemed like everywhere in that entire city was somewhere we had been before, some memory that was tainted with my inability to just be a normal person. For most of that time, she tried to get me to be open with her, but I just . . . couldn't. Maybe some part of me knew that if I said the wrong thing or had too much baggage, it would be over. That I would just be too much."

Zeno's brow furrowed deeply, and he stopped walking for a moment. "Cora, you could *never* be..." he trailed off, running his fingers through his hair. "My apologies. I didn't mean to interrupt. Please, continue."

"It was a pretty bad breakup. She said she had tried everything, but I was incapable of being open with someone. It wouldn't have stuck with me so much if she was wrong, you know? Even before we got together, I knew it wasn't possible for me to have love or a happy relationship. That's why it isn't lonely in the abbey, you know? I've always known there isn't anything out there to miss."

Zeno went quiet, his expression grave and eyes low. We walked another wordless lap around the museum before leaving, but to my horror, gloom seemed to stick to us as tightly as the sweat on the back of my neck.

The unease was latched onto us even as we exited into the cool night and ducked into the warm, cozy car. Every tiny dip in the road felt like it would jar me from my seat. The scratching of branches sweeping over the roof sounded razor sharp, and even my perfume turned pungent. And my God, did the silence itself gnaw at my skin.

Fuck. Shit. Fuck. What's wrong with you? Why are you being so weird? Why would you talk about something from so long ago? All that mopey bullshit! You must look pathetic!

The thoughts sprung out faster and faster, the sorts of self-conscious scoldings I hadn't given myself after months of therapy. They were enough to start that dreadful ringing. I squeezed my eyes shut as tightly as I could.

Zeno's cool hand rested on mine, and all the noise in my head stopped.

All I could hear was the gentle whir of the engine and my quickening heartbeat in my ears. I turned to Zeno, who was staring out of his window at the rolling hills. Even so, I saw the redness of his ears.

"I, uh—there is something I must tell you. I wanted to say it way back there."

It is human nature to predict the ends of sentences and connect dots to fill the silence. And yet my mind was blank, for I knew there was no way to predict his words. I held my breath.

"Someone will love you like you're meant to be loved, Cora," Zeno said in a low but certain tone. "You're one of those people the universe has chosen to be cherished."

Anxiety pulled at Zeno's brow and caused it to furrow heavily over his eyes—those beautiful coral eyes I had painted so many times but could never fully capture. Would I ever get used to them?

Impulsively, I kissed him, then pulled away moments later, alarmed by my own actions.

Now it was my turn to try reading his expression. Luckily for me, it was easy. Zeno's mouth parted and allowed a small breath of relief to escape, then curled at the corners. Clearly, he was trying to conceal his elation—and just as clearly, it was showing.

"Your lips are dry," I whispered, not knowing what else to say.

The vampire held my gaze for a second, then replied, "I'm sorry. Yours are soft."

His sincere tone made me chuckle, and just as I was about to say something else, his lips were suddenly on mine.

One hand rested on the small of my back while the other gently cupped my face. I swept my tongue across his teeth, feeling the fangs that had bore holes in my wrists, and Zeno countered by drinking me in and catching my lower lip with his.

I pulled away to catch my breath for an instant, and he pressed his forehead against mine.

The heat of his breath and the gentleness with which he caressed my cheek made warmth smolder in my chest.

"I've wanted this—you—for a long time."

"Really?"

"Yes. Since the moment I lit that first candle in front of you, and you told me about Vivaldi."

I laughed and said, "Oh, I didn't know nineteenth-century composers got you going."

He smirked in return, planted a small kiss on the corner of my mouth, and replied, "Only when you talk about them."

I pulled back and gestured pointedly toward poor Signora Rafia, who was presumably horrified at our open display of intimacy.

"Who gives a fuck?" Zeno's voice was a low growl, though not devoid of mirth.

I smiled despite myself and pulled his face closer to mine.

By the time we got home (much to the relief of Signora Rafia), the clouds had cleared, and the night sky glowed with thousands of stars. I paused in the garden with Zeno's hand in mine. We stared at it in silence for what felt like hours, until I struggled to keep my eyes open.

He led me to my room, lingered at the door for a moment, then departed for his own.

Curled up beneath my sheets, I wondered how I would bear that week apart before our *ritus sanguinous*, and if I would ever have it in me to leave the abbey.

BOOK TWO:
VERISMO

Chapter Twenty-Six

Intermezzo

As much as every bit of me wanted to curse Catherine de' Medici for popularizing the steel corset in the late sixteenth century, I had to admit I was gorgeous. My boxy frame had been transformed to fit perfectly along the contours and curves of the Renaissance-styled dress. The bodice pressed around me seamlessly, creating an hourglass figure topped in deep crimson and embroidered gold. The high neck and low sleeves of the dress acted as a ruffled line across my arms and made my square shoulders appear elegant. I didn't even want to think of how much velvet and red dye had been used to create a billowing effect at my waist and fold into the individually embroidered panels that ran from my waist to the floor.

"Did Signora Carbone really make this?" I whispered sideways to Lucia, unable tear my gaze from the graceful figure in the mirror.

"Yes! Isn't she so talented?"

I swiveled and watched as the layered skirts billowed. "How did she even come up with such a pattern? And make it in only a week?"

"Signora Carbone just does that. I've always felt so lucky she took me in. Signora Carbone has always been so kind to me. She's firm, of course, but I owe her everything. I hope one day you two can be close."

Though her demeanor was dreamy, Lucia's deft pace continued on, lightly maneuvering me rather than giving me instructions. I still wasn't used to being so casually touched, and I wasn't sure I would ever be. Initially, I had wondered why on earth I

was getting dressed at the venue, but now the reason was obvious: no matter how hard I tried, I wouldn't be able to keep the train of the dress clean outdoors. Beyond that, I probably would have ruined my makeup by sleeping against the window; Noor had dragged me out of bed with a cocktail of anxiolytics that afternoon, with the rationale that I couldn't panic about leaving the abbey if I wasn't awake to do so. The room I woke up in for the second time—the one I was still in now—was unremarkable, with flagstone for walls and floors. It felt as though it could have been some unfinished room in my sanctum.

I turned to see what preoccupied Lucia now. A trio of golden, U-shaped pins shone between her fingers, with gem-encrusted lilies. I wondered if I would get the time to count the diamonds and rubies on each miniature petal, or if the pins would disappear wherever all my jewelry tended to after their one use. Lucia put them between her teeth, freeing up her hands to work on my hair. I tried not to wince every few seconds, reminding myself that the result would be some masterful updo.

Lucia plaited and tamed my curls into a crown braid tied into a low, looping bun. A few stray ringlets framed my face, with several strands hanging strategically out of my bun. The pins, though methodically placed, appeared like an afterthought. *How paradoxical*, I thought as I tried to ignore my stinging scalp, *that endeavor and pain had given such an effortless appearance.*

She took a step back and spun my chair to marvel at every angle of her work.

"How lovely!" she exclaimed in Italian, clasping her hands together. "Don't you look like a treasure? Now . . ." She rushed to the other side of the room to grab the final accessory: a bracelet.

I took it from her and held it up to the light. The stones were cool and smooth between my fingers, silky beads formed from a dark red-and-brown mottled crystal. *Tiger's eye*, I remembered from Emily's book on crystals, but for the first time in months, I didn't linger on her.

"Who gave you these?" I asked, trying to ignore the fluttering in my chest.

Lucia gave me a strange look. "Duca de' Medici, of course. He chooses all of your clothing."

"I see. Tell him I said thank you."

I ran the bracelet through my fingers. The beads were the same thickness, the same weight, the same smoothness as the rosary on my nightstand. I would probably never feel ready for the onslaught I feared, but with my safety net literally in hand, this was the closest I would get.

Lucia helped me up and moved away with a small, sad smile. For whatever reason, I knew this meant she would not be at my side tonight. I wasn't sure if that made me feel better or worse. I twirled in the mirror one more time, confidence bolstered once more by the majestic cascade of velvet.

Even if I was an imposter in this bourgeois world, the skin fit over me well enough. I gave one final glance at the beads in my hands—my hands, which Noor had correctly predicted would be smooth so long ago. I nodded at Lucia, whispered my thanks to her, then went to the doors to the main ballroom.

They were as heavy as the pit in my stomach. With a deep breath, I pushed both of them away.

Chapter Twenty-Seven

Se vuol ballare

The ballroom was massive, saturated in creams and lace, more magnificent than I could have painted. The floor was made of inlaid marble tile, with fine details embossed in gold leaf. The expansive walls were painted with ornate floral murals and draped in satin curtains. A colossal crystal chandelier bloomed overhead, filling the room with warm, brilliant candlelight. Long tables covered in hors d'oeuvres flanked the sides of the room in the distance, each surrounded by small crowds. Placed perfectly to take advantage of the acoustics was a full orchestra, complete with a grand piano, barely audible over the countless voices.

Just as majestic as the ballroom itself were the people who filled it. The vampires and *beniamini* looked straight out of a historical drama, with the women wearing billowing hourglass ball gowns over hidden corsets. Now surrounded by all these stiff collars and petticoats, my own skirts felt normal. The men were dressed a bit more modernly—from the 1800s, as opposed to the 1500s—and wore long waistcoats over frilled shirts with cravats. A colony of top hats perched on hangers at the entrance.

All the conversations and laughter that had filled the air quieted. As innumerable eyes fell on me, everyone's voices hushed into whispers. I had never felt so naked.

I shut my eyes tightly and focused on the now-audible music. A song had just begun, presumably marking my entrance, and by now it was blossoming into an elegant piece. I recognized it as Rachmaninoff, *Rhapsody on a Theme of Paganini*, Opus 43, Variation 18. I could tell it was him because of the wide chords and the use of "Dies Irae."

My stomach flipped and swirled with an inscrutable wash of feelings that mirrored the swell of the orchestra. I opened my eyes. These feelings were more overwhelming than all those eyes on me were. It was only when the murmur of voices grew louder and returned to their previous volume that I remembered none of these people knew the significance of this piece.

Keeping a watchful gaze on me, the crowd returned to their former conversations.

I had broken out into a cold sweat. The sharp sting on my wrist made me realize I was digging my nails into it. Instinctively, I searched the room for Zeno. In any other situation, finding him would have been easy, but here, I was surrounded by vampiric nobility. Rather than attempt to distinguish my would-be savior from others by appearance alone, I tried to look for someone who had an unusual air to him—someone who carried himself with a dreamy yet intense air, who gestured broadly but was visibly closed off. Most importantly, someone who was probably failing to hide how desperately they wanted the occasion to be over.

I found someone who fit the description near the center of the room, but once he broke away from his present conversation, sifted through other nobility, and sauntered toward me, the discrepancy became clear. The person approaching me had an alien air of confidence and charm; he was comfortable in this situation. And while he had the same jawline, nose, and brow, his frame was broader than Zeno's, and there was a vulpine glint in his eye.

"It's a pleasure to meet you, Signorina Bowling," the vampire said once he was within earshot. I could smell his deep, musky cologne. "I've heard quite a bit about you."

"From who?" I failed to conceal my incredulousness.

The man tossed his head back and let out a melodic laugh. "Why, from everyone, signorina! Who wouldn't be enchanted by the unusual American who managed to become the *beniamina* of our dear Zeno? I think I've heard your lineage and history a dozen times over!"

I bit my tongue when he said Zeno's name. My silence elicited yet another chuckle from him.

Finally, I asked, "And you are?"

His smooth veneer cracked for a brief moment. I noticed a

scar that ran from his right nostril down his chin.

"Ah, I suppose it isn't fair that I know so much of you, yet you don't even know my name. I am Barone de' Medici, Zeno's older cousin."

Without warning, he stepped toward me and grabbed my chin. How I had spent so long in Italy without encountering *il bacetto*—the air kisses Italians used as a familiar greeting—was an oddity, to be sure, but I certainly wasn't expecting it.

Even with little experience, I knew Barone de' Medici's kisses were atypically . . . intimate. He turned my face from one side to the other, and his lips slightly grazed my cheeks, touching me so lightly I was almost convinced it was an illusion. I had to bury my fists in my dress to avoid the urge to push him away.

When he pulled back, Barone de' Medici was looking past me with a devilish grin.

"Don't touch her," a familiar voice snapped.

Behind me, Zeno was glaring at his cousin so fiercely, it was a wonder the other vampire wasn't ablaze. Instead, he was utterly dripping with mirth.

The baron ran his hand along my chin to my shoulder, all the way down my arm to my fingertips, where his own lingered. "What's all this hostility for? I'm just greeting your *beniamina*, dear cousin!"

Zeno gritted his teeth and lowered his voice to a growl. "Words would have sufficed."

"I'm sorry, Zeno. I didn't realize I needed your permission for a simple greeting." The baron's fingers slid between my own. His other hand hovered near my waist. "Should I beg you to dance with Signorina Cora as well?"

In a rapid movement, Zeno smacked away his cousin's hands and grasped me by the wrist. "No need, Basilio," Zeno spat as he dragged me past his cousin. "There are more pertinent people for her to speak with."

The baron threw back his head to guffaw and called over his shoulder, "You wound me, dear cousin!"

So that was the Basilio Zeno had described to me—the one he spoke of with genuine hurt, the one who had somehow betrayed their

friendship in his youth. I looked back, but the swarm of people had already engulfed him.

We wove through the crowd, spinning and turning around couples and small circles of conversation. I only picked up brief snippets of each, but I heard my name and Zeno's countless times. Now and then I saw Basilio's head bobbing over the crowd, circling us yet never growing nearer. I got the sense I was staring back at a stallion on a carousel—one that wouldn't end anytime soon.

"Where exactly are you taking me?" I asked, feeling dazed.

"Away from that asshole," was his bitter reply. "Beyond that, I don't care."

As we wound through a particularly compact group and his grip on me tightened, my wrist began to ache. Once we cleared them, I pulled back my wrist. "Well, *I* do."

The anger vanished from Zeno's face, and he quickly composed himself. "You're correct. This ceremony has its raison d'être, and I shouldn't forget that."

It was astonishing how instantaneously he could shed all visible emotion. I held my arm in my hand and wondered if I should pair this observation with admiration or apprehension.

Zeno took my hand now, more gently. "Allow me to introduce you to a few opportune individuals."

As soon as he spoke those words, there was another shift in Zeno. The man I had studied and painted for so many months now transformed into something entirely different. I watched as his movements became more fluid, his gait was lighter. Even the way his eyes raked across the crowd was different.

A stranger appeared before me, a short vampire in his sixties with coiffed, creamy-white hair and wide, scarlet eyes. His name eluded me entirely—I was too distracted by the alien smile on Zeno's face, the exaggerated Florentine accent and broad hand gestures. They spoke of the weather and wine, and the stranger's latest trips.

"Oh, dear, how impolite of me! I have yet to introduce my *beniamino*. Why, we just had our *ritus sanguinous* the other month. Why didn't you attend?"

Looming behind the stranger was a beautiful man—a boy, really. The Spaniard must have been in his early twenties at most,

with the last remnants of baby fat still rounding what would soon become a sharp jawline and a thin frame that had yet to fill out entirely. Despite his youthfulness, his eyes were devoid of anything but weariness.

"My apologies, Barone Sforza!" Zeno let out a practiced laugh. "I did not realize that my invitation was for yet another *ritus sanguinous*. How many have you had now?"

The other vampire mirrored his mirth. "Pah, just three! And I promise, this was the last. Regardless, this is Rafael."

"Of what family?" Zeno countered.

"He is from the Borgia family. Second-born."

"I see!" Zeno spoke with a voice so genial, I hesitated to believe it was him speaking. "They are stockbrokers, correct? If memory serves, I believe the eldest Contessa Visconti has a *beniamino* from the family as well."

"Yes, Rafael's younger brother. I had hoped to make a deal with the family for him, but this creature is lovely enough!" Sforza slapped the back of the boy in a gesture I knew was meant to register as playful but filled me with dread. The Spaniard was limp and expressionless. It was unusual but not unheard of, I knew, for some vampires to have multiple *beniamini*, or even to share them, mostly because of the practical need for multiple donors. With the way Barone Sforza's hand lingered along Rafael's lower back, I felt his intentions were more pederastic than pragmatic.

How many years, I wondered, had Rafael prepared to be a *beniamino*? What did life look like for him? And what had happened to Sforza's previous two?

Could it happen to me?

As I stared at his hand, my stomach turning, Sforza's rambling faded into the background. It wasn't until someone said my name that the conversation came back into focus.

"Signorina Bowling has made for quite the stimulating interlocutor," Zeno said. "In fact, she's gormandized the entirety of my library. Why, I fear the poor thing will become ennuied!"

"Dear Medici, if you came to my estate more often, you would know that I have quite a grand library myself! Perchance our

librarians can get in contact and share inventories? Oh, and you *must* attend my Christmas party!"

Zeno clasped his hands together in faux jubilance. "What a brilliant idea!"

While Rafael and I stared at one another in silence, Zeno managed to pivot the conversation elsewhere and then end it entirely.

"Thank you again, Barone Sforza. I would love to speak with you longer, but I can't be rude to my other guests. My people will be in contact with you next week regarding that proposition of yours with the library."

Barone Sforza said his own parting words and gave me a bow before Zeno introduced me to more names. I knew many from my studies—Medici, Sforza, Visconti, and countless other ancient families. Zeno's conversations echoed that initial one with Barone Sforza, with nearly identical greetings and repeated small talk.

When possible, I stood on the sidelines. I had shown up to a masquerade without a mask or a script. Occasionally, I would be asked a few simple questions, such as what my family did ("Nothing"), how I could tolerate such a remote abbey ("Quite well, thank you"), and what my accomplishments were ("I have very few"). Zeno would help me dodge invites while collecting literary inventory. As often as I could, I snuck off to the hors d'oeuvres table to try and eat a cube of cheese or a small sweet, but I wasn't able to swallow anything with such anxiety.

The butterflies in my stomach proliferated by the minute as stressors piled up. There was the *ritus sanguinous*, of course, persistent in the back of my mind, plus the fact that I was not at the abbey and was instead thrust into this bizarre environment, straight out of a historical drama. And finally, there was the familiar face that lingered in the periphery of my vision, a fox waiting for a moment to strike.

Basilio finally cornered me at the table with a macaron in my mouth. To my horror, Zeno was off talking with some Visconti nobleman.

"Hello again."

I mumbled a hello, crumbs jetting from my mouth. I wiped my lips roughly with a handkerchief.

"Careful," was his smooth response. "You don't want to ruin your makeup."

"Oh." As anticipated, the handkerchief was covered in a thin layer of vermillion.

"It's a shame Zeno absconded with you so, signorina," Basilio stated, broadening his shoulders. "I meant to speak with you further."

I tightened my lips into a line. "About?"

"Zeno, of course. You managed to bring him out of the shadows, and I wanted to thank you for that. We did, actually."

"We?"

"Yes, myself and my guest, as it were. What a pity she's running behind." He gave an exaggerated sigh, then widened his eyes as he looked past me. "Ah, speak of the devil!"

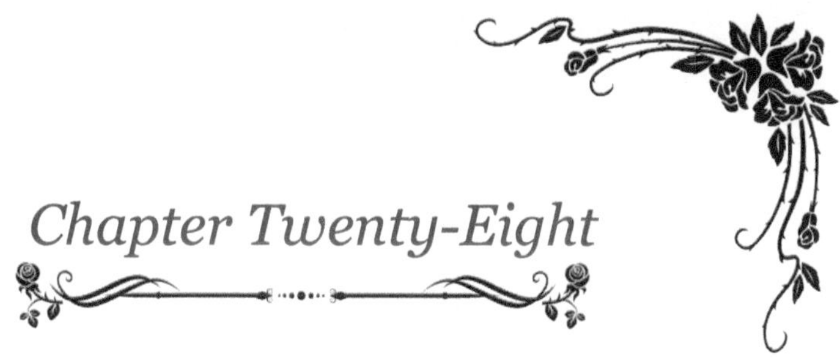

Chapter Twenty-Eight

Nessun Dorma

Even if I hadn't seen photos of the woman with those unmistakable heart-shaped lips and ethereal profile, I would have recognized her from her magnetism alone. Serafina Rosa Salviati, the woman who had shown up to my wedding in a white dress.

The conversation hushed as Serafina descended the stairs toward me. Even with her in flats and me in heels, she towered over me. As beautiful as I had believed I was this afternoon, I now felt the opposite. I remembered I was a short, plain, poor student surrounded by aristocrats, wearing a dress valued at several times my net worth. She looked like a masterpiece in a simple, blue cocktail gown. I didn't know if tearing off my dress would make me feel more or less naked right now. Serafina's eyes traveled inchmeal across me, piercing through each freckle and flaw before finally landing on my face.

"You must be Cora Bowling." She leaned down, washing me in the fragrance of her spicy perfume.

Was I? With such an otherworldly person so close she could have kissed me, it was hard to remember anything at all.

"I, uh—yeah."

Serafina recoiled, one of her ringlets brushing across my shoulder. Hers was the softest, lightest hair I had ever felt. "*You* are to be his *beniamina*?" she scoffed, then looked above me with a smile. "Oh, hello, you."

A warm hand rested on my shoulder, and Zeno pulled me toward him. I exhaled a breath I hadn't realized I'd been holding.

At the sight of Zeno, Serafina's eyes blazed. In an instant, she transformed from a lovely cherub to a beautiful Lucifer. No wonder he had loved her.

The thought sent yet another pang of dread through me. But when I looked behind me, he didn't appear to share the sentiment. Rather, Zeno regarded the woman with the same cool impassivity he would give a mere object.

"Don't follow us, Serafina," he said in a monotone.

Her lips tightened and trembled, like her mouth was full of embers. Slowly and deliberately, she enunciated, "As you wish."

Zeno led Baslio and me back to the room where I had awoken. It was cramped, of course, having been barely big enough for Lucia and me, but I felt much less suffocated there than amongst the crowd.

Zeno motioned for me to sit on a bench in the corner, leaving him and Basilio to stand as they conversed.

Zeno straightened his sleeves, held his hands behind his back, and smiled warmly at his cousin. "Why did you bring Serafina here? I didn't invite her," he said evenly, even sweetly, but the sharpness in his tone was undeniable.

Basilio leaned against the wall and folded his arms over his chest. "What do you mean? Obviously my *beniamina* would be my plus-one."

Zeno narrowed his eyes. "I hadn't gotten there yet, but in case you weren't aware, I didn't invite you either."

Basilio smirked. "Your father extended an invitation to me on your behalf. I'm family, am I not? Who else is more equipped to bring you back? It isn't my fault the only time I could reach you was now."

My chest tightened. Zeno was leaving the abbey?

Why did that hurt so much, when I might do so myself one day?

The vampire let out a mirthless laugh and shook his head. "Stop speaking nonsense. You both know I have no plans of returning. Why did you even come here? What's changed?"

"What's changed, Zeno, is that Uncle Vincenzo learned you not only took someone like *her*—" he gestured to me "—as a *beniamina*, but more importantly, you dared to present her in public when you denied such a position to Signorina Salviati. Do you know what that will do to the company stocks?"

The people who had crowded outside of the room to listen in did not even bother to whisper any longer. I heard my name in dozens of voices at full volume, spoken with shock and disdain.

Basilio continued in his suave manner, "You chose to make this *ritus sanguinous* public and bring your name to the forefront. It's time to return to proper society. I'm tired of holding your place, Zeno. You can't hide in backwater Italy and wallow in your own misery forever."

"I can't wallow in my own misery forever?" Zeno sneered. "As usual, Basilio, you underestimate my abilities."

"I think *you're* the one underestimating here." Finally, Basilio cracked and his voice rose above baseline. "Since you made this foolish decision, Uncle Vincenzo has given me orders. He wants you to leave this girl, leave backwater Sicily, and come back with a reputable *beniamina*. I pulled innumerable strings and even broke apart an engagement to bring Serafina here. I can make it so this gathering never even happened, as far as high society is concerned."

Zeno's brow flattened, and the corner of his lip twisted in disdain. "What an utter waste of everyone's time. You're a fool, Basilio."

It was Basilio's turn to step closer to his cousin. Now the two were so close, they could touch.

"Insult me all you want, but I'm just trying to help. I'm worried about you—leaving suddenly like that, with no phone number, no mailing address, no way of contacting you? This is the first time I've actually even been able to talk to you."

"Maybe you should have taken that as a hint."

"Look, even if you hate me, I still care about you. You have an entire family that wants you to come back and just . . . be normal. I miss you. I truly do."

Suddenly, Zeno's demeanor lightened—not to brightness, but to nothingness. Expression blank, he turned his back to Basilio and faced me.

"I don't care about any of that. To me, there is only Cora. Everyone else and everything else is meaningless. There's only her."

My heart fluttered so violently, I felt it would burst from my chest.

An incredulous laugh escaped Basilio as he watched Zeno hold out a hand to me. "You're actually serious, aren't you?"

Once he had helped me up, Zeno glanced over his shoulder and replied, "Of course. When it comes to her, I always am."

Basilio's voice took on a hint of panic. For the first time, he addressed me. "I'll pay you, Cora. However much Zeno is paying you, I'll double it." Zeno pulled me gently but firmly past Basilio, who continued to speak to me rapid fire. "You don't understand what you're doing to the Medici name, what you're doing to my cousin. How could you? How could a commoner understand what a travesty this union is?"

When Zeno threw open the door, Basilio's voice was quickly eclipsed by the mass that had aggregated around the small room. Zeno squared his shoulders and pushed through the crowd roughly, eyes fixed on the exit across the ballroom.

I was surrounded by horrified gasps and whispers of confusion.

"We're done here," he announced, not stopping. "Everyone go home."

The people around us got even louder. Although I could pick out some sentences, the voices and sentiments overlapped. Finally, Serafina emerged from among them, burning even brighter than before, and blocked our path.

"What do you mean, go home?" she exclaimed. "Are you seriously going to kick us out—all of us—after we've gone out of our way to come to this farce?"

Zeno glowered at her. "It seems," he sneered, "you've retained some basic comprehension skills. Congratulations. Now move aside."

She didn't move but directed her yelling elsewhere. "What is the meaning of this, Basilio? You told me Zeno was going to take *me* as a *beniamina* once he talked to you!"

The crowd, now an aggregate of cursing, gasping, and laughing, quickly enveloped the interloper. Basilio shoved in beside Zeno. "I—I didn't realize just how senseless he'd be."

"You made a fool of me! You let *him* make a fool of me again!" Hot, fat tears rolled down Serafina's face, which was now contorted beyond recognition. She addressed me for the first time, jabbing her finger in front of my nose. "You! What makes you think you're better than me?"

I didn't respond. My surroundings felt far away, and it seemed like I was watching everything unfold around me on a screen.

"Can't you talk?" she demanded. "What do you even want with Zeno?"

My chest felt tightened and I broke out into a cold sweat. I could see and feel the blood vessels in my eyes pulsing, my fingers going numb. I knew what was coming.

So I ran. I shoved through people, ignoring all the yelps and protests. Darkness and dizziness creeped into my vision, a familiar sense of dread clawing at my rib cage.

"Please, I can't—"

Someone stepped on the train of my dress, which tore off in a clump behind me. The final word, *breathe*, was cut off when my chin hit the floor.

I vaguely heard peals of laughter beyond the ringing in my ears. Once I felt blood rush from my split lips, it was too late—my breath escaped me entirely. I gasped hard, but my breath was shallow. I tried again with the same result, over and over, until I was hyperventilating. I curled up into a ball on the tile.

"Everyone out!" Zeno roared.

A pair of powerful hands reached under me and scooped me into the air. My body fell limp into his arms, and then everything washed away.

Chapter Twenty-Nine

E lucevan le stelle

"Breathe in, two-three-four, hold, two-three-four, out, two-three-four . . ."

Despite how the words blurred behind the screen of screaming in my ears, an instictual response began. It took several seconds and several attempts, but my breathing evened and slowed. The tingling faded from my fingers, and I could finally feel the beads between them.

One-two-three-four, inhale, turn a bead. One-two-three-four, hold my breath.

The blackness finally disintegrated, and the air felt heavy again.

"Tell me five things you can see."

I flickered my gaze around. "The sky. Stars. Your face. My hair. The tops of trees."

"Well-done. Tell me four things you can hear."

"A water fountain. Crickets. Your voice. My breath."

"Three things you can feel now."

"Water on my face. Warmth. A finger rubbing my cheek."

"Good. Two things you can smell."

"Your cologne. Night air."

"One thing you can taste."

"Blood?"

I shifted slowly, finally out of it. My heart was still racing, hands still trembling, but the feeling of dying was gone. I was now curled up in Zeno's arms on a stone bench outside of the ballroom.

The vampire stared down at me with a complicated array of emotions across his features: sorrow, fear, peacefulness. But behind it all, blazing within: wrath.

I pulled away from him, and something fell to the ground. A handkerchief covered in blood. Zeno grabbed my chin and pulled me close to him. My entire body burned at our proximity, at the soft feeling of his breath on my lips. He tilted my head slightly. Just as I couldn't take it any longer, he released me. "Good. I was afraid you'd need stitches."

"Oh." For an entirely different reason than before, my heart was racing. I grabbed the fabric on my lap and fidgeted with it. "Um, where did you learn those things? Box breathing and five-four-three-two-one?"

Zeno leaned forward so his arms were resting on his legs, and he looked at me sideways. "I read about them. After that time in the church, I read about panic disorder."

Why? I almost asked, but even before the word left my lips, I knew there was no need, not when he had already told the world. He just hadn't told me to my face.

"Hey, Zeno?" I tried to speak casually and hide how much my heart raced as I dusted off my dress and pulled confetti from my hair.

"Yes?"

"Did you really mean that? About there only being me?"

Zeno was about to answer calmly, it seemed, but as some sort of recognition hit him, he froze, eyes opening so wide I could see the reflection of the crescent moon in them. He took a staggered breath, then a slightly deeper one, and ran his fingers through his hair. I wondered if Noor would have been able to hear his heartbeat without a stethoscope.

To force Zeno to respond when I knew the answer seemed cruel, so I spared him whatever horror he seemed to be going through.

"Zeno, I still want to have a ritus sanguinous," I said once it became clear he wouldn't be able to reply. Despite what Serafina and

Basilio had said, despite wanting to finish my thesis, I needed to stay with him and be his.

I would figure out how to make everything turn out well.

The fear on his face was replaced by relief, which was, in turn, replaced by confusion. How strange it was that Zeno had seemed so unemotional earlier tonight, when now every single emotion was so transparent to me.

"I don't understand," he scoffed. "You want to go back in there? After all that? I can't allow—"

I shook my head quickly. "Of course not."

Zeno loosened his tie and sat forward, expression grave. "It isn't ritus sanguinous without an audience."

"We have an audience. All the stars are out for us tonight. Do we need anyone else?"

I think he saw the sky for the first time in that moment. It was cloudless, with the blues and purples of distant galaxies mottled together. Every constellation was bright and visible, as though straight from a textbook. It was one of those night skies that made the earth seem small, one of those nights that made the events that had transpired feel insignificant. Just like that night we'd shared before, where I spoke with him candidly for one of the first times. Our sky.

Yet when I looked over at him again, his face was the antithesis of my expectation.

Zeno's brow was furrowed heavily. His mouth quivered in a way I had never seen before, and his eyes darted around the ground. He blinked several times, each one clearly punctuating every rapid thought. Zeno's lips parted, letting out the soft, guttural creak of words on the verge of being spoken. Then, with no more than a resigned exhale, they closed once more. He gave one final, small breath, then his gaze slowly traveled up to meet mine, burning into my soul.

"I'm sorry, Cora," he whispered hoarsely. "We shouldn't do that. We shouldn't do any of this."

"What?"

Zeno cupped my cheek carefully and caressed it. He smoothed down my hair with his other hand and gave me the smallest, saddest smile I had ever seen.

“My beloved Cora,” he murmured, brushing his thumb across my lower lip. “I did really mean what I said earlier. For me, there is only you. No one and nothing else. That’s why—”

Zeno’s fingertips lingered for a precious instant longer before he parted from me and rose to his feet. All the softness in tone and movement was gone. All that remained was a husk. “It’s time for you to go back.”

For several excruciating seconds, all I could do was blink. I desperately searched his face to see if he was joking, but it soon became clear he was dead serious.

“You mean for us to go home, right?” My voice came out as little more than a pathetic squeak. “Aren’t we going to ride back together?”

“I’ll walk you to the car.” Zeno took my hand, his touch mechanical, and helped me to my shaking feet. On instinct and desperation, I squeezed his hand, but he shifted it so we were walking arm-in-arm with a palpable space between us.

The path felt simultaneously short and long by the time we reached its winding end through the garden. Signora Rafia had pulled the car up so closely, the tires were practically touching the curb. Maneuvering me into the already open door was a seamless process.

The passenger-side seat—Zeno’s side—felt wrong, every setting incorrect. Most of all, the car seemed bizarrely open.

“Wait, what’s going on?” I cried, my nails digging into the leather seat. “Why are you acting like this?”

“I’m going to stay here a bit longer. I have . . . matters to attend to.” Zeno looked over his shoulder at the ballroom, which was already clear of guests. “You don’t belong in that world, and you don’t belong at my side.”

“What?”

I looked up at the vampire, who returned my gaze steadily and folded one arm across himself. He gave me a deep bow, then straightened with his eyes looking beyond me. “Good night, Signorina Bowling.”

With that, he shut the door. Even before the car began to move, I knew that beyond the tinted windows, Zeno had already walked away.

Chapter Thirty

Volti Subito

I traveled on a train for the first time when I was nine years old. I had religiously read a chapter of *Around the World in Eighty Days* to Pa every night that summer, waking him up to hear every last word if he dozed off. He got train tickets for all of us near the end of the book, and when Ma told him he should have waited for my birthday to get them, he joked, "But she might'a got 'round to readin' *Murder on the Orient Express* if I waited any longer!"

It was all I could think or talk about for days: being like Phileas Fogg. The tickets were for a nice passenger train, and it was the first thing I had ridden other than a rusty pickup or a bike too large for me. As far as I was concerned, going on that ride was the most exciting thing that had ever happened to me, or ever would.

My first panic attack was on that train, right after I saw dirt underneath my nails. I tried to figure out for years what exactly made it happen, to no avail. Maybe it was something about the floating sensation of wheels on rails beneath me, or maybe seeing the grit on my hands was a subconscious reminder that I was out of place beside the tourists.

Now, with the subtle, rhythmic jerking of the car beneath me as we navigated through paneled roads, I knew both were to blame.

You don't belong in that world, and you don't belong at my side.

I stared down at my hands. My fingernails had been painted, and my palms had been scrubbed meticulously. But neither got rid of the dark hue of my skin, the freckles that washed over them, or the old burn scars I'd gotten working in the bakery.

Of course you don't belong with nobles, you idiot, I thought, tightening my fists into balls and burrowing them in my skirt. *You never belonged anywhere.*

No—I had belonged once, or I'd felt like I did, at least. When I was gardening in the abbey, sitting with Zeno in the aviary, or just wandering the gardens. If nowhere else, that was a home.

"Where are you taking me?" I asked Signora Rafia, lurching forward in my seat.

Signora Rafia hadn't said a word the entire time, or even looked back at me. She simply sat there with both hands on the wheel, head fixed forward. That was how she remained even now, seemingly unaltered by my outburst.

"Because," I continued, leaning back in my seat and forcing my tone to soften a bit, "I—I don't know what Zeno meant when he said I should go back. I don't know if he meant the abbey, or London, or . . . somewhere else."

"I have been given orders to drive you to the Abbazia di Santa Dymphna," Signora Rafia stated. "I do not have any further orders."

I closed my eyes and tried to convince myself I was asleep and that the events of the night were all some hydroxyzine-induced nightmare. I could have that, I decided, at least until after the ride back. Perhaps I could even convince myself that the blood on my chin—which had just reopened—was actually drool, and the pressure behind my eyes was a sleep mask worn slightly too tight.

Despite my efforts, I couldn't drift fully into this fantasy. My phone, resuscitated for the first time in nearly seven months, sat against my thigh beneath my dress, and some part of me waited for it to buzz. Maybe, just maybe, in that brief span of Wi-Fi going through the city, Zeno would call me and explain that this was some misunderstanding. Even the clarity of being told he wanted me to leave forever would have felt better than this limbo.

Eventually, the ground beneath the car felt familiar, and it slowed to one final stop. Signora Rafia helped me out, and I was shuffled from person to person like some package on a conveyor belt. Based on how delicate the words and movements of everyone around me (even Signora Carbone) were, FRAGILE, THIS SIDE UP was clearly plastered on my forehead.

I was led by Signora Rafia to Signore Urbino, to Signora

Carbone, to Lucia, and finally, Doctor Ntumba in the clinic. She sat me down squarely, already prepared with her wound-care supplies.

Zeno had been mostly incorrect in his assessment of my wound. It was a thin yet deceptively deep cut from the right corner of my mouth to the middle of my chin. I had landed on a chipped piece of tile, which had unfortunately shattered and lodged into the muscle of my chin, but fortunately not into the bone. After a lidocaine shot and quick extraction of the pieces, Doctor Ntumba informed me the rest would be easy.

"How did you know I got hurt?" I asked as she flushed the laceration on my chin with saline.

Doctor Ntumba did not look up from what she was doing and moved on to washing the skin around the cut. "Zeno told me," she answered curtly. "He said that the night went poorly, and you fell and hit the ground." She leaned back and tilted my head to the side. "Hmm. We'll try some butterfly bandages. It will likely still scar."

"Do you know what's going on?" I said to her back as she dug the bandages out of her bag.

Doctor Ntumba returned and pinched my jaw between her fingers. "Hold still."

"But—"

"Stay still and I'll tell you."

I did as she said, but it was difficult to steady myself when I was shaking so much. A few minutes and two butterfly bandages later, however, she was successful.

"Now," Doctor Ntumba finally said, taking off her gloves, "I can tell you what I know."

I folded my hands in my lap and nodded eagerly, urging her to continue.

"Zeno did not tell me very much, truthfully. He stated you were injured and that I should expect you in a number of hours, but that he would not return until Monday."

"Where is he? And what will he be doing for two days?"

Doctor Ntumba sighed and slumped ever so slightly. "That, I do not know. I could likely track down his precise location with ease, as I'm sure he is aware. He is still nearby, I assume. Doing what, however, is a mystery I do not wish to know the answer to."

She quickly gathered up the remnants of the kit, then extended the step from the base of the exam table, a clear signal it was time for me to leave.

I tightened my jaw so much that the pain broke through the steadily decreasing numbness. "What am I supposed to do, then? Just sit around and wait for him to explain what the hell is going on?"

With the kit fully packed up, Doctor Ntumba tossed it over her shoulder and started for the exit. "It's late, Cora. Get some sleep for tonight," she replied somberly, hand on the doorknob.

She gave me a small smile and shut the door softly. I remained in that room for a long time, and for once the chill felt comfortable.

When I staggered to the dining hall the following evening, I wondered if I would find breakfast, lunch, or dinner. I quickly discovered my meal to be a hybrid of the former two. My stomach gurgled at the sight, and with nobody around, I was free to scarf it down. Nobody met me for my bath.

Nobody but Lucia spoke to me at all.

Signora Carbone worked twice as fast as usual and busied herself with cleaning every inch of the house. Signore Urbino became utterly infatuated with specks of dirt on the wall or took far too long with a basic task whenever I entered the room and was constantly off doing "duties." Doctor Ntumba didn't show up for tea and had seemingly disappeared from the abbey. Lucia attempted to converse with me as usual, but any time she thought I couldn't see, she would gaze at me sadly from a distance. Even Leonore treated me differently, her coos ever so slightly somber, her movements more delicate.

That night, I heard the low voices of Zeno and Doctor Ntumba coming from his room, intense and snipped and far too soft to decipher. But I never heard music.

Chapter Thirty-One

Nel cor più non mi sento

Years of practicing compartmentalization had come in handy, it seemed. I could dismiss that entire night as some distant nightmare. But with each passing hour, once-fleeting thoughts finally amalgamated in my stream of consciousness.

What's going on? Why won't anyone talk to me like before? Why haven't I seen Zeno? Does he hate me now? Will he leave the abbey? Will they kick me out?

Midway through the second day, it became clear distraction was my only option.

It was strange to see the hill during the day. The way the afternoon sun peeked through the leaves and cast askew shadows made it almost an entirely different landscape. I chuckled as I first emerged into the clearing. Only in this strange country would flowers be in full bloom in late November, and only in this strange country would I reminisce on rainy days in London.

After trying and failing to find a patch of plantless dirt, I patted down the yellow sea of fennel and set my blanket down.

After plopping down, I laughed for the second time in a while—with the grass up to my nose, it was impossible to see the pond I had gone all this way to sketch. I tossed my sketchpad aside and stretched out onto the blanket. If I couldn't draw, I could at least soak in the sun.

I rolled to the side, brush shifting around me. When I looked up, a trio of purple stellate blooms were dangling above my head. I pushed away the borage flowers and sighed. "Even during the day, the stars are taunting me."

At the sound of my voice, something in the distance shuffled audibly. "Signorina Bowling?" a familiar, deep voice called out just as I sat up to see her.

"Oh, uh, hello, Signora Carbone." I quickly pulled the grass from my hair and straightened my skirt. "What are you doing here?"

It was a stupid question, considering the shears in her hands, but it felt better than nothing.

"Tending to the graveyard," she answered, a frown creasing her shaded face. "And you?"

I tried to formulate a straightforward answer, but the second I opened my mouth, questions poured out. "What's going on with Zeno?" I asked, sitting up. "Why is he avoiding me? What's going to happen to me?"

I thought she would avoid my gaze like she had for the last few days, but she returned it, both her eyes and voice razor sharp. She thrust the shears into the ground and tossed aside a glove to offer me a hand.

I took it hesitantly, and she pulled me to my feet.

"For once in all my time working here, Signorina Bowling, I do not know what is happening under this roof. Do you understand how that feels for me?"

"No," I replied just as quickly. "I have no clue whatsoever what you're feeling. But honestly, I care much more about what you're thinking. Or, if not a guess, *any* shred of information about what's going to happen to me."

The woman looked to the side, watching a deer lap at the pond with a strangely serene expression. No, not serene—hopeless.

"No one knows what's going to happen to you, not even Duca de' Medici," she muttered. "All I can tell you is that I have been given orders to pack and unpack your bags several times."

To hear it said so candidly brought a chill down my spine. For a long, extended silence, all we could hear was the mild breeze and the deer lapping water. It looked up at her, seemed to see something fearsome in her face, and quickly dashed away into the forest.

When Signora Carbone looked back at me, eyes ablaze, I could empathize with the creature.

“You’re going to need to talk with him soon,” she said. “Otherwise, I have a feeling I’m going to be packing your bag for the last time.”

The room was even darker than usual when I entered, a feat I hadn’t known was possible. The only thing preventing pitch darkness was the distant candle in the lounge.

After grabbing the unlit lantern on the table, I navigated the room by memory into what little light there was.

Zeno’s shoulders rose and fell slowly as I approached, as though breathing became burdensome upon my entrance. The candle’s flame flickered in response to his audible, breathy sigh, and the light shifted dramatically across his features. His coral eyes gazed at me intently from above his arm, reminiscent of Cabanel’s *The Fallen Angel*.

“Cora.”

That single word, a strange greeting of sorts, sounded heavy in his mouth. Heavy and bittersweet.

“Zeno,” I whispered back, mouth taut around his name. I took a few steps forward, closing in on him. “What’s going on?”

With yet another sigh, he formed his fingers into a triangle, lowering his chin onto his thumbs and pinching the bridge of his nose with his forefingers.

“I told you already.” His voice was hoarse, that specific hoarseness that emerged from hours of not speaking. “You don’t belong in that world, or at my side.”

I restrained myself and placed the lantern on the piano instead of slamming it down, then further restrained myself to speak in a low voice. “Why? Because I grew up poor? Or because I’m not Italian?”

Zeno sat up and looked at me as though I had said the sun was out at midnight, then flattened again. “Of course not!” he responded. “You deserve *better* than those worlds. You deserve so much better than being torn apart by shitty, two-faced people and rotting in this abbey.”

“I’m not rotting! I haven’t felt this at home in years.”

"Maybe right now," he mumbled, returning to his former pose. "But I told you before, Cora, I'm a husk. That feeling won't—"

I folded my arms tightly against my chest and cut in sharply, "Do you think I haven't seen your eyes go empty? Do you think I'm not aware that I'm living in your casket? Look, if this is just some self-sacrificing bullshit—"

"It's not," he snapped, emotion finally returning to his voice. "I don't have a sacrificial bone in my body. Every ounce of flesh beneath my skin is as selfish as a man can be."

"Then why?"

He pinched his nose again, cursed sharply under his breath, then said, "I care for you too much, Cora. And I can't handle that feeling."

Everything in me softened all at once. "Zeno," I whispered.

"Solitude is a delicious poison. I'd rather drink it to death than have you for just a taste."

I finally neared Zeno, who did not turn to look at me. He flinched when I placed my hand on his shoulder. Every muscle tightened. Like I was a stranger.

"I told you, I'll be here as long as you'll have me. I meant that when I said it. Either as friends, or something more."

With those words, he loosened up, even leaned into my hand slightly, so slightly that it seemed as if on instinct. Slowly, I withdrew it and returned it to my side.

Zeno didn't move from his former position or sit up to look at me as I continued, "But I can't sit here and be dangled back and forth. I'm not trying to give you an ultimatum or force you into anything you don't want. If it's what you want, I can leave. No hard feelings."

Zeno slammed his hands on the desk and leaped up.

"Of course I don't want you to leave!" he cried. "I *want* you to stay here. I want to see you finish your thesis and enjoy sweets and smile. I want you to hear my music. I want to watch you and your garden grow to their fullest beauty. I haven't felt happy in years. You're everything. You're all there is."

"Then why?" I asked. "Why can't it be that easy?"

Zeno met my gaze, eyes ablaze. He took a step closer to me, then another, expecting me to back up. But I stood square. Zeno looked me up and down, eyes softening, then slowly took one of my hands in his. His hands, which had been clenched so tightly moments before, were warm for the first time. "I don't have it in me to love in parts. If I have you, I need every inch of your soul and every inch of your body. I can't settle for less."

At the genuine frustration and despair in his tone, my resolve was finalized. "Zeno," I whispered, putting my other hand on his.

He searched my face, then softly replied, "Yes?"

Though I paused, though my words were shaky, I knew what I wanted. "Drink from me."

With a staggered breath, Zeno bit his lip so hard I feared he'd draw blood. For a second, I thought he would decline, but then he looked deep into my eyes and clutched my hand. "Are you sure? Do you know what you're asking?"

I gave him a slow nod. "Yes. I know who you are. I know what I'm signing up for."

"God, I hope you never do."

Chapter Thirty-Two

O soave fanciulla

Zeno trained his gaze on me unapologetically, his eyes visibly trailing along the curves of my body. His fingers grazed against my cheek, snaked slowly along the veins in my neck, and lingered for just a whisper over the hollow of my throat. Only then was his path blocked by the oppressing lip of my high shirt collar.

His hand froze, and I became acutely conscious of the rise and fall of my chest as he puzzled out the predicament we were in. He fumbled with it for a moment, trying in vain to move the fabric. Then, after a few excruciating seconds, he finally growled, "Fuck it."

In a swift motion, Zeno pulled me against him with one arm, hooked his fingers into my shirt, and yanked. A chill ran down my spine in perfect unison with the sound and sensation of tearing fabric. I gasped as cold air met freshly bare skin, my shirt now torn in a jagged V so that my shoulders and the tops of my breasts were exposed.

Zeno's grip around me tightened so that we were flush against one another, and he pinned my arm to my side before I could cover myself with it. The vampire sank his fangs into my neck, and searing heat washed over me.

Zeno grasped feverishly at me, using every ridge of every rib to claw me closer. His nails dug so tightly into my back that I feared the rest of my shirt would be torn to shreds within seconds.

I squirmed at the electricity in his fingertips, and Zeno frenzied at the movement, drinking me in further. My skin fluttered every time he moaned, and it took only a few greedy gulps of my blood before the entirety of my body was a numb, shaking mess. Once every crevice of our bodies was pressed as tightly as possible

against each other, we were trembling statues.

There was a moment that seemed both endless and fleeting, where the only thing I could feel was the pulsing of my veins and Zeno's warm breath on my neck.

He pulled away from me slowly with a shaky breath. Our faces were now inches apart, our noses touching. I could see my blood on his parted lips, and within his eyes burned a fire I had never seen before. I had been clutching his shirt tightly, had been pressing my body into his and digging my nails into his arms. Though I loosened my grip and untangled myself from him, the exhilaration coursing within me had not abetted.

Slowly, deliberately, he swiped his tongue across his lips, savoring the last drop of me. I took one step back, then another, until I was touching the desk behind us. He was panting now, excitement coursing within him, waiting to pounce the moment I gave him the go-ahead.

I nodded.

With a fierceness I didn't know he possessed, Zeno threw his arm across the desk, sending books and papers flying. An inkwell tipped over, black ink pouring down the far corner of the desk.

And then he was on top of me, feverishly kissing the spot he had drunk from me. His lips traveled along my collarbone, and his hands were everywhere, tearing off the rest of my blouse, pulling at my skirt, unbuttoning his pants.

Then he placed his arm just above my head, hovering above me so closely, I could feel the warmth emanating from his chest.

"God, you're beautiful," Zeno whispered, cupping my face with his other hand, trailing his thumb across my lips. "Those eyes will undo me. Those lips will be the death of me."

The soft movement of his fingertips along my jaw sent a wave of shivers through my body. My breath caught in my throat when we locked eyes. Were mine just as dark and desirous as his? Was I looking at a reflection of my want?

But then, beneath the wanting, I caught a moment of hesitance in his movements. He loosened from me, and something stormed between us—some unseen dilemma within him.

"Please," I whimpered, wrapping my arms around his neck. "Don't stop."

There was a moment of silence. I bit my lip, and something in him unraveled.

Zeno pulled my hands off his neck and pinned them above my head. "How can I resist such pretty pleas when I've already waited so long?"

I let out a gasp, and he smothered my cries with his lips. I arched my back, pulling him into me.

Indeed, how had we waited so long?

I woke up the next morning in his bed, his arms wrapped around me. His skin felt real, his breath on the top of my head felt real, and the soft beating of his heart in my ears felt real. But I had dreamed of being in Zeno's bed so many times, I dared not move, or even breathe. I held my breath as long as I could until finally, I couldn't help but nestle into him. If this was a dream, I should savor it. And on the off chance that this was reality, I needed to savor it even more.

He planted a soft kiss on top of my head and pulled me in tightly. "Good morning, *passerotta*."

My face grew hot. *Passerotta*—"little sparrow." Being given a pet name seared what happened last night into reality.

"G-Good morning, er, Zen—Duca de'—" I stammered desperately, then admitted defeat by burying my head into him.

Zeno laughed and caressed my hair. "No need to get flustered. You don't have to call me anything but my name."

"That's probably for the better." I giggled. "I don't think you'd want the kind of nicknames from where I grew up. Unless Tater, Squirt, or Sugar Pie make your heart skip a beat."

He feigned a contemplative look. "I could get used to Sugar, I think. Especially if you used that pretty Southern accent of yours."

I rolled my eyes but still smiled. "It's either Zeno or Q-tip. That's definitely what you would have been called. Take your pick."

The vampire scoffed and gently pinched my face. “Cheeky, aren’t you? Zeno it is, then.”

He sat up in bed, taking me with him. The change in position shifted the feeling in the room, and I wondered if our banter was a prelude to something a bit more serious. The events of last night had been unexpected, and so many questions were still unresolved that talking through them was clearly warranted. What were we now? Were we supposed to tell anyone, or was this meant to be a secret? Where would we go from here?

But when Zeno looked down at me, every question was answered with a single known truth—I was his *beniamina*, in every sense of the word.

We still needed to talk, I decided, but it could wait a bit. We could just enjoy simplicity and one another’s presence.

Unfortunately, my counterpart had other ideas.

“I’m leaving tomorrow for a trip to Puglia for a few weeks,” he said plainly. “I plan on bringing you with me.”

Yet another curveball. The sheets rustled as I shifted away from him to make eye contact.

“Tomorrow?” I asked, brows raised. “What? Why? What’s wrong with the abbey?”

“Who said you were allowed to get out of bed yet?” Zeno grumbled playfully. In a motion equal parts gentle and swift, he pulled me back into his chest. “I have no qualms with the abbey,” he added after nuzzling his head back onto mine. “Rather, the Puglia residence is one of the oldest Medici properties, and it rarely sees any guests. I went there only once as a child, when my family went to visit Sforza’s villa. Seeing him was why I remembered that place. He’s been quite . . . amicable, despite it all. Regardless, there have to be countless untouched documents there, ones which hold many secrets.”

I remembered my bags. I felt cold despite the warmth pressed along my back. I moved my hands, which had been wrapped around his forearm, to my side.

“You were going to have me go there, weren’t you?” I demanded. “And send me off under the guise of ‘temporary research.’”

He sighed and ran his free hand through his hair. “It was a fleeting thought during those first few hours when we got back. One of dozens. I decided the more appropriate option was for me to go and send them back to you here. Either that or send you away fully stipended and buy you some house to live in wherever you wanted.”

Taking advantage of the gap between us, I crossed my arms. “But you *know* where I want to live. And you know I don’t want some allowance. That would just make *you* feel better about it all, not me.”

Zeno scoffed and gave me a bittersweet smile. “I told you, didn’t I? I’m a selfish man.”

The rumbling sensation of someone laughing while pressed against me was too sweet, and despite myself, I loosened up again. Of course, my emotional guard remained. “How do I know that me being there isn’t just a fleeting thought? How am I supposed to believe that you aren’t going to change your mind?”

“Oh, *mia passerotta*, that will never happen,” he murmured, wrapping his arms around me tightly. “Now that you’ve agreed to be mine, I have no intention of letting you go.”

Ba-dump, ba-dump. I didn’t know whose quickened heartbeat I was hearing, but I got the strange feeling they were synchronized. That was all it took to give in to it once again—that intoxicating feeling of infatuation.

“I’ll go with you.”

I pulled his face closer, threw aside the sheets, and breathed him in. He pulled back to meet my eyes and assess my intent, and I gave a smirk and nod.

Released from self-restraint, Zeno lowered me onto my back and stared down at me, already teeming with electricity. I caught a glimpse of his eyes in those few milliseconds before he kissed me, full of passion.

I could spit in his face and cut his throat, I realized, and even to his dying breath, he would love me more than life itself.

Chapter Thirty-Three

Pensato

My vision was blurred, but I could still see the faint movement of rolling along my nose and cascading to the water's surface. I could have gotten goggles or trained myself to open my eyes more widely within the mineral water, but it didn't matter—more important than that was the feeling of simultaneous weightlessness and fullness. Finally, when my lungs burned and the stream of bubbles ended, I surfaced.

"Are you ready yet?" Lucia grumbled at my side, making a point to hold the pitcher of milk and honey within view. If Lucia had caught me leaving Zeno's room rather than my own that morning, she didn't say anything.

Regardless, she was acting oddly bitter.

I smiled at her and nodded. Lucia poured the pitcher, and I watched as the milk swirled around the tub and shrouded me in an opaque cloud.

"Do you think the other residence has a tub like this?" I asked. Hopefully some small talk could brighten her mood.

Lucia gave the water another stir for good measure, then replied, "I don't know. I've never been to any of the other houses."

"I guess we'll find out," I said, holding my arm out to her to scrub.

Lucia paused and gave me a strange look. "Didn't Duca de' Medici tell you? Signora Carbone and I aren't coming with you."

Under her harsh gaze, I couldn't help but pull my arm back against me and hug my legs. "I, uh, didn't hear about that," I admitted.

"Not even Doctor Ntumba is coming with you," Lucia said. "I don't like it, signorina. I have a bad feeling about this entire trip."

I gave her a weak smile. Her words were dark, but I refused to let them touch me. Not when I felt so happy for the first time in days.

"It'll only be for a few weeks. It should be fine."

Lucia went back to scrubbing me, and a painful silence hung between us for several minutes. Once she began to scrub my legs, she spoke once more, her voice now somber. "I've seen people around the abbey the past few days, signorina."

I pulled my legs back in and sank deeper into the hot water in an effort to stave away burgeoning goose bumps. I had seen them, too—glimpses, really, but I had seen them nonetheless. They were different from the others. As clear and realistic as the fleeting sights of my family were, they were clearly not real. Just like dreams upon waking, there was a clear disconnect from reality. In contrast, the silhouette I had seen in the moonlight yesterday, and the shuffling I had heard in the grass that morning, were very real.

No, I told myself. *That can't be true. They must be shadows from the abbey.*

"The Abbazia di Santa Dymphna shows you your ghosts," I said, echoing Signora Carbone's words from months ago. I wasn't sure if I was saying them to comfort Lucia or myself.

The bag on my shoulder was lighter than it had ever been. My day bag had traveled with me from Red Creek to London, London to Sicily, from Sicily to the Abbazia di Santa Dymphna. And now it would come from the Abbazia di Santa Dymphna to Puglia.

The inside of the bag was dented from the corners of books, and there was a pocket I had sewn in to hold pill bottles. The zipper always caught midway through its track, which was swollen from where it had been overstuffed with all of my clothes. Now my bag held only pill bottles, the bracelet Zeno had gotten me, and a few sundresses.

Pack lightly, Zeno had told me. *I'll buy you everything you*

need.

The roar of the private jet was starting up (who would have ever guessed I'd ride in one of those?), audible even through stone walls, and I could already imagine Zeno's impatient huffing at my delay. I rolled my eyes at the thought and quickened my pace.

I passed by his desk, and my eyes lingered as they usually did. It was human nature, I hoped, to be nosy, especially when I was accustomed to seeing pages full of lyrics and sheet music. I hoped they could be some precursor to the wondrous documents I would uncover.

This time, however, the desk was covered in something entirely different. Rather than loosely scrawled script, there were pages full of typed-out charts. I saw names, dozens of names, many of which I recognized. I remembered, albeit vaguely, many of the nobles from the ball. All of these names were attached to faces that had whispered and pointed at me, even outright jeered. The columns next to the names contained addresses, names and ages of family members as young as six, and names of their businesses and frequented areas. Some of this information was underlined, starred, highlighted, or otherwise annotated.

I stopped at the desk and flipped through pages in a desperate attempt to find some information that could explain these lists in a normal way, but as the pit in my stomach told me, there was no normal explanation. More pages revealed more names and more intel. Secrets and scandals.

Blackmail material.

Behind me, Urbino's familiar footsteps echoed through the halls, and before me, my shadow grew darker and shorter with the approaching light. Shit. I threw my head from left to right in the hopes that if I waited long enough, I would know what to do. The steps grew louder, and the light brightened. I was still shrouded in darkness, but only for a few more seconds.

In a panic, I clutched the papers close to my chest, then finally arranged them as closely to the position I'd found them in as possible.

Just as the footsteps were about to turn into the closest hallway, I managed to sneak off.

I rounded the corner, hugging the wall, then slid down until I was sitting. My ears pounded, and I closed my eyes as tightly as I could, forcefully suppressing gasps of air into shallow, quiet panting.

There is no normal explanation for those lists, I thought once more. *There is no normal explanation.*

Chapter Thirty-Four

Ecco, ridente in cielo

The inside of the private jet was nothing like I had expected, though I wasn't certain what those expectations had been. Its exterior was relatively straightforward—a white, striped plane that resembled most of the commercial airplanes I had seen. The inside, however, could have easily been mistaken for a business meeting area. Directly in the middle of the room was an oval-shaped coffee table, bound to a carpeted floor with a gold-plated base. The walls were paneled in wood, combined with gold accents and bejeweled lights overhead. A partition almost entirely obscured the inner workings of the cockpit, save a small window showing the back of his head.

Behind me, Zeno ducked into the jet and placed a hand on the small of my back. I jumped at his cool touch, as I had made the mistake of wearing an open-backed dress—or at least that was the excuse I planned on giving, anyway, when I saw the frown on Zeno's face after he shed his balaclava.

I rushed to sit in one of the chairs and buckled myself in immediately. Unable to access the portside chair beside me, Zeno sat on the opposite side of me.

"Not fond of flying, I take it?" he asked, placing a hand on my whitened knuckles.

That's what I'll tell myself, I thought, nodding to us both. *That's the only reason I feel sick and jumpy right now.*

Zeno scowled and grumbled to himself, "I knew I should have taken a larger jet for less turbulence."

Despite myself, I laughed and turned my hand to grasp his fingers. "Pfft. Spoken like a true plutocrat. I'm pretty sure I would get lost on anything larger."

He chuckled and gave me a sideways glance, a combination that never ceased to make my heart skip a beat, then rested his chin on his free hand and stared out the window. "We couldn't have that, could we?" he mused.

"Yeah. If I went missing, you'd get even more mopey."

"I am *not* mopey," he scoffed, tilting his head up with a grin. "I'll have you know I'm delicate and refined."

"Is that why—"

A harsh roar and an equally harsh motion cut off my words. My stomach lurched as we raced down the track and climbed into the air. I squeezed my eyes shut and hugged my arms to myself. Maybe if I shut them tightly enough, I could block out the blackness before it entered the periphery of my vision. Maybe if I grasped my arms closely enough, I could squeeze away the tingling before it pricked my fingers. But unfortunately, the ringing in my ears was audible above the rumbling of the jet, and I could sense the tightness deep beneath my skin.

Something bumpy and cold was pushed beneath my fingers. Opening my eyes, I ran the unknown object through my fingers. My bracelet.

I spun the beads slowly between my fingers, counting and breathing. My breath sounded loud in my ears, but as the ringing diminished and the spinning sensation stopped, I could notice changes. The engine reduced to a steady whir, and the plane itself was flying level.

My stomach churned once more, now from vague motion sickness rather than pure dread.

All this is worth it, I told myself. *All this is worth it to see what my destination holds.*

My shoulders fell away from my ears, and I forced out a shaky exhale. Though still slightly blurred, I could see Zeno still staring out the window, trying to look nonchalant. He usually did when panic attacks struck me, likely to not heighten my anxiety. Unbeknownst to him, the subtle quiver of his jaw, the irregularity of his breath, and the minuscule furrow of his brow brought me a strange comfort. He cared. Quietly, of course, but he cared.

I made the mistake of looking at him too long and glimpsed clouds rushing beside us. At the sight, I choked on nothing in particular and almost fell back into it.

"Five things you can see, Cora," Zeno's voice cut through.

I forced my eyes open. "Clouds. The vase. My bracelet . . ."

We worked through the entire exercise along with another, and by the end of them, the brief trip was nearing its end.

"I'm sorry," I murmured, giving Zeno's hand a small squeeze.

"For?"

I shrugged. "I don't know. Being like this, I guess?"

Zeno's gaze darkened, and he clenched my hand. "Don't apologize for an ounce of yourself. After all, I lo—" he cut himself off, growing beet red, and cleared his throat. "I, um, am fond of every aspect of you. Anyhow, you put up with my moods."

I lo—? It was impossible not to finish the sentence in my mind. I tried to tame my racing heart, to remind myself it was probably just a slip of the tongue.

But would it have been so bad if he said it? Would it have been a sin to have said even more?

"Thank you for helping me through this. It means a lot to me. *You* mean a lot to me, moods and all."

Just as I finished, the jet faltered, its wings catching, then forcing its way through a pocket of hot air. My stomach flopped as we began our descent, and Zeno squeezed my hands. "Five thi—"

"No," I said quickly. "I'm all right. Going down is kind of the opposite of the part of flying I hate."

He narrowed his eyes, overtly skeptical, but loosened his grip when my breathing evened out. He gave a small huff from his nose and smiled. "You make very little sense, you know. *This* is the part I despise. Then again, I suppose you've never landed in a private lane, have you?"

"What does that mean?"

"We're going somewhere rather remote, far out from any city. But I promise, the rough landing will be worth the destination."

I tried semisuccessfully to squint out the window at the rapidly approaching landscape. True to Zeno's word, the land was a plateau, mostly barren of houses, right along the coastline. Altopiano delle Murge, if memory served correctly, was the Italian name for this rocky coastal region.

I wondered where on earth we could land with all the olive trees and grass, but it was only a few more minutes before I found out. The jet circled around a few times, bucking irregularly as it caught pockets of hot air, then closed in on a loosely manicured gravel road.

We touched down on the rocky ground, and the jet jerked once violently, then evened out with the skillful hand of the pilot. My vision blurred for just a moment, but the shaking was over before I could go into anything.

Zeno gave my hand a small squeeze and pulled his balaclava back over his head as the jet whirred to a stop.

Sunlight poured in as the door opened, and Zeno held out his hand to me. "Are you ready to see where we're staying?"

Chapter Thirty-Five

Appoggiatura

"Oh."

The house itself was small, remarkably so. I knew the region was famous for its *trulli*—small, cone-shaped huts made of stacked limestone that historically housed rural peasants. Even so, I had become accustomed to the realm of the Italian nobility, with ornate columns and stained-glass windows in lieu of one-room, windowless dwellings that were theorized to be designed with tax evasion in mind.

Stranger yet, this *trullo* was the middle building of a cluster of three, and the *trulli* on either side of it were in different states of disrepair. The westernmost *trullo* was mostly reduced to rubble, with hoary roots embedded within it. The easternmost *trullo* had been more recently felled, but it had still been decades since it was in a livable condition.

I tried to hide both my disappointment and confusion, but they must have been evident, as Zeno laughed. "Just wait, *mia passerotta*," he said, giving my hand a small squeeze.

Despite its rustic exterior, the *trullo* had been outfitted with a modern set of locks, and it took Zeno quite some time to work through them all. As expected from a windowless, airtight hut, the inside was pitch dark. He entered without hesitation, and I did my best to follow his footfalls. Who knew what was in there, after all? There could be countless valuables to accidentally step on, or some tapestry to slip on.

A previously unseen lantern flickered on, impressively illuminating the entire interior. It was practically without decor—bare brick walls, untouched slab floors, and a simple cot within a curtained alcove. Would it even be large enough for the both of us? In the center of the room was a low, dusty coffee table that appeared on the verge of collapse over an equally disheveled rug.

Before doing anything else, Zeno locked the doors behind us—the digital lock, dead bolt, and two latch locks.

"Bit excessive, don't you think?" I muttered mostly to myself. "Not much to protect here."

Zeno chuckled and repeated, "Just wait."

He dropped his suitcase beside the door, got on his knees, and shoved aside the table. It overturned with pathetic ease, as did the chairs. I scampered back. "What are you—"

He threw aside the rug, revealing a large trapdoor. After entering a few numbers on yet another lock flush with the floor, it opened with a satisfying *pop*.

Zeno grinned up at me and gestured to the open door with a flourish of his hand. "Signorina, your destination awaits."

"Holy shit."

I peered down into the door, mouth agape. It was deep and dark, a pit of blackness only a bit larger than me, carved cleanly into limestone. A single ladder, old yet sturdy, was propped against the side, and it wasn't until Zeno held the lantern over it that I could even see its bottom about twenty feet down.

Despite growing up in the mountains, I was never good with heights, so I only felt reassured enough to enter when Zeno gave me an approving nod upon touching the ladder.

"I'll be right behind you," he said.

I gulped, ducked beneath the lantern, and descended. It was a surprisingly quick trip to the bottom

When my feet touched the ground, my lantern and concern were both rendered unnecessary. Dozens of ceiling lights flickered on, revealing a long, perfectly symmetrical tunnel, complete with decoratively carved reinforcements. The floor itself was embossed in a simple yet meticulously laid pattern; the curved walls were painted.

But questions remained, as the tunnel ended in a solid wall.

Zeno scaled the ladder quickly and hopped to my side. After giving my shoulder a squeeze, he walked in front of me, staring at the ceiling.

"One, two, three . . ."

Midway down the hall and midway through the twenties, he stopped and crouched. He trailed his finger along an unseen line on the wall, then pressed an inconspicuous divot.

With a hiss, a previously unseen entrance propped open.

Zeno gestured for me to follow him across the threshold.

I had come to know Italian wealth over the past several months—its good, its bad, and most of all, its beauty. There was the showy decor of houses that doubled as public exhibits, the celestial buildings of religious devotion, and now this: rustic luxury.

We entered a living room covered in countless exotic furs, mahogany wood, and plenty of landscape paintings. There was an enormous marble fireplace opposite a plush couch. For a moment, I wondered if it was for show, considering our underground dwelling, but the fine layer of soot outlining the stone proved otherwise.

Zeno leaned against the doorframe, his arm curved around its surface.

"There were fears among the Medici circa the nineteenth century that Italy may follow in the steps of France and have her own Robespierre emerge from the woodwork, hence the acquisition of this place." He gestured toward a chandelier in the middle of the ceiling. "I suppose they could have found a place to hide *without* spending millions to excavate, but I doubt they could have survived without a wine cellar or fine decor. Not that I'm complaining, of course."

I peered around and discovered two additional doors, both with their own locks. I neared one and could open it with relative ease, as the padlocks were already unlocked. The door creaked open, revealing yet another long hallway.

"How big is this place?" I asked, closing it.

"I would not be able to attest to that. I left the room to your left only on a few occasions during my stay. In truth, I know very little about this residence."

I looked at the door of the aforementioned room and noted that it differed from the others—scratched, with chipped paint. I fought the urge to look inside, somehow knowing it wouldn't be right to do so in his presence.

"I'm heading out," Zeno said.

"Huh?" My eyes fell to the floor. I mumbled, "Oh, you're leaving."

"I have some loose ends to tie up. I need to send off a few people to town for clothes, food—"

"By food, you mean chocolate," I cut in.

"Chocolate *and* wine, I'll have you know," he teased. "Regardless, I'll be back in a few hours." Though obscured by his mask, I could sense Zeno wore that crooked, bemused smirk of his. "Is that disappointment I see on your face?"

I felt my cheeks grow hot and put my hands on my hips. "So what if it is?"

"Careful, Cora. I might get an even bigger head than I already have."

I masked a smile with a huff. "Don't worry. I'll keep you humble."

"A job I wouldn't entrust to anyone else," he said, ruffling my hair. "The time will go more quickly if you look around a little. I'm relying on you to pick out some music, too, of course, as well as our next book."

A grin spread across my face. "We're going to keep reading together here?"

"Of course. Nothing gives me more pleasure, *passerotta*." He lifted his balaclava just enough to expose his lips, grabbed me by the chin, and planted a rough kiss on my forehead. "I'll be back soon. Don't leave the house, okay?"

I nodded, a bit taken aback but too excited to look around to ask questions. The moment he left, I eagerly began my search.

Chapter Thirty-Six

Stagione

As I soon discovered, each room felt different in design, and the house must have been steadily built from a hiding spot into a proper dwelling.

The hallway itself was far more lavish than the one that had brought me into *la cantina*. Its walls were covered with such intricate crimson-and-gold Moroccan wallpaper, I felt compelled to stop and admire it. Even more beautiful were the massive romantic landscapes and golden sconces between each door. I peered into the first room on the left, and upon seeing bookcases, quickly shut the door again. Who would eat dessert before dinner, and similarly, who would see the archives before the rest of the house?

The room beyond it was a straightforward dining room, decorated in traditional 1920s Italian fashion. Though small and rustic in feel, it housed a crystal chandelier, crystal glassware, a porcelain vase, and countless other fragile things that gave me the same swell of anxiety as the china section of an antiques store. Holding my breath and sucking in my stomach, I stepped around a Queen Anne dining chair and into a modern kitchen. Granite and steel surrounded me here, and I couldn't help but wonder if the stoves had ever actually been used.

Across from the kitchen and dining room was the master bedroom, a familiar sight. It carried the essence of Zeno's room at the abbey, a Renaissance-style bedroom with crimson and black, satin and lace. A single four-poster canopy bed with matching nightstands on either side.

I gulped. One bed. We'd be sleeping in one bed.

I stepped slowly in front of the vanity and stared long and hard in the mirror. This was the face he'd wake up to, and the small, slender body he'd hold at night.

One part of me was terrified of sharing a room so soon, while the other part wondered why it had taken so long.

I was deep in thought when I first noticed birdsong, so distant I almost thought I was imagining it. My attention went to the massive curtain covering the entire opposite wall. I crossed the room slowly, brow knitting, and took hold of the curtain. The cloth was heavy and thick, and I could not easily cast it aside. Instead, I had to swim into the dark curtains, only to be plunged into light.

Utter confusion stunned my muscles, and the curtain fell over my back. Before me was overwhelming light—*sun*light. I rushed out of the room and forced my way into the most tightly locked door of all, beside the bedroom. It gave with great effort, revealing an outdoor courtyard on the other side.

I realized *la cantina* had been built into a mountain, and this courtyard had been carved into its outer face. Much of the natural stone had been preserved in the outcrop, now fashioned into sculptures and the bases of topiaries. Local clay formed the pottery and vases which housed small but flourishing fruit trees and flowers. How the greenery had been so well-maintained on such a remote estate was a mystery, but something I appreciated nonetheless. It wouldn't feel like I was living underground.

A set of chirps greeted my arrival and drew my attention to the nest of sparrows in a persimmon tree. Now I wouldn't miss the finches or Leonore so much either.

I took a seat on a bench and breathed in the cool mountain air. A glass wall similarly partitioned the other side of the courtyard, but the sunlight made it impossible to see the interior. With no other option but to satiate my curiosity, I abandoned my place and went to examine this new room.

The bathroom consisted almost entirely of a modern open shower, with that half of the room formed of marble, except for the courtyard-facing wall. Instead of stone, two sliding glass panels made up the courtyard-facing wall of the bathroom, allowing the shower to open up to the outside. The first panel was clear, and the second was tinted, so vampires could shower while still being able to see the courtyard.

I was tempted to abandon my search then and there, to stand beneath the rainfall showerhead and let warm spring water flow over my body while watching birds flit across the mountains. Or perhaps I could sink into the whirlpool tub built into the stone itself and let the world wash away.

Both options sounded divine, yet neither of these earthly delights could overshadow my excitement for the penultimate room of the house: the archive.

The door to the archive had almost as many locks as the entrance to *la cantina* itself, but those had been unlocked for me by Zeno prior to his departure. I tossed aside padlocks and used all of my bodyweight to push the door open.

Based on the dust that permeated the air and covered the furniture, it was unlikely anyone had entered it since Zeno was a child. In the corner was a large desk and matching chair, but the rest of the room could more accurately be called archival storage than anything else. Floor-to-ceiling shelves were packed in tight rows with loosely organized documents and folders stacked on top of one another in small cubbies. The papers ranged from slightly yellowed to nearly falling apart, and I cringed to think of what would happen if book louse or mold were to enter this place.

I whipped out my phone and typed out a text to Zeno, knowing full well I'd have to wait until surfacing to for it to deliver:

I'm going to need a dehumidifier, pesticide, cleaning supplies, a respirator, and soejbewsdfg

The message had already been sent. I frowned and started another one.

Sorry, I sneezed. Anyway, all that and some notebooks and pens, STAT. xoxo

I erased the last four characters, pressed send, then pocketed my phone.

Even though I was too nervous to properly examine anything until I had my tools, I carefully stepped between the shelves to glance over what I would work with the next few weeks. Rather promising were several stacks of what appeared to be letters, so old they would have been dust by now if they hadn't been laminated. Beside them were several hand-bound notebooks stuffed with receipts, envelopes with old photos peeking out, and leather-bound books.

Tucked in the corner, on top of a shelf, was a dark box. It was cleaner than the rest of the room and had clearly been handled within the past few years. Despite my initial intention to deep-clean the room before touching anything, I was too curious to wait.

A ladder was necessary, but nothing in the room looked remotely trustworthy to stand on. Eventually, I settled on testing my luck with a shifty-looking crate in the corner. My stomach flopped, and I clutched onto the shelf as the crate wobbled beneath my feet. I took a deep breath and reached up but was still a bit too short.

Every bit of me knew how bad of an idea it was to continue, but I rationalized it by telling myself the sooner I got the box, the sooner I'd be out of danger.

The crate creaked and whined when I shifted my weight to stand on my toes and creep my fingers along the shelf's edge. Then finally—

"Oof!"

The box, far larger and heavier than expected, crashed into my stomach the second I slid it down, sending me toppling.

Against all odds, I landed on a pile of furs, but this did little to save me from pain. When I hit the ground, the corner of the box jabbed sharply into my sternum, knocking the wind out of me. Even with my body to cushion it, the box slipped through my fingers and the wood scratched against the side of my hand. It bounced off the floor with a hollow *thud* and disappeared out of view.

"Shit," I hissed under my breath. I touched a hand to my chest, then recoiled at the budding pain. A massive splinter about the size of my pinkie had implanted itself at an acute angle in the base of my thumb, sticking out like the quill of a porcupine.

I contemplated pulling it out in the archive itself but thought better of it. Even as a child, my parents had boasted about my high pain tolerance. Throughout most of my life, bottles of painkillers had remained unopened on my account. But I knew the truth even then: my pain tolerance itself was abysmal, but distraction was the most powerful analgesic of all. And of course, my greatest talent was the ability to abandon reality.

The blood and annoyance could wait.

Instead, my attention turned to the fate of the box itself. Up close, I could see it was clearly handmade, but I couldn't tell exactly how recently. Decades at least, if not centuries. The black paint was chipped, revealing some sort of hardwood and yellowed glue. I could only imagine how vibrant the portrait on top had been. It, too, was faded, but I could make out the pale-white figures of vampires crowded beneath the Medici crest.

The only modern thing was the nearly new padlock tightly bolting it shut. It was massive, with a twelve-letter code.

A quick tug showed it had been scrambled, and I didn't bother guessing any codes. College algebra told me I was looking at a billion possibilities if the letters were entirely scrambled. I dug into the wood around the hinges to reveal that a layer of metal was welded beneath it. Burning and forcing weren't options, it seemed.

Feeling a bit like a child on Christmas Eve, I shook the box next to my ear. The faint shifting sound suggested it was full of papers, photographs, or a mixture of the two.

I huffed and peeled myself off the ground. If I had merely heard the jingle of coins or jewelry, I would have given up on opening it, but now I wanted to look inside more than anything. I put the treasure back, then returned to the living room.

In my peripheral vision, I saw the door to the room where Zeno had stayed. Something about the old, chipped wood reminded me of the room I had spent the past half hour staring at. Any sort of clues would presumably be in the documents, but I felt better looking into this room with Zeno gone.

With a deep breath, I put my hand on the cold metal knob and prepared myself to look inside.

Chapter Thirty-Seven

Ostinato

I opened the other door and found a small, simple bedroom on the other side. The walls were a strange shade of yellow, the floor stripped of carpeting, and the room barren of the sort of decor that characterized the other rooms. The furniture consisted of a mostly gutted bookcase and a nightstand beside a single twin bed with linen sheets. All bolted down, just like the pair of shackles on the wall.

"Ah, so you've found my old room," a voice said behind me.

I gulped.

"I was unfettered during my stay," he stated calmly, as though needing to clarify such a thing was commonplace. "I largely opted to remain in here of my own accord."

Before I was able to say anything, our conversation abruptly halted. Zeno's gaze fell to the chunk of wood stabbing into me, and the nothingness in his countenance was replaced with pure horror. He dropped all the bags he was holding, causing produce to go flying across the room in a burst of color.

"Jesus, Cora!" he cried, grabbing my hand. "What happened?"

Now, with my wound in sight, my entire body ached, and I blubbered like a baby. "I—I fell, a-and—"

"Where else are you hurt?"

I pointed to my torso, hands, and back. In a swift motion, Zeno grabbed something from one of the bags, swept me off my feet, and carried me to the couch.

He sank quickly into the plush, and I sank into him. Zeno crossed over me with his arm to hold my wrist, tossed aside his jacket, and began scavenging through the box he had gotten. When his slender hand neared my own, I instinctively tried to pull away, but his grip on me was firm.

"Stay still," he ordered sternly.

I let out a pathetic squeal and blinked back tears as Zeno plucked it out of my hand and immediately pressed gauze to the wound. The pressure stifled the acuity of the pain, and I finally relaxed into him.

"Good girl," he said. "Let's get this washed now."

He led me to the sink and messed with something, back turned to me. The cold water brought back all the pain tenfold, and I bit my lip to hold back tears. The amalgamation of dirt, dust, and general grime all flowed off, and brown flooded the inside of the sink. I tried to watch Zeno from the corner of my eye, already suspicious of what was happening and already aware it was necessary when I looked back and the water was running red.

He neared me and smeared a cream on my hand. I didn't bother asking what it was, and the lidocaine's numbness set in soon enough. With my head hung low, I walked to the couch and curled up on it.

Zeno gave me a sad smile and nudged a table beside the couch with his foot. "So, you've parsed what's about to happen."

I stared into the cushion of the couch as a pair of nitrile gloves audibly snapped beside me, followed by the crinkling of unwrapping. I pinned my hand to the surface of the table and shut my eyes tightly. I recognized the sickening click of a needle holder grasping onto its target. It was easier to not look, to pretend the nearly imperceptible back-and-forth tugging on my arm was simply Zeno pulling on my hand rather than forceps grasping at the needle piercing through my skin.

In a shockingly short amount of time and surprisingly few clicks, there came a final, rough tug, followed by a snip. I slowly opened one eye, then another, to reveal a series of clean, even stitches across the wound.

I held my hand at different angles to marvel at his handiwork. "How did you learn how to do this?" I asked. "It looks almost professional."

Zeno glanced up at me briefly, then nonchalantly returned to cleaning up the supplies. "I've had plenty of practice on myself and Basilio. Who knows how many sets of sutures I've done? Noor taught us both when it became apparent they would be required, even in her absence."

"Were they . . .?" I couldn't finish the sentence, as my mouth was too dry, and the words were too sharp. He pressed a bandage over the stitches firmly, and I winced even though I couldn't feel it.

"If you're wondering if those wounds were self-inflicted," he murmured, sealing the border, "or afflicted on one another, the answer is no."

Something about his tone, which mirrored the strange calmness he'd displayed earlier, made me remember the shackles on the wall in his old room. I gestured with a shaking hand. "Does that room have anything to do with it?"

Zeno didn't bother to follow my motion and instead continued to gather up the trash. He replied, "In an abstract sort of way."

Frustration furrowed my brows. "What do you mean?"

He sighed with equal exasperation. "Cora, I do not think words suffice, and alas, I am quite poor with them when it comes to this topic. It was the sight of shackles that brought about this line of questioning, and it would be another sight that would best answer it."

"Then show me already!" I pleaded.

"As you wish." His fingers went to unbutton the collar of his shirt, and he worked his way down. I widened my eyes at the sight of his bare skin. "Wha—"

"You don't mind, do you?" he asked, gazing up at me through his lashes. "I'm trying to answer your question, you know."

Blood rushed to my face, and I tried to keep my thoughts chaste. To my combined confusion and relief, he turned his back to me as he finished the last few buttons. His shirt rippled to the ground, revealing lean musculature.

Despite how smooth and porcelain his skin was elsewhere, long, silver lines covered his back. They formed overlapping, jagged X's that crossed from the tops of his shoulders down to his hips, with an apex on the prominences. I touched them, and my fear was confirmed. They had the unmistakably silky texture of scars.

Some were deep, others raised, many were merely thin lines. All long-healed but likely years apart in origin. My heart sank.

"Basilio doesn't have quite as many as I do, and most of his are on his chest," Zeno said in a strangely lighthearted manner. "And of course, I must brag that his wounds were sutured much more cleanly than my own. He may have a way with words, but I've always been keen with a needle."

I was utterly speechless.

Zeno shrugged his shirt back on and stated, "I assume you still have questions."

No shit, I thought, but the words could not escape my mouth. Nothing could, not even my breath.

He chuckled, nearing me, and cupped my cheek in his hand. "Ah, Cora. You're so horrified already, yet I haven't begun to scratch the surface. Even so, you wish to know the context, the truth, and the foundations of my cruelty? It is a rather wretched truth."

Frustration broke through horror. "Isn't it obvious already? I want to know everything about you! I don't care how wretched!" I fought the urge to tear his shirt back off, to see the proof of a secret that had never truly been concealed.

He took a seat beside me. "What do you recall from what I told you of my past?" he asked, tone soft once more.

"I'm not sure," I muttered. "Everything you've told me, I suppose. I know you are a bastard and that you never knew your mother. I know you and Basilio were close as children, and now, for some reason, you are not." I halted for a minute, waiting for my words to be corrected or expanded, but Zeno gave me a reassuring nod. "I know your father brought you to the abbey when you were young, and that since then, you wanted to live there. And I know you were in love with Serafina Rosa Salviati—" At her name, silly jealousy burned within me, and I forced it back. "That's it."

That wasn't entirely true. I had seen how easily coldness came to him, and how difficult it was for him to exude radiance. But I had also seen that he *could* play the game with nobility, say the right words, and generally charm them. I had seen how hollow he was any moment he was not listening to music or looking at me. And of course, I knew he would die in an unknown number of years.

Zeno's eyes flickered across me, full of mixed emotions. "It seems you have the basics, *passerotta*. Shall we start then, from the beginning?"

Chapter Thirty-Eight

Vissi d'arte

"You guessed the origins of Enzo Armando correctly. Like myself, he was a bastard child secretly sired from the unholy union of blood relations. How else do you think this horrid combination of mutations that afflict me is possible? Whether my parents were siblings, or cousins, or mother and son, I do not know—and I do not wish to know. More importantly, none outside my immediate family would have ever guessed that the woman who raised me for the first few years of my life was anyone other than the woman who birthed me and raised me for a year before she, too, died."

The lidocaine had faded, but my fingers were number than ever. All of his words and even my own life felt fake right now. The incest, affairs, and secrecy all just seemed like more research into the distant past. But as soon as I placed my hand on his wrist, I could not deny that a racing pulse was coursing through it.

I remained silent, and he continued, "Unlike myself, Enzo Armando had the luxury of living in anonymity throughout his childhood. My father needed an heir, and despite living in our household, Basilio would not suffice. His own mother was a known adulteress, just as his father was a known philanderer. Speculation of his true parentage was a public pastime, and him being taken under my father's wing was the charity work of a demonstrably pious man. My father raised us both in the Vatican, after all, rather than Florence.

"As I'm certain you've discerned, both Basilio and I were mere tools for him—pawns in the game of noble politics. I never once questioned whether he loved me, as I knew he did not. An echo, probably, to his own upbringing. Frankly, I don't give a shit why he is cruel, and I never have. Love and joy were vague, foreign concepts to me, and nothing to really aspire for. Sometimes I forcefully emulated them, as with Serafina, but they were never true. Beauty and knowledge, on the other hand, were the best aspirations. I stopped trying to play the game early on—perhaps out of an inability to do so, and perhaps out of stubbornness. Perhaps out of spite for being birthed with all these aberrations, then being forced to waste the short life I was granted."

He took a slow, deep breath, and I knew by the quickening of his pulse beneath my fingertips this was the part he dreaded sharing most.

"For many years, the discipline—a seven-corded whip typically meant for religious self-flagellation—was the punishment of choice for my refusal to play along. The sin of sloth was usually cited. As it became evident that Basilio was an especially skillful puppet master in our preteen years, envy was the preferred rationale. My father had hope in me for a moment when it finally clicked. I discovered it *was* quite easy to say the correct thing at the correct moment, or turn people against one another with the simple power of knowledge. So many lovely symphonies I was able to attend! The intoxicating wine tastings, and the pleasure of social power. Then the sin attributed to my whippings became gluttony and greed, as I only bothered using social manipulation for my own Machiavellian gains. It got boring after that, you see, once I realized music could be listened to and chocolate could be eaten alone in my room, away from the annoyance of it all. My last few whippings were for wrath, and those were the ones that weren't stitched. I hope you never learn why those were given, or what I am still capable of. It was only a few occasions before my father decided it was far easier to groom Basilio into his heir than to domesticate me."

I clenched my fists and forced myself to stay still. Right now was not the time to make this about me, no matter how much I wanted to throw myself onto him and embrace him. I must have done a good job at concealing this, or else Zeno pretended not to notice, for his voice did not falter when he spoke.

"Shortly after that, I turned to religion for some sort of happiness, but of course, it brought nothing. I do not think I will ever see Heaven, you see, with what I truly am. What, then, would be the point of a life of asceticism in the priesthood, especially when it's full of politics as well? Sometimes I still prayed when I was able to convince myself that it had a purpose, that He could bring me

happiness." He slowly shifted away from me, pulling his hand back into his chest.

The eyes staring into me belonged to a being of strange contradictions. A scared child and a jaded old man. A blazing flame and frozen solid ice. An angel and a devil.

When Zeno spoke again, his voice wavered and cracked in a way I had never heard before.

"That's why I started praying again, Cora. Because when I found you, all of this suffering made sense finally. Every lash, every tear I tried so hard to shed, and even my own mortality. It was finally all worth it when I heard you laugh, when you ran your fingers through my hair, and when I drank from you the first time. I am aware I sound crazy, I am aware I *am* crazy, but it's the horrible truth. You are my sanctitude."

His voice had risen, a crescendo of volume and passion. My own was soft and gentle.

"I know, Zeno. I've always known, and it doesn't scare me."

"It should. It scares me. Before you, I've never wanted, or needed, or . . ." he trailed off and averted his gaze from me, trembling slightly. He shook his head as though to refuse the rest of the sentence, then, with some strange resolve relaxing his features, took in a heavy breath and forced it out. "Or loved."

How strange it was to have love declared to me in such a tone of guilt and defeat. How I knew such a thing could only come from this anomalous man, who had somehow managed to understand and treasure the entirety of my being. Who I cherished speaking with every day, who I trusted more than anyone, and who I wanted to share every moment and thought with.

Of course the darkness didn't matter. Of course the tragedy and isolation associated with living with such a man were irrelevant. Of course I didn't care that he would die decades before me.

I moved so I was sitting in his lap, my forehead pressed against his. I slid my hands beneath his shirt, and embraced him with my skin flush against his scars. "I love you, Zeno."

He embraced me tighter and pulled my head into the crook between his neck and shoulder. I wouldn't tell him that despite his effort to hide them, I still felt his tears roll onto my cheek.

"I love you too," he said. "I have for so long."

I gently peeled him from me. His cheeks still felt sticky when I kissed him, but his lips tasted as sweet as ever.

He cupped my cheek with one hand and put his other on the small of my back. In turn, I grasped the back of his shirt, but when Zeno pulled away to catch some air, I became more impatient. The warmth that emanated through his shirt wasn't enough. I wanted to feel the closeness of skin on skin.

I slid my hands beneath the fabric, and once they reached the ridges of scars beneath his shoulder blades, he tensed.

We've been through this, I said by catching his bottom lip in mine. *I love you regardless.*

He kissed me harder and faster. His hands traveled down my body and found a comfortable spot on my waist. It was all the leverage he needed to press my hips against his and make me feel impatient in another way entirely. I became more liberal with my hands and lightly bit his lip.

Zeno pulled away, grazed his teeth along my earlobe, and sent a shiver along my spine as he whispered, "You're a wicked little thing, *mia passerotta*. How pure and chaste I promised to be with you, yet here you are, making me do this again."

"I have no clue what you mean," I whispered back with a grin. "Why don't you show me?"

"It would be my pleasure."

Chapter Thirty-Nine

Messa di voce

S*nap.*

"Ugh."

Still seated on the floor, I straightened out my legs and tapped my ankles several times to restore a bit of blood flow to them. A pang of pins and needles rewarded my efforts, and I resigned myself to sitting on the ground a while longer.

Dozens of documents were fanned out in front of me on the floor, each in various stages of notation. Empty pens punctuated the border, freshly drained of ink. As indicated by the graphite smears on the side of my hand, I had switched to pencil after having to run back and forth for new pens, but this had proven problematic in its own right. *At least*, I thought as I dusted up shattered lead, *this is all for a good reason.*

After another experimental tap resulted in tingling in the tips of my toes, I hobbled to my feet and went to fetch a dustpan. It had taken me several days to touch many of the papers; those that were deliciously yellowed and musty in that strangely aged yet timeless manner all but told me outright they were unarchived relics. I had been cautious about transferring them to the scanner Zeno fetched me, but it was all worth it now.

Upon entering the kitchen, my stomach gurgled, and the fridge called to me immediately. I took a large gulp of cold water and it hit the back of my mouth, as searing as vodka. Yet another punishment for neglecting my body. I wished I could say the reason for skipping meals was all passion driven, but I knew a substantial part of it was that I had become horribly reliant on Signora Carbone's cooking.

I grabbed a handful of chips, shook out the last of the numbness, and strode to the window. I started to untuck the blackout curtains, then abandoned the task immediately. What would greet me on the other side, besides an empty courtyard? Only once had I seen anyone out there—a flash of Urbino. Not even birds flitted about anymore. For all I knew, I was in the middle of some masterfully crafted set.

How many days had it been? How many hours? I glanced at my phone for some clarity—12:37—but was surprised to realize I didn't know whether this was past noon or past midnight. I counted on my fingers, and found that I knew, at the very least, I had been spending my time in the archives for two weeks.

I hadn't left *la cantina* other than to go on walks or explore on foot, and Zeno never expected me to join him on his various excursions. I was a homebody and reading in the courtyard and taking open-air showers was enough for me on most days. Zeno, therefore, delegated himself the task of going on errands for the both of us.

Increasingly, I saw the car drive off into the distance just far enough for his phone to access cellular connection, but whatever phone calls he was making were incredibly brief. As of late, other cars from town had met him to deliver food, amenities, and a terse exchange of words. I didn't bother to ask what was going on; in truth, I was far too distracted in my world and our shared world.

I considered going outside to reorient myself but instead stuffed the chips in my mouth and trod back to the study, dustpan in tow. In the pursuit of knowledge, time had proven meaningless. I was so close, I could taste it. Whatever was in that box, I sensed, was the key to all the secrets the family held.

I reviewed my work once more. To the untrained eye, I had tossed the documents around carelessly, but I knew the order of the chaos. Four segregated areas of documents. Front and center were a highly annotated set of letters between Ferdinando and La Bambagia beside photocopied diary entries. Ferdinando often wrote his journal free-form, and trying to chronologize various entries with these letters had proven to be a challenge in its own regard. Then there were some old family photos with loose captions scrawled on the backs, many of which were relevant and many of which would make

for little more than pretty decor.

I briefly scanned over the set of documents to the right of all this. An old report card from the 1970s, notes between high-school sweethearts from the 1940s. Precious ephemera, sure, but not relevant to my work. After tidying up my snapped pencil, I noted their contents on a folder and slid them into it. I focused on the contents in the left pile, sorting them into the center and right based on theorized utility. With the left freshly emptied, it was time to refresh my four groupings—leads, possible leads, probable dead ends, and things to assign into the above categories.

I returned to the corner of the study, where I had left off, dustpan still in hand. I had just cleared off a shelf, and it was the least I could do to tidy up a bit. Though more successful at scattering the dust than gathering it, my handiwork had revealed something I hadn't noticed before: strange indentations on the back wall of the shelf. I squinted at it for a bit and ran my finger along the edges to no avail. Then, just as I was about to give up, I remembered what was in the dustpan. With the end of my fresh pencil, I ground up some of the broken lead into a coarse powder. I coated my finger in the graphite, then smeared it over the writing. With the carvings contrasted with the darkness, it was easy to read now:

Festina lente.

Make haste slowly. The family motto of the Medici.

The omniscient phrase was scratched grotesquely into the wood, as if by a pocketknife. I didn't recognize the handwriting at all—it wasn't the flowery, slanted hand of Zeno, nor was it the quick writing of Doctor Ntumba. Despite being carved out with a knife, it was uncannily square and soulless, as if produced by a monospace typewriter.

Why would the family motto be written here?

My ears had been poised to expect the sound of feet on a ladder, so it cut through all of my thoughts when I heard it. I physically and mentally tossed aside what I was doing and ran to the door.

"Zeno!" I cried, rushing toward him with a grin.

How he had learned to climb down the ladder with bags in his hand was a mystery to me. Luckily, his feet had already touched the ground by the time I arrived, and he allowed me to take a few of

them in my arms and rush them inside more quickly. I set them on the kitchen island with a huff and looked inside. "Did you get everything?"

An astonishing number of bags joined the ones I had brought in, answering my question.

"I certainly hope so. You know, you don't have to cook for us, *passerotta*. I am more than happy to have dinner brought to us."

"I know," I said with a smile. "I like cooking for you, though."

It feels domestic, like we're really a couple.

"I'm certainly not complaining." He returned my smile with one of his own and smoothed my hair. "It's not as if I can find Robert 'n' dumplin' soup anywhere in Italy."

My face burned, and I feigned annoyance as I poured chicken broth into a pot. "That's a low blow, considering you don't leave a single drop."

Zeno scoffed and did not riposte any further. Perhaps he knew *I* had the high ground here. Instead, he set a stalk of celery onto a cutting board and attempted in vain to puzzle what knife would be appropriate to chop it.

"I don't want you chopping your finger off." I nudged him away toward the hallway. "Go and pick out our music for tonight."

"So you're requesting that, instead of doing manual labor, I listen to music?" With a crooked smile, he tilted his head toward me. "My, what a dreadful thing you ask of me, Cora! How shall you repay me?"

I rolled my eyes but couldn't help but smile as well. "Isn't the soup enough?"

Zeno playfully scoffed, "For *my* musical expertise? No earthly pleasure is comparable."

I brought the produce to the sink, and I shot him a coy look over my shoulder once I began to wash them. "No earthly pleasure, huh? I'll remember you said that."

"That isn't what I—" His entire face turned red in an instant. "You *know* my weakness, you wicked little thing!"

I grinned and began to peel the carrots. "And what would that be?"

Zeno brought himself so close, I could feel his body heat emanating onto my back. "I have but one, and it's one I refuse to let you forget."

The steam rolling out of the pot probably would have cooled my face down.

"En-enough of that," I stammered. "I need to cook."

"All right, all right." Zeno grinned his tilted grin and returned to his station at the island with his chin up, having successfully enacted his revenge. "What is the occasion I'm selecting music for tonight?"

I bit my lip, now flustered for a different reason. "It's kind of embarrassing, but I'm afraid I'll get too excited and read ahead of you in *Madame Bovary*, so I thought we could talk about the most recent chapter tonight instead of tomorrow."

In my peripheral vision, I could see Zeno rest his chin on his cheek dreamily. "I should have known that would be the case, considering how you discussed it this morning."

"Was it that obvious that I liked it?"

"Yes," he answered seriously. "You were enchanting."

The tension in the room peaked, and despite the heat, I was frozen. To my side, the broth gurgled with the beginnings of a boil. I quickly returned to preparing vegetables. "I think something from *Carmen* would be fitting. Not that I'm trying to tell you what to pick or anything. Um—you should go now."

"As you wish, signorina." Zeno returned to his feet, and I returned to an efficient chopping beat. "I guess I have two weaknesses." He chuckled to himself, leaving for our little library. "How troublesome."

Chapter Forty

Vesti la giubba

The morning was beautiful, so beautiful it felt like a sin to spend it indoors. I peered beyond the curtain, watching voluminous clouds roll through the sky. It was never truly cold in this part of Italy, so it was a wonder every plant and animal knew it was spring. Even through the glass, I could practically feel the gentle yet crisp breeze glide over my skin and smell the flowers in early bloom.

The shower door slid shut just loud enough for me to hear, and I quickly jumped back from the curtain. All at once, the delightful sunlight vanished, leaving only the dull, yellow, artificial lighting.

Zeno entered the room with a towel tied around his waist. Without thinking, my eyes trailed across him, causing him to smirk. I immediately looked away, face burning.

He burst into laughter, sweeping on a plush robe. He tied the sash loosely, much of his white skin still entirely exposed.

"There, better?" he asked, plopping down on the bed and lying with his head resting on his hands.

"Just hurry up and get dressed already!" I grumbled, heat lingering on my cheeks. "I want to talk about the next chapter."

"What, will the robe have you distracted with unchaste thoughts or something? Or must I finally charge you a fee for a proper figure painting?"

I contemplated throwing my book at him but opted to glare instead, eliciting another melodic laugh.

"Fine, fine," he crooned, making his way to the dresser.

I wish you weren't so pretty sometimes, I thought, stealing a glance at him in those few seconds before he slipped the shirt on. I wished desperately that just once, I could see him outside during the day, that I could draw his entire body immersed in the essence of spring and paint the way the daylight highlighted every muscle and curve. That I could just walk out the door with Zeno and have faith he wouldn't die long before me.

I let out a sigh without thinking, and Zeno immediately homed in on it, turning to give me an inquisitive look.

"It's nothing," I said before he could ask, forcing a weak smile. "I'm just impatient, is all. I, uh—I'll go heat up some tea and wait in the dining room."

Without waiting for a response, I quickly left the room. I splashed some water on my face and put our usual kettle on the stove.

It wasn't a possibility, not for us. But even though it was such a simple, inescapable reality, it didn't feel any better.

With the glowing orange fire beneath it, the water heated almost immediately. I had scarcely stepped to the other side of the room when the kitchen became filled with steam and the strangely pleasant singing of a harmonica teakettle. As if compelled by its melodic peer, the smaller pot of milk also began a light boil. I quickly got to work, pouring the steaming water over Earl Grey tea bags and breathing in the satisfying smell of bergamot. I frothed the milk and poured it over as skillfully as I could, which wasn't very. Even with the mess of semifrothed milk all over the countertops, the mere presence of my slapdash London Fog made me feel better.

Walking slowly so as not to lose a single drop, I carried both mugs to the dining area and put them in our respective places.

Zeno was still getting dressed in the bedroom. Even though it was just the two of us at home, he never neglected to properly groom himself. Just as I was meant to wear whatever dress he had picked out for me, he always took the time to iron his pants, comb his hair, and properly fold his shirt cuffs. Whether this was due to the propriety cultivated in childhood, Zeno's own flair for panache, or a combination of the two, I did not know. All I knew for certain was that I would have ample time to gather my thoughts and orient them toward our future conversation.

Just as I settled into my mind, I heard a noise I hadn't in weeks: a knock on the door.

The mug in my hands suddenly felt searing, and every other noise felt loud, including my own irregular breathing. The mere act of standing felt as though I were breaking out of my skin. Everything about this felt strange and wrong. I knew each door of this place had copious locks for a reason, that we were in the absolute middle of nowhere. And yet with how calm the knocking had been—barely audible, from where I sat—I couldn't help but hope it was Lucia or Noor.

I considered waiting for Zeno, but the siren's song had grown too powerful. I didn't think I had it in me to wait for Zeno to put on his sun-protective gear. Setting aside my drink and caution, I crept into the hallway and climbed up the ladder. The trapdoor opened and shut silently when I emerged, and my own footfalls were inaudible. If I wanted to, I could go back without being detected.

You should just go back anyway. Someone being out here is ridiculous. Nothing good can come of it.

I sighed to myself and reached for the trapdoor again but froze immediately. Behind me—three more raps, softer than the first.

No matter how conflicted I was, I felt compelled to answer. "Hello?" I called, approaching.

No response.

I cupped shaking hands around my face and repeated, "Hello?"

I was met with a further trio of wraps. I tiptoed closer, pressing my ear against the door and holding my breath.

I could hear heavy breathing on the other side. I braced myself for another knock but instead met something entirely different: footsteps fading into the distance.

I listened for several moments longer, and none returned. My shaking hand rested on the doorknob.

I opened the door and screamed at the top of my lungs.

In front of me was a dove, cleanly decapitated. Blood still fresh across white feathers, wings folded neatly across its breast and tied with a ribbon. Her head—for I knew this bird—was at her side

atop a silver platter, a fan of rose petals beneath her. Her feet were still twitching, and as I discovered upon collapsing to my knees and picking her up, her body was still lithe and warm.

"What the fuck?" I repeated in alternating whispers and screams. "What the fuck?"

I pressed Leonore's head against her body. They fit together perfectly. She looked so at peace, eyes closed loosely, beak slightly ajar, feet curled into her. But when I let go, everything fell apart again.

At the sight of her head tumbling onto the ground, I broke into hoarse, painful sobs.

"Cora?!" Zeno bellowed from the bedroom. Footsteps thundered behind me.

I dropped her body on the ground, staggered back, and slammed the door shut to protect Zeno from the light, then I fell onto my back.

At the sight of me lying supine with semicoagulated blood covering the front of my chest, Zeno grew even paler than I knew possible. He gaped at me, and we were both frozen.

"It's not—" I had to force the words out of my trembling lips and pointed to where I knew the body was. "It's not my blood."

Each of his muscles loosened, though only slightly. "Are you hurt?"

"N-no." A flashbulb memory of Leonore's head as it rolled away struck me, and I brought my hands to my face. It was already sticky with tears and snot, and now grime and blood joined it. "I'm not."

It felt like a lie and the truth all at once. I smeared away what little I could with my sleeve, and when I looked back at Zeno, I was horrified to see him staring at the door with a look of resolve. He was going to go outside in the middle of the day in cloudless Florence without a shred of protection. If I didn't stop Zeno, he would burn irreparably within seconds. He looked composed, utterly at peace as he spoke with a gentle smile to the door.

"I'm going to rip his fucking throat out."

My shoes squeaked against the floor as I tried and failed to scramble to my feet. I gasped in a mouthful of air, just enough to scream out, “Zeno, no!”

To my relief, he faltered, but his hand remained glued to the doorknob. I crawled on my knees toward him and pulled desperately at his clothes.

“Zeno,” I said, doing my best impression of him that night in the church. “Please stay.”

He joined me on the ground and wrapped me in his arms.

“I’m sorry,” he whispered into the top of my head. “I’m so sorry.”

Chapter Forty-One

Soggetto cavato

That night, I dreamed of her. The dream itself was vague, more abstract than a full experience. Flickers of light combined with the scent of flowers and sweet tea in some unknown time. She and Zeno were both vivid, though—every feather, every pore, like I could touch them. In my dream, she was together, alive, and breathing. It was like those early days in the aviary, when she startled at my every movement and watched me closely. But no matter how wary, Leonore was happy. And holding her in his hands, so was Zeno.

Beside me, across the veil of sleep, the real Zeno shifted beside me in bed. I tried desperately to go back to that place and could for a few wonderful minutes. Then my mind drifted across the events of the past few days and lingered momentarily on the carvings in the bookshelf.

Festina lente. The words entered my mind the minute I opened my eyes.

I was able to restrain myself enough to sit up slowly in bed. I immediately shielded my eyes, as the bed was covered in sunlight, the curtains having been opened. The smell of slightly burned pancakes wafted into the room, but it was faint and old.

Squinting, I leaned over to peer out the window and saw the light had taken on the orange hue of dawn.

Zeno must have left a while ago, and given the sun protection he would have had to wear to open the curtains, he would be gone a while longer.

When I brushed against a piece of paper, all of my sleuthing became irrelevant. It was covered in the unmistakable flowery script of Zeno—one of his morning love letters that kept me company when he left for a day trip.

Cora,

I mourned not being able to share the day with you, or see the look in your eyes this morning when you awoke. I curse that I cannot see you shine as you speak about our books. I may have departed, but my heart remains with you. I will come back to you soon to fetch it in exchange for kisses. Please keep it safe, and smile while I am gone.

I love you.

—Zeno

P.S. Sorry I burned the pancakes. I tried my best.

If not for the enthusiasm coursing within me, I would have probably taken the letter with me and eaten pancakes. Instead, I roughly pulled a dress over my nightgown and raced to the archive.

The stool wobbled and threatened to overturn when I leaped onto it, but the risk of toppling over was one I was willing to take. I grabbed the box and pulled it into my chest, and the movement was enough to stabilize me. I let out a breath and slowly climbed down with my treasure.

I rushed to the living room, placed it on the rug, and sat cross-legged before it. The dials resisted against my fingers initially, but each one slowly turned.

F-E-S-T-I-N-A

I moved onto the next set, which was equally stubborn, but similarly gave in.

L-E-N-T-E

Click.

"Holy shit," I whispered. "It actually worked."

Slowly, gingerly, I slid my finger into the crevice of the lid. Though the hinges were slightly rusted, it opened all too easily.

As I had suspected, the old box was full of photographs and

papers. I dumped them on the floor and rifled through. Photographs, dozens of them, from different time periods.

Even at a glance, a pit fell into my stomach. These photos featured harsh lighting, askew subjects, and blurred focus. They were clearly candid, to put it nicely. I held one up to the light.

It was a moonlit portrait photo of a woman smiling over her shoulder beneath a large willow tree. The woman was beautiful, pale and delicate as a porcelain doll, with wavy, white-blonde hair and crimson, doelike eyes. Her stomach was strangely bulbous on her slender frame. Upon her full lips was a crooked smile, showing a single fang.

I did not know this woman, but I knew her smile. It was one I saw every day.

I flipped it over and discovered the photograph was dated from early September, almost three decades back. *Dolores with child.*

I recognized that name, but it took me a bit to register from where. Dolores d'Orléans, a famous theater actress who had faded into obscurity after a few plays. But I knew her mostly as a member of the Medici family—and half sister to the current head of the family.

The photo slipped through my fingers and fluttered to the ground.

I quickly grabbed another one, which showed a face I knew very well. A school-aged Zeno was beside his cousin in some sort of fancy Italian building. Zeno sat on a piano bench with a trophy almost as large as himself in his lap. He was blank and unsmiling, as icy and stony-faced as I had seen him. Next to him was Basilio, grinning broadly despite the much smaller trophy in his arms. Behind both, staring with watchful eyes, lingered Signore Urbino. *Cousins in competition*, read the caption on the back, in that small, square handwriting I assumed belonged to Zeno's father.

I pulled yet another one from the pile. This one featured no caption, only a date from a decade and a half ago. Signora Carbone, with a toddler Lucia waddling toward her. I had never seen her smile like that before. With a similar smile finally gracing my lips, I looked at another photograph.

It was crudely taken, with fingerprints on its edges indicating it had been roughly pulled from the camera far before the image set. The photo itself was shaky and slightly crooked, but what it showed was unmistakable: a man in a suit, lying in an uncomfortable position on the ground. But based on the fresh bullet holes in his head and chest, and the even fresher blood pooling at his throat, he probably didn't care. The only brightness in the photo came from his eyes—downturned, baby blue, and horrifically empty.

Bile stung the back of my throat and my stomach lurched, but I swallowed it roughly and winced at the burn. I squinted through tears to discern anything other than a corpse. Part of the caption was scrawled across the photograph itself—some coordinates and a name I did not recognize.

On the back, in that same tight script, was only one word: *First.*

I'd had enough of the photographs. I couldn't stomach them any longer, couldn't bear to see whether the reminders showed corpses or memories.

Convincing myself I didn't see the others, I shifted my focus to papers. I discovered doctored ledger papers, quickly scrawled maps of unknown purpose. And worst of all, stapled packets with names on them.

I was struck with the memory of the list I had seen on Zeno's desk, as well as the realization that doing such a thing had come so easily to him.

I rifled through them, and one stuck out immediately: *Noor Ntumba.*

A trio of candid, stealthy portraits of her taken decades ago, per the date scrawled on the bottom of the photograph that had been taped above more recent photos. All of them had been clearly taken without her knowledge and were attached to pages of information on all of her children and distant relatives, and every address she had lived at. Every client she had worked with. Warrants for her arrest in various countries. Beneath it, several informal contracts.

My hands trembled so violently that the papers became a horrid blur, and my mouth grew painfully dry.

I squinted past the blur as best I could, picking out snippets.

Duca Zeno Giovanni de' Medici is to be the exclusive patient of Noor Ntumba.

During employment, full international amnesty shall be granted, but upon dissolution . . .

Then, a sentence that made my heart stop.

Administering physician-assisted suicide to patient Zeno Giovanni de' Medici is a mandatory action should 1. It be determined via a combination of physician examination, laboratory findings, and third-party pathologists that the patient's condition is terminal, and 2. The patient request it.

Physician-assisted suicide. So that was her unusual specialty.

A pair of ambling footsteps neared, the unmistakable cadence of my other half, as light and casual as ever. I whipped around to face him.

"Hello, *mia passerotta*," he said, smiling as warmly as usual. "What are you—"

"Zeno!" I cut in, gesturing to the mass of photos and documents. "What is all this?"

With a confused frown, Zeno knelt and examined the photos. He barely had to rifle through them to come to a conclusion. He met my eyes and spoke, evenly and slowly. "Where did you find these?"

Words eluded me. I gestured toward the box, which had been tossed aside, then pointed to the library.

He followed my motions, darkening by the second. "So that's what that month here was for. My father was tying up some loose ends from afar. But what . . ." Zeno's words petered out, for he discerned the answer from the trembling papers in my hand. He took them from me and flipped through them quickly, then shifted around the photos and documents on the floor. "Oh, how touching. So while he was arranging my death, Father did make me my own box," he said bitterly. "I guess he does care after all."

A horrified combination of a laugh and a "What?" escaped me. At my expression, Zeno softened and reached out to place a hand on my shoulder. I flinched—and he utterly unraveled at the gesture.

"Oh, Cora." Zeno slowly rose to his feet and walked off. I raced after him and grabbed him by his wrist, but he pulled away.

"You don't understand," he said through gritted teeth. "This is me. This is my blood."

I grabbed his hand. How fragile it felt in my fingers, yet how powerfully it was clenching. "What makes you think you're anything like your family? You're nothing like—"

He looked up at me, gaze darkening more than I had ever seen before, his eyes shooting icy daggers into me. "Your ghosts are gone. They've been gone."

Eyes wide, I took a step back, then another, until I had backed into the wall. For several seconds, all I could do was shake my head. The people Lucia had seen, that I had seen since our *ritus sanguinous*—they weren't our ghosts at all, but flesh and blood.

"So what I saw around the abbey . . ." I whispered.

"Men. My men. I had them patrol around the abbey, at least two keeping watch of you at all times you were alone."

"What?" My voice was weak, strength having vanished from my entire body. My legs gave out, and I slid down the wall. "Why would you do that?"

Zeno neared me slowly with his hands raised, as though I were some rabbit on the verge of flight. The way my heart was racing, he was likely not mistaken.

Once he was within arm's length of me, he lowered to his knees, and I drew my legs into my chest. "I do not trust Basilio, or any of my family, for that matter. Least of all, my father. I cannot trust men with the same blood as me boiling in their veins. I thought you'd be safe here, but clearly, I was wrong."

"Wrong? Surely they wouldn't harm me."

The words I spoke carried no weight behind them. They were, if anything, more of a desperate plea for reassurance. When Zeno gazed into my eyes and clenched his jaw, I knew it was a solace that would be denied.

"I know their cruelty firsthand. I have felt it in every sense of the word. You have seen the contents of the box. You have seen my scars. My father's hand has been behind them all." He slowly reached forward and caressed my cheek, sending a chill down my spine. "To them, you are little more than one of my birds. And when it comes to you, Cora, I am little more than a rabid dog. I shall act accordingly."

“What are you planning on doing?” I managed to ask through quivering lips.

“I intend to do what any beast does to the vermin that nears its treasure,” he replied with a warm, sweet smile. “If they dare touch you, I will tear them limb from limb.”

Chapter Forty-Two

Ch'ella mi creda

Superficially, things between us remained the same for the next few days. We didn't speak of any of it again—not of the contents of the box, not of his morbid words, not even of Leonore. We had our usual conversations and our usual banter. He brought me trinkets and clothes and sweets and fancy dinners from town. He held me close in his arms and whispered sweet words to me in bed every night.

I still cooked for him. While I was in the abbey, my hands had become soft and my technique poor, but I had luckily regained some of my former skills. The *trullo* felt the safest when I cooked, like I was in an entirely innocuous summer home. But when I caught glimpses of the scar on my hand from where the box had impaled it, the illusion was shattered.

Even if I couldn't see the scar, the shadow that had overcome our household of two was undeniable. There was a tension beneath all of Zeno's actions, and I became anxious whenever I was alone, which was becoming more frequent. Zeno left the house often, but for only minutes or, at most, an hour at a time. When he returned, there was always a strange weight upon his shoulders. I had plenty of chances to ask what he was doing, but I never did. He always brightened when asking me about my day, and I didn't have it in me to deny him that bit of relief.

At one point, I wanted to go with Zeno into the city and go to a bookstore, hoping it would hearken back to old times. I wished for little domestic dates with him, those which the *trullo* had stolen from me: walks in the park, boat rides, even just grocery shopping. But when I proposed such an idea, I saw his jaw tighten, his eyes following an imaginary line to where I had discovered Leonore's

body.

It wasn't the *trullo* that had stolen those small, prosaic dates from us, I remembered, but the Medici name that had lured me into this world in the first place.

"Not now," he said. "But soon. It will be safe enough soon."

I forced a smile and forced myself to remain optimistic, if not for Zeno's sake, then for my own. I didn't want to dig into the archive anymore, partially because I had everything I needed to support my thesis, but more because I was terrified of what I could find.

Unfortunately, that meant plenty of free time once I finished reading all the novels I had brought with us and run out of drawing supplies. Upon realizing this, Zeno furnished the corner of our bedroom into a small library, which comforted me quite a bit. He filled its shelves with a delicious variety of novels and provided me with plenty of canvases and paint. To my great joy, I began to paint Zeno again, often at night.

One of these nights would be my downfall.

Spring had fully ripened, and the flowers in the courtyard were fragrant in full bloom. The bushes, ever thriving, had become a pleasant challenge to maintain, growing every which way. I circled one of them to decide the best way to prune it while sparing every flower. However, the vibrant azalea consisted more of blossoms than leaves, and it was with a heavy heart that I acknowledged there was no way to spare them all. But how was I meant to choose a sacrifice when every bloom had such an elegant blush and spiced aroma?

I took a step back and noted that the shadow of the plant had grown longer and the tiles had taken on an orange hue. With a smile, I turned to the setting sun and thanked it for prolonging my choice. *It's too dark to see well enough to prune*, I argued to my nonexistent detractors. I set my gardening shears aside and plopped beside my satchel to retrieve my sketchpad from its innards. I flipped to a loose sketch of Zeno from behind and filled in his figure with enough detail to become the base of a watercolor. Once it took form, I tilted the pad toward the skyline to imagine how the orange and pinks would play along his shoulder blades and glimmer in his hair, how the low sun would reflect on the edges of the scars revealed by the linen shirt I had chosen.

With a huff, I slammed it shut again. I hadn't gotten the curls at the nape of Zeno's neck correct, and no amount of collecting eraser dust would help. I tucked the sketchpad beneath one arm, carried the satchel with the other, and held the pencil in my teeth.

My model waited for me in the bedroom, sitting at a desk with his head curved slightly over a book. From where I stood, the angle and pose were utterly perfect. Even candlelight was hitting him at just the right angles.

The pencil hit the ground with my satchel when I opened my mouth to order, "Don't move!"

Once I saw Zeno freeze per my command, I gathered my supplies and quickly got to work. The curls that had eluded me moments ago proved easy to capture, but now that he was in front of me, I realized I had gotten the borders of his scars all wrong. Squinting for that extra bit of detail, I neared Zeno, only to find the hues I had hoped to evoke were already present. The outer perimeters of large, yellow splotches freckled in reds and blues peeked out from his collar.

Were those . . . bruises?

How long had it been since he had drunk from me or had any sort of blood replacement? I counted the days on trembling fingers once, then again, getting two different numbers. I didn't bother with a third time. Both numbers were far too large.

"When was the last time you got blood?" I demanded.

Zeno didn't turn to me or give any sign he had heard me, but his forced stillness was evidence enough. I forced my hands under his arms and reached around his body. Zeno stiffened at first, then resigned himself to being cooperative as I unbuttoned his shirt and tore it off.

It was the first time I had seen his bare body in the light in weeks. A body which I thought I could have sculpted by memory, which I thought had been fully impressed upon my brain. How hadn't I noticed before?

Beneath paper-thin skin was purplish-brown mottling. Bruises at various stages had pooled into a yellow gradient on his torso in a way that was impossible to produce with any sort of blunt trauma, and tiny fireworks of red bloomed from burst capillaries. I

had seen such bruising once before on my mother, when her liver stopped producing clotting factors.

Just before she died.

Air rushed out of my chest, producing a staggered, horrified exhale. With my vision blurring and hot tears already forming, my arm was little more than a violently shuddering line in front of me. Depth perception rendered nonexistent, I overshot, fingers pressing into a fleshy spot beneath his shoulder blades. He recoiled at my touch, the first acute movement he had made since he returned.

"I wish," he whispered, tugging his shirt back up in a movement as sharp as his tone, "that you didn't paint me so many times. Maybe then you wouldn't have noticed the differences."

"Why haven't you—" Some combination of a hiccup and an unwanted sob interrupted my sentence. I wiped my face roughly with my sleeve. After another *hic*, I tried again. "Why haven't you drank from me?"

Zeno finally gave me a sideways glance, and there was nothing in his eyes but distant defeat.

"I can't," he replied in a soft yet certain tone. "I can't hurt you, not even that small amount. Not anymore."

"But I'm your—"

"You're so much more than just my *beniamina*, Cora. I will figure things out soon. I can get blood. I *will* get blood."

Ice ran through me. I remembered the photograph of the man in the suit, with his throat torn open. Even if that wasn't Zeno's doing, it was easy enough to gather blood from corpses. I knew the answer to the next question, but I asked it anyway. "Are you . . . going to go to the hospital to get transfusions, then?"

Silence. Dead silence. I put a hand on his shoulder and implored him with my eyes. He finally acquiesced and answered, "The whole blood transfusions I require take two to four hours on average. I don't have that sort of time, especially not to leave you alone. Not until I find them. Not until I can ensure your safety."

Basilio and Vincenzo and the entire Medici army versus the two of us were odds I wasn't fond of. Especially not when Zeno was visibly falling apart. I bit my lip, furrowed my brow, and made a big

show of grappling with inner turmoil. Then I gazed into his eyes, communicating as much trust as I could with them.

"I'll wait until then, Zeno," I lied with a smile. "No matter how long."

"Of course, *mia passerotta*," he whispered, cupping my face in his hand, eyes full of adoration and resolve. "I have no intention of conceding."

That's the problem, I thought as I pressed my lips to his and entangled my fingers in his hair. *That's why I have to act on my own.*

Chapter Forty-Three

Rubato

It had only been a few days since I'd confronted him, but every minute had been excruciating.

I opened my eyes slowly, having relied on nothing but the slowing rhythm of Zeno's breathing to inform me when it was safe to do so. The room was lit by a single lantern in the far corner of the room, and with such little visual acuity, it would have been easy to pretend that things were normal. Zeno was snoring softly, crickets were chirping, and the bed was still warm. But I knew if I tore the blanket off and brightened that little lantern, I would see a body mottled with yellows and greens.

For the dozenth time, I considered rolling back over, drifting off into sleep, and trusting that somehow, everything would get better. That a letter would show up in the mail saying, *Hey Zeno! This is Basilio. We're going to leave you alone forever,* and Zeno would actually believe it. But we had waited for weeks, and while the danger continued to escalate, Zeno continued to deteriorate.

I moved across the bed, featherlight, and crept outside the room. I had prepared for these next three minutes over the last three days.

Three days ago, I tested every drawer in the kitchen to see which creaked the least and used it to hide my backpack. I peered inside and went through my mental checklist.

I looked in the largest pocket: plenty of food and water, a flashlight, my medications, a first aid kit, my phone (powered off currently, of course) and a phone charger. There was only one final step before departing now.

I placed a pile of neatly folded sun-protective clothing on a table beside the door, and set a note on top:

Zeno,

If I make this note too long, it might seem weird or final, so let me assure you it isn't. Just think of this like your love letters, because when I see them, they remind me you'll be back. Similarly, I'll be back once I've figured out this situation. I want us to be able to spend our days safely back at the abbey, and I want you to get healthy again. If you plan to go after me (which we both know you will), please wear the clothes beneath this message, even if it's still dark out when you find this. I won't forgive you if you're careless.

I love you,

Cora.

I had hoped seeing all of these things together would give me some greater sense of preparedness, but it did very little. I swallowed down my anxiety, drew on the heavy backpack, and emerged from *la cantina.*

Then, for the first time in months, I left the *trullo* through the front door for more than a few minutes.

Tonight the air was heavy with humidity. The road before me was carved from rugged stone, a smooth and seamless path with streetlights illuminating it as bright as day. Obviously, walking or riding down the main road would likely go poorly, but that meant traversing the rocky, unlit crags.

When I took a cursory step out to see where I was going, the door shut behind me loudly. I couldn't go back now.

I ducked quickly around the *trullo* and out of vision. It was astonishing how after walking only about twenty feet, I could barely see where my feet would fall next. A curtain of light rain sprinkled almost imperceptibly, shrouding my route even further in darkness. I thanked my past self for having scouted the region out earlier that day but still kept one hand on my flashlight if need be. The *trullo* was built on the edge of a plateau, whose flat face sharply tapered to form a steady lip a ways down. There was a single traversable divot between these points, but it was narrow and steep.

Already regretting my decisions, I pushed through bushes of

rock roses to begin my descent. The gravel beneath me was loose and crunched beneath my feet. My old sneakers had zero traction, so it wasn't a matter of *if* I fell, but when. I flickered on the flashlight and propped it awkwardly under my chin, as if my arms would actually be of any help when I tumbled.

Halfway down, my feet slipped out from beneath me. I groped helplessly at the surrounding terrain, grabbing at shrubs and stones, but it all slipped between my fingers. When my flashlight threatened to free itself from its place under my chin, I was forced to lean entirely into the dirt and slide the rest of the way down to save it. I hit level ground, and I sat for a bit.

"Ugh."

Only minutes into the journey, and I was already aching. My palms stung from stems slicing through them, silt encrusted my rock-indented elbows, and the buckles from my backpack had pushed uncomfortably into my shoulder blades. I knew without looking that minute cuts and scrapes covered me, but I could attend to them later. For now, I had to focus on continuing.

I staggered to my feet and squinted ahead of me. Though plenty bright, my flashlight did little to cut through the fog, casting only a dim orb of light on the crag immediately ahead of me.

I would have likely felt disoriented from the get-go if not for being so close to the shore. Waves beat heavily against stone, and keeping the water to one side of me was the easiest form of navigation. But then, when the rain and fog cleared, I made the brief but horrid mistake of shining my flashlight off the side of the cliff.

The light could barely reach the bottom, and what little I could see consisted of white water lashing at daggerlike stacks of limestone. An intrusive, horrific query struck me: Would the ocean carry my body away, or would it remain impaled on stone?

The thought of both outcomes made me press my body even closer to the face of the cliff.

It seemed like hours passed as I walked heel to toe, but I knew it could have only been a couple of miles. Either way, relief flooded me once I could turn off onto a pedestrian footpath. The dirt path had been excavated between the backs of neighboring farms. Wild grasses and crops reached far above my head on either side, forcing me to focus my gaze on the wavering line a wheelbarrow had carved.

This should have been peaceful—time to spend with nothing but me, the road, and the sky above. But the moon was deep into its nightly journey, and all the animals around me seemed aware that the hours before sunrise were dwindling. I reached the apex of a hill and could finally assess my surroundings. My efforts revealed nothing but miles of rural land in every direction, barns and houses interspersed between greenery.

But then, to my pleasant surprise, I spotted an anomaly in the rustic scenery: a cell tower.

I sat on a rock and dug out my phone. It was a 2G connection, of course, but that was far more than I had expected.

I had typed out the message I was going to send to Noor long ago—had written and rewritten it several times—so all I had to do now was push a single button.

> *Hello, Doctor Ntumba. It's been a long time since we've spoken, and I miss talking to you. I hope you, Lucia, Signore Urbino, and Signora Carbone are all well right now, since I fear that my and Zeno's safety is in jeopardy. He is refusing to drink from me and has not gotten any transfusions. I think the only way all of this will end is if I figure something out. If Zeno asks, let him know that I am safe and I plan on all of us meeting again soon.*

My thumb hovered over the button, and I was tempted to rewrite it for the umpteenth time, but pressed send before I could.

I didn't expect any sort of response until later in the day, but for the first time in nine months, my phone rang.

Chapter Forty-Four

Va tacito e nascosto

"Hello?" My voice sounded hoarse and strange.

The voice that answered me was low and steady. "Is he visibly bruising now? How compromised is his health?"

"I—" I sucked in a deep breath and exhaled the next word. "Very."

The phone crackled as she sighed into it. "I should have known. His calls to me have gotten fewer and further between. Is he refusing to have a transfusion at a nearby hospital?"

"Yes."

"Cora, you're making a mistake. Zeno did not tell any of us where you have been staying. He wants to keep your location secret."

Even in the cool spring weather, I felt myself flush. "I know that, but—"

"What I am telling you, Cora, is that although I do not know where you or Zeno are, I am certain there are others who do. There are no secrets within the Medici family, and every Medici is a demon with many eyes and ears. Why Zeno is hiding from them, or what will happen when you are found, is unknown to me. What I do know is that it's only a matter of time until you *are* found. If you continue to act this reckless, I am confident the two of you will just become caged birds for Zeno's father and cousin."

Caged birds.

"Did someone break into the abbey?" I rasped. "And steal Leonore?"

On the other end, I could hear her moving around. When she spoke again, the eclectic chirping of various finches became audible.

"The bird? I don't see her often, but no one has broken in. Why?"

My mouth felt painfully dry, as if cotton balls were stuck in it. "I found her the other day outside the door. Killed."

There was a prolonged silence, and I might have thought we were disconnected if not for the sound of steady breathing on the other end. "How long ago was that?" she asked.

"A few weeks ago."

I heard the door shut, and the birdsong quieted.

"So they've known exactly where the two of you are staying for 'a few weeks and have made no further attempts to contact you?"

Somehow, with my mind so focused on watching Zeno fall apart in front of me, I hadn't connected such straightforward dots. I paced the same short length back and forth. "Yes."

"Have either of you left the house?"

My pace quickened. "Zeno leaves a lot."

"And you?"

"Outside of yesterday and today, I haven't even been aboveground."

"So they've been waiting for *you* to leave," Noor said so gravely, it made me stop in my tracks. "Cora, you need to turn the phone off and go back now."

I spoke quickly and loudly so she wouldn't hang up. "I know they want me alone, but Basilio offered to pay me once. It might be possible to make some kind of arrangement now."

"'Arrangements' with nobility take a lifetime to learn to navigate," she replied with a scoff. "People like *them* do not make 'arrangements' with people like *you*. Be smart, power your phone off, and go home before they track you."

I pulled the phone away from my face and considered ending the call and going home. It would be quite easy. Embarrassing if Zeno had already awoken, perhaps. I could already imagine him fretting and holding me. But now that I could imagine that, I could also imagine the bruises gathering beneath his skin.

I spoke into the phone once more. “Thank you for your advice, Doctor Ntumba. I know chances are we won’t come to any sort of truce. But I need to at least try.”

Once again, a low, deep crackling came through the phone. I could practically see Noor on the other side, pushing up her glasses by their base and pinching the bridge of her nose to stave away the beginnings of a migraine, her umber skin turning russet, a single vein visible in her forehead.

“Are you certain?” she asked, words prickling with annoyance.

“Yes.” My answer was firm and quick, immediately tailing the last word of her question.

Yet another groan. “As you wish, Cora. I know better than to try to talk you or Zeno out of something once you’ve resolved to do it. No matter how ill-conceived it is.”

I tucked the phone between my chin and shoulder, returning to the rock I had been sitting on. I felt the need to grip it with both hands, to ground myself as much as possible while literally sitting on the edge of my seat.

“So will you help me?” I asked.

“What exactly are you expecting me to do from here?”

“I imagine you have some way of contacting Basilio, right?”

“I will send you his contact information,” she responded. Then, an unexpected plea: “Cora, promise me you’ll be careful.”

Now it was my turn to be silent. Lying had become an unwanted skill of mine, one I didn’t want to continue practicing. So I simply said, “Thank you for sending me that, Doctor Ntumba. Goodbye.”

“Goodbye.”

The chattering of night animals, which had once seemed so loud, now sounded like a whisper. Everything about my surroundings seemed more remote than ever, but I felt no more in danger. After all, I hadn't truly been safe in a long time.

She sent over everything a few minutes later—email addresses, a mailing address, and multiple phone numbers. I tried the first one, and it didn't get the chance to fully ring even once.

"Signorina Bowling, what an unexpected delight!"

Despite his enthusiasm, Basilio's voice was raspy, and I could tell that he had just woken up. "What on earth are you doing in the middle of all those farms?" he chuckled. "Surely my dear cousin didn't drag you out there on some peculiar hike?"

Of course he knew I wasn't at the trullo. Of course it had only taken minutes of me being connected to 2G for him to track me.

I curled my knees up to my chest and set my phone on top of them on speakerphone. "No, I'm alone."

"Ah, brilliant, just what I love to hear!" he purred. "Now, to what do I owe this immense pleasure?"

The strange lightness of his voice irked me, and I didn't bother to hide it in my reply. "I'm tired of waiting for things to get better."

The answer came quickly. "Of course! I, too, tire of this game of cat and mouse, especially since my dear cousin has mistakenly assumed *he* is the cat."

I wished he could see me roll my eyes. "Can we talk in person, then? And figure something out?"

"As nostalgic as a visit to the old Medici summer home sounds, I must admit I'm not in the mood to travel to whatever pile of leaves you're hiding in. Why don't we have a helicopter fly you to—"

"No," I snapped. "I'm not flying again, least of all in your helicopter. You've been waiting to talk to me for months. You can wait until I've walked to the nearest city. I should be at Cisternino by sunrise if I keep up this pace. If you must be picky, I can catch a bus to Fasano, then a train to—"

"No, no, Cisternino works perfectly! There's an utterly delightful little cafe where we can grab some coffee. It's a date!"

I grunted in acknowledgment, then hung up the phone, pocketing it before I even got the chance to see it shut off. I had estimated that I'd be at Cisternino at sunrise, but sunrise was in four hours. I took a few gulps of water and a small snack—sour grape candies—before starting the first leg of what I knew would be a long day.

Chapter Forty-Five

Segue

Just as the sun was emerging from the horizon, the small city of Cisternino came into view over the steady incline I had been traveling along.

The small town, surrounded by scenic dairy farms and olive groves, was an island of whitewashed stone. Narrow brick streets were sandwiched between angular buildings stacked beside one another and joined with steep staircases. Greenery interspersed the structures, massive trees marking the corners of various town squares. Every inch of the city was lovingly decorated, with each house surrounded by tropical plants, brightly painted doors, and windows against the walls of white. It would have resembled a cute pastoral diorama if not for the rare scooter skittering in and out of the streets. Old-fashioned streetlights had just flickered off, bringing my focus to the way the sun twinkled on the surface of the distant ocean.

Dirt road transitioned to gravel, and in the distance, I could even see paved sidewalk. With how quickly my legs gave out when I sat on a pedestrian bench, it was a wonder I had even remained upright so long. Now in cellular range, I retrieved my phone again.

To my relief, the only message was from Basilio. No rebukes from Noor, and none of the hundreds of messages I knew I'd get from Zeno when he finally woke up. Just the same old photo of a rose that had been my companion for months, with a single notification from Basilio covering its surface:

> *Here's the address to the cafe. They aren't open yet, but tell them that Basilio de' Medici will be dining with you at eight and they'll let you in. Sorry I'm late! Looking forward to our date~*

I rolled my eyes at the message but plugged the address in. The cafe was on the very edge of town, on the corner of its street.

In any other context, the little restaurant would have charmed me, with its traditional decor and the fresh flowers on every wrought-iron table. But now I wondered how on earth I was supposed to even have a sip of water with the turmoil in my stomach. I grimaced at the CHIUSO sign hanging against the window and knocked on the door a few times.

It took a minute or two for the owner to open the door. He was a young, handsome man with an apron tied loosely around his waist and flour covering his hands. He looked confused, then annoyed, then something else entirely.

"Oh!" he said, his full lips curling into a tiny *O* to match. "Are you the one sent by—"

"—Barone de' Medici," I finished his sentence for him, trying not to show how bitter the name was on my tongue. "Yes. I am."

He pulled a seat out for me immediately, skittering about in that same desperate-to-please manner I had seen from the shopkeeper of the plant shop months ago. The man rambled to me at length, but with how preoccupied I was, I only caught the bare skeleton of his explanation—something about how he was the youngest son of some noble family that was closely allied with the Medici, how he had opened a store in this quaint little town with the blessing of his parents, and so on. I didn't even latch on to his name. It was only when I saw he was looking at me expectantly that I realized he had asked a question.

"Sorry, what was that?"

He frowned for a split second, then forced a smile. "It's all right, Signorina Bowling! Basilio told me he is about fifteen minutes away. Please let me know what you would like to drink in the meantime. My treat." He rattled off various options, but once again, my mind was elsewhere. Had I introduced myself? Would Basilio have told him who I was by name?

Once the man's voice lilted in that way that foretold the end of my options, I made deliberate eye contact. "I'll take that last one, thank you."

"Of course. I'll make that for you right now."

When he retreated into the kitchen, I relaxed the tiniest bit. My shoulders were still midway to my ears, but at least I didn't have to worry about making small talk at a time like this. What good would being this tense do for the creation of a peace treaty?

Just enjoy yourself and forget about the enemy, Cora, I told myself, closing my eyes. *For the next fifteen minutes, it's a normal morning at a normal cafe.*

The drink that materialized in front of me when I opened my eyes certainly helped with the illusion. I had apparently ordered an affogato, and the smell of vanilla ice cream drowned in hot espresso was delightful. I turned the drink from side to side, marveling. Despite the speed at which the man had made my drink, his attention to detail was remarkable. Elegant curls of chocolate shavings were just beginning to melt, save those shielded from the heat atop a fresh leaf of mint.

"I made the whipped cream this morning," the man said, gesturing to the generous dollop on top of the ice cream. "The milk is from one of the local dairy cows."

I picked up a straw and a spoon, eager to dissect the meal, but before I could dig in, he stopped me.

"Wait!" the man cried, holding a hand up.

I froze in place, brow raised.

He let out a shy chuckle, hand returning to the nape of his neck. "It may be silly, but I enjoy honoring the traditions of this place. While in Rome, you know?"

I gave an understanding nod and tried not to make it obvious that my attention was mostly focused on the ice cream sinking into espresso. To my relief, his explanation was quick enough. "There's a single coffee bean hidden in the whipped cream, and you're meant to eat it first."

As he wiped down the tables around me, I dug into it and quickly found the aforementioned bean.

"Hmm," I replied, popping it into my mouth. "Like the plastic baby in a king cake."

Though still preoccupied with cleaning, I could see the man make a strange face. I realized it did sound rather unusual if you hadn't done the tradition before. Warmth crept over my cheeks. I

chased the bitter bean with two heaping spoonfuls of ice cream. Beyond being a stranger, this was a friend of Basilio's. Did it really matter what he thought?

I shoveled down the ice cream and drank the espresso, savoring every bite and sip. It had been a good ten minutes at that point, but instead of feeling energized, I just felt . . . foggy. That was when it hit me.

This was a friend of Basilio's.

Even ten minutes later, the bitterness of the bean still lingered on the back of my tongue, but it didn't taste like the acidity of a coffee bean. I picked up the drink to examine it closer, then widened my eyes. "Oh—oh no."

On the napkin he had set my drink on, in the halo of condensation, was a quickly scrawled, *Sorry*.

I turned to see the man, but he had already vanished, and everything was already beginning to feel dreamlike.

As the whirring of an electrical vehicle grew near, an overwhelming heaviness passed over me. With all my effort, I peeled my eyelids apart with my fingers, but even my arms struggled to remain upright. I cursed to myself aloud and pushed up against the table, hoping against all odds that I could take advantage of the last spurt of adrenaline to run away. But even the screeching of the chair right under me sounded distant, and the sight of the silver car pulling up beside me looked blurred. I couldn't tell if the lines darting across my vision and tingling of my arm were some benzo-riddled hallucinations or a sudden torrent of rain.

Shit. Shit. Shit.

The world tilted, and the streetlights transformed into diagonal lines as I fell. I never hit the ground.

Chapter Forty-Six

M'odi, e trema

The concrete floor was chilly beneath me, yet warm enough to tell me I had been lying on it for a while. I was on my side, arms tied tightly to my side, shoulders aching against the hard floor. There were two men before me.

Even in the dim lighting, I recognized the first man instantly. Who else could those gleaming, crimson eyes and broad, fanged smile belong to but Barone Basilio de' Medici?

Unlike the pristine grooming he'd undertaken during our first meeting, the nobleman looked unusually disheveled. His long hair was mussed, there was dirt along his jaw, and he wore a muddy button-down instead of the suit I had originally seen him in. Despite the mess, he still looked just as composed as when we had first met, if not more so.

To his side was a stranger in somber dress and visage. He stood behind Basilio and to the side, an elegant shadow.

"Who—" I began to ask, then stopped. I knew the answer.

The man was broad-shouldered and glowing with health, despite his age. He was a normal Italian through-and-through, sun-kissed even in the shadows, with curly salt-and-pepper hair. There was something I recognized about his high cheekbones, his defined Cupid's bow, and most of all, the look in his hazel eyes. Utterly dead and yet intensely ablaze. Zeno's father.

He folded his arms behind his back and bowed slightly at me, and the dim light glanced across a scar—a thin, silvery streak where his lips had been split down the middle at one point. I fought against the ropes harshly as his leather shoe appeared at my nose, but they

did not give in the slightest. I wriggled desperately, then gave in as Basilio sat me up and propped me against the wall, clutching my cheeks in his grimy hands.

I squirmed out from his grasp and pulled my face back as far as I could in those ropes.

"Why are you doing this?" I demanded, holding back tears. "I thought we could talk this over!"

Basilio sighed, straightened, and tilted his head to the side with a genuine frown. "Talk? Don't be ridiculous. I undid the existence of your *ritus sanguinous*, you know. I pulled every string I needed to pull, and not a soul has spoken your name since that night. Company stocks have been unaltered. But I still know."

I didn't say anything, just glared and pretended his words didn't feel like daggers in my chest.

With a small sigh and shake of his head, Basilio continued, "I won't lie to you, Signorina Bowling. Beyond protecting the Medici name, this may not be personal to Uncle Vincenzo—" he paused and pointed at the man at his side "—but it's personal to me. You made me break promises, and more importantly, you've stolen someone dear to me."

"Why are you telling me all this? Aren't you wasting your breath when you're just going to kill me?"

He laughed a genuine, mirthful laugh and shot a glance at Zeno's father. "Oh, Cora. If we wanted you dead, you would be. But Zeno would find out that his *everything* is *nothing*, and I assume the worst for him."

"Then what do you plan on doing to me?" I asked, squirming again. The ropes burned against my arm, which made me want to squirm even more. But of course, the rational side of me knew there wasn't a point, so I instead opted to glare as hard as I could.

"I plan to make you leave, Cora. If money doesn't, and if a dead bird doesn't, perhaps pain will."

"Nothing will—" I began to say, but he slapped me hard, so hard that he knocked me over.

I tried to say something, any sort of stinging response, but all that came out of my mouth was a staggered wheeze. Basilio scowled down at me, holding his hand with disdain, as though it were my

fault it stung—as though it were my fault there were parallel tears in his eyes, and even guilt on his face. He reeled back again, and I squeezed my eyes shut, bracing for the blow.

"Basilio," Zeno's father snapped, voice low and harsh. "Do not dirty yourself. You have done enough."

When the blow did not come, I cautiously opened an eye. In the brief instance I had closed my eyes, the man had transformed. Now, the Basilio before me stood erect with a cool and calm expression, focused more on fixing the cuffs of his sleeves than anything else.

"Of course," he replied to Vincenzo. "I'm wasting time messing with her."

"Correct. It is as I've always told you," Vincenzo said, taking a few steps toward me with his hands clasped together behind his back. "Medici do not dirty their hands. That is what the help is for."

As the patriarch neared, I held my breath. If he wanted to, he could kick my face, or pull out a knife and kill me on the spot. I craned my neck up to see him, but this effort was meaningless. Vincenzo bent over, folding at the waist, strangely formal. He gave me little more than a cursory glance and sighed, looking disappointed with what he saw. With a small nod to his nephew, the pair walked off into the distance.

Upon flickering off the sole light in the room, their footsteps diminished into silence and darkness.

After it became clear they wouldn't return, I considered trying to sit up again but gave up without even trying. It wouldn't make me feel better. I had never felt colder and darker and more alone, and cutting up my arms by wriggling around wouldn't help. It was easier to close my eyes and pretend this was some horrible dream.

Just as I had resolved to sink into the concrete, a light shone on me. I squinted into it and perceived the outline of an approaching figure. My eyes adjusted, and a familiar set of features became discernible just among the visible edge of the light.

A tall, barrel-chested man with a meek look in his beady eyes and a strange nervous quirk in his lip and brow. He had a well-groomed russet beard and finely combed hair.

"Signore Urbino?"

I had seen this man so many times over the past year in the abbey but had never truly spoken to him. He had become something of a strange accessory in my mind, a piece of furniture shifting around the same few locations hourly. But I realized he looked entirely at home standing in the shadows, more so than he ever had in the abbey.

Urbino approached me slowly, his expression strangely flat. The distinct scent of shoe polish grew stronger.

"Signorina Bowling." Urbino's greeting was in the form of a strange, low growl. He peeled his gloves off slowly, and for the first time, I glimpsed his hands. Thick scars covered the surface, and the undersides of his palms were entirely and evenly burned.

Urbino roughly grabbed me by the ropes and jerked me upright. The action came easily to him, and I broke out in a cold sweat with the horrifying realization that this seemed far from the first time he had done such a thing.

Pleas poured from my quivering lips. "Please don't hurt me! I'm begging you, please! I'll do anything—I'll give you anything!"

He tilted his head at me in the distinct manner of a hawk before it dove. *How is the best way to do this?* his eyes said. *Where is best to sink in my claws?*

"I'm telling you, don't hurt me!" I tried to force my shaking voice to be as stern as possible. "Someone will notice I'm gone, Zeno will—"

Urbino tossed his head back in a scoff. "Zeno will what? Hurt me? Zeno and I have played many times. He never even tried to fight back! Lash after lash, he just sat there, shivering. The weakling didn't even try to fight when his father installed me in the abbey."

I could see Zeno in my head, a young boy hugging his legs, his shirt tossed aside in a heap on the ground, with dead eyes that did not cry and a body that did not flinch when the whip came down.

The reason for my trembling had changed. More than scared, I was furious.

I leaned forward and spat on his shoe. Urbino stared down at his feet, eyes wide and jaw open, and glowered at me. Then he unleashed.

He grabbed my head, slammed it against the wall, then pulled it back and slammed it again. I felt a sickening crunch, felt my incisors gnash through my tongue. Grasping my head so tightly with his hand I thought it might burst, he ground the side of my face into the wall, so that dirt and stone joined the pulp of broken teeth and blood in my mouth.

Every ounce of me knew I should scream or fight, but I was a limp, breathless from the pain and adrenaline coursing through me. He released me, and as I slid down to the floor, my vision became blurred. A foot rammed into my stomach, and I felt something snap. He kicked me again in the same spot, and instead of a crack, all I heard and felt was a hollow squelch.

Black spots clouded my vision, and the universe seemed monochrome, except for all the red around me—the red I was coughing up, the red pooling around my chest. My whole body was one dull ache, like a hand seared to the bone. I felt the occasional sharp pain—my fingers being snapped, my hair being yanked—but none of it drew me out of the feeling of floating. Every snap and thud echoed outside of my body, unable to fully penetrate the pool of darkness and nothingness I was suspended in.

Eventually, the vague sensation of spinning was all there was.

I don't know how long I was in that pool. Brief vignettes appeared before me, but I struggled to process what they meant before they faded away.

The first few times there was only the floor. Then, a door opening. Screaming—but not from me. A bang reverberating from across the room, along with the smell of gunpowder. The man who had been kicking me, but now on the ground with his throat torn open. White hands pulling apart skin and muscle and fat as though they were layers of a quilt. Being lifted into the air by trembling arms. The click of a seat belt. Inertia pulling me back into a seat. Trying to pull something off my eye, but discovering it *was* my eye, only bulbous and swollen shut. Being lifted again. Several voices, both familiar and new. A sharp prick in my inner arm, my jaw being forced open, a stern voice saying, "18 etomidate and 125 succinylcholine IV stat. 7 millimeter tube."

Then the full descent into nothingness.

Chapter Forty-Seven

Conservati fedele

I faded in and out of sleep several times and was distantly aware of my surroundings over the course of an hour, in the way an insect was. A sterile scent overpowered the base notes of stone and mustiness—the unmistakable fragrance of the abbey. I was sitting up in an uncomfortable bed, and every time I moved, cotton rasped against my arms. There was a weight in my lap and heavily blunted pain all over my body. Eventually, however, whatever had numbed the pain wore off.

Finally, I became fully conscious. I was back in the abbey, tucked in a room I hadn't seen before. It had been rendered into a makeshift hospital room, with a monitor at my side and a web of wires and sensors everywhere. Zeno was softly snoring through parted lips with his head in my lap and his arm reaching over my body to hold my hand. At the sight of him, the machine beside me beeped loudly.

The door creaked open, and Noor's head poked into the room, followed by the rest of her.

"Good," she said, setting a glass of water at my bedside. "You're awake. I hoped it would go well."

"I—" I tried to speak, but that single syllable came out as little more than a harsh rasp. My throat was painfully scratchy. I reached for the water at my bedside. It felt like sand going down. I blinked back tears and tried not to cough.

At my movement, Zeno's lashes flickered open, and he sat up immediately.

"Cora," he murmured, grasping my hands. "I was terrified you'd never wake up. I was *terrified*."

I went to speak and could not once again, but for an entirely different reason. I had known Zeno for months and had seen him at his highest and lowest. Only twice had he cried in my presence, and now, before my eyes for the very first time. At the sight of my loved one so despondent, it was impossible not to cry myself.

"Hey," I whispered, catching one of his tears with my lips. "I know better than to go and do something like that."

Zeno took advantage of my proximity and tilted his head up to kiss me. There was restraint in it, frustration at the web of wires holding him back from embracing me outright. I cupped his cheek in my hand and skillfully navigated him closer to deepen the kiss. I made my movements as fluid as possible to mask the fact that many of my tears were in response to the pangs of pain throughout my entire torso, the throbbing in my bandaged fingers, and the burning ache of my entire throat and jaw.

"Zeno," Noor scolded. "Leave the room."

The vampire pulled away from me and shot such icy daggers at her that, for a split second, I was convinced he'd murder her. But as I should have known, Noor had a vague understanding of how to herd the beast within the man.

"For Cora's own good," she added a bit more softly. "So I can focus on healing her."

He shot me one last longing glance, then left the room like a dejected dog with his tail between his legs. If not for the confusion and searing pain, I would have laughed.

As soon as Zeno left the room, I let my body wilt.

"Give me a number for the pain," Noor said, approaching.

"Nine," I whimpered in return.

She held up a syringe of some sort of medication. "Would you like—"

"Anything!" I interrupted. "It hurts."

She flushed my IV and then administered medication slowly. I already felt relief by the time the plunger met the barrel, along with

a general feeling of ease. Another flush left me feeling warm, and it pleasantly numbed every ache. I exhaled and closed my eyes, tempted to drift away once more. Through my eyelashes, I could make out Noor's impatient expression, jolting me back.

"What . . .?" I stared down at my body, utterly perplexed. I was a mess of wires and tubes, bruises and bandages.

Noor sat on the edge of my bed, which creaked in protest. "My knowledge of how you came to the hospital is secondhand. I will tell you that if you want, but I'd like to start with your medical state."

Both were, I supposed, equally valid lines of questioning. I gave her a nod to continue.

"You arrived at the hospital nine days ago in critical condition with a variety of minor injuries, such as broken fingers. More concerningly, you bit through your tongue. Unfortunately, you inhaled quite a bit of blood when you lost consciousness. That, combined with four broken ribs—one of which punctured your lung—and an unknown amount of blunt trauma."

"Jesus Christ." I touched my hand to my side and found a massive bandage along it.

"That's just from the chest tube," she said, as though that would comfort me. "It came out two days ago. I'm going to monitor the sutures for a bit, but your lungs are looking quite healthy, especially considering the intubation."

My hand moved to my throat. "I was *intubated*?"

"Yes. Twice, actually. You were extubated for the second time two days ago."

"That explains how terrible my throat feels," I croaked. I was trying, semisuccessfully, to mirror the casual nature in which Noor was speaking. "What happened to me?"

Noor frowned. "Do you not remember? You were taken by Zeno's family and beaten."

Flashes of Basilio, Urbino, and Zeno's father came to mind. A shiver ran through me at the thought of them.

"I do remember," I responded. "I just didn't know if I could trust that it really happened."

She gave me a strange look. "What *can* you trust, if not yourself?"

"A lot. Or maybe nothing. I don't know."

Noor held my gaze and allowed me to parse one of many questions. "I remember seeing Zeno. Was that—"

As I spoke, my mouth felt even drier. I certainly remembered *someone* tearing Signore Urbino apart as I was drifting away. Someone with blood covering their hands and rolling down their chin, like I had seen in old medieval paintings of vampires. Maybe that was all this memory was: just some distant recollection of an artwork I had looked at.

With a pit in my stomach, I tried to approach the burning question from another angle. "Where is Signore Urbino?"

Noor darkened, and her expression alone immediately granted my answer. "He doesn't work at the abbey anymore," she replied dryly.

"What about Basilio?" I demanded. "What about Zeno's father?"

"They won't bother you anymore."

There was a prolonged silence between us, as heavy and dry as the lump in the back of my throat. The beeping of my heart rate had spiked, and as the silence dragged on, it gradually plateaued. Doctor Ntumba didn't move at all, just maintained eye contact with the wall behind me.

"I wish you would just tell me outright," I whispered. "I wish you would tell me that Zeno tore them limb from limb like he told me he would."

Her response came quickly and sharply: "Zeno did no such thing."

I knew Doctor Ntumba well enough to know that such a response wasn't very meaningful. She was an incredibly honest woman, but her honesty was hollow. He hadn't literally torn them limb from limb, but that didn't mean they weren't killed by his hands or by an order. That didn't tell me if they were even alive.

I also knew Doctor Ntumba well enough to know prying would be a waste of time beyond this point. Zeno would tell me the truth if I asked—every horrid ounce of it.

But as I stared down at the well-worn indent in the bed where Zeno must have spent countless hours resting in lieu of his own bed, at the closely annotated copy of our most recent read, and at the mess of wires along my arms, I felt a new resolve. Doctor Ntumba had already given me the only truth I needed: *they won't bother you anymore.*

By my actions, we were free. It didn't matter how.

"Can I see him now, then?" I asked softly. "Just for a bit?"

"Of course. I'll be back in half an hour and we can discuss your treatment in depth. For now, just know that these next couple of days will be excruciating in many ways, but by the end of them, I'll have you disconnected from all these wires and lines. The next two weeks without morphine will be even worse, but by the end of them, you won't have any bandages under your clothes."

I winced at the thought of it. Even now, with morphine coursing through me, I could tell that the pain was still present beneath the warmth. It was waiting just beyond the threshold, ready to pounce and consume me the moment it got its chance. But as certain as I was of this, I was certain of something else.

"I can handle it. I can handle anything now."

Chapter Forty-Eight

L'istesso tempo

Doctor Ntumba was probably right about those next two days being excruciating, but I couldn't say for certain. They were a blur of rotating medications. A steady dose of hydrocodone every so many hours, complemented by my frequent pressing of a morphine pump. A cocktail of medications to counteract the side effects of said painkillers, like an embarrassing dose of laxatives and plenty of ondansetron for nausea. Then, just before bed, a dose of prazosin for the nightmares that had already begun.

I had the unfortunate feeling I'd be on the last two for a very long time.

Zeno was at my side more often than not, a watchful yet doting bandog. He was even at my side when he received a transfusion, joking about our matching IVs. I employed him to reread the same few verses of the *Aeneid*, which he stumbled through in ancient Greek. More comforting, however, were the gentle caresses I demanded regularly and occasional soft *I love you*'s.

As I quickly discovered, what Doctor Ntumba *was* right about was that the next couple of weeks were excruciating. I was only on day four and already on the verge of asking to be knocked out.

After several minutes of working up the motivation to do so, I pushed myself off my bed. I hobbled into the bathroom, letting out a staggered moan, and immediately had to lean onto the bathroom wall.

"Can you open a window?" I managed to huff out between pursed lips.

The condensation pouring out of the shower, typically a

source of comfort, was now stifling. With little more than a small *mm-hmm*, Lucia climbed on a step stool designated for just that. I sighed in relief as steam rolled out of the small window and the air immediately lightened and cooled.

I pulled my belt and my robe fell into a heap on the ground, just as I wished I could. Though I wanted to fully emerge myself in the downpour, Doctor Ntumba's scoldings the first time I got my chest-tube dressing wet were still fresh in my mind.

I stepped halfway into the shower, contorting my body in various directions. While awkwardly washing my body, I couldn't help but wonder if I'd even get the technique down by the time the sutures came out.

I stepped out the second I finished scrubbing, half of my body searing with pain and the other half searing from the hot water.

Outside, Lucia had hardly moved. She remained sitting on the stepladder, her knees drawn to her chest and holding her cheeks in her hands.

With the added lighting, I could finally notice the spidery veins in her eyes and the purplish collar beneath them. As long as I had known Lucia, I had never asked her exact age. To me, the only thing that mattered was that her spirit was that of a child. Looking at her now, I wondered how much the human soul weighed, and if it was as much of a struggle to carry it as it looked.

At the sound of the glass door sliding shut, Lucia's eyes flickered up at me and away from whatever distant plane they had been in. Though her step lightened as she darted across the room, it was clear whatever miasma possessed her had not been exorcized. I tried not to wince as she slid my arm into a sleeve with the same speed as she always did, and if she noticed, it didn't show. When would my medicine kick in? Had I even taken any?

I huffed to myself as I buttoned up my shirt, fully aware that double-dosing wouldn't be a good idea. Lucia would remember in my stead, I realized, as she was the one who had brought me breakfast that morning.

"Hey, Lucia, do you know if I took the medicine this morning?"

"Yes, Signorina Bowling," she answered, returning to her spot by the window, all the way across from the bathroom.

So the strange distance Lucia kept between us upon my return hadn't been in my imagination after all. She had tidied the house from afar these past two days, and when she spoke with me, it was oddly tense small talk.

"Is something wrong?" I asked outright. "You're being different."

Lucia didn't look at me. She just sighed and continued to stare out the window. The gesture was on the verge of being too overt, so much so that I wondered if it was just for show. But when she finally glanced over, I knew it was at least partially genuine.

"I heard you learned a lot about the Medici family while you were away." She sighed again. "I did as well."

"What exactly does that mean?"

"The house got lonely while you were gone. I asked Signora Carbone about what happened to my parents."

Lucia gave me a small smile, but it didn't reach her eyes—those downturned, baby-blue eyes from the corpse in the photograph. *Oh.*

I tried to open my mouth and ask for clarification, but nothing came out.

She held up her hand and shook her head, dismissing my question quickly. "Don't worry about it, signorina. Getting better is your job right now. Things will be back . . ." She didn't finish the sentence, but it was implicit: *to normal.*

I manually turned the gears in my mind to convince myself she was right, that once these stitches were out of my side, we'd all be happy again.

If only because my medication started kicking in, it worked. "Yes, I'm sure they will," I said, putting on my shoes to head to the main hall. "See you later!"

She gave me a small wave as I left. Shortly down the hall, Zeno was leaning against the wall, one foot propped up and a book in his hands. At the sight of me, he tucked it into his arm with a smile. "Good morning, *mia passerotta.*"

I grinned back and said, "Can you believe it, Zeno? I'm finally disconnected from them all!"

I moved my arms around me for emphasis and Zeno winced on my behalf, evidently remembering the sutures in my side before I did.

"I know, I know," I muttered before he could say something himself. "Just because I'm not hooked up to anything doesn't mean I'm totally fine."

"How kind of you!" Zeno teased, ruffling my hair. "You saved me the effort of saying it myself."

I rolled my eyes but couldn't help but smile. "Enough scolding. I'm off to garden now. I'm sure my roses desperately need pruning."

He tensed at my words. "Don't forget to wear gloves. No matter how precious, those roses of yours have thorns."

"Uh, sure," I replied, raising a brow at his words.

Doctor Ntumba had told me as much as well, but never so gravely. Zeno spoke as though I were at risk of impaling myself straight through my hand, and I was half convinced he'd change his mind and explicitly forbid me from dirtying my hands. Instead, he huffed in dismissal and returned to his book with a glower.

"Gardening, then tea with Doctor Ntumba," I reminded myself as I immediately put on a pair of gloves before even examining the clearly overgrown shrubs in depth. "Then lunch, tea in the aviary, dinner and time alone. Like always."

Chapter Forty-Nine

Scordatura

Snip. Snip. Snip. The shriveled head of an old bloom joined the rest of the old foliage littered across the ground. I took a step back and glanced at my watch. An hour had passed, and the smell of fresh cuttings filled the air, but I still had plenty of work to do. Tea roses had reached crookedly to the grow lights, prairie roses crawled lopsided on its trellis, and a young addition to the garden had overextended itself by focusing on flowering before developing a healthy root system. Most pertinently, *La Rosa di Santa Dymphna* had not only germinated while I was gone but had already begun its awkward adolescence.

"Sorry, but I'm already late for tea," I said to them, sitting on my heels. "I'll be sure to take care of you first thing tomorrow." Then, just before leaving, I added, "I'm proud. All of you were so brave and strong while I was gone. I'm sorry it took me so long to come home."

As I soon discovered, tea and cookies were waiting for me in the library, but Doctor Ntumba was not.

Sorry. Won't make it, read a simple note folded neatly beside the plate. I didn't even see Signora Carbone drop it off—it was as though the still-brewing chai and cookies, so freshly baked they were still hot to the touch, had *poof*ed into existence. They were as fragrant and spiced as ever, but rather than digging in, I watched the steam. Whether it was because of medication in my system or anxiety, the thought of eating or drinking anything in front of me was nauseating. Worse, it brought flashbacks to that affogato that Basilio's friend had given me in Cisternino, and the *Sorry* written on the napkin beneath.

The plate screeched in tandem with my chair as I pushed it away and left. A walk was in order, I decided. Some fresh air to settle

my mind and stomach.

The door to the courtyard was heavier than I remembered, or maybe I was weaker. I was forced to ignore the pain and lean into it, but the result was immediately worth the effort.

It had been a long time since I had been to the abbey, and yet everything appeared as it did the first day I arrived. The fountains burbled with their usual crystal-clear water, the statuaries grinned down at me from above, and even the sky itself was the same marbled mixture of orange and pink. There was a distinct, sweet fragrance—the final, desperate blooms from Sicilian flora trying to attract wildlife.

Signora Carbone (and, I realized with a chill, probably Signore Urbino) had maintained the shrubbery almost identically as when I had arrived long ago. The sight made me feel as if I were transported back to that simpler time, but this only lasted a few seconds. I could ignore the annoying swishing of the hospital gown, could mask the lingering taste of medicine on my tongue, and could even push away the steady ache that had started up the moment I tried to walk again. But the thing that brought forth chills was the realization that there was no audible wildlife. Though I hadn't always paid much attention to it, the Abbazia di Santa Dymphna was always bustling, especially at this time of year. Birds called to one another at dusk, rabbits grazed, and countless other animals had their typical schedule around the abbey. This evening, however, I heard nothing.

I paused to examine the tree line and discovered there was no avian movement there, either, or hopping among the grass. In fact, not even the wind was blowing. I felt excruciatingly small.

Not again.

There was a good excuse for this, I convinced myself, just as the tingling began. I glanced at the door, ensuring it hadn't magically locked behind me, and walked further. I had just finally felt at ease when suddenly, a soft, barely audible coo rang out in the distance.

My heart raced, and within seconds, my fingers were tingling. There were several species of doves in Sicily—in fact, I used to watch a nesting pair of wood pigeons from the abbey. But this coo belonged to none of them. Within this country, I had only heard the gentle song of a Barbary dove within the walls of the abbey.

Then, despite everything I knew and despite that sinking feeling in my chest, I saw *her*. A white Barbary dove fluttering in the distance, a collar of red around her neck.

"No—no, no, no!"

I staggered back but was able to catch myself on a pillar. When I looked back, she was gone, not even a white dot in the distance.

I blinked back tears and focused on my breathing. *Nothing is there. It's just the painkillers.*

A contralto voice reverberated behind me. "You shouldn't be out here."

My breath hitched at the sight of Signora Carbone. I couldn't help but associate her with Signore Urbino and his duplicity. Of course, I logically knew that if she were involved, Zeno would have already sent her away. Yet days later, the association was as strong as ever.

"O-oh, Signora Carbone!" I stammered. "I didn't see you."

She softened at my expression, and part of me felt the need to apologize for wounding her. Instead, I averted my gaze and festered in the guilt.

She repeated, albeit in a gentler tone, "You shouldn't be out here."

"I came outside because I heard . . ." I trailed off.

"It isn't wise to follow ghosts," Signora Carbone warned. "Especially not into places you aren't meant to be."

But my ghosts were gone. Zeno had said so himself. I had not seen my parents or Peachy for weeks, and for all intents and purposes, the abbey should have been entirely unhaunted. But I had just seen Leonore, and now I wondered if I would have to see others. I got the terrible feeling that Basilio, Urbino, and Zeno's father would now inhabit the Abbazia di Santa Dymphna. Perhaps worst of all, maybe I would have to face the bruised and swollen version of Zeno that had haunted me weeks ago.

I shook away the distressing thought and instead inquired about the second half of her sentence: "Why am I not supposed to be out here?"

Signora Carbone looked over her shoulder at the manor, gaze boring into Zeno's room, then back at me. Like Lucia, her eyes were unusually bleak with heavy circles beneath them, and she blinked slowly as she answered me. "He doesn't want you outside of the abbey."

"That doesn't exactly answer my question," I responded with a frown.

Her eyes lingered on me a moment longer before she responded, "He said you aren't well and should remain indoors."

"Isn't fresh air supposed to be good for me?"

"I am telling you what he said, not what I believe," she said gravely. "What I believe does not matter in this household. It never has."

So whatever possessed Lucia was contagious, it seemed. And I feared it was spreading to me as well.

Something is wrong. Something is very wrong.

I shifted from foot to foot, as though the movement would shake words loose from my mind. I finally murmured an awkward goodbye and went back inside, tail between my legs.

The hall seemed darker than only moments before, the air heavier. With little else to do before my time in the aviary, I returned to the library, where the tea and cookies awaited me. That lukewarm chai, drank alone in dead silence, was the bitterest I had ever had.

If not for the knowledge of my next destination, I probably would have just gone back to bed. Beyond the usual drive to see Zeno or discuss the *Aeneid*, there was something greater that kept me awake. It would be the first time I had been in the aviary since returning to the abbey. And even though Leonore would not be among them, I missed the birds—and the normalcy.

When I entered the room, the quiet and stillness of the library vanished in an instant. In the aviary, the chirping was loud as ever, and the room was as vibrant as usual, if not more so. The plants I had picked out many months ago were flourishing, but even more vibrant than the blooms were the birds that flew between them. Every bird teemed with energy, taking full advantage of the breadth of the room. Their bright summer plumage gleamed in the grow lights. A trio of strawberry finches flitted over to me, tilting their heads at me with evident curiosity.

It took me a moment to see Zeno sitting among the white stone, to remember that the aviary did not have any statues in it.

"You're early," I noted, sitting beside Zeno. "Or not five minutes late, I guess."

"I've waited long enough for you," Zeno responded in an equally casual tone. "I can't bear wasting another minute." I turned toward the bird to shield my flustered expression, and Zeno picked up his copy of our book. "Which verse do you remember us reading last? Shall we start there?"

What were words? What was the *Aeneid*? The way Zeno was looking at me, I couldn't remember any of that. I just wanted to soak in a past comfort and then take advantage of a newfound treasure. I tossed aside my copy.

"As much as I'd like to talk about the *Aeneid*, I don't think I can today. I've really missed this place," I said with a small smile. "Not *just* the aviary, I mean. All of it. I'm just happy to be here right now with you."

Zeno chuckled, resting his hand on his chin and giving me the warm, crooked smile I adored. "I know. Me too." With far more boldness than I remembered having, I crawled into Zeno's lap. He scooped me up immediately and kissed the top of my head. "I was hoping you'd do that."

I laughed and nuzzled into him. "There's no way you could've known I would!"

Zeno huffed in response. "I'll have you know I have an *exquisite* imagination. There were plenty of things I was hoping you'd do. This was the tame option."

For whatever reason, this lighthearted tone—likely intended to enlighten me—had the opposite effect. After holding my breath for a few beats, I asked him, my voice low and wavering, "Is it really over now? Are we really safe?"

Zeno's breath grew hot on my neck. "I promise you, Cora, not a soul will hurt you again. I will make certain of that."

While I wanted to take these words for fact, not question him further, and sink away from this fear, I couldn't.

“Is this different from the last months in Puglia?” I asked. “Will you fade away from me and stop drinking from me?”

“It *is* different.” The answer to my question came immediately, and I wondered if he had been expecting it. Considering how grave and intense his tone was, he must have. “I am having transfusions. I will drink from you when you are well,” Zeno explained. “In the meantime, I will make this abbey impenetrable. I will make you untouchable to anyone but me.”

The intensity of his words took me aback. They were likely meant to inspire certainty from me, to quiet any dissonance, but they had the opposite effect. *He* wanted the abbey impenetrable, but did I?

“We should go to town soon,” I suggested. “I haven’t seen it in the summertime before.”

Zeno’s reply was as sudden as it was firm. “That isn’t a good idea. You aren’t well yet. You could get sick, or someone could bump into you and burst open your stitches. I can’t permit that.”

I shrugged, feeling foolish but resolved to continue testing this invisible boundary.

“I’m sure a small bookstore would be safe. It would be nice to have some more books. I think I’ll likely go through them more quickly now—” I cut myself off, but the implication remained. I would go through books more quickly now that I wouldn’t be researching the Medici—a name which used to signify fascination and even adoration, but now served only as the harbinger of nightly terrors.

Despite my ever-growing discomfort, Zeno seemed unmoved, eyes as distant as before.

“We’ll have outings when you’re better,” he said finally. “In the meantime, tell me anything you want. A new library, a closet of dresses, a private theater. As long as you are here and as long as you are safe.”

“Just books are fine,” I muttered, nestling into his chest as an excuse to dismiss myself from that fiery gaze. “Like you said, we’ll go once I’m healed. It’s okay. We have forever, however long that is.”

“Yes,” he echoed. “Forever, however long that is.”

Chapter Fifty

Per pietà, non dirmi addio

I had always been told deep-breathing helped with discomfort, but it seemed to have the opposite effect right now. So many months ago, I had winced at the tightening of strings on a corset, and here I was, on the verge of tears from strings being cut. I was scared to look down, scared that once the last stitch was removed, I would see my skin unfurl in a heap on the ground.

There was a tug—the first of many stitches to be removed—followed by the uniquely sickening sensation of string being pulled through skin. I held my breath.

"Please stay still and breathe normally," Doctor Ntumba scolded, not bothering to hide the annoyance in her tone. "The more you move, the greater likelihood I'll actually cause pain."

I let out a small *mm-hmm* and fought the urge to say what I was actually thinking: that Zeno, who was not a doctor, had at least waited for the lidocaine to kick in when he gave me stitches.

"You really were right," I said beneath my breath, suppressing both a laugh and a wince as she wormed out the next few stitches. "These two weeks have been horrible. I didn't think the pain and discomfort was ever going to end. It still hasn't, all the way."

"But you did well, Cora," she replied with a smile in her voice. "You were a star patient."

"Was I?" I scoffed. "I was crying every five minutes once you tapered me off hydrocodone."

"As would anyone else in your circumstance."

There was one final tug, and then she shifted away. I looked

down to see not a pile of my skin, but a mostly healed line of reddened skin along my side. The sight of my body, free of wires and free of stitches, solidified the fact I had crossed a threshold.

"Do you need anything else from me?" I asked, sitting on the edge of the exam table. "Are there any more procedures or medications?"

"Not unless you develop an infection of some sort. No, I would say that while the pain will linger for a long time, you are quite healed."

I shrugged my shirt on. The area where she had removed the stitches was still quite sensitive, yet feeling the fabric rub across my skin with little resistance was strangely relieving.

"Thank you for all of this, Doctor Ntumba," I whispered.

She chuckled and continued to gather up her supplies. "Of course. It was a refreshing change of pace to have a patient other than Zeno. I had almost forgotten one's blood work could look any different from his." Then, after giving me another smile, she added, "Have a nice day, Cora. Enjoy yourself now that you properly can."

I beamed from ear to ear and leaped off the exam table, murmuring more thanks before rushing out into the main area of the abbey. I entered the abbess's suite, a room I had only really passed through as of late, and paused to marvel at its majesty for the first time in months. It was still early morning, a time Zeno would still be fast asleep, when I would normally sleep beside him. Perhaps I should have simply gone back to bed and gotten up as normal, but I couldn't. Every part of me felt as bright as the light pouring through the bay window, and I was all too eager to catch the tail end of dawn. For once, I could even draw it in pastels.

I filled a satchel with my old art supplies, a small book, and a few snacks. Then, as I walked out the door, it hit me: I could go anywhere. I was unimpeded by wounds or danger or anything, so why limit myself to painting the sunrise from within the abbey walls? I scoured my mind, considering countless possibilities, then decided on a small area I had driven past several times before.

The spot was little more than a small grove on the cliffside, with barely enough room to set out all of my supplies, but the view it overlooked was immaculate. At this time of day and year, Poggioreale would be an undeniably beautiful contradiction to a

ghost town. Mature wildflowers and ivy would frame the lifeless stone architecture. Orange hues from the heavens contrasting with cool blue grass undulating amongst the ruins. Perhaps I could focus on making a realistic landscape, or I could hint at village ghosts in an impressionistic work.

With these ideas and more bustling around in my head, I headed down to the parking area to seek Signora Rafia.

The sun shined directly in my eyes, but I could squint through it somewhat. In the shaded alcove tucked between the abbey and the main road, I saw a woman preoccupied by something as she stood between two cars. *Perfect timing,* I thought, holding up a hand. *Who knew this would be such a short goose chase?*

I broke into a light jog, taking full advantage of the sloped terrain. "Signora Rafia, I—"

After ducking into the shade, I realized the person was not Signora Rafia after all, but someone even more elusive. I hadn't seen Signora Carbone since that night in the garden, at least not up close.

She looked worse than before, even more exhausted than I could have imagined—and, suspiciously, crouched beside the cars. She straightened slowly, her expression flat.

"Oh, hello," I said, slightly out of breath. I tucked my satchel behind my back, as though I were the one with something to hide. The fabric scratched as I tightened my hands and tried not to stare at hers.

"Hello, Signorina Bowling," came the low reply. "You are up earlier than expected."

"Uh, yeah." I rubbed the back of my neck. "Do you know where Signora Rafia is? I was—"

"Why?" The question was as immediate as it was harsh. I blinked once, twice, thrice, and stammered an incoherent reply for a painful amount of time before Signora Carbone sighed and shook her head. "The reason doesn't matter. Shouldn't you be eating breakfast soon? Lucia has it ready."

As if on cue, my stomach gurgled, and I considered acquiescing until an enormous cloud floated overhead. I tightened my lips.

"It's fine. I'll eat when I get back. I really should be going soon. I don't want to miss painting the sunrise."

She shook her head. "Duca de' Medici would be quite upset to learn his *beniamina* is skipping meals. Especially while she is unwell."

I folded my arms tightly, and my tone finally broke into overt impatience. "I'm not *that* unwell anymore, and he *would* understand. Now, please tell me where Signora Rafia is."

Signora Carbone's nostrils flared. "She is the only remaining driver who works here, and she is attending to her duties. I am simply obeying orders when I tell you to return to the abbey and resume your schedule."

It wasn't as though I could drive myself. Beyond not knowing how to work this electric car, and beyond not having a driver's license in this country, I had the sinking suspicion the remaining car keys were in her pocket, and I would have to pry them from her if I wanted them.

"What orders?" I snapped. "And what duties? Zeno is asleep, and you're here fiddling around with the cars!" What could she possibly be up to?

Silence, dead silence. Frustration on her face—but something beneath that. Her pupils were dilated, her lips quivering ever so slightly.

Fear. That was fear beneath that frustration.

My arms fell slack. "I-I'm sorry. I understand. You're just doing your job. I'll go now."

She let me leave without another word. Head held low, I walked back into the dining hall. Rather than bothering to set it down, I let the satchel slide out of my hands into a heap on the floor. Several of my pastels toppled out, but I didn't chase after them.

Breakfast was my favorite, clearly meant to be a celebratory meal. Two *treccine*—fried dough topped with sugar, so fluffy and delicious it made donuts jealous, and ice-cold, freshly squeezed orange juice and a hot cappuccino.

Even with the massive feast before me, the room looked emptier than ever, and I felt sicker than I had been with all those tubes and wires. Normally, my mouth would've been watering, but it

felt as dry as when I had first woken up two weeks ago. I prodded at the food with the fork for a painfully long time.

I didn't notice them at first, watching me from afar—Lucia's eyes, which had often flickered to the ground in my presence for the past two weeks, were now staring at me intently beneath a deeply furrowed brow.

"Jesus, Lucia!" I cried, startling.

"Sorry, signorina!" she whispered as she came nearer. "I didn't mean to scare you."

"Not that I'm complaining, but what are you still doing here? You usually run off before I even get the chance to say good morning."

Lucia nodded slowly and looked around. "Is Duca de' Medici here?"

I glanced at my watch. "No, he's probably still asleep." I realized then that the last time I had left bed before Zeno awoke was in Puglia. Would he panic when he woke up without me beside him? Would he go mad?

"Good," she said quickly. "I have some car keys. We need to go."

"Uh—why?"

"This is your only chance to leave! All the footpaths will be blocked soon, and Signora Carbone is already shutting off the cars. Duca de' Medici is going to make it so you can't leave!"

The only way I would have been more taken aback was if Lucia had told me she'd be serving chicken-fried unicorn for lunch.

"Zeno is what?"

Her voice rose to a desperate pitch. "He says you're not well, and that someone could get you sick. You need to leave before he wakes up!"

My fingers felt numb. The world felt strangely cold.

"But I don't want to leave, Lucia. This abbey is my home. I was here for *months* without leaving. I'll be fine!"

Lucia scoffed and threw down her arms. “I know you love him, but please don’t be blinded! There’s a difference between not wanting to leave and not being able to.”

She couldn’t be right. This was everything I wanted. *He* was everything I wanted. I didn’t even need to finish my thesis now, did I? We would all be happy here again. Everything would be normal again.

“I—I need to think.” My voice was soft, shaking furiously, along with the rest of my body. “I can’t talk about this right now.”

“You don’t have time to—” Lucia froze. She stared behind me, jaw agape, trembling as much as I was. A shadow rose from behind me. “Oh,” she whimpered. “Duca de’ Medici. What a pleasant surprise.”

I felt the warmth of him lingering long before I saw him or heard his voice.

“Yes,” he said in voice devoid of emotion. “A surprise indeed.”

She forced a toothy smile that looked like it pained her. “I’ll go make you a plate as well.”

“It’s fine!” I said quickly. “We can share!”

“No, please do, Lucia,” Zeno replied, taking a seat beside me. “I don’t want to eat any of Cora’s. She isn’t well yet.”

Lucia bowed so deeply and shakily, I thought she would fall over. Then, with that same terrified grin, she replied, “Yes, sir!”

She skittered away, leaving me alone with the person I loved most.

“Now then, Cora,” Zeno purred, clasping my hand. “What shall we do today?”

“I want to go back to sleep for now,” I whispered, staring down at my food. “I’m so exhausted. Maybe after that we can just relax?”

Zeno cupped my face in his hand and tilted my head up. The rage in his eyes melted away immediately. He looked at me with the sweetest of smiles, with utter love and adoration. With eyes that worshiped me.

"Of course, *mia passerotta*. The world is ours. Not another soul matters."

Chapter Fifty-One

Il mio tesoro

For the next week, I didn't leave the bedroom on account of being "sick." In truth, I felt perfectly fine—better than I had in months, in fact. But the entire household whispered about me as though I were a hospice patient. I had meals in bed, tea in bed, showers in the small bathroom attached, books and music curated to my desire. The finches were even trained to hop into travel cages to greet me.

It was someone's will keeping me in those walls within walls. Someone had decided that I would isolate myself for three days, that the outside world would cease to exist. I did not know if this idea was Zeno's or my own, nor which scenario would have been worse.

Just as I had awoken three days ago with the resolve to remain in bed, I awoke on the fourth intent to spend some of the day outdoors.

I had faded in and out of sleep, with Zeno at my side on occasion and the bed vacant on others. The final time I sat up, he was not there. A meal of some sort—I wasn't certain if it was breakfast, lunch, or dinner—sat on a tray on the bedside table. Some sort of flaky pastry, warm and still steaming, paired with a creamy soup.

I had come to know most of the dishes served in the abbey. There was plenty of variety, of course, yet all the food was in the form of rustic Sicilian dishes I had researched before my first interview. Signora Carbone was fond of following the tradition of the land. Something about this dish, meanwhile, seemed vaguely French. I frowned and mentally went through my past few meals.

How hadn't I noticed it before? Caprese salad, minestrone, and ribollita. They were all mainland Italian, or even outright foreign.

I tried in vain to parse the significance of this for a few minutes but gave up. My food and the bed were now cold and equally unappealing, so I abandoned them both.

Without a window or clock, the time of day was indiscernible as I stepped out into the hallway. The floor felt like ice beneath my feet, and the house had that strange, ethereal stillness that felt nocturnal. But as I peered into my old bedroom and saw light pouring through a gap in the curtains, my suspicions were confirmed to be wrong. It was simply an unusually still afternoon, much like the one during which I had seen Leonore.

But even on that day, there had seemed to be some sort of life in the abbey, with Signora Carbone and Lucia moving around in the background like mice, attending to the unforeseen machinations of the house.

I hobbled into the room, my breath eluding me. The air was heavy, full of my anticipation and something else entirely—a musty scent that was alien to this room, yet one which had been a close friend of mine for many years.

I ran my finger across the top of a bookshelf and found a fine, gritty layer on my fingertip. Dust. Something a conservatrix would have never permitted, even in a vacant suite. Signorina Carbone made Lucia clean the suite daily, and this degree of dust, though slight, did not accumulate with a single missed cleaning.

I slammed the window into its sill and yanked aside the curtains, which tore with a sickening sound and fell, limp, onto the ground. The room, now fully illuminated in many senses, was a wreck. The blanket and pillows had been scattered across the floor, every drawer thrown open and ravaged. Even the crosses had been torn from the wall.

"Lucia?" I called, as though she would be in the other room. "Signora?"

No reply, of course. I staggered out of the room, leaving the door ajar. The second it hit me, my heart raced, a terrible drum beating accelerando as all the clues unfolded.

When was the last time I had seen either of them? When had

I last eaten the sort of food they cooked? When had my bedroom last been cleaned?

Badump-badump-badump-badump. Louder and faster my heart beat, the tiny vessels behind my eyes and within my ears visibly and audibly pulsating. Just as the tempo reached allegro, I became faintly aware of a song behind the drum—the gentle, steady first movement of “Moonlight Sonata,” played with the emotive yet skillful touch of Zeno’s fingers.

Vision darkening, I relied on the melody itself to guide me to our bedroom.

It took everything within me not to collapse back into the bed and allow myself to be lulled back to sleep by the music, to instead push beyond my sanctum and into Zeno’s. Through a haze, I could see him at the bench, head tossed back and eyes closed in a look of utter peace.

Anger swelled in me, rage at being unable to feel so calm myself.

I exhaled shakily, and the sonata seized midmeasure. “Ah, Cora,” Zeno said, glancing back at me. “What’s the ma—”

“Where’s Lucia?” I asked, balling up my fists.

Zeno looked away in the obvious manner of a guilty dog. It was one of those times where, in any other circumstance, I would have found the overtness endearing, or even adorable. But in this case, my greatest question was whether the beast had bared its teeth.

“Gone,” he replied after a painful silence.

My immediate question, and the realization that it had come so instinctively, rolled over me in a wave of nausea. “As in . . . gone-gone?”

“Are you asking if I killed her? Of course not!” Zeno scoffed, rising from the piano bench and tossing himself onto a chair. “You told me long ago she wanted to open a salon in the city. I simply funded her venture.”

“And Signora Carbone?”

He shrugged and took a long sip of wine. “Barone Sforza needed another conservatrix. She gladly took a position there.”

“And Signore Urbino?”

Silence. Dead silence, for God knew how long. Then, equal parts begrudging and matter-of-fact: “He’s dead, Cora. I shot him.”

Zeno might as well have knocked the wind out of me, the way my breath escaped me. I had always known, of course, but now the truth was inescapable.

Yet now that it was out in the open, Zeno held my gaze steadily. From here on out, I knew the answers would come out as smooth as silk, as though he were answering the time of the day. I wished I could stop myself from asking them.

“What about Basilio?”

“I caught up with him shortly after, once you were on the way to the hospital. He hadn’t gotten far.”

With each sentence, my voice rose, and now I spoke on the verge of yelling. “What did you do to him? How did you—”

“With a concrete block.”

I could practically see it: Basilio with his pretty face bashed in, arms and legs bent at horrendous angles, chest concave. Several ribs protruding from his chest, others impaling freshly burst organs.

Bile rose in my throat, but I couldn’t stop asking, “And your father?”

“I haven’t found him yet.” He sighed. Remorse showed on his face for the first time, far too late.

“And when you do?”

He darkened, eyes ablaze, nails digging into his armchair. “I don’t know. He almost killed you. Nothing I can imagine is sufficient justice. Regardless, I’d like to deal with him myself, unlike the others.”

I almost laughed at the surrealness of it all and could only echo his last two words. “The others?”

Zeno bore a hole into the floor with his eyes and gnashed his teeth. “What happened to you was no small operation. There were many others involved, like the man who drugged you. I don’t know if any of them met their ends swiftly, but even if they did, my father will not be afforded the same luxury.”

Faced with this realization, all I could do was look back at the beginning of our conversation. "What about Doctor Ntumba? Are you going to make her leave too?"

In only a sentence, I pulled him out of some sort of depth. "Noor? She has done nothing wrong. More importantly, she's still treating—"

Finally, something in me snapped. "Come on!" I cried. "Let's give up the act. We both know I'm healed! I don't have a single goddamn stitch in me!"

Never had I spoken to Zeno in such a manner, and I regretted it for an instant at the sight of him genuinely wounded by the harshness of my words. But when I looked closer and saw that beneath the injury was his own guilt, I knew those words needed to be spoken.

I took a step back and turned away from Zeno, unable to meet his eyes. When I spoke next, my words were scarcely above a whisper. "I'm not better, and I never will be, will I? You're never going to drink from me again, you won't let anyone but Doctor Ntumba near me, and I'll never leave this abbey."

His silence was my answer.

I was once more left alone with only the gentle drum of my heart to break the silence. Discordant against its rapid rhythm, Zeno's gentle footsteps slowly approached me. In a swift movement, he wrapped his arms around me and pulled me close to him. He, too, was trembling.

"Even if it means sending away every other soul, locking you away, and barring every window, I will do what I must to keep you safe," Zeno said, voice husky in my ear. "I will repent for the harm that befell the most important thing to me of all. I will make the world burn."

I hadn't ever believed it was possible for words to become reality, and yet these words, spoken so vehemently, must have been bewitched. For the first time in my life, I truly feared what Zeno was capable of. Not in that unsettled way as when he spoke vacantly, or even in the flashbang manner as when he told me about his father, but truly.

"No!"

Zeno froze, and I took the opportunity to break away from him roughly. I tried to spin on my heels to see him, to step out and away from his grasp, but I fell to the floor. I tried in vain to stagger to my feet and put space between us but succeeded only in landing on my ass and skittering back.

Chest heaving, heart pounding, I stared back up at his crestfallen expression.

Zeno crouched on his heels and gave me a long, sad look. Just as he opened his mouth to speak, I cut in, “Zeno, I need to think.”

With a small sigh, he turned his head away and closed his eyes. His voice came out, low and shaky and just audible above the ringing in my ears. “Cora, I—”

“Zeno, no.” I rose to my feet and dusted off my skirt. “I need to be alone.”

He didn’t call out to me as I left. He didn’t do anything at all but sit there, already starting to disintegrate.

Chapter Fifty-Two

Un bel dì, vedremo

I locked myself in the abbess's suite for several days, not reading, not painting, not doing anything at all. Just being suspended in a strange, dissociative state. Zeno gave up trying to talk to me, for he quickly learned I wouldn't respond. But before bed, every day, he gave me an unanswered, "Good night. I love you."

He slid letters under my door, but I didn't read them or even pick them up. I cried. A lot. Despite it all, I missed him furiously, worried about him furiously. Loved him furiously. I allowed Doctor Ntumba alone to see me and bring me food.

Until one day, she didn't.

I was sitting in bed, cross-legged, doing nothing and everything. Analyzing the pores of my hands, counting the bricks on the wall, watching the rise and fall of my eyelashes as I slowly blinked and did anything else I could think of to slip into a strange meditative trance. A trio of soft knocks jarred me from it, and I nearly fell off of the bed. I walked slowly and shakily to the door, and the scent of freshly baked bread wafted beneath it.

My stomach gurgled so loudly, I was certain whoever was on the other side would be able to hear it. Who that someone was, I knew, was not Doctor Ntumba, for she had the habit of unapologetically bursting into my room with her skeleton key and arms full of prepared meals.

I hadn't eaten today, I realized. I had skipped two meals entirely, despite the chiming of a bell beckoning me downstairs for breakfast and lunch.

Closing one eye, I pressed my head flush to the ground and peered beyond the tiny gap beneath the door. On the other side, Zeno's shoes greeted me for an instant, only to be blocked off by the sight and sound of a tray being placed gently in front of my door.

"Cora, please eat something. I'll leave you for however long you need. Just take care of yourself."

True to his word, Zeno did not linger for even an instant. Instead, his footsteps retreated into the distance, all the way to the other side of the abbey.

After several minutes of silence, I finally cracked the door. The sole guest awaiting me on the other side was a metal tray topped with a round loaf of sourdough, a bowl of tomato soup, and cucumber water. I opened the entrance to my domain just enough to snatch the meal through, then locked it behind me.

My fingers burned as I tore savagely into the loaf, but I did not care. I drowned a large hunk in the hot soup for several seconds, relying on its creamy moisture to allow me to swallow unchewed bites so quickly it made me feel sick. Once I had engulfed the sourdough, I lapped up what little remained of the soup and finally chased it all down with large gulps of cucumber water.

"Ugh."

Regret set in just as quickly as the bloat. I considered sneaking out for a few spell, taking advantage of Zeno's absence and tracking down Doctor Ntumba to ask for a cocktail of antacids and salicylates.

But then I remembered I hadn't seen her at all today, just as I hadn't seen Lucia or Signora Carbone. Confident that Zeno was still keeping his distance, I abandoned the tray on the ground and left the suite for the first time in almost a week.

The main door to the abbey was wide open. Light poured into the entrance. Trees gnashed back and forth, spurred by the same ferocious winds that whistled through the halls. The cool blue gradient of moonlight across the tile was broken by the silhouette of Doctor Ntumba, whose massive shadow appeared engorged. The bag in her arms was misshapen, all of her belongings clearly forced inside.

For Noor not to have every shirt folded and every item packed as economically as possible defied all my expectations of her, so in a

strange way, the shock on her face made sense. She wore sneakers in lieu of her usual high heels, her shirt was buttoned a row off, and her hair was disheveled.

My heavy footfalls were a staccato above the ever-present hum of a motor just outside. Doctor Ntumba turned to face me.

I stared, slack-jawed, and continued to approach her slowly, as though she were a skittish animal.

"Cora," she said, gathering her composure poorly.

"What's going on?"

Instead of answering, Noor set down her bag and smoothed her hair, arranged her clothes, and otherwise tried to look put together. Then, just as I was about to prod further, she spoke in an undertone. "He asked me to leave."

"Who did?"

It was a stupid question, given our household of three, but perhaps if I was lucky, some inhospitable phantom would materialize, and she could blame it on anyone other than Zeno.

She responded with the look the question warranted.

Doctor Ntumba stepped into her shadow, and the door rattled against its hinges, refusing to close. It remained as ajar as my mouth. She placed her hand on my shoulder, and though her touch was light, it felt immensely heavy on me.

With a swell of rage inside me, I couldn't bear to look at her. I tightened my fists and held my breath. How cruel of her to allow me to have these terrible thoughts. How wicked of her to make me process this truth. For the first time in my life, I wished I could smack her across the face, and the gravity of this thought startled me. Never had I wanted to physically harm another person, no matter how upset I was.

This must be, I realized, an ounce of what wrath had brought all the scars upon Zeno's back.

"Can I ask you a question?"

Noor nodded. I was thankful that she did not speak, for it would make my wavering voice even more pathetic in comparison.

"I know all of this is because he's terrified, and he wants to keep me safe. But once he thinks I am truly safe, will he stop?"

Though I was still unwilling to meet her gaze, Noor continued to bore her eyes into me. I didn't have to look up to know the look on her face.

She removed her hand to gesture for me to follow and passed me at a slow, ambling pace. Too confused to ask what was going on, I joined her side.

As we walked down the hall, things felt the same as they had long ago: Noor walking with her hands behind her back and her chin up, just like she did during conversations when I first came to the abbey. Like clockwork, she guided me down our usual route, and I could almost smell the chai brewing as we neared the tea room and hear Lucia's laugh in the distance.

When Noor finally spoke, it was with that conversational tone from bygone times.

"As a child, I had a fascination with many of the street dogs in my neighborhood. Despite having been thrown to the streets and beaten, they desired nothing but companionship. Even if they guarded their treasures ferociously, they were still creatures forged of nothing but utter adoration for their companions. But there was a common disease that plagued them all. Time and time again, I would watch how perfectly reasonable and loving creatures could so quickly deteriorate into irrational shells. What I learned early on, Cora, is that rabid beasts act on nothing but insatiable bloodlust."

As we continued along the path and into her memories, I let myself slip into my own. I pretended her words were another story on our way to tea, that I still felt strange sleeping in the bed in the abbess's suite. The room we neared now was one I used to only imagine entering at this time of night. Zeno's door was tightly closed, locked by a set of keys I had become more and more familiar with.

"What if it's just Zeno and me here?" I asked as Noor dug through her pockets. "What about once you and everyone else leave?"

She found it finally: a small, silver key. Even in the dim light, its metal surface radiated as brightly as its significance.

She held it up to her face in a strangely contemplative manner. Then, after a small click and a slight pull, the door gave with ease.

Before we entered, Noor turned to me and spoke, every word dripping with gravity.

“I have seen that when a rabid dog has destroyed everything around it, it begins to bite its own leg. For the last two decades, Zeno has been my only patient, and for the last two decades, I have loved him as furiously as a mother. But I know what he is, Cora. Do you?”

I wish I was silent for longer and been forced to contemplate my answer, but I did not. “Yes. I have for a long time.”

She led me into the room, and we lingered beside his bed. “You know about my . . .” She trailed off for a moment, eyes lowering to the ground. Finally, she looked back up at me. “. . . medical specialty, do you not?”

I held her gaze, studying her eyes for any sort of intention, but could identify nothing but a vague sense of sadness. Regret for her actions, perhaps? Guilt for not having told me about it?

Unable to discern any further information, I replied, “Yes. You specialize in physician-assisted suicide.”

Wordlessly, she led me to Zeno’s bedside drawer, took another key from her pocket, and unlocked it.

For whatever reason, the last things I would have expected the vintage furniture to house were modern medications. Despite my limited scopes of view and knowledge, I recognized a few of the bottles: narcotic-level pain medications, sedatives, and even specially bagged chemotherapy drugs.

Without needing to search for it, Doctor Ntumba pulled out a bottle easily and placed it in my hand. “Then you must know what this is.”

Pentobarbital oral solution, I read on the label. With shaking hands, I opened the bottle and peered in. A thin liquid swirled around the bottle, amber-hued.

How strange it was, I thought, *that such an innocuous syrup has the power to end a life.* That the drug of choice to allow a man to kill himself was placed in the same kind of bottle with the same type

of label as the liquid ibuprofen at my bedside. I returned it to her hand.

"It's a very bitter syrup, I've heard. Unfortunately, an effective dose for euthanasia is one hundred milliliters for this specific concentration." Doctor Ntumba spoke slowly and deliberately, making sure I was catching each and every word. "Of course, for the sake of euthanasia, it is typically mixed with vodka and sugar to mask the taste. My former patients have stated they couldn't even tell."

Ice ran through me.

"What are you implying?" I whispered.

"I am implying nothing, Cora," she stated plainly. "I am simply providing information."

I stared at the spot in my hand, still cool where the bottle had been, and sat on her words for several moments.

"Thank you for the information," I said finally, meeting Noor's eyes. "But I don't think I'll need it. Words have gotten me this far. I won't need anything more."

Noor wrinkled up her nose and gave me a disgusted look. For a second, she looked like she'd argue back. I could practically see the bitter words on her tongue: *How foolish you are to think a rabid beast can be reasoned with. How conceited.*

But then, with little more than a breathy sigh, the anger faded into something entirely different: grief.

"Information cannot hurt you, Cora. Just as I provided you with information, I am providing you with this key."

She placed it in my hand, and it sickened me to feel it was warm from her touch. How could anything so horrid feel like anything but ice to me?

But just as strangely warm was Doctor Ntumba's expression before she departed. "Goodbye, Cora, and good luck."

Chapter Fifty-Three

Ch'io mi scordi di te?

Despite having been gone only a handful of minutes, when I entered the abbess's suite, I was met with pillows overturned, the bathroom door thrown open, and a desperate hound sniffing every leaf in search of its master.

One of the unopened letters crackled beneath my foot as I stepped into the room, immediately drawing Zeno's attention.

"Cora!" he breathed with a combination of shock and relief. "I thought you had—"

"I'm leaving, Zeno," I cut in before he could say it himself. Before either of us could deny it was happening. "I just came back to say goodbye and grab my bag."

It was waiting for me under the bed, already filled with my essential belongings and topped with a car key. I realized with a pang of guilt that Noor must have packed while I was asleep—or perhaps, in a somnolent state, I packed it myself. Either way, one of us had known. Now it was time for Zeno to know too.

He stood, a frail, quivering barricade in front of the door. He hadn't had an ounce of blood in God knew how long. I despised Zeno for an instant, for making me speak and act so coldly, until I remembered it was myself I hated. Who I would hate even more by the end of the night.

"Please, Zeno," I said, trying in vain to muster any sense of authority as I approached. "Let me go."

"Cora—" When he said my name, even in that haughty tone and even under these circumstances, my heart still fluttered. I still wanted. Perhaps it was upon seeing this that his demeanor

hardened, and he finished his sentence. "—I can't. You gave yourself to me to love you, to keep you safe. To have you. I can't rescind *any* of that."

"Zeno," I replied sternly, pushing him aside with just as much force as was necessary. "Goodbye. I mean it."

Goodbye. Two syllables pierced him, brought him to his knees at my feet.

"I love you," he whispered, his voice now as soft and shaky as his grip on my wrists.

For the first time in days, the man at my feet felt like more than just a whisper of the one I would have given everything for. And every ounce of me then wanted to fall to my knees and press myself into the crevices I could have traced with my eyes closed, even now. Every instinct I had was screaming at me to comfort him and hold him and forget this had ever happened. I had swallowed the words *I love you* so many times, they were now a mouthful of bile threatening to erupt from my lips.

But all that came out was an emotionless, "I know."

I had never known before that moment that it was possible to see a heart break, nor how horrible it would look. I half expected to see crimson bloom across his shirt. Now I was forced to carry the knowledge that it was entirely my fault that Zeno looked on the verge of disintegration.

"Please tell me you love me too," he whimpered. "I'm begging you."

I couldn't bear to look at him a second longer because I knew I would fold. Those four words, *I love you too*, had the power to end his anguish, to mend together his heart and practically unwind the last few minutes.

I looked away and said nothing. The desperation in his voice heightened tenfold. "I'll chew off my own hands. I'll cut my throat. I'll do *anything*."

"I know you would!" I cried, looking at him for the first time in what felt like an eternity. Looking at a reflection of my own agony. "But I don't want any of that."

"Then what do you want? Please. Anything."

With a shaky exhale, I let my hands go limp, and they slid out from his fingers. Fighting back tears, I turned from him and forced my eyes to the spot on the floor, where my heart was residing. "You're going to devour everything around you. You're going to devour us both."

I expected him to argue with me, to question a single word, but he didn't. Instead, he asked a question that tore into me: "You do love me, don't you? Even after all this?"

Maybe things would be easier if I lied and said I hated him. Maybe that way, I could shatter his heart irreparably and leave no chance between us. Or maybe it would be easy in another way, and it would spur Zeno to double down on his efforts to keep me in the abbey.

But easy wasn't necessarily right.

"I do," I whispered. "I really do."

The opposite of my expectation happened. I had seen countless times how, when cut off from its base and placed in water, a rose would slowly die. No matter how lovingly maintained, once snipped away, there was no choice but to watch the once-vibrant blooms wilt and wither.

With roses, this process took days, or even weeks. With Zeno, it took only seconds.

"You need to leave," he murmured, staggering to his feet. "You need to leave me here and leave the key with me."

Despite the weight of our conversation and how everything else had faded away, I hadn't forgotten the key was against my hip. I reached into my pocket and grasped it so tightly, it threatened to draw blood. Maybe if I held it tight enough, the tiny key would embed itself into my skin, and I wouldn't have to give it to Zeno.

But hadn't I known deep down that this was a possibility?

"I—are you sure?"

"Yes," he said with utter resolve. "You love me, so you must. And I love you, so I must."

How strongly I wished that he was wrong, that I could argue any of it. But I couldn't. I shut my eyes tightly, freeing a torrent of

tears, and held out my hand. Once I felt the warmth of his own beneath it, I peeled apart my fingers and let the key fall out.

"Thank you, *mia passerotta*."

I could hear the smile in Zeno's voice, just as much as I could the tears. I broke away from him, hugging my arms tightly around myself in lieu of him.

His hand—the one not holding his mortality—gently folded in mine, and I allowed him to walk me over to the bed.

"Just stay a little longer. Please. Just for a few more minutes, hold my hand, and listen to me. That's all I ask of you."

I bit my lip and slowly nodded, joining him. The plush was soft, the light was soft, and my hand clasping Zeno's was as firm as I could make it.

"It scared me when I was younger, how little I felt," he said, closing his eyes. "I used to think that maybe feeling had been trained out of me, but now I think I was just born with something missing. Some piece in my brain or my soul that was supposed to make me alive. Maybe my body had the knowledge that I never would really be alive." Zeno's pale lashes flickered open, and a small, strange smile crossed his lips. "I was able to find some things that made me feel, when I got older. But no one and nothing made me feel as much as you."

I tried to pull away my hand. "What are you—"

Zeno firmly held mine, looking into my eyes with full sincerity. "I'm not saying any of this to make you stay, Cora."

"Then why?"

"I just need to say it. I've thought this so many times, and I need to say it for once. I need someone to hear me one time in my life."

"How can I believe you?" I cried. "Don't you know . . .?" *How this makes me feel?*

He laughed a short, bitter laugh. "Of course I do. Allow me to be selfish, just for now. See me as I am for a breath. I know you're the only one who can."

I tightened my jaw and looked back up at the ceiling, hoping the angle could disperse my tears and prevent them from rolling down my cheeks. Zeno did the same.

"I thought about a lot of ways to make you stay. I considered reinforcing every inch of this abbey, employing dozens of guards. Tying you to the bed, making you look at me every morning and night, just to make you think of me. But—" Zeno placed the key onto his chest and ran his newly freed hand through his hair in a strangely casual gesture. "—I knew I could never truly have you. And I always knew it was my destiny to die alone."

"It didn't have to be like this," I whimpered once I could stifle the words.

"No, it did. I don't have it in me to love in parts." He sat up more, foretelling the end of his confession. "This abbey was always my casket. Even if you made me feel alive for a while, I was supposed to die here. I'm ready now, though. I've been ready to die for as long as I remember."

I finally let the sobs break free, so ragged and wretched they wracked my entire body. It was Zeno's turn, I knew, to have to restrain every muscle in his body not to hug and comfort me. He simply held my hand as I cried until I couldn't produce tears any longer.

Then, after one final squeeze, he released me.

"Will you take the finches with you?" Zeno asked, eyes flickering over to where the cages resided. "They don't deserve to be here either."

"Yes. I'll take good care of them."

"Nobody else could do it better."

Lying back down, he grasped the key tightly again and let out a long breath—the strange, final breath of a dying beast. It was hollow compared to the sharp whistle of a gale just beyond the window. He turned his back away from it and hugged his arms to his chest like a scared child.

"My God," he said to the wind. "I'm terrified."

That was the end of our conversation, I knew. That was all there was to say.

And yet, just as I was about to leave the room for the last time, Zeno spoke with the most pain, fear, and love I had ever heard in a man's voice.

"Please . . . just know I'll love you forever. Remember that my bones will love you."

I looked over my shoulder at him, etching his face into my mind, searing his eyes into me. "I love you too," I whispered. "I always will."

Finally, I realized there were tears in his eyes as well, glinting like the key in his hand. A man mourning himself.

"Can you open the window before you go?" he asked with a genuine smile. "I want to see the stars tonight."

Epilogue

Non temer, amato bene

Doctor Cora Bowling expected the Abbazia di Santa Dymphna to look the same as when she had inherited it so many years ago. The idea that, like her, the abbey would age, had somehow never struck her.

Even before she reached the apex of the hill, the discrepancy between her expectations and the reality of the abbey was undeniable. The olive trees, so ancient and gnarled she had thought it impossible for them to grow any larger, had done just that. Serpentine roots had unfurled through the maze of tiles, now cracked and overgrown with encroaching wild grasses. The statues and architecture had been overtaken by vines and moss and ivy. More so than even in Puglia, the air had a distinct, dusty odor to it, and the sisters got the sense that the main building itself had remained untouched by the elements by the same magic that had allowed it to survive the earthquake so many decades ago.

Not that it was in prime condition, of course. Dead branches and small animals alike had found ways to nestle in its dusty crevices, some of the facades had smoothed with time, and even a few nonessential bricks had toppled out of place. All in all, however, the skeleton of the looming building was an unchanged artifact.

A gust of icy wind sent a wave of freshly fallen leaves spiraling toward them, and as if to beckon them from afar, the rusted main gate to the abbey creaked open noisily.

With her long dress billowing around her, Opaline pulled her tan cardigan more tightly across her slender frame, trapping several russet locks of hair. Already in front of her sister, Opaline's pace quickened even more, as she felt strangely compelled by the imagined gesture.

"Slow down, Peachy!" Cora yelled. "I'm not in as good of shape as I used to be."

Opaline slowed her speed and tried not to turn and look back at her sister. Cora hadn't cried very many times in front of Opaline since they started speaking again, but the mere mention of this place always seemed to make her eyes glaze over. Opaline knew the ragged breaths of her sister behind her were not because of physical strain, but she wanted to grant Cora the excuse.

Opaline couldn't help but wonder at the significance of the items her sister was carrying. Such disparate things could only have one unifying factor: a person she knew little about. Cora had told her so much about the abbey itself, about its gorgeous architecture, its curious history, and the hill beside the graveyard, but only in the sense of the historian she had come to be. The name *Zeno* had slipped out of Cora's mouth by accident once or twice, and an immediate change in topic always followed. But these objects, so light they had to be carried in a box for fear of being blown away by the slightest gust, were some of the heaviest things the doctor had ever held.

The two finally reached the entrance, and only once tucked into its mouth did Cora realize the abbey would be locked. She juggled the box from arm to arm to dig into her pockets, cursing to herself all the while at the clumsiness of the movements. In most circumstances, Opaline would have waited for her sister to remember that it was she who had the key and take full advantage of the opportunity to tease Cora back for once. Today, though, she opted to pull the freshly copied skeleton key out from her pocket and show it to her sister before unlocking the door herself.

The key fought with Opaline, and it took a few deft movements to maneuver the old lock into submission. After a soft *click,* the door opened on its own accord, far too quickly.

The hallway, which utterly engulfed any shred of daylight, illuminated itself. Row by row, the sconces flickered on, casting the vacant room with a low, amberish hue. With chills running down her spine, Opaline glanced back at her sister, half expecting her to be terrified, half expecting her to mutter some excuse about how the building's foundation must have shifted. What Cora *actually* did was entirely outside of Opaline's imagination.

She brightened, even laughed as if seeing an old friend, and stepped inside slowly.

“Sorry, Peachy,” Cora said over her shoulder. “I forgot to warn you that this place has a tendency to show you ghosts.”

The younger sister quickly vanished further into the hallway, hugging the box tighter than before. Opaline peered back outside at the bright, sunny Sicilian landscape, and then back into the belly of the beast. Opaline could not deny the abbey was beautiful, despite the decrepit state of its exterior. It was as though the baroque room had been factory sealed centuries ago, with ornate marble flooring and a celestial fresco of a cloudy day overhead, joined by sinuous columns that also acted as frames for the murals painted across the walls.

Red, velvet curtains marked every open entrance. Portraits and sculpted busts alike stared at her expectantly, so lifelike it seemed like they would scold her for leaving the door open. Opaline wanted to say something to Cora, but instead she sucked in her breath and kept her eyes to the ground. She didn’t know why her sister had brought her along, and she didn’t know what was the right or wrong thing to say.

Silence, Ma had always told her, was a lot easier to apologize for than misplaced words.

“Isn’t it beautiful?” Cora said in front of her. “I don’t think a more beautiful place exists in this world, and I’ve looked for a long time, Peachy.”

Opaline couldn’t argue with her sister if she wanted to. Cora led the pair into a smaller, plainer hallway that was more functional than decorative.

“I’ve always preferred this portion, though. It feels more like home.”

“What are we doing here, Birdie?” Opaline finally mustered the nerve to ask, following her sister into what seemed like the umpteenth corridor.

Finally, with a small, strange smile gracing her lips, Cora turned to face her sister. “I’d like to show you around my home.”

That didn’t answer Opaline’s question fully; instead, it raised even more. How long had her sister lived here, and under what circumstances? If Cora had inherited such riches, why did she insist on hopping from apartment to apartment in London and Partanna, even crashing with her for weeks at a time at their childhood home in

Red Creek? And why hadn't she been told anything of its former owner?

Yet the housewife didn't have it in her to press any further. She simply followed her sister and wondered at Cora's beaming face.

After setting down the box on a side table, Cora turned into a small room, one that was plain compared to every other place they had traveled. There were no true decorations, just barren stone walls and floors and ceilings, all lit by a window so small, it looked like a porthole. Undecorated shelves were crammed across every wall, stuffed to the brim with old books and files, and a plain wooden desk and chair. Covering it all was a thick layer of dust, much of which stirred at their entrance.

The sisters sneezed in rapid succession, and Cora burst into laughter. "I didn't think this place could get any dustier! I should have brought a shovel!"

Opaline pulled her cardigan over her mouth and nose as her sister ventured in further.

"This is the little library. We won't stay here long. After all, I've studied every document in here back and forth! Most of my ideas for my thesis came from this room." Suddenly, Cora grabbed Opaline's hand and grinned broadly. "Are you ready, Peachy?"

"I—" Before Opaline could respond, her sister broke into a run, dragging her along effortlessly, although Opaline towered over Cora. "Hold on!" Opaline giggled, barely able to move her legs fast enough.

Cora stopped in front of two large doors, and Opaline nearly crashed into her. They were visibly heavy, and Cora had to lean into them to make them budge. Finally, just as Opaline had decided to help Cora, they gave.

Opaline was already a little out of breath, but what little breath remained was stolen from her in an instant. Realizing her sister was too stunned to walk, Cora dragged her in behind her.

Though not much of a reader herself, Opaline could still certainly empathize with the utter rapture possessing her sister. The library itself was two stories tall, the room larger than the largest church Opaline had ever been in. Shelves upon shelves of gorgeous leather-bound books, perfectly organized, were illuminated by the largest chandelier she had ever seen. Vases and bronze busts had

been placed in every corner in such a manner that they were still easy to navigate around, forming a clear path that reminded her of the museum she had seen on a field trip. Even the floor beneath her feet, every stone carefully carved with patterns so delicate she was horrified at stepping onto them, was its own work of art.

Cora picked up a jog once more, and instead of one of the hundreds of gold-leaf books, she sought something entirely different: a spiral-bound binder, utterly innocuous other than how tightly it was stuffed.

"My reading list, past and future," Cora said to her sister with a smile, flipping through both the front and back of it. Then, mostly to herself: "I wonder if I'll feel differently about *Il Canzoniere* after so long." Despite its size, Cora managed to put the binder down gingerly. "All right," she said. "I guess it's time."

The room between the little library and the main library was a bedroom that balanced utility and beauty to be luxurious, but the two only lingered for a minute. Compared to the jovial air the dusty room had conjured between them, and the elated tone of the main library, a somber miasma permeated within this room. Though it was stately, what with its velveteen, king-sized bed, mahogany furniture, and Tiffany glass lamps, something about this room was clearly lived in.

Cora trembled as she neared the bed, her hand visibly wavering on its path to the mattress. Her fingers barely touched a faint outline.

"I wonder if this was the room they found his body in," Cora whispered shakily. "I never asked Doctor Ntumba. I never went to the trial."

Another name Opaline had heard occasionally but seen on a few letters addressed to her sister. As far as she knew, Cora had only written back to the penitentiary once.

Cora spoke, hands still caressing the indent, back turned to Opaline.

"It's been fifteen years since I've been here, Peachy. In those fifteen years, I've done everything I've ever dreamed of and become the person I've always wanted to be. And yet through it all, I've felt . . . nothing."

For a long time, Cora's eyes lingered on the floor. When she finally met Opaline's again, they were brimming with tears. "When I inherited this place, I told myself that if my feelings had changed, I'd donate it to some historical society in a heartbeat. But if my soul still felt as empty as the day I closed that door, I'd return and care for it for the rest of my life. Here we are."

"Oh, Birdie." For the first time since they had reunited, Opaline embraced her sister just like she did when they were children. And Cora sobbed just as she did as a child, and Opaline rubbed her arm.

"I'm sorry," Cora said, half laughing and half crying after a few minutes. "I didn't mean to make this awkward."

Opaline gave her a squeeze and stepped back. "It's like I used to tell you. Having feelings isn't something to apologize for."

Once more, Cora let out her half laugh and wiped away a tear. "You're right. That's all I have left, isn't it?" Then, resuming that serious tone, she placed a hand on Opaline's shoulder and said, "Sorry, but I have to visit this last room alone."

"I understand," Opaline replied. "Do you want me to wait for you?"

Cora shook her head. "You don't have to wait for me. Do you remember the way back?"

"To the car, you mean?" she asked, tilting her head to the side. "In Poggioreale?"

"No, you can go all the way back to Lucia's place. I'm . . . going to be a bit."

Despite her internal protests, Opaline didn't argue with Cora. She gave Cora an understanding nod and departed after giving her sister's hand a single squeeze.

Cora stayed in the room for several minutes longer, finding several trinkets left untouched. Her beaded bracelet, she discovered, fit her perfectly still. She was so lost in her thoughts, so lost in memories, that it took her a long time to hear the music. It was suspended in the air around her, and its origin was impossible to ascertain. At first, Cora assumed it was being played from her old record player in the bathroom, but soon she noticed that the

keystrokes vibrated in the air in the way that only a live piano could produce.

"I see," she whispered with a smile. "So this isn't the room you died in."

Her limbs feeling heavier than ever, Cora retrieved the box and hugged it tightly to herself. She considered going back, saving herself from more tears, and never coming back to this painful place. It was gorgeous outside, beautiful and bright and simple. But the idea vanished the second she recognized the song: *Rhapsody on a Theme of Paganini*, Opus 43, Variation 18.

Zeno's room was unchanged. More than the rest of the house, it was exactly as she remembered it. The scent of his cologne, woody and musty, still lingered as if he had sprayed it that morning. The scarce light of an already lit candle played across the furniture in the dramatic lighting she had painted so many times, shining through a wineglass that still bore the imprint of his lips. The song Leonore sang for her departed mate had long faded away, leaving Cora in a peaceful silence as she ducked into the innermost sanctum. The curtain ran across the nape of her neck as she entered like a gentle caress.

Cora moved aside sheet music and set the box on his desk, opening it carefully. One by one, she retrieved its contents and placed them on top of his piano.

Dried rose petals, a page of sheet music from Liebestraum No. 3, an old copy of the *Aeneid*, and a single dove feather.

"I told you the truth, Zeno. I told you the truth when I said I'd always be yours. Forever, not just for a taste."

Acknowledgements

To Dylan, for your unwavering support, endless love, boundless advice, and rabid insistence that I share my work with the world. I don't think there is anyone else who will appreciate how much my work means to me as you, nor anyone who will dissect every line and examine every metaphor with such fervor. I continued every step of writing and publishing this book with you and the beautiful way you would read this book in mind. Please forgive the fact that I killed off a character so clearly inspired by you and don't feel the need sleep with a knife under your pillow. After all, I need you alive to read everything I write in the future.

To my mother, for always encouraging my creativity at a young age and making me feel like my thoughts were worthwhile. Some of my earliest memories are running back and forth to you to ask you how to spell words for my childhood books, and helping me make the most ridiculous crafts. I never stopped writing from the moment you let me sit at your computer and use the word processor.

To my father, who is probably going to joke about the fact that his acknowledgment is under my mother's and is significantly shorter, but who gave me a refined taste and fed my bookish appetite early on.

To Jamie Barry, for showing me that *Just for a Taste* was something worth publishing. When I began to write, I told my loved ones I didn't care about money or success—all I wanted was one person who didn't know me or who I didn't pay to truly understand it. And while I may have paid you for your beta reading services, your deep understanding of my novel, from its basic prose to all of its underlying themes and characterization helped me realize this dream.

To Siobhan, for beta reading my work and allowing me to read yours. Your thoughtful comments and suggestions transformed the entire first half of this novel, and I can only hope my own were helpful for you too. I cannot wait to hold a copy of *The Princess and the Tailor* in my hands when it is published!

To my work colleagues, friends and family members, for showing genuine interest in this process and making me more confident putting this book out there.

About the Author

Vera Wolfe is a lover of all things dark, strange, and romantic. Native to Texas and invasive to Nebraska, she spends her time crafting, playing with her bird, and reading dark academia. When it comes to writing, Vera explores the relationship between dark and light, bitter and sweet, and romance and suspense. As a nurse with a degree in psychology and minor in neuroscience, she enjoys weaving accurate and academic elements into her character-driven stories. She is especially passionate about realistic and empathetic mental health representation.

Visit my website and join my mailing list for promotions and updates on my writing at:

Verawolfebooks.com

www.ingramcontent.com/pod-product-compliance
Lightning Source LLC
Chambersburg PA
CBHW060810310726
48980CB00002B/294

* 9 7 9 8 9 9 2 1 8 0 6 3 3 *